BLUE KANSAS SKY

FOUR SHORT NOVELS OF MEMORY, MAGIC, SURMISE & ESTRANGEMENT

MICHAEL BISHOP

WITH AN INTRODUCTION BY
JAMES MORROW

GOLDEN GRYPHON PRESS 2000

DEDICATIONS & ACKNOWLEDGMENTS

As a collection, *Blue Kansas Sky* is for my agent, advisor, and friend, Howard Morhaim.

The story "Blue Kansas Sky" is for my brother-in-law, John Gregory Whitaker, Jr., who recommended that I read Robert Bly's *Iron John*; for my sister-in-law, Linda Whitaker; and for their sons, my nephews, John, Jeff, and Kevin.

It is also for Peter Crowther and Edward E. Kramer, who commissioned it for an anthology, *Heartlands*, that never saw print. It therefore appears in this volume for the first time anywhere, copyright © 1999 by Michael Bishop.

"Apartheid, Superstrings, and Mordecai Thubana" is for Lewis Shiner, who, mercifully, did a merciless line-edit of a shorter earlier version.

It is copyright © 1989 by Michael Bishop and first appeared as book no. 10 in the Axolotl Press series, copyright © 1989 by Pulphouse Publishing.

"Cri de Coeur" is for Geoffrey A. Landis, who wrote the five haiku attributed to "Gulam Sharif." Geoff provided good advice about both textual and technical matters; he is *not* to blame, however, for any errors, literary or scientific.

The story is copyright © 1994 by Bantam Doubleday Dell Magazines. It first appeared in the September 1994 issue of *Asimov's Science Fiction*, with a subsequent appearance in *The Year's Best Science Fiction: Twelfth Annual Collection*, edited by Gardner Dozois (New York: St. Martin's Press, 1995).

I dedicate "Death and Designation Among the Asadi" to the memory of the late Ejler Jakobsson, who bought my first story in 1969, for *Galaxy*, and who showcased this subsequently Nebula and Hugo Awards short-listed novella in the February, 1973, issue of *Worlds of If*.

It is copyright © 1973 by UPD Publishing Corporation, but later appeared, revised, as a portion of my Berkley/Putnam novel *Transfigurations*, copyright © 1979 by Michael Bishop.

Copyright © 2000 by Michael Bishop

Introduction, copyright © 2000 by James Morrow

Edited by Marty Halpern

LIBRARY OF CONGRESS CATALOGUING-IN-PUBLICATION DATA
Bishop, Michael.
    Blue Kansas Sky : four short novels of memory, magic, surmise & estrangement / by Michael Bishop — 1st ed.
      p.   cm.
    Contents: Blue Kansas sky — Apartheid, superstrings, and Mordecai Thubana — Cri de coeur — Death and designation among the Asadi.
    ISBN 0-9655901-0-0 (hardcover : alk. paper)
      1. Science fiction, American. 2. South Africa—Social life and customs—Fiction. I. Title.
PS3552.I772B65   2000
813'.54—dc21   00-037147

All rights reserved, which includes the right to reproduce this book, or portions thereof, in any form whatsoever except as provided by the U.S. Copyright Law. For information address Golden Gryphon Press, 3002 Perkins Road, Urbana, IL 61802. Printed in the United States of America.
First Edition

CONTENTS

INTRODUCTION
by James Morrow

vii

BLUE KANSAS SKY

3

APARTHEID, SUPERSTRINGS, AND MORDECAI THUBANA

62

CRI DE COEUR

132

DEATH AND DESIGNATION AMONG THE ASADI

192

INTRODUCTION
"SUCH GUILELESS BEAUTY IN DEBRIS":
THE MORAL UNIVERSE OF MICHAEL BISHOP

To drive off the spleen, regulate the circulation, and keep himself from succumbing to despair, Ishmael takes ship on the *Pequod.* The rest of us settle for more prosaic possibilities. Whenever it is a damp, drizzly November in our souls, we yell at our children, break dishes, drink vodka, watch professional football, go into politics, or join support groups. Sometimes we write fiction. And if the spleen of the moment boasts a proper Melvillean mixture of ire and melancholy, the resulting story or novel might be a very fine work indeed.

Can there be art without spite? Many painters, composers, and writers would answer no. Accepting his National Book Award in 1952, novelist James Jones lamented the flight from irony and skepticism that marked so many artists' responses to the hyperpatriotism of the war years. "The only thing wrong with literature in our time is that it lacks malice, envy, and hate," said Jones. "This fear of rascality in our writers is unwillingly turning them into moralists."

A quarter century later, another National Book Award winner, novelist-philosopher Walker Percy, weighed in with a similar brief on behalf of bile. Conducting a self-interview in a 1977 issue of *Esquire,* Percy called fiction writing "a very obscure activity in which there is usually a considerable element of malice. Like frogging." (Frogging, he explained, is "raising a charley horse on somebody's arm by a skillful blow with a knuckle in exactly the right spot.") Later in the piece, Percy argued that the knack for writing fiction entails theological, demonic, and sexual components: "One is aware, on the one hand, of a heightened capacity for both malice and joy and, occasionally and with luck, for being able to see things afresh . . ."

We turn now to the case of my friend and colleague Michael Bishop, whose fiction exhibits a decided dearth of rascality, a remarkable absence of malice, and absolutely no inclination toward frogging. To be sure, there is darkness in the novellas that follow, not to mention physical pain, psychological torment, wry humor, and impassioned outrage over human stupidity, but the ruling ethos is a generosity of spirit that belies the formulations of our two National Book Award winners. So where does that leave us? If Jones and Percy are right, it would seem that Bishop's qualified optimism and essential sunniness—not by accident is the hero of the lead-off novella, "Blue Kansas Sky," named Sonny—are fundamentally at odds with the higher varieties of literary ambition.

At this juncture, a remarkable little book by novelist John Gardner comes to our aid. The central thesis of *On Moral Fiction* is that the best writers function not as malice-meisters but as bearers of universal values. In the first chapter, Gardner makes his classical bias explicit:

> The traditional view is that true art is moral: it seeks to improve life, not debase it. It seeks to hold off, at least for a while, the twilight of the gods and us . . . That art which tends toward destruction, the art of nihilists, cynics, and merdistes, is not properly art at all. Art is essentially serious and beneficial, a game played against chaos and death, against entropy. It is a tragic game, for those who have the wit to take it seriously, because our side must lose; a comic game—or so a troll might say—because only a clown with sawdust brains would take our side and eagerly join it.

As his argument deepens, Gardner further antagonizes the merdistes:

> Great art celebrates life's potential, offering a vision unmistakably and unsentimentally rooted in love. "Love" is of course another of those embarrassing words, perhaps a word even more embarrassing than "morality," but it's a word no aesthetician ought carelessly to drop from his vocabulary. Misused as it may be by

pornographers and the makers of greeting cards, it has, nonetheless, a firm, hard-edged sense that names the single quality without which true art cannot exist.

At the risk of embarrassing Michael Bishop, I must declare that I, for one, cannot read passages like these without thinking of his oeuvre: not just the collection before us, but also such thematically rich novels as *No Enemy but Time, Ancient of Days, Unicorn Mountain,* and *Brittle Innings,* as well as the stories gathered in *Blooded on Arachne, One Winter in Eden, Close Encounters with the Deity,* and *At the City Limits of Fate.* While *On Moral Fiction* is not a wholly persuasive treatise (in the second half, Gardner goes off the deep end, equating serious novelists to divinely inspired priests), I shall always be grateful to its author for placing the literature of affirmation on a par with the pessimistic calisthenics of Samuel Beckett and Kurt Vonnegut. In Gardner's view, the maker of authentic "moral fiction" is an entirely different creature from James Jones's creepy "moralist." And *Blue Kansas Sky* tacitly makes the case for this distinction as powerfully as any book I know.

If all of this sounds a bit high-minded, I should hasten to add that Gardner's aesthetic readily embraces the sort of "category fiction" with which Michael Bishop's name is usually associated. In the final chapter of *On Moral Fiction,* Gardner celebrates "the intelligent and sensitive writer" who has learned how to bend genre conventions to his purpose: "As John le Carré, Isaac Asimov, Peter Beagle, Curtis Harnak, and many others have shown, one need not be a fool or a compromiser to write a mystery story, a sci-fi or fantasy, or a book about growing up in Iowa." If the four novellas that comprise *Blue Kansas Sky* didn't deliver the reliable delights of speculative literature — if they didn't offer uncanny encounters and canny extrapolations — I wouldn't be discussing them right now, mainly because Bishop wouldn't have written them in the first place.

Beyond its sophisticated picture of social interactions aboard an interstellar wheelship, "Cri de Coeur" gives us a hard-science space adventure replete with stunning vistas and heuristic mishaps. Counterpointing its subtle anthropological ruminations, "Death and Designation Among the Asadi" (a Nebula Award finalist) offers up aliens so deliciously incomprehensible that they linger in the mind long after the plot details have dropped away. To accomplish the critique of racial oppression that drives "Apartheid, Superstrings, and Mordecai Thubana" (also a Nebula finalist), Bishop deploys an astonishing amalgam of magic realism and quantum mechanics. Even the fundamentally mainstream "Blue Kansas Sky" is shot through with a sense of the fantastical—to the young Sonny Peacock, the world feels more numinous than Newtonian—and it's even possible to regard its various rainbow and tornado images as soliciting a return to Oz.

How does Bishop accomplish this feat? How does he create viscerally pleasurable works that nevertheless participate fully in the universe of "moral fiction" while simultaneously eschewing the pamphleteering impulse? The answer, it seems to me, lies in what Percy calls the "cognitive" or "diagnostic" dimension of fiction writing. In each of the works before us, Bishop takes hold of the same two interconnected themes—the same two grand ideas—and addresses them with all the intellectual honesty he can muster. As Percy puts it in his *Harper's* essay called "The Diagnostic Novel," "the serious novelist is quite as much concerned with discovering reality as a serious physicist." It is Bishop's relentless urge toward discovery, his insatiable appetite for surprise, his insistence on wrestling his thematic obsessions to the ground, that enables him to avoid the sentimentality and moralism that Gardner, Jones, and Percy—and Herman Melville—would all agree is the enemy of art.

Early in "Cri de Coeur," Dr. Abel Gwiazda, the geologist-poet who narrates the story, has yet another unpleasant encounter with Kazimierz Mikol, the space ark's sour fuel-systems specialist. The principal object of Mikol's hostility is Abel Gwiazda's son, Dean, afflicted with Down's syndrome. When Abel expresses pride that Dean has made a compelling intellectual connection between the shape of a geode and the ship's fuel spokes, Mikol asks, sarcastically, "Do you think that on that basis I should declare the kid a genius?" To which Abel replies, "Human would do. Just human."

Human would do. In that stark plea for cognitive enlightenment lies the first of the two themes that animate these novellas, a plea that we might call—to borrow the title of Jürgen Habermas's most recent book—"The inclusion of the other." For Mikol rejects Dean not only as an individual (at one point he dismisses him as a "hairless baboon"), but also as the avatar of all Down's-syndrome individuals. "I dislike mongoloids," he tells Abel. "In my view, an entirely rational prejudice."

In Abel's eyes, meanwhile, not only is Dean fully human, his soul partakes of a palpable brightness. "Cri de Coeur" vibrates with images of luminosity, beginning with the wonderful opening line, "Why, once, did moths singe the tapestries of their wings in candle flames?" While Dean is in utero, his extra chromosome a matter of public record, Abel speaks of his desire to "call Dean's pent-up spirit from the dark." After Dean is born, Abel marvels at the child's belief that everyone loves him: "In a universe of swallowing dark, and despite the eclipse of his reason at conception, he scatters a property so similar to light that it dims my vision." Observing Dean trying to manipulate his cybernetic doppelganger inside a virtual-reality chamber, Abel composes a poem that begins:

> *A starchild in a VidPed cage*
> *Unwraps himself, with deadpan glee.*
> *Such fragile tissues disengage,*
> *Such guileless beauty in debris.*

Just when all this rhapsodizing threatens to become a bit much, Bishop reminds us that there is more to raising a child, especially a Down's-syndrome child, than the mutual exchange of unconditional love. In one especially memorable moment, Dean's habitual wailing carries his father past the snapping point: " 'Damn you, you little defective! Shut up!' " Even after Dean grows quiet, Abel's anger remains: "Repeatedly, I shoved him in the chest with my knuckles, herding him toward the exit."

Racism is the most obvious way that human beings violate the ideal of inclusion, and each novella in this collection addresses the issue at some level. The preadolescent Sonny of "Blue Kansas Sky" studies the Kansas-Nebraska act and the abolitionist movement in school. The pathetic Mikol of "Cri de Coeur" calls Abel, who is Tanzanian, a "selfish Sambo." The extermination of the African pygmies hovers like a malignant ghost over the events in "Death and Designation Among the Asadi." But Bishop's richest meditation on racial injustice is "Apartheid, Superstrings, and Mordecai Thubana," in which Gerrit Myburgh, a smug Afrikaner, becomes an unwilling witness to the murderous policies that have polluted his country for so many generations.

At the climax of this meticulously researched novella, Bishop piquantly inverts the light imagery that suffuses "Cri de Coeur." Newly aware that the luminous white city of Pretoria is infested with oppressors, Myburgh comes to regard all its streetlamps, incandescent bulbs, and blazing automobile chrome as negative innovations. These things belong to a universe "contaminated by light." Pretoria's complacent glow has prevented Myburgh from perceiving the excluded others, "the shadow-matter armies bivouacked in their shameful invisibility out there beyond the electric bonfires . . ."

With "Death and Designation Among the Asadi," Bishop expands the ideal of inclusiveness into the extraterrestrial realm. Throughout his investigation of the cryptic Asadi who inhabit the planet BoskVeld, the cultural xenologist Egan Chaney is a man at war with himself. By defining the BoskVeld aborigines as "an alien people," wholly commensurate with *Homo sapiens*, Chaney hopes to achieve an oblique expiation for what his own people did to the pygmies. Yet Chaney's efforts to bring his subjects into the fellowship of the intelligent are continually thwarted by the Asadi themselves—by their antisocialness, their troublesome diet, their seeming lack of language, their bedeviling prismatic eyes, and, most especially, their bestial familiars (who turn out to be far stranger than you are likely to imagine). Early in the novella, Bishop offers a "dialogue" between Chaney's two psyches, an exchange that climaxes when one of the selves declares, "I hate the Asadi . . . They curdle my essence with their very alienness." That this outburst comes from Chaney's "soul" half, not from his presumably colder and less compassionate "self" half, is a measure of Bishop's refusal to strain thematic complexity through the comforting filter of dualistic reason.

In "Blue Kansas Sky," Bishop explores the social and moral ambiguities entailed in our attempts to include those "others" commonly termed "ex-convicts." A coming-of-age story set largely in the 1950s, "Blue Kansas Sky" frequently echoes *Huckleberry Finn* and *To Kill a Mockingbird*, and, as with those earlier works, the child-hero apprehends certain ethical imperatives that elude the grown-ups around him. Entering the story as a brutal and unattractive figure, Sonny Peacock's Uncle Rory repels the local citizens, who see him as just another unsavory exemplar of convicted criminals everywhere. It is only Sonny who accepts Rory from the first, not because children possess an innate moral superiority—Bishop will have none of such mawkishness—but because, like Dean Gwiazda, Sonny is heir to a kind of unfocused curiosity, a "guileless beauty," largely unavailable to the adult world.

Let me add parenthetically that I regard "Blue Kansas Sky" as one of Bishop's finest achievements, and I'm pleased that he decided to make it the flagship of this collection. Keyed to the primary colors—the blue of the sky, the yellow of the ballcaps

Rory's mother naively sends her imprisoned son, the red of the blood-ties that bind the characters in reluctant constellations — the novella is a *tour de force* of tension, tone, and tongue:

"Potatochips fell around him, petallike in their beauty."

"These tall flowers, with their brown clockfaces and their lionlike manes, did not lend themselves to comfortable bicycle transport . . ."

". . . Neil and Pike angled off in different directions, the wind howling after them, shrapnel storms of snow glittering and whirling all about the cottonwood-studded pasture."

"Chili, as everyone called the captain, struck Sonny as an okay guy, but his orange suit made him look less like an airman than a swashbuckling clown."

The second time I read "Blue Kansas Sky," the last line made me cry.

Complementing Bishop's insights into "the inclusion of the other" is an allied theme that we might call "the redemption of the outsider." Each novella in this collection gives us at least one important character who finds himself, either through conscious intent or metaphysical accident, standing outside a normal human frame of reference. This dislocation finally has an instructive effect — sometimes on the outsider, sometimes on his fellows — though the lesson is never simplistic, and its full implications remain mysterious.

The outsider in "Blue Kansas Sky" is the ex-con Rory Peacock, who upon his return to Van Luna takes up residence in the town dump. Having banished himself to this bizarre and unsavory landscape, Rory can finally reflect on his life, and he gradually enlists the understanding and even the admiration of the Van Lunans, effecting various reconciliations we would never have thought possible at the beginning. While "Blue Kansas Sky" remains Sonny's story throughout, the parallel narrative serves Bishop well, permitting him to mirror the child-hero's maturation in Rory's progressive domestication of the odiferous wasteland.

"Cri de Coeur" features an outsider far less sympathetic than Rory Peacock. Exiled by his bigotry, Abel's nemesis, Kazimierz Mikol, rejoins the human community aboard the wheelship only after his aunt's death forces him to reevaluate his past. While the exact mechanism remains obscure, Mikol's redemption evidently occurs once he connects his instinctive hatred for the handicapped Dean with his beloved sister's own sort of neurological pathology.

"Apartheid, Superstrings, and Mordecai Thubana" presents a searing literalization of the situation described by Ralph Ellison in the memorable opening lines of his first novel: "I am an invisible man. No, I am not a spook like those who haunted Edgar Allan Poe; nor am I one of your Hollywood-movie ectoplasms. I am a man of substance, of flesh and bone, fiber and liquids—and I might even be said to possess a mind. I am invisible, understand, simply because people refuse to see me." In Bishop's novella, however, it is a *white* man, the Afrikaner banker Myburgh, who suffers from invisibility (as the plot would have it, he is temporarily translated into subatomic shadow matter), so that, for the first time in his life, he truly *sees* the blacks with whom he grudgingly shares a nation. Written during a period when the fall of apartheid was by no means a foregone conclusion, "Mordecai Thubana" avoids any easy implication that Myburgh will now spend the rest of his life championing racial harmony. But he is still a man transformed.

For Egan Chaney, the xenologist-hero of "Death and Designation Among the Asadi," detachment comes with the job. I suspect that, in naming the protagonist as he did, Bishop intended to evoke silent film actor Lon Chaney, whose brilliant portrayals of the deformed and the misbegotten made him a hero to outsiders everywhere. In his mad attempt to comprehend the denizens of the BoskVeld rain forest, Egan acquires an "invisibility" almost as literal as Gerrit Myburgh's, for it so happens that Asadi cultural norms permit him to assume the role of pariah, "psychological outcast": no matter what Egan does, the natives will be obliged to ignore him. The more vigorously the xenologist pursues his ideals, however, the more unrealizable they become, and I'm not giving away anything vital—indeed, the fact is announced on the dust jacket of *Transfigurations,* the full-length novel Bishop eventually spun from "Death and Designation"—when I reveal that Egan ultimately finds the Asadis' irreducible otherness more attractive than "normal" human community.

Egan's epiphany not only provides the novella with its marvelous conclusion, it furnishes an appropriate coda to my appreciation of the present collection. "I belong among the Asadi," Egan writes to his colleagues shortly before returning to the rain forest, "not as an outcast and not as a chieftain—but as one of the milling throng . . . I'm one of them. I feel for them."

A former outsider, equivocally redeemed. An alienated empiricist, now connected to the other. Moral fiction.

Egan's message continues: "... I'm a great slow moth. A tiger moth. And the flame I choose to pursue and die in is the same flame that slowly consumes every one of the Asadi."

A flame-drawn moth—the exact sort of creature, you will recall, that singes its wings at the beginning of "Cri de Coeur." Such strange affirmation. Such oblique optimism. Such guileless beauty in debris. Human will do. Enjoy.

James Morrow
March 2000

Blue Kansas Sky

BLUE KANSAS SKY

ONNY PEACOCK MEASURED THE GOODNESS OF EACH day by the amount of blue in the sky. Total cloudlessness — smooth blue bellyskin from horizon to horizon — meant adventure, a win in tetherball, a smile from Maggie Vy Medders, a helterskelter romp with some mutt in Buffalo Bill Park, a precarious trek around the rails of Van Luna's bandbox. Partly cloudy meant partly happy, and deep overcast — an irongrey tent over the yellow prairie — meant scoldings at home, Fs in spelling, the straying of Maggie Vy's gaze, mystery meat for lunch, stomach cramps, the unshakable glums.

Today Sonny crawled over his pillow, tweezered one Venetian blind, glimpsed robin's-egg blue.

Okay! he thought.

Even before his mother Jenniel came in to coax him up for some toast and wheatmeal, he had dressed and sauntered into the galleylike kitchen, where sunlight spilled like buttermilk over their dinette set.

Straight home from school, Jenniel said. You can watch Flash Gordon and the Mouseketeers.

It's pretty out, Sonny said. Craig and me may want to take our BBguns to the dump and bust some bottles.

Listen to me, Sonny: *straight home.*

Sonny ate a spoonful of stiffening cereal. But why?

Jenniel worked in personnel at McConnell Air Force Base southeast of Wichita, twenty to thirty minutes away depending on traffic. Sometimes she didn't get home until six or sixthirty. Sonny could pedal a slew of miles and dent a mound of tincans between school's last bell and his mother's eventual homecoming.

Rory Peacock just got out of prison, said Jenniel, wiping her hands on a dishtowel. She seemed primed to expand on this news, but stopped. Stopping—staying stopped—required her to clamp her lips and to clutch her own shoulders.

You think he'd come here?

Yeah. Yeah I do.

Sonny said, Then wouldn't it be better if I was somewhere else till you got home?

Jenniel unfolded, glided up behind him, propped her chin on his collarbone. Course it would. I'm not thinking. It's hard to think with Rory getting out and things at work so crazy all of a sudden.

He wouldn't hurt us. I'm your second dad he told me once.

Once he maybe believed it. I don't know how he is now and mostly don't care to find out.

Sky's blue, Sonny said. Real blue.

Jenniel pulled back and regarded him as if he'd just said Ike himself had given him a national citation: Smartest Twelve Year Old in Kansas. Then she telephoned Mrs. Whited to ask if Sonny could stay at her place after school the rest of this week and a few days into next. Mrs. Whited agreed. Jenniel shrugged on her tweed jacket and hurried out to her '56 Nash Rambler, a snazzy charcoal-and-pink twotone, for her daily drive up Rock Road to McConnell.

Sonny washed dishes. After locking the house, he bestrode his battered Schwinn and raced like an Italian cyclist toward Van Luna Elementary. As he pedaled, the sky behind the town's grain elevator graded from robin's-egg to luminous Dutch-china blue.

Directly overhead the tiny silver cross of a B-47 laid down wispy contrails: clouds of no real substance or clout. *Peace is our profession!* shouted Sonny, waving at the unreachable pilot.

In an aisle seat at the bus's center hulked a curlyheaded giant in leather boots, denim pants, a sheepskin vest. The matronly woman beside him leaned away, like a highschool girl on her first date to a drive-in. Their bus, meanwhile, cruised east on Highway 50 past the wheatfields and cattlepastures of the tamed Great

Plains: a motorized schooner running its course counter to that of the pioneers.

This is some dull crowd, said the curlyheaded man.

The matronly woman grimaced, but in agreement rather than disgust, peering out her window at the wheat flaming green and torchlike in the late April gusts. Her mangy foxstole wrapped her throat like a muffler. Tugging on it, she hunched her neck to set the stole more securely.

Dull dull dull, said the man.

The woman kept her eyes on the hurtling wheat.

Makes no sense, said the man. Open road. Beautiful day. No cuffs on our wrists or legs. But we git, well, this crabby glumness.

Mmmhmmm, said the woman.

Abruptly the curlyheaded man stood up, filling the middle of the bus like a pillar. Okay, everbody, he said. Whaddaya say we sing?

Siddown back there, said the driver, showing a no-nonsense scowl in the rearview.

Row Row Row Your Boat, said the curlyheaded man, still standing. We can do it in rounds. He hummed, as if to locate the song's proper pitch, then raised his hands like a symphony conductor and sang: Row row row your boat, Gently down the stream. . . .

The driver said, Mister, I tolya to siddown.

Merrily merrily merrily merrily, Life is but a dream, sang the curlyheaded man, conducting no one but himself. Then he said, It aint mister. Name's Peacock. Rory Peacock. Rory H. Peacock.

Well, Mr. Peacock—began the driver.

Rory said, Everbody over to my side'll start it out. The rest of you'll come in when we hit Gently down the stream. He repeated his pitchpipe hum and began again. No one bothered to join him, but Rory finished the stanza. Then he said, Boy is this some chickenshit crowd.

The driver hit the bus's brakes, twice. Passengers jolted forward and back, forward and back. Rory, despite a grip on the headrest in front of him, staggered and fell to one knee. Three women gasped, one squawked brightly, a young child began to wail.

I don't cotton to rulebreakers, said the driver. And I don't put up with nobody usin scuribous language, Mr. Peacock, you savvy?

I don't like brakers period, said Rory, pulling himself upright again. And what you just did cain't be legal neither, you sorry snot.

The driver tapped the brakes a third time. Rory sprawled face forward down the aisle. An insectfaced young man with a blond pompadour and a pack of cigarettes in his Tshirt sleeve jumped on Rory, struggled to twist his huge arm into the small of his back.

Rory raised his butt and flipped the kid over his head toward the driver, then got up, placed a foot on the kid's rear end, and shoved him on a collapsing stagger to the dashboard, where he hung like a cat-o'-nine-tails victim, now cursing, now wailing. Cries of alarm and outrage reached the decibel level of marching piccolos and tubas.

How is it yall cain't sing but you can bitch n moan wi the best of em? Rory stared balefully around. Lord but you're a gloomy crew.

This time the driver stopped the bus dead. The rustling of wheat made itself audible over the wind, through the ticking bulkheads. A farmer in a pickup passed them going west. The expression on his face reminded Rory of the sewer guy's on The Honeymooners after an argument with Kramden. Likewise, the expression of the driver's face in the rearview reminded him of old Ralph's after a run-in with the sewer guy. This comparison made perfect sense: Kramden and the fellow up front both drove buses, didn't they?

Get out, the driver said. I won't have a nutzo on board with decent paying customers. I mean it, *off!* He opened the accordionpleated door beside him.

Rory stood crucified between two seats with cowering human beings in them: decent paying customers. He glanced back. The long rearseat had no occupant at all; neither did the three or four paired seats in front of it. Rory grabbed his duffel by its draws and pointed one thick finger at the driver's mirrored features.

I may not be decent but I damn sure paid, he said. Dibs on that spot back there till we git to Van Luna. He retreated down the aisle and sprawled across the seat beside the narrow lavatory. Don't try to throw me off fore we're there, he said. You do, I'll have to crunch you.

No one said a word.

Eventually the driver levered the frontdoor shut and drove them off again.

No one ventured into that part of the bus to which Rory had laid claim, not even to use the toilet. He began to hum, then to sing.

Take me out to the ballgame, he crooned. Take me out to the crowd. . . .

Rory opened his duffel and removed from it a canary-yellow ballcap. In his massive hands it looked like a baby's cap; he could've worn it on his head no better than he could've worn a thimble. It did fit his knee though, and so he wore it on one knee, with its bill pointing down and its soft felty yellowness imparting a weird glow to his vest and shirt, to his wide chest and face.

Sonny had the last desk on the windowside row in Mr. Hugh McKinley's classroom. This seat allowed him to play with the plastic pullcone on the Venetian-blind cord and to keep an eye on the everchanging faces of the sky. Today the sky stayed blue, feeding and sustaining in him a feeling of contentment, of control. He flipped the thimblelike cone up the long cord with his right index finger while with his left hand he pulled the blinds cord taut.

This game—his own invention—reminded Sonny Peacock of the ring-the-bell-with-the-sledgehammer attraction at carnivals and fairs. The harder you swung the hammer the nearer the bell you sent the weight on the ruled-off upright supporting the bell. *Sissy* said the lowest of the ruled levels. *Lightweight* said the next. And so on up to *HeMan*. Anyway, the harder Sonny flicked the pull, and the tighter he held the cord, the closer to the top of the blinds rocketed the pull—only to spiral back down, even as he looped the cord to keep it aloft, like a coin on a mad edge-to-edge wobble.

Craig Baldwell, Pike Kennerly, and Neil Stroyer (Sonny's chief rival for the necklace ring of Maggie Vy Medders) envied him his ready access to the pullcone game, but Sonny had won the right to choose his desk by making the best grades in class over the last sixweeks period. Amazingly, then, he could play his game virtually all day, even under the frazzled glances of Mr. McKinley as he made crossing-guard assignments or led them through the answers to yesterday's math problems. The only times Sonny had to stop were tests, writing assignments, lunch, and recess. Once, in fact, he'd lined up on the con side in a general classroom discussion on the morality and effectiveness of capital punishment (which in Kansas from pioneer days onward the state had carried out by gallows and rope) while repeatedly flicking the fluted pull up the blinds cord. Mr. McKinley had not rebuked him, and the alternate rocketing up and spiraling down of the pull had seemed to almost everyone on hand to twin the agitated rhythms of their debate.

Today Mr. McKinley talked Kansas history: that series of events after the Kansas-Nebraska Act of 1854 which resulted in counter-massacres among abolitionists and proslavery advocates, and which earned the state the nickname Bleeding Kansas. Old Osawatomie Brown. John Brown's body lies amouldering in the grave. And so on.

Sonny half listened as he flicked the pull up the cord and let it back down in lurching spirals. John Brown had less historical interest for him than did the latterday careers of Cullison Peacock, his father, and Rory Peacock, his uncle. With the half of his mind that could not listen to McKinley or bring itself to focus on his blackboard cartoons, Sonny mulled the tidings of Rory's release and the long-ago doings that had led to the brothers' troubles with the law.

Five years ago, as Jenniel had explained to Sonny after the trial, Rory had talked Cullison, the older and wiser brother, into crossing the Colorado line and waylaying an armored Wells Fargo truck traveling between Pueblo and Rocky Ford. This was just a couple of years after an Eisenhower-approved reduction in force, or RIF, had separated Cullison from the airforce and sent him back home to Van Luna and a demoralizing succession of deadend jobs, from grocerystore clerk to sadsack apprentice roofer. Anyway, Rory had—

Mr. McKinley, I can't *think* with Sonny doing that, said Cynthia Zook. He's gone a poco loco this morning.

Sonny, stop fiddling with the cord, Mr. McKinley said.

More dazed than defiant, Sonny made the cord twang.

I asked you to stop, said Mr. McKinley. Keep that up I'll have to send you to Mr. Medders.

Joel Medders, Maggie Vy's daddy, reigned over Van Luna Elementary as principal. Once he had played forward on Kansas University's basketball team. Today he stood at least a half a head taller than any other citizen of the community. Most of the boys in the sixthgrade, when not in Maggie Vy's hearing, called him Joel the Pole: a reference to his height, not his nationality. He wielded a paddle with holes in it, and once he had nearly wrenched Pike Kennerly's arm out of its socket when Pike came Keds-clopping fulltilt down the hall past him after recess. (In those days no one had even thought about trying to sue either.)

Sonny let go of the cord. Through the windowblinds' dusty slats he saw a glacier of irongrey clouds pushing aside a broad wedge of blue.

Crap, he thought.

The spiel on Border Ruffians, abolitionist guerillas, and the sack of Lawrence resumed, as did Mr. McKinley's outlandish chalk cartoons, a feature of his teaching that set him apart from his female counterparts at Van Luna Elementary and usually garnered him his students' admiration. Sonny shut down to the drawings though and dredged from his wallet a tiny album of black-and-white photographs, including recent snaps of Craig, Maggie Vy, Pike, and friends. These he flipped straight past, for they had the numbing familiarity of Cream o' Wheat. The photograph he wanted—a shot of himself on Cullison Peacock's knee in an Amarillo motelroom— was pressed between Craig and Pike in one clear-plastic sleeve. Sonny pulled it out and flattened it on his desktop.

Cullison, his daddy, looked about eighteen but was really closer to thirty. He wore a wild patterned shortsleeve shirt and smirked in openmouthed tongue-to-teeth pride at his six- or seven-year-old son, an imp in broadstriped pajamas, with a CocaCola bottle in one hand, as if they had together agreed to shill for the softdrink. Except for their stylish tailoring, the pajamas on the kid in the picture resembled prisongarb, exactly what Cullison would later have to model when convicted of armed robbery and attempted murder of the Wells Fargo guard, whom either he or maybe Rory had gutshot with a Ruger pistol—although Rory, according to Cullison's testimony, had served only as a reluctant accomplice and thus received the lighter sentence.

Rory wasn't married, Jenniel had said, telling this story. He didn't even have a girlfriend. He should've taken the fall for Cullison.

But of course Rory hadn't taken the fall, and it pained Jenniel to admit that his doing so might not have spared the Peacocks of Van Luna even a sliver of heartache: Cullison would have gone to that Colorado prison anyway, and in his seventh month there, a freak flashriot had occurred in his cellblock. During this fracas two prisoners on an upper tier had pushed a metal trashdrum over the rail onto a random huddle of inmates including Sonny's dad, the only man killed in the melee or in fact injured beyond the therapeutic reach of a quick stitch and some Mercurochrome. It was on their visit to fetch Cullison's body home for burial that Rory told Sonny, Don't fret, kid—in me you got yourself a second daddy.

Sonny remembered that. He remembered Rory, a giant with a head like a great lichen-flocked stone, a man probably fifty pounds heavier than Joel Medders despite spotting him five or six inches in height. Sonny searched among the pictures in his insert for a snapshot of his uncle. If he had ever had one (he remembered once caching away a lopeared print of Rory clanging the bell at the sledgehammer challenge at the Sedgewick County Fair), he could not find it now.

Time for spelling, Mr. McKinley said. Take out a sheet of paper.

With stiffly uncooperative fingers, Sonny fumbled the photo insert back into his wallet, the wallet back into his pocket. He laid a sheet of notebookpaper on his desk, where, a moment past, the snapshot of him and the gone-to-dust Cullison Peacock had rested. Here, then nowhere. Weird.

This is a hard one, Mr. McKinley said. *Cumulus*. Sound it out by syllables: *cu, mu, lus*.

Sonny, like his classmates, knew what the word meant. He looked through the slats and saw that the pewterhued invading clouds of twenty minutes ago had obliterated every reassuring gulf or inlet of blue.

In Wichita two uniformed policemen came aboard the bus and ordered Rory to grab his stuff and beat it.

I'm goin to Van Luna, he said. It's still on down the road a piece.

You caused a disturbance, said the smaller and somewhat friendlier-looking policeman. Your driver wants you off now. Ditto your peacelovin bus company.

I paid to git to Van Luna. If it's *my* bus company how come they're puttin me off shy of my git-to place?

We know who you are and where you've just come from, said the less amiable policeman. Screw around with us, Mr. Peacock, you may wind up back in stir.

Rory stood up, expanding like a paradeballoon before the two policemen. Merrily merrily, he muttered. Gently down the stream.

He stuffed a yellow ballcap into a vestpocket, pulled his duffel up by its draws, and exited the bus humming. Inside the buttstrewn depot, a company employee gave him two dollars as a prorated return on his unfulfilled ticket. Rory asked this man directions, then left the waitingroom to walk through town and out Highway 15 to Van Luna.

The city smelled of gasfumes and rain; the small-aircraft plants south of town, of sheet metal and synthetic rubber; the wet fields beyond them, of silage and cow manure. If Rory had hailed from this part of Kansas, he might have relished these smells; today they merely recalled to him Cullison and the many burdens of kinship.

Outside Fedora, a town midway between Wichita and Van Luna, a man wearing a John Deere cap stopped his pickup to give Rory a hitch. The rains commenced. Rory asked the man if he knew the Peacocks. Nope, the man said, he was passing through Van Luna to Winfield. He let Rory out on Main Street though, and Rory ducked under the torrent-drummed awning of a drugstore as the man saluted him and drove away over the street's glistening brokenbrick cobbles. Rory slipped inside.

Ingram Zook, the pharmacy's owner, recognized Rory from his visits to town before the botch-up with the Wells Fargo truck. He approached Rory fearlessly and ordered him to leave Jenniel Peacock and her boy alone if he wanted to move on from Van Luna with his hide untarred.

We'll fletch you up as purty as a Kaw warbonnet if you try anything smartass, Zook said.

Rory smiled. Bold talk from a man not much bigger than a pekinese, but Rory registered its force. Got any shelfstockin or sweepin up I could do? he said.

Oh yeah, said Zook. Like I need a killer sweepin up. Git out. I got to close.

It's still rainin.

Eventually it'll stop, Zook said. Git long gone from Van Luna fore it does. I intend to tell Tony Loyal you've done a tarnished-penny trick, turnin up here. He'll put an eye on you right tight.

Since before the Second World War, Tony Loyal had served as Van Luna's chief of police. Rory recalled his Popeye forearms and easy cowboy squint. Once past the symbols of his badge and pistol though, Loyal conveyed the same degree of menace as a neutered chowdog. Still, Rory had no strong ache to cross his path tonight and so let the feisty Zook maneuver him out to the sidewalk.

Under the pharmacy's sodden fluttering awning, Zook locked up and opened a plaid umbrella. With a grudging nod he marched off toward his '52 Hudson.

See ya, Rory said.

Zook turned back around. No, he said. No with a capital N. The clatter on Main's cobblestones drowned the sound of his retreating footsteps.

* * *

Expectation dogged Sonny through the next two days, on both of which it rained. If his uncle Rory had served his time (a lesser sentence than Cullison's, owing to Cullison's insistence that he and not his hulking little brother had shot the Wells Fargo guard, and at a point in the robbery when they could have escaped without bloodshed), why didn't Rory come see them? Why didn't he come to their house and stay for supper? Or, failing that, why didn't he walk over to Van Luna Elementary and take Sonny out of class for a sundae at Zook's Drugs or a milkshake at the Dairy Blizzard?

The rain, thought Sonny. The rain has something to do with him not showing up.

Jenniel's angry with him, he thought a moment later. Her anger's the big thing. She thinks Rory suckered Daddy into the robbery and then played babyface after it all went haywire on them. Surely, though, a man who had outlasted his prison term and declared himself Sonny's second daddy would find rain and a woman's resentment silly fleabite annoyances, not great jagged stumblingblocks.

At his desk Sonny flicked the pullcone and stared outside at the empty street, the wet maples, the sheetmetal sky.

In fact, Rory had tried to make contact with Sonny on his second day in town. After a miserable night in the bandbox in Buffalo Bill Park (an oak- and elmshaded commons between the Pix Theater and the city library) and no breakfast at all, Rory found a pay telephone with a mostly intact directory and looked up Jenniel's address. She and Sonny had moved twice since his imprisonment, and their new residence was at 159 Franklin. He reached the house as Jenniel climbed into her Rambler and drove off to work, but could not nerve up to step into the car's path without the buffering presence of the boy, whom he intuitively knew for an ally.

Rory did however step into the street to stare after the Rambler, preliminary to approaching the house to say hello to Sonny. In the street he stood exposed in the spotlight from Loyal's patrolcar, which floated toward him through the foggy drizzle.

Figgered you'd drop by, Loyal said through his rolled-down window. *Feared*, actually.

Rory was waterlogged up to the neck and heiferfaced above it. His arms hung down like a greasemonkey's chains. Ingram Zook phoned you, didn't he?

Yep, said Loyal. And I tol Jenniel. Said I'd mosey over this morning to innercep you if you took a notion to see Sonny.

Is Sonny home? Rory said.
None of your beeswax. Stay clear of em both.
Loyal escorted Rory off Franklin, making him walk in the drizzle, pacing him through town to the citylimits sign beyond which a gravel road skewed parallel to the Oklahoma-tending flow of the Arkansas.
Where'd you spend the night last night, Peacock?
The bandbox, Rory said wearily.
Never again, Loyal said. Thass public property.
I'm part of the public.
Thass doubtful at best. You're a convicted felon.
Then where can I go?
Outta town, outta sight, outta mind, said Loyal the way someone else might murmur, See no evil, hear no evil, speak no evil. He permitted his patrolcar to idle as Rory walked down the puddle-splotched road to the dump, a halfcircle of hell on the banks of a bullhead-haunted river.
Sonny answered Here to Mr. McKinley's roll about the time Rory wandered into the city dump to survey it and consider its possibilities.
Merrily merrily, Rory said, looking at the pocked leathery waters of the Arkansas just beyond some low ramparts of trash. Merrily merrily . . .

Jenniel said nothing to Sonny about Rory's return to Van Luna. She did her job at McConnell, one of the Strategic Air Command bases devoted to deterring Soviet nuclear attack, and trusted that Police Chief Loyal had scotched Rory's belligerent reappearance in their lives. She trusted that Loyal had run the curlyheaded fool out of town. Where would he go, though? Maybe back to Coronado, the West Kansas podunk where India Peacock, Cullison and Rory's aged widowed mother, still lived. Jenniel hoped so. She trusted so. It was too soon to forgive Rory the cruel injuries he'd inflicted on her family. Even when Van Luna's threeday soaking ceased and blue arched again over the fields of Red Turkey wheat hemming the town about, she felt no sunnier toward him.
Sonny perked though. His gloom, a gloom rooted upsidedown in the ashen overcast, broke up like the shredding clouds. He began to believe the rumors of Rory's release from prison had no substance to them. Or that Rory had set sail for Tahiti or Shanghai. Or that, like Cullison, he'd got caught in a riot, expiring in a great red lake of his own blood before reaching his discharge date. Bad possibilities — abandonment or death — but, look, the sky had

turned blue again and blueness counted for a lot. Also, Jenniel had finally stopped making him walk or bike over to Mrs. Whited's after school. He'd sidestepped that humiliating state of dependence for over a week now. His adventure sense had begun to spark again.

That Friday afternoon Sonny corralled Craig Baldwell near the softball backstop and suggested some targetshooting at the dump.

No way. Craig's lipcorner fleered.

How come? I figgered you'd like to.

Yeah, well, some strange stuff's happenin out there.

Like what?

Like Neil Stroyer's dad sayin he saw a bear when he went to unload this ol refrigerator.

There's no bears round here, Sonny said.

Like a lot of wailin at night. Like all the stray dogs out there takin off for other parts. Craig ducked his head, rubbed his sneaker through the gravel.

It's clear daylight, Sonny said. You fraid to go out there this afternoon?

Pike's folks've gone to Wichita to see his grandmama. He's ast me over to look at his dad's cutie mags.

Crap, Sonny said. You've seen em already.

Yeah and I've busted bottles at the dump already too.

Then I'll just go do it alone, Baldwell. Sonny pedaled home, got his BBgun out of the garage, slung it over his shoulder like a GI's carbine. Then he pedaled licketysplit to the dump, his butt never once touching his rockhard triangular seat.

The dump sat by the lolligagging river in all its tedium and stench: the smells of vegetable rot, mildewed upholstery, decomposing newsprint, spoiled meat, damp clothes, discarded carpets. Four men in the back of a highsided truck—Sonny knew them by their faces—used flatnosed shovels to push crumbling cinderblocks into one of the riverside pits, and the sides of the truck rocked steadily higher above its chassis. At last the men finished.

Sonny set up some bottles—whiskey bottles, mayonnaise jars, widemouthed pickle containers—and potted them with a lot of lovely breakage from thirty or forty yards. Several large rats scurried amid the trashpiles, but (only belatedly did he pick up on this) no dogs. The oddness of the dogs' absence touched him as lightly as the sweat on his back.

Later, to clear his head of all the stink, Sonny hiked a weedy tire-rutted road south along the river. Among the pines and widely spaced oaks he saw a ribbon of smoke uncoiling from behind a clayey rise. He toiled up it, sweating more seriously now, then looked down on a scene out of Robert Louis Stevenson: a scene piratically troubling.

A curlyheaded giant in ragged denim shorts tended a spit on which the carcass of a mediumsized animal—a pig? a bearcub? *a dog!*—gleamed pink and charcoal: the very colors of Jenniel's trendy Rambler. A mouthwatering smell came off the carcass. As for the halfnaked guy cranking the cottonwood spit, Sonny knew him for his uncle, Rory H. Peacock. Discovering him here, though, was a lot like happening upon, well, Robinson Crusoe. The river eeling by, manyforked and languid, did sort of seem to island-strand him. At length, probably inevitably, Rory saw Sonny standing above him and made a slow git-down-here motion with his hand.

You can have some if you want, he said when Sonny stood two or three feet away. I figger it's some sort of spaniel-collie mix.

Rory, Sonny said.

Seems like you heard a me. Zook and Loyal must've spread the news I made it back.

Uncle Rory, Sonny said.

Even if I haven't stepped a toe back into town since Loyal gave me the bumrush out. The bastid.

Uncle Rory, you shouldn't be eatin dog.

Rory stared at Sonny.

It's uncivilized.

Rory said, My brother Cullison said the Koreans ate dog. I'd fish but I don't much like it— fish. It's fishy. Rory stared in evident bewilderment at Sonny. Who're you to tell me what to eat?

Sonny said, I'm Sonny Peacock, your nephew. Don't you know me?

No, Rory said. You're too big, way too big.

Uncle Rory, you went off to prison five years ago. Last time you saw me I wasn't even eight. I had a butchcut, but now my hair's long and I part it.

Rory shook his head. He wouldn't let some smart preteen— *almost* preteen—kid dupe him into believing they were kin. A kid like this one would do a lot to prove himself related to someone as famous as a prodigal excon.

Lookere. Sonny raked the hair at his temples back into a makeshift ducktail. My ears don't show like they did. See? See em now?

The spit handle cranked once. Rory wiped his forehead with

his knuckles. The dogmeat above the flames blistered, split, crackled. Sonny raked his hair forward again, fumbled to pull his wallet out.

I got a pitchur of me and my dad. With the barrel of his Daisy tapping the back of his head, Sonny flipped out the photo insert and paged through it looking for the shot of Cullison and him. No luck. He checked every packet, digging between the back-to-back photos. Still no luck. His wallet lacked even one picture of himself with his name on it. It didn't even have a membership card—Cub Scouts, Mouseketeers, Captain Video's TV Cadets—featuring his name. Even if it had, Sonny now believed that Rory would have accused him of picking its rightful owner's pocket.

Whadda I have to do to prove I'm Sonny Peacock?

Let me see that pitchur of you and Cullison.

It's lost, Rory! It's done got itself lost! I can't show you what's lost, can I?

Your mama's bound to have another un if you're really Sonny Peacock. Git me a pitchur of you and your daddy from Jenniel. Once upon a time she kep one in their bedroom.

Sonny cried, *Geez!*

Lifted both arms. Cried *Geez!* again.

Clambered up and over the low clayey dune, hiked back to his row of busted bottles, snatched up his Schwinn, and, awobble with frustration and enmiring ash, ground his molars all the way home to Franklin Street.

In Jenniel's bedroom Sonny felt like a peepingtom and a thief. Lingerie hung from an old hattree like captured silk banners. The fragrance of cologne and the scent of bathsoap lingered. A photo of Cullison in his airforce duds stood in a gold frame on Jenniel's dresser, but that was not what Rory wanted.

Sonny found what Rory wanted—a blowup of Cullison and son—by kneewalking across the partly made bed and sliding back a panel on the blond headboard. He grabbed the photo, removed it from its frame, put the frame back in its cubbyhole, closed the panel, wiped his kneedents from the coverlet.

In twelve minutes Sonny was back at the dump, in the hollow where Rory still oversaw the broiling of his dinner. He showed Rory the proof he'd asked for.

Rory studied it, occasionally comparing the kid in the photo to the twelve-year-old fidgeting before him like a gnat in an updraft.

I don't know, he said.

Uncle Rory, lookit the shape of our mouths. That's a black-

and-white photo but you can tell from it the kid there's got light-colored eyes. Like mine.

Rory conducted his photo assessment as methodically as a tax-audit. At length his eyes widened, kindled. He clasped Sonny to him, lifted him, turned him around, squeezing and shaking Sonny so that Sonny's sneakers swung at Rory's knees like ugly pendulum bobs.

You're him, you're him! Yipee, boy, I found ya!

It seemed to Sonny, even in his captive and shaken state, that he had found Rory rather than the other way round, but the thrill of proving himself overrode any urge to challenge Rory on this, prompting instead a string of triumphant whoops and yodels. These, along with Rory's hosannas, echoed over the riverside dump like peacock cries—which, of course, describes them literally.

Sonny said No to an invitation to dinner, but promised to come back to the dump for visits after school and on weekends. However, he must keep these visits secret from Jenniel or disguise them as junkets of a different sort. If he didn't, Rory explained, Chief Loyal would learn of Rory's disobedience and run him out of the county. The hostility of Sonny's mother had grown that sensitive and poisonous. Sonny accepted these conditions. To remain true to his Peacock blood, it seemed to him he had to.

Out of respect for Sonny's squeamishness, on that first afternoon Rory put off his own dinner. He offered to show Sonny what he'd done to make his voluntary exile in the dump more hospitable and convenient.

Sonny said okay, but accidentally hooked one of the spit's uprights with his foot and dropped the broiling dog into the fire. Flames crackled, ashes flew, dirt and char clung like scabs to the fallen carcass. Sonny put a hand to his face and began to wheeze. Rory knelt to reset the post and to steady his dinner on the weakened spit. Sonny tried to help, but burnt his left thumb. He rocked back on his heels to suck it, whereupon his wheezing got worse.

Never mind, Rory said. Accidents happen, God knows. Come see my place.

They walked to a bridge of hardpacked sand, then crossed over it to an island on which Rory had built a twostorey hovel of discarded lumber, cinderblocks, linoleum, roofing shingles, even an upended Amana freezer. The house—it looked a little like a house—had a big hinged door, two lopsided windows, a skylight. Sonny admired it. When he trotted to the door for a peek inside, his wheezing ceased entirely.

Why'd you build it out here? Sonny indicated the way the Arkansas eddied around the peninsular sandbar supporting it. Come a big rain, your place'll wind up broken to nubbins and covered over.

Rory said, Just cuz you've built once don't mean you should never have to again.

Oh. For a brief moment this fatalistic pronouncement made deep sense to Sonny.

The next afternoon he visited Rory again. This time he stood on the roof of the hovel's upper storey and tried to catch a fish—a bottom-dwelling bullhead—for Rory's dinner. (Rory proposed to eat some of the dogmeat that he'd cooked yesterday, even though he'd kept it all day in the worn-out freezer functioning for him now as an unorthodox cornerstone.) In working to position himself over a likelylooking pool, Sonny stepped through a linoleum roofpanel and almost plunged through the resulting hole.

Rory caught him, pulled him to safety, and said he could repair the hole easily enough if Sonny would just get down and leave him to secure and cook his own meals.

Sonny returned the following day with a bag of potatochips that he had bought at Reddick's Grocery with some of his own allowance. He regarded this offering as a friendship gift and as repayment for his gaffs of the previous two days. Rory probably thought him a total doofus and screw-up. Before Rory spotted him, Sonny saw Rory on the hovel's weird tower filling in the hole that Sonny had made. Sonny's earlobes flushed, his heart swung like a gong inside his ribcage—but, still unseen, he crossed the sandbridge and took up a position just below the repair work.

Hey! he said, taking two steps back for a better throwing angle. *Think fast!*

With that, Sonny hurled the bag of potatochips up to Rory, whose face had appeared moonlike over the edge of the roof. The bag hit Rory in the chin, dropped back down the flank of the tower, ripped open on a nail protruding from the eave of the lower storey, and spilling chips like featherweight coins flapped with the fury of a screech owl into Sonny's face. The shock more than the force of this blow caught Sonny offguard. He stumbled back again, windmilling his arms, and fell into the river.

Potatochips fell around him, petallike in their beauty. When he broke the surface coughing, many clung to his dripping hair and many more floated south or eddied about briefly before saturating and sinking from view. Rory jumped well out into the river past Sonny, dogpaddled back toward him, tried to help him scramble back onto the mudpack.

I can do it, Sonny said, fighting him. Really.

They reached the bank, Rory pushed Sonny out, they sprawled chuffing like trains in the hovel's shade.

Eventually Rory said, Third time's the charm.

Sir?

Look, Sonnyman, mebbe you don't need to come out here *ever* afternoon.

Sonny put his forearm over his eyes.

Not cuz you got no more grace than a tacklin dummy — that's bout standard for boys your age. But cuz the more you come out here the more certain it is Jenniel or Chief Loyal's gonna find out I'm still hangin round Van Luna to see you.

Sonny said, You want to see me less so folks won't figure you're here to see me?

Right. Or we may not git to see each other atall.

For now, they had a problem even more pressing than Chief Loyal's likely unhappiness with Rory: Sonny's soaked clothes. Rory took them from Sonny (who squatted in front of a fire in his sagging briefs) and draped them from angled broomsticks or over his ramshackle eaves. They had very little time to dry before Jenniel returned from work and expected Sonny home for dinner, but Sonny hoped for a slight diminishing of their dampness and some boys-will-be-boys charity from his mother. Meanwhile, he shivered, glad that a bend in the river and a high muddy bank hid him from anyone visiting the main dumping areas. Rory busied himself aloft, then disappeared into the heart of the structure. When he came out again onto the roof, he fetched in Sonny's clothes, grimacing at their clammy feel, and popped each garment a time or two in the breeze. Then he brought the stuff down to Sonny, along with a perfectly dry yellow ballcap.

What's this? Dressed again, Sonny puzzled over the cap.

For you, Rory said. Don't let your mama see it. Before Sonny could ask why, Rory told him a story:

The Colorado prison to which Cullison and Rory had reported after their trials offered its inmates the chance to compete in several different intramural sports. The very month of their arrival, the warden was organizing a baseball team that would play the highschool squads of several nearby towns. This team would eventually wind up a regular part of these schools' spring baseball schedules, or so hoped the progressive warden and the inmates' elected liaison. The team needed equipment, uniforms, solid coaching.

What we didn't need was travel expenses, Rory said. Ever one of our games would be a home game.

The Peacock brothers had played ball for Coronado Senior High School in their small Kansas hometown (but at different times), and they tried out for, and made, the prison team as an outfielder (Cullison) and a catcher (Rory). Cullison would coach as well as play. When he wrote their mother, India, to tell her about the team, mentioning their need of equipment and a nickname more dignified than either the Rockbreakers or the Cons, India went to work.

She headed up a bakesale and quiltraffle in Coronado and donated the proceeds to the prison team. She also sent a box of fourteen stacked ballcaps of brilliant yellow—in sizes small, medium, and large—and the suggestion that the team call itself the Canaries. Her two boys' old highschool squads in Coronado had played under that name. Neither Cullison nor Rory had the bighouse smarts or maybe just the simple common sense to recognize the folly of India's wellmeant offerings. They hauled out these caps at their team's next practice and touted Canaries as a really hightone moniker.

The Canon City Canaries, Cullison said. Has a nice ring to it, don't you think?

The other ballplayers—two of them lifers, several of them veterans of other penal facilities, including Leavenworth, SingSing, and Alcatraz—traded looks. Then they either broke into laughter or grumbled like unfed stomachs.

I don't sing, said one of these inmates. And I shoor as hell aint yellow.

Another inmate threw his cap down and began to grind it into the yard under his heel. Another pulled his cap apart with his hands. Another separated the bill from the brim with his teeth. A tussle ensued, with Rory just barely managing to salvage one cap from the shipment by snatching it out of the hands of a utilityman of such childlike stature that everyone called him Little Bit. It was this cap that Rory preserved throughout his whole fiveyear sentence and presented to Sonny on the afternoon of the potatochip caper. Sonny was not to allow Jenniel to see it because she had seen Rory behind the plate for Coronado during Cullison's courtship of her, and if anybody could put two and two together from a complex jumble of clues with only a passing resemblance to four, it was Sonny's mama, Jenniel Kempton Peacock.

Sonny did not wear the Coronado Canary ballcap anywhere near his mother. But every morning he tucked it inside his notebook or stuffed it into the front of his jeans so that he could wear it at school. He believed he cut a swashbuckling figure in the cap, and this suspicion found support in the fact that Maggie Vy Medders, the principal's daughter, a compact and pretty girl with soulful halfcircles under her eyes and oddly snowy skin, took nearly every occasion at recess to watch him playing catch or dodgeball and in the classroom to work as his partner on art or history projects — much to the disgruntlement of Neil Stroyer and Pike Kennerly.

Mr. McKinley always asked Sonny to stow the cap in his desk when he saw Sonny wearing it indoors. (In those days wearing a cap indoors had the approximate social cachet of spitting on the carpet.) Sonny would oblige for ten or fifteen minutes before the changeover from math to social studies, or social studies to spelling, gave him an excuse to rummage the cap out again and slap it cockily back on his head. And wearing it — flaunting it, more like — Sonny had a charismatic sheen wholly unavailable to Mr. McKinley.

On Sonny's third blatant disobedience Mr. McKinley splintered a yardstick across his desk and ordered Sonny to report to the principal's office with his confounded yellow hat in his hands, *not* on his head, there to confess his deliberate crime and its indefensible repetitions. Sonny removed the cap and, holding it next to his leg, strolled to the classroom door. Maggie Vy followed his progress with her falsely debauched-looking eyes and a smile of both encouragement and approval. Sonny did not resent this smile, as he might have other sixthgrade girls', for Maggie Vy had suffered her daddy's paddlings at home and well knew their humiliating sting. He smiled back at her. In the hall he set the Coronado Canary cap squarely on his head before marching quicktime to Mr. Medders' office and telling his secretary that Mr. McKinley had sent him for creating a disturbance.

What sort of disturbance? Mr. Medders said when Sonny was ushered in. What's with the cap? Take it off.

Sonny said, That's the disturbance, sir. I kept putting it back on after Mr. McKinley said not to.

Why would you do that?

To keep my head warm?

It's almost May, Peacock. Take the cap off.

Sonny sat stockstill on his chair. Nosir, he said.

Mr. Medders beheld him mildly, as if Sonny had merely taken a bite of tapioca or changed the station on a radio. Well, he finally said, two or three good swats with Billy Bumbuster will probably knock it off. After which I'll confiscate your pretty cap until the end of school.

Yessir, Sonny said. But a better punishment would be to make me do lunchroom duty for a couple of weeks—carting trays, wiping tables, scrubbing pots for Mrs. Cavan's cafeteria crew. That'd last longer and teach me a lesson too.

Mr. Medders did not understand Sonny's preference for two weeks of kitchen labor over a couple of rapid swats, but he saw it as a way to satisfy young Peacock while providing Mrs. Cavan and her overworked lunchroom staff a willing drudge. Sonny did not want Jenniel to know about the yellow cap, and Mr. Medders did not want to inform her of Sonny's misbehavior because that could undermine his planned technical violation of federal and state child-labor laws.

Deal, he said. And he shook hands with Sonny, who scarcely came up to his hip but who kept his yellow cap on even as they shook.

Uncle Rory had to stop eating dogs, Sonny figured. Sooner or later he'd kill, clean, and broil somebody's darling, like Craig Baldwell's bluetick Josiah or Dot Ward's cocker Wiggles. Then somebody with a keen suspicion and an oiled shotgun would go prowling for, and blow the head off, the culprit. On the other hand, Rory refused to eat fish and had too much pride to scrape the vegetable tins that wound up relatively fresh in Van Luna's landfill.

Mrs. Cavan, said Sonny on his first day working, if I do a good job for you can I carry some leftovers home?

Pudgy and florid, Mrs. Cavan ruled her lunchroom domain in a hairnet and a stretched-taut apron that on her ample figure resembled a bib with a mudflap. She seldom denied seconds to anyone, uttered a scolding word, or shirked her own turns at oven cleaning or pot scouring. The two other women who worked with and for her regarded her a virtual saint of the scullery; they saved their disagreements and backbiting for their off hours. Students in the lunchroom frequently heard Mrs. Cavan whistling Ragtime Cowboy Joe or Pistol Packin Mama, the vibrato of her whistle bumbling in her cooking pots like a distraught hornet.

You and your mama come on hard times? she asked.

No mam, not exactly, but we've got a neighbor who's out of work.

Mrs. Cavan patted Sonny's shoulders with her floury hands and kissed him drily on the forehead. Law sez nuthin not eaten on the premises goes home, but the law's full of it. You're a kindly Christian boy who can bet your big toe I'm not about to let no neighbor of yours starve.

She didn't either. Sonny worked two weeks for Mrs. Cavan, primarily washing dishes and hauling trash, and at the end of each session—before shooing Sonny back to the classroom—she handed him a plastic bucket, quartered with plastic dividers, containing meat, vegetables, bread, and dessert for his jobless neighbor. After school Sonny would swing by the kitchen, long since abandoned by its workers, rescue this bucket from the double-doored refrigerator, and hang it from his handlebars for a quick jaunt out to the dump. On these rides, he inevitably wore his Coronado Canary ballcap as he slid through the shadow of the town's grain elevator and jounced over the brain-jogging ridges of the railroad tracks.

Rory accepted these buckets with amused rather than abashed eyes. He liked the fact that Sonny had taken on a daily labor beyond his regular homework; he liked the devotion behind this labor. He did not like playing the helpless beneficiary and told Sonny that he could not remain forever as a vagrant crazy man in a homemade shack on an eroding sandbar in a bend of the Arkansas south of Van Luna's dump.

So eight days into his voluntary servitude Sonny said, Whaddaya plan to do?

Rory said, Still gotta figger that out.

The two Peacocks sat next to each other on a twisted bench of driftwood as Rory gorged himself on handsful of dumplings and beans from Mrs. Cavan's—no, Sonny's—charity bucket. (At least, thought Sonny, he's stopped eating strays.) The coming weekend would pose a supply problem though and Rory might lapse as he had last Saturday.

Friday was Sonny's last day of punishment, Mr. Medders reminded him just before the first bell. Mr. Medders would not allow him to continue in thrall to Mrs. Cavan's crew even if he stuck his ballcap to his head with a gallon of Elmer's Glue and a thousand surgical stitches. Given such defiance, he would suspend

Sonny from school and see if he and Mr. McKinley could concoct a semilegitimate scheme to deny him promotion to junior high.

These threats convinced Sonny to pocket his cap again. One bright aspect of the situation lay in Mrs. Cavan's willingness to prepare a daily charity bucket for the Peacocks' neighbor as long as that neighbor needed help and whether or not Sonny went on pulling scullery duty.

That Friday afternoon Sonny picked up Rory's bucket and freed his Schwinn from the fitted-pipe bicycle rack in front of the school. As he started to mount, Maggie Vy tapped him on the shoulder and asked him what'd happened to his pretty yellow cap. Her frank expression and her puzzled tone told him that she intended no taunt.

Your daddy sez he'll suspend me if I wear it.

Even *outdoors?*

Sonny reddened. A principal's authority did not extend to dictating student clothing away from the classroom, did it? He rummaged his notebook out of his saddlebag and his cap out of the notebook, and fitted the cap to his head. He had the sense that its felt crown had suffered some denting, and its bill was cocked noticeably to one side. Maggie Vy smiled, but with more goodwill than sarcasm.

Yellow's my favorite. You look . . . sporty.

Sporty, Sonny thought. *Sporty.* Before he could flush any redder or withdraw his hand, Maggie, gripping his wrist, shook sunflower seeds into his palm from a cellophane packet. When he clasped his fingers over the striated grains, they clicked against one another faintly.

Energy for your trip, Maggie Vy said. Sunflower energy.

Sonny put a seed between his teeth.

What happened to your thumb? Maggie Vy said.

Burnt it. It's okay.

Maggie Vy kissed the tip of her index finger, then touched that tip to Sonny's thumb.

His thumb tingled. He could hardly move.

Maggie Vy said, You should ride by later to see if I'm on the porch with Cynthia or Irene.

And do what? thought Sonny, cracking the seed. A wheelie? A curbjump? Wave from the street? Make myself look like a lovesick pup? He cracked another couple of seeds, discreetly but manfully spitting the shells to one side, then funneled the rest of the grains into his shirtpocket.

Maggie Vy hailed her friend Darla Westfall at the crosswalk and slipped away before Sonny could reply. So he had plenty to think about pedaling to deliver Rory's dinner and then sitting beside him as Rory chewed gamely away at a slice of fried liver and several rubbery stalks of broccoli. One of his thoughts centered on the forest of sunflowers across the jeepruts from the dump and so by association on the seeds that Maggie Vy had given him. While Rory ate, he cast these seeds about the perimeter of Rory's house. Then he rinsed the bucket in the river, told Rory goodbye, and pedaled across the road to pull four or five of the virile shaggy sunflowers.

These tall flowers, with their brown clockfaces and their lion-like manes, did not lend themselves to comfortable bicycle transport, but Sonny managed to struggle with them all the way back to town without capsizing. To his own huge surprise, in less than ten minutes he found himself at the curb in front of the Medderses' house. Maggie Vy did not occupy the glider on the porch, but he could hear someone plunking out Heart and Soul on the piano beyond the open window behind the glider. He listened to this piece in a trance, as if it were as sublime as any Puccini aria, starting from it only when Joel Medders himself hitched around the corner dragging a gardenhose the color of balogna. Catching sight of Sonny, Mr. Medders paused and squinted hard.

Sporty hat, he said.

That's what Maggie Vy said, Sonny said. Here. These're for her.

He cast down from his handlebars the sunflower stalks he'd ridden into town from the dump. Then he pumped off recklessly down the street with Heart and Soul and a thunderstorm of blood hammering in his ears.

Uprooted sunflowers! Mr. Medders shouted after him. Classy gift, Peacock! She'll be swept off her feet!

Some of the seeds that Maggie Vy had given Sonny sprouted and came up around Rory's sandbar-rooted hovel. They grew fast and tall. By July they had attained Sonny's height at least, with a few of those ornamenting the house only a head or two shorter than Rory. Sonny thought them as graceful as rain and more cheerful than a parley of chipmunks. In even the softest breeze they rustled and flashed.

Surprising Jenniel, Sonny had planted a stand of sunflowers

behind their house on Franklin Street. Also a small garden of carrots, squash, cabbages, sweetpeas.

The sunflowers he liked for their own sakes, but he grew the vegetables out of an inchoate notion (now that school had ended and Mrs. Cavan's catering group had gone on break until September) that he might pick a few to help feed Rory. The impracticality of this scheme dawned on him relatively early though, and well before June Rory had taken steps to see to his own provisioning and upkeep.

I've paid my debt, he told Sonny a week before summer. And it's foolish for a grown man to hide himself in a stinkin dump on the outskirts of happiness.

Whaddaya gonna do? said Sonny: his favorite question.

Waitnsee, Sonnyman. Waitnsee.

Rory ventured into the onsite construction business, using thrownaway materials—discards of all kinds—and his own wit to build a fence around the entranceway to the landfill and a manager's booth just inside the armlike gate. Then he used a sandfilled drum to roll out a series of flats deeper into the landfill—runs, he called them—and built a stockade of barbed wire, chickenwire, and brambles around these runs. He did most of this work—saving back the installation of his gate until last—in the final week of May, and at no point in this flurry of earthmoving and building did he try to cloak his activities from the bewildered Van Lunans who came out to the dump to strew their garbage or to shoot rats. By now Sonny understood that Rory *wanted* the townspeople to see him, and to wonder, and to report his weird doings to either Mayor Goodroe or Police Chief Loyal. The placement of the railroad-style lever-arm across the dump's entranceway, a task to which Sonny had lent his aid, guaranteed a run-in with city authorities, for it appeared to deny taxpaying citizens, with trash to unload or rats to shoot, their inalienable rights to do such things.

Go home, Rory told Sonny when the gate was set. Go home and watch Flash Gordon.

Why?

Cuz I don't want you here when the dung comes flyin off the fan. Rory smiled. Merrily merrily.

Although he pretended to, Sonny did not go home. He could not watch Flash Gordon if he wanted to. He had already watched chapters of these serials so religiously on their afternoon broadcasts from Wichita that, during a crucial head-to-head between Flash and Ming, the Peacocks' Motorola had burned out a tube and shed an acrid stream of sawdust through a pencilsized hole in the console bottom. Besides, the coming set-to between Rory and whoever came out to challenge his improvements to the dump would illuminate the Flash-vs.-Ming showdown as the dopey makebelieve crisis it actually was. So Sonny pretended to go home, but biked left just shy of the railroad tracks, hid his Schwinn in a waste of sorrel and curled dock, and sneaked back along the riverbank until he could climb a mound of tires and peer down on Rory standing arms akimbo next to the guardbox he had erected inside the gate.

It took an hour—Sonny sweated through his shirt and got tire-black on his palms and kneecaps—but at last Chief Loyal arrived. Rory lifted the arm for his patrolcar as perkily as a cadet saluting a colonel.

Hell're you doin here? Loyal climbed out and slammed his door. How long you been back?

I never left. Let me show you some stuff.

Before he could protest, Rory led Chief Loyal from the gate to the entranceway fence to the odd stockade so near Sonny's perch among the tires that, in spite of all the other stinks, Sonny caught a whiff of the chief's aftershave. He prayed not to sneeze or nudge a tire off the mound. He noted that it was less animal force than animal magnetism—Rory's personality—that pulled Chief Loyal about the dump and kept his firearm in its holster.

This dump needs a keeper, Rory said. A caretaker.

Peacock, I—

Folks tote in crap they ought not to. Rake n plow heads. Ol medicine. Busted frigerators. Even brokedown jalopies that ought to go to junkyards. A keeper could watch out for that and make this place last a long time thout stretchin it down the river like a runnin eyesore.

Loyal said, Peacock, we've never—

And whoever took the job could double up as animal-control officer. The town aint got one right now.

We've never had one, Chief Loyal said. Nobody pens their dog here. Folks *live* here so they won't have to.

No, Rory said. They just don't know no better. See these runs. Strays and runaways—dogs, cats, even ferrets if folks start pettifyin em—would git held here till their time ran out or their owners anted up a fine.

Hold on.

Runamoks're dangerous. They can bite, or topple trashcans, or dash in front of traffic, or turn rabid. Community health's at stake. Mebbe even community dignity.

Lissen to the jailbird sing of dignity.

I stand free and sing free, Rory said. I've paid my dues. Now I want to row my own boat, merrily merrily. I've showed you how I can so that all of Van Luna can prosper along with me. Don't be a stick-in-the-mud grudger, Tony.

Loyal crossed his arms and surveyed all that Rory had done to bring a modicum of order to a facility whose root rationale embodied the opposite of order. His right hand rubbed his left collarbone and his sunburned throat.

You'd do all this for free?

Like hell, Rory said mildly. I'd want a salary—say forty bucks a week. And the right to come into town proper thout any hassle, like any other loony Van Lunan. *Ha!*

Forty a week? A hunnerd-sixty a month?

A peon's wages, Tony. Think of all the jobs I'm gonna do. And how I'll always be on call.

Chief Loyal massaged his neck again. Guess I could take it to the city council. Might solve a few problems for me. He knuckled Rory almost affectionately on the arm, and after a slow stroll back up to the guardbox piled into his cruiser. He promised—this was faintly audible to Sonny—to propose Rory's hiring to Mayor Goodroe tomorrow. Then he drove away.

Sonny popped up and threw three quick punches at the sun. Hip hip hooray! he cried. Hip hip hooray! Hip hip— A tire slipped out from under him, and he and the tire bumped down the pile like basketballs down a bleacher tier.

School dismissed for the summer, and when the city council accepted Chief Loyal's recommendation to hire Rory H. Peacock as landfill caretaker and animal-control officer, Jenniel learned from the *Van Luna Vanguard* that her brother-in-law had either returned to town or resurfaced after a long period of hiding out. She said nothing to Sonny, refusing to believe—despite his many outings to the dump and his crazy fascination with Rory—that he knew anything about this event. The news in the paper enraged her though. Rory had seduced Cullison into crime, wounded an innocent man, and, by laying the blame on Cullison, stolen from her a beloved husband and from Sonny a gallant if sometimes foolish daddy. Now he jumped up—where was justice?—as a new city employee. Damn him.

Wasn't it hard enough raising a boy to manhood as a single mom? Daryl Strohm, her new department head at McConnell, once a filing-system specialist in the Pentagon, thought that two or three times a week Jenniel should bring him cinnamon rolls from home, along with her intellect and expertise. Twice in the past month Strohm had had Jenniel chauffeur him into Wichita on private errands. So the only attractive use to which she could think to put Rory Peacock was seizing Strohm by the neck and cracking a few of his upper vertebrae. With a job-candidate roster to revise and another TDY unit to outprocess, Jenniel could hardly imagine worse blows to her role as parent than the almost simultaneous appearances of the Boss from the Pentagon and the Brother-in-Law from Stir.

She wanted to cry, to light out from Van Luna, spiriting Sonny with her to an apartment in—*Paris*, there to teach him piano, cooking, creative stitchery, the punctilious rudiments of the romantic duel. He would wear linen suits with ascots, pocket handkerchiefs, Italian shoes. She would wear flowing silk, elegant shawls, pearled slippers. Kansas—the Great Plains—the Air Capital of the World—all the frustrations of motherhood—would fade before the sophisticated splendor of the Old World like a match flame in full sunlight.

Sonny, seeing the *Vanguard* on the breakfast counter, knew that Jenniel knew that Rory had returned. He knew that she also knew that he and Rory had communicated, even if she chose to bury that knowledge under several layers of denial. Sonny figured that one good way to make her see the truth would be to put on his Coronado Canary ballcap, but he chickened out. Like that cap, he was a deep-saturated yellow. Or else he loved her too much to let the cap declare him a filial turncoat. Three weeks into June, then, both members of the Peacock household on Franklin Street conspired to pretend that neither of them knew what they actually did know.

The Motorola TV set remained unrepaired. As a timepasser, Sonny went to his bedroom and started writing a Robert Service-style ballad about the Klondike goldrush. As Angus Bigfoot McKyle, Sonny's hero, was about to hit the motherlode, Jenniel began playing her upright Mendelssohn in the parlor. Sonny automatically lifted his pen. These days Jenniel played only when a blue funk had taken her, and she played until the mood passed or she exhausted herself at the keyboard.

Sonny would have enjoyed listening except that Jenniel's

music spoke not of her delight with the world but instead of her edginess and despair. She never played hymns or Heart and Soul, she played Autumn Leaves, Unchained Melody, Prisoner of Love, and popular transcriptions of the grandiose concerti of Rachmaninoff, almost always with the keypounding dynamics of a piledriver.

Angus Bigfoot McKyle would not hit the motherlode, at least not tonight. Sonny set his pen aside and tossed his ballcap onto a high shelf in his closet.

For several days Sonny stayed away from the dump. Rory had found work. He could buy groceries. Charity buckets, halted at the end of the school year, need never again provide his chief source of the four major food groups. Besides, Sonny had biking, hiking, and other stuff to pursue with Craig, Neil, and Pike, Van Luna's Three Musketeers. (Sonny regarded himself as D'Artagnan.) All for one and one for all, so long as Maggie Vy or Irene Burden didn't step in and provoke a wrangle.

Then, in July, Pioneer Days struck the town like a weeklong plague of cattledrovers, furtrappers, sodbusters, Indian fighters, frontier women, saloon gals, potionpushers, and rope-galluses scalawags. Male citizens grew beards and pulled on boots. Females wore calico dresses and soft floppy bonnets that pretty much hid their faces. Conestoga wagons stood at each end of Main as rallying sites; between them stretched a gamut of attractions, from foodbooths to tool displays to art shows to bakesales and canned-goods competitions. In Buffalo Bill Park a kid could ride ponies, a spinning bullet capsule on a huge rotating arm, or a Ferriswheel with gondolas penstriped like customized hotrods. The whole business district reeked of manure, boiled peanuts, fried meats, cottoncandy, sweat.

Jenniel took half a personal day one Thursday and asked Sonny to go to town with her. He had already spent a month's allowance on the games on the cobblestone midway and despised even the thought of appearing downtown with his mother. Worse, she planned to go as herself, not a pioneer woman, and expected introductions to any of the carnies or vendors with whom Sonny had become familiar. He argued that you didn't get buddybuddy with tattooed hucksters who only wanted your money.

But Jenniel said, They're people too. They appreciate a smile as much as the next guy.

I doubt it, Sonny wanted to say but didn't.

On the midway in the three o'clock sun amid all the dubious games of skill, Jenniel said, Which is your favorite?

Sonny took her to some empedestaled aquariums with toy steamshovels or cranes inside them. The cases held no water, only a twoinch stratum of corn kernels on which lay a number of cheap prizes: bubblegum, toy cars, Chinese fingercuffs, and a few shiny silverdollars. A pair of fluted metal wheels on the case operated the crane, one to swing the arm over a prize and one to work the pincers and pick it up. Silverdollars slid like water through these pincers, but bamboo fingercuffs gummed right to them. Corn kernels *plooshed* whenever a poorly grasped prize—often a silverdollar—dropped into them.

After watching some young gamblers, Jenniel said, What a swindle. You sure you want to play?

Yes mam.

Jenniel gave Sonny a dime to give the carnie, who, thank God, had too much else going on to talk. Sonny twiddled the knob that swung the crane arm over a silverdollar. Then he twiddled the pincer wheel and grasped the coin. He coaxed the arm toward the chute that would toboggan his prize to him if he could maneuver the coin into place and let go. Amazingly, he seemed to be doing okay. Better than okay.

Ssssss! Jenniel hissed, laying a hand on his neck. *Lookout lookout! It's slipping it's slipping!*

I know I know, he said, but could do nothing to stop it and so prepared himself for failure.

Swing it! a male voice said. Turn that knob sharp!

Sonny obeyed. The pincers on the crane arm flung the coin into the chute; the silverdollar rattled into his hand.

Rory, Sonny said.

Rory and Jenniel faced each other for the first time since she had seen him through a pane of glass in a prison visiting room. (Cullison had just died.) She liked what she saw today no more than she had liked it then.

Jenniel took Sonny's arm, but he shrugged her hand aside, hunching his back as if to fit it into an invisible carapace. Then he saw that Rory had a great shaggy beard, grown in mere days, to match his curly hair. He also wore a trapper's garb, fur from boots to coonskin cap, with only his sleeveless tunic as a concession to the sweltering heat.

Come on, Jenniel said to Sonny. Let's go. You've got your precious prize.

I live here now. Rory nodded. Just over the tracks. A snail of sweat crept down his brow.

I guess if you're not in the hoosegow it's a free country, Jenniel said. Sonny, come *on*.

I do good work in this town, Rory said as she gentled Sonny away from him. Ask Chief Loyal. Brent Noah just ran some lines out to my place. I've even got me a phone. (Brent Noah was a power-company man.)

Jenniel turned back around. Hooray for you. Now tell me why you think I give a flip.

Rory looked at Sonny, bending forward to cut the distance between them. You ought to see my sunflowers now. They scrape the blue blue sky. Any little breeze, they rattle like velvet swords.

Poetry becomes you no more than that beard, Jenniel said.

Rory spoke to Sonny: Call me if you ever need help. I'll come through like gangbusters. . . .

After this Pioneer Days collision, Jenniel asked Sonny not to associate with or in any way make himself subject to Rory's influence. (Sonny respected her tact in declining to command him outright.) She restated her objections to the man, listed his many betrayals, said that his finagling of a place in city government, even as dogcatcher and first minister of trash, revealed him plainly as a conniving s.o.b. To mess with Rory, she said, would constitute a wilful slam at Cullison's memory. She loved Sonny with an ache strong enough for any two mothers because she had to make up for Cullison's lost love. It killed her to think that Rory had succeeded in hoodwinking Sonny, that he had preyed again on the first victims of his greed and power lust. So saying, Jenniel Kempton Peacock sat before Sonny with her head up and tears running down her face.

The result? Sonny, despite his love for the dump and the river and the nearby willow copses, avoided all those places beyond the tracks. He crossed the street or changed directions or hid upon seeing Rory on Van Luna's maindrags or in Buffalo Bill Park. These tactics had a cost: they hurt. Many times, avoiding Rory, Sonny understood that Rory had seen him avoiding him. After many months, the hurt deepened when Sonny realized that if Rory saw him first, Rory either pretended not to have seen him or hurried to get away. Worse, Sonny surmised that Rory sidestepped him not from resentment or indifference, but a desire to spare Sonny discomfort if Sonny had to act first to keep them from meeting.

One Saturday in October Sonny ducked into Harry McCullohs' barbershop next to the Pix Theater. He sat down to wait his turn. Men and boys crowded the narrow shop, a lot of the men overalled codgers, a lot of the boys preschool tadpoles. Sonny recognized several faces the way an ardent moviegoer recognizes the bit players in most 1940s Hollywood releases, but he could not call the names of many of them. Meanwhile, McCullohs was rat-a-tat-tatting about trade subsidies to foreign countries, bending the ear — actually holding it down to clip a few stray hairs behind it — of a customer rotated away from Sonny. Then McCullohs swung the chair around, and Sonny, who had noticed something familiar about the hair on the linoleum, looked up to find Rory, semishorn, regarding him.

Hey there, Sonny.

Sonny knew that he should say something, but he could not. He patted his pockets as if he had forgotten his money. Sorry, Mr. McCullohs, he said. Sorry. After stumbling over several customers' feet, he exited with a glass-shuddering slam of the door.

That year he attended junior high some three blocks from Van Luna Elementary. The junior high housed only two grades — seventh and eighth — and dominated a neighborhood mostly notable for its black maples, its squat clapboard houses, and a general air of gloom that made Sonny think of the forest primeval in Longfellow's Evangeline. Blue skies seemed rare, with so many days of leaden overcast or warring fleets of thunderheads that the birds hushed and the purr of tires over asphalt hinted at sinister errands: a hearse to the cemetery, a patrolcar to the bungalow of a wife beater.

One hearse did make it to the cemetery that fall. Junior high principal Arnold Binelli suffered a heartattack in the lunchroom one Thursday and died popeyed and thrashing in front of a table of seventhgraders disgusted with their cold beans and franks. The school nurse could not revive him, and when the ambulance carried his faintly lavender body away, many students believed they had witnessed a complex stunt, a pretext for shutting down for the afternoon, and that Mr. Binelli would return on Friday to help administer a battery of standardized tests. He had faked his heartattack, to relieve his student body's stress levels.

But Mr. Binelli had really died. School did not meet on Friday, and on Saturday the board of education held a special session to issue a memorial proclamation in Mr. Binelli's honor and to appoint Joel Medders to replace him. Sonny, along with most of his classmates, approved of this appointment. Despite or because of his holey paddle, Mr. Medders had his students' respect. Most liked him as much for his pokerfaced wit as for his powerforward height.

Maggie Vy contributed to his popularity. Her soulful eyes — the eyes of a madonna on too much caffeine — and her good grades, not to mention her house parties, her pet horse, and her stylish clothes, made *her* popular. Her popularity fed her daddy's, and vice versa, until it seemed only right to almost everyone that Mr. Medders should oversee whatever school his daughter attended and that she should attend whichever school he oversaw.

In many ways though, the months after Mr. Medders' arrival circled toward Christmas break like a scratched 45 rpm record that sticks and then plays, repeatedly, until the needle retrieving its sound winds up tracking the whitenoise spirals at its hub. Sonny heard October, November, and December that way. The day-to-day song of that period lurched and grated; it had no consistent rhythm, no hummable melody, no joy to give. Sonny kept his Coronado Canary ballcap in the closet, hidden away, and Maggie Vy never asked him why he no longer wore it or when he planned to fetch it out again.

Of course Mr. Binelli's death had dampened everyone's spirits. In sympathy the sky brooded over Van Luna in tones of grey and dust-heavy umber. Meadowlarks clung in silence to the wheatstubble in outlying fields. Or so it seemed, even though Sonny realized that this bleak impression of the world had less to do with reality (for days of sunshine and overcast recurred almost exactly as they had in previous years) than with some startling changes among his classmates and his own reactions to those changes.

First of all, over the summer Neil Stroyer had shot up like a sunflower potted in pigdung. He had also put on muscle, and anyone looking at him could see that he needed to shave — not just to clip the scraggly hairs that popped out randomly on his chin, as Craig Baldwell and Pike Kennerly did, but to apply a bonafide razor on a daily basis to the entire lower half of his face. Neil looked like a man, not a boy, and every girl at Van Luna Junior High, including Irene Burden and Maggie Vy Medders, had noticed his metamorphosis.

Sonny, meanwhile, had determined that no one at his school, male or female, stood closer to the ground than he did. In short, he was the shortest kid on the premises. Maggie Vy — as a girl, and as a powerforward's daughter—had grown almost as much as Neil had and could look him in the nostrils, if not the eyes, without mounting a stepstool.

The Three Musketeers, with Sonny as D'Artagnan, found fewer occasions for weekend adventuring together. Neil had moods, weird moods. He telephoned girls, or hung around their houses, or met them at Zook's Drugstore or the Dairy Blizzard.

Pike got interested in breaking down automobile engines and painting rebellious designs—skulls, flames, cobras—on the hoods and flanks of highschool boys' souped-up jalopies, skills that his older brother Zach had taught him.

Craig, who read sci-fi novels and astronomy texts, began messing around with telescopes, microscopes, model rockets, insect collecting, chemistry sets. Maybe because he remained close to Sonny in height, he palled around with Sonny more than with Neil or Pike and frequently included Sonny in his weekend rocket launches and chemical-mixing experiments.

For his part, Sonny had no abiding passions but thumbing through his Topps baseball cards, writing rhymed poems, and sleeping. Sleep he loved. He slept like a seed, continually probing and reorienting throughout the night.

Early in December a snowfall blanketed Van Luna and the empty fields surrounding it. By some askew happenstance Sonny and the Musketeers came together that Saturday. Just east of town they built a snug fort in an anomalous fivefoot declivity in Graham Richardson's cowpasture. Long cardboard strips—from packingcases for refrigerators or stoves—provided them their walls, their floor, and, held aloft on counterpropped boards, their ceiling. At a different compass point, each boy lay bundled in parka, scarf, and woolen cap on the cardboard slopes of this fort, facing inward and listening with glee to the wind keening harmlessly above them and the periodic lowings of Richardson's disgruntled cattle.

A kid could hibernate in such a hideout, Sonny thought. A kid could sleep down here forever.

Instead—almost as eagerly as they had as fourth-, fifth-, and sixthgraders—the Musketeers talked. About an Enchanted Bluff in New Mexico. About cruising either east or west on Route 66 in a snazzy Corvette Stingray until they ran smack up against the end of America. About goldeneyed Martians and the mysterious chesspiece cities that stood reflected in their canals. About oneman bathyscaphe excursions to the bottom of the Mariana

Trench. About uniformed bands of spidermonkeys in the orchid-hung rainforests of Brazil.

For Sonny, the only out-of-whack element in the Musketeers' underground reunion stemmed from Neil Stroyer's newfound size — he had to scrunch to keep his head below their wind-rippled ceiling — and from his faint but detectable air of superiority. A smirk, an ugly lipcurl, accompanied his every remark, just as it met every claim or adventurous suggestion that any of his friends put forth. Sonny fell silent and grew even more sure of Neil's judgmental detachment.

Finally Neil rocked forward and said, Cmon, you guys, show me yours.

Craig looked sidelong at him. Show you our what?

You know, Neil said. Your shortarms. Your peckers.

Sonny, Craig, and Pike looked at one another as if Neil had asked them — well, just what he had asked them.

Pike vented a highpitched guffaw. Why would you want us to do that, Stroyer?

Cuz I've got a man's now, Neil said. When it stands it's right at half a foot.

Half a foot? Craig said. How do you know that?

Come on, Mister Wizard, can't you guess? I measured. I put a ruler to it.

Pike giggled in spates. Sonny and Craig regarded Neil with faces utterly blank. The Enchanted Bluff, the cities of Mars, and Brazil's uniformed monkeys all evaporated from Sonny's mind like pictures in a shortcircuited dream.

So what do you guys rule off at? Neil said. Or just slap em out and show em so's we can say who's king.

Criminy, Craig said. It's too cold for that kind of crap. And nobody else here's bothered to break out a ruler for such a job, Stroyer.

Not even you, Mister Wizard? Cmon. On the other hand, *why* would you? Neil barked a laugh and reached over his head with both hands to jostle their cardboard roof up and down. A gust caught one corner and whirled the whole panel on a bucking cartwheel over Richardson's pasture. A two-by-four in the hole toppled, and the remainder of the roof fell in. Snow blew down on them, scarves of gauzy white dust.

The roof's collapse ended not only their discussion but the entire outing. Sonny and Craig left together, but Neil and Pike angled off in different directions, the wind howling after them, shrapnel storms of snow glittering and whirling all about the cottonwood-studded pasture.

Eventually Sonny separated from Craig and got home to find a note on the table: *Visiting Blanche. Home soon.* Blanche worked with Jenniel in personnel at the airbase, and the two women were best friends. Snowstorms—snow itself—frightened Blanche, a native of Florida, and she insisted on company when drifts began to migrate, even if they discouraged and sometimes thwarted visits.

Sonny had the house to himself, at least for a while. He recalled that last summer Rory had told him, Call me if you ever need help. Like Blanche, Sonny felt that he needed help. However he also strongly felt that for all her tenderness and wisdom Jenniel would provide him neither the solace nor the counsel that she always brought Blanche. Sonny decided to call Rory. Rory still had no book listing, but a local operator patched Sonny through manually. The next small miracle was that Rory answered.

Sonny talked to Rory as if they had last seen each other only yesterday. Rory replied in kind. Static—from the wind, from the kicking flurries—crackled behind his words without obscuring them: What's eatin you, sport?

Sonny told him about the cardboard fort and Neil Stroyer's boast. He confessed that what was bothering him was that very boast and his own stalled development.

The static on the line and Rory's oceanic laughter became indistinguishable from each other.

Sonny held the receiver at arm's length, listening to its seashell roar. For a moment he considered hanging up, a form of rudeness that Jenniel despised as much as she did the petty lewdness of her current boss. Finally Rory stopped laughing.

Forgive me, Sonnyman. You still there?

Yeah.

You hate me, I bet. Your face aburnin?

No. Yes.

Forgit what Neil said. Do this: Go outside, find a good clean drift, grab you a coupla handsful, and take em into your mouth till they begin to melt. Swallow the meltage. Come back inside and warm up.

Sonny stared at the ebony handset.

You hear me?

Yessir. I suppose I do. And he obeyed Rory to the last specification. His face cooled, his anger at Neil waned, his self-doubt departed. He resented Rory's laughter though and dreamt that night that he had pushed Rory into a whirlpool in a shoreward stretch of the Arkansas and watched him corkscrew into its depths like a needle tracking a 45 rpm record all the way to its innermost hub.

After this telephone call Sonny lost every inclination to visit or talk to his uncle. He fell into a volition-killing winter trance. The world acquired for him the outline and substance of gauze. He sleepwalked through its soft contours oblivious to the necklace ring — Maggie Vy's — that Neil Stroyer now wore daily to school. He sleepwalked through Neil's weird hallway dances, poetry recitals, impromptu political rants. He remained heedless of most social matters until spring tornado season, when funnelclouds hurtled through the southern Great Plains as often as freighttrains but without their coherence or predictability.

One night in March the town's emergency siren began to wail, keening from watertower height, shivering almost every Van Lunan right down to the bones. Jenniel hurried Sonny out of the house in his pajamas and down into their combination cannedgoods vault and stormshelter — beneath a dromedarian berm next to the still untilled garden. A battery-operated radio broadcasting skywatches and twister sightings went with them, goosing Sonny's anxiety. Once under the corrugated tin door, Jenniel set the radio on a high musty shelf where it would not lose its signal. (Various announcers' strangled voices cut off and resumed with maddening irregularity.) Filthy canning jars lined the walls, and the hole itself smelled of damp earth and an unplaceable rot.

Sonny, sitting bent forward on the edge of an unbalanced canvas cot, trembled in his slippers. Jenniel dialed in a new station every time an old one dwindled away. The cellar door whined or clattered as the winds dictated, and the sounds of thrashing trees and tumbleweeding gardentools or lawnchairs seemed endless, unimaginably so. Sonny's ribcage ached. His stomach roiled. Not wanting to shame himself, despising an act he could not resist, he hawked up a viscous string of bile and tried to unhook it from his bottom lip. Jenniel wiped his mouth with the sleeve of her robe and made him stretch out on the cot. Sirens other than the Civil Defense emergency siren — firetrucks? patrolcars? ambulances? — yowled out and dopplered away in the machinegunning rain.

Two hours later there was neither rain nor wind. Jenniel helped Sonny — a thirteen-year-old invalid codger — back into the house. His stomach had stopped cramping, but he lay awake till morning scolding himself for cowardice. Then Jenniel came in and told him that a tornado had hit Fedora, seven miles up the road, visiting upon it at least twelve deaths and hundreds of thousands of dollars' worth of damage. Shamefully, this news eased his conscience a little about the extent of his babyish anxiety in the shelter. . . .

Sonny's juniorhigh career ended unspectacularly. Even as one of the shorter boys on roll (by March of his eighthgrade year he had reached fivefootthree), he did play guard on the basketball team, which Mr. Medders coached and which also featured Neil Stroyer at center. But his gradepoint average dropped and Maggie Vy and the other popular girls in their class now looked to the new highschool on the Wichita Highway for boyfriends, to the chagrin and annoyance of most of the eighthgrade boys, who tried to compensate by playing court to doe-eyed seventhgraders.

Over the summer before his promotion to the highschool as a freshman, Sonny's mother began to date a bachelor officer at McConnell, a B-47 pilot who sometimes showed up at their house on Franklin in a luminescent orange flightsuit, a garment so stitched together with zippers that Sonny once dreamt of the man — Captain Chillicothe Smith — with zippers on his mouth and eyelids. Chili, as everyone called the captain, struck Sonny as an okay guy, but his orange suit made him look less like an airman than a swashbuckling clown. Sonny almost always felt embarrassed around him, whether because of the flightsuit or a powerful suspicion that he cramped the captain's woo-pitching, Sonny could not have said. Usually, then, unless Jenniel told him authoritatively not to, Sonny left the house during Chili's calls and rode around town on his increasingly dilapidated and undersized bicycle.

One evening in August he took a ride to the dump, which he had not visited in months. His fresh sight of the riverside landfill amazed him, for Rory had supervised a massive cleanup and beautification project. Inside the frontgate Sonny saw a neat blondbrick house with cobblestone paths and flowergardens around it. Above and beyond the expanded runs of the animal compound, which a fluttery rank of staked poplar seedlings bordered, loomed Van Luna's brandnew motorpool of heavy yellow equipment: a garbagetruck, a backhoe, two or three bulldozers, a snowplow, a tractor, and a converted schoolbus for carrying volunteers to regional disaster sites.

The dump's old middens reposed on the edges of these new

buildings or in some cases between them, but Sonny could find no sign of the mountain of tires that had once overlooked the river. Moreover, bulldozers had pushed the latest deliveries of garbage, construction rubble, and discarded appliances into low escarpments. Sonny could not tell from the gate, but he would have wagered that Rory's original hovel no longer existed either. The dump still reeked, but it looked almost habitable, and by creatures other than bottleflies, rats, and stiffnecked turkeybuzzards.

Sonny slipped past the lever arm controlling admittance, then ducked both himself and his Schwinn under a long chain from which hung a placard announcing the facility's hours. Several dogs in the pound began to bark, leaping against the chainlink or pacing back and forth along it with indecisively wagging tails. Rory appeared before Sonny as if out of the dust and haze of sunset, wearing ashpowdered boots, a pair of creased beige slacks, and a ribbed undershirt with no arms. Sonny felt that his uncle *hulked.* His hair and beard glinted, the sunset outlined him in salmoncolored light.

Many months no meetings, Rory said. Like to come in? He gestured toward his house and headquarters. The dogs stopped barking. Just beyond a ridge of trash, the silken flow of the Arkansas asserted its music.

Sonny said, No thanks.

Well?

You've fixed it up nice, Sonny said. But it's still only a glorified dump and I couldn't live where you do. You know, the horrible *smell.* Out of nervousness Sonny pushed down on the higher of his two pedals. His chain slipped abruptly off the rear chainwheel, folded up on itself, dropped into the greasy dust.

Crap, Sonny said. That's always happenin.

Mebbe I can fix it. Rory knelt, took the chain in his big hands, spread it out, labored to resprocket it.

For no good reason Sonny could think of, he told Rory about the storm that almost a year and a half ago had made him sick on the scary night that a killer tornado slammed Fedora. His story flowed as irrepressibly as a river: his fear, his shame, his helplessness. While Rory worked, Sonny fixed his gaze on a bulldozer in the motorpool even as he unabashedly elevated Rory to the status of confessor. By the time Sonny had finished his story, Rory had reset the chain.

That should git it, he said. For now.

Sonny waited.

The next time a twister like that Fedora storm dances past Van Luna, tell yourself you've done been nauzjiss on account of one. Scairt's okay—that storm scairt *me*, Sonny—but sick's humiliatin, not for what people think but for the way it drops you low.

So whaddaya do? To keep from gettin sick?

Like I said, tell yourself you've done been sick, then do something else. Spot twisters for a neighbor, mebbe.

Sonny considered this. Rory wiped his hands on his ribbed undershirt, not his clean pressed slacks, and invited Sonny in again, this time for a lunchmeat sandwich and a sodapop, but Sonny decided that in inadvertently betraying Jenniel's wishes to avoid Rory, he had gibbered long enough with the enemy. He shook his head, mounted his bike.

No matter how nice it looks, he said. No matter. I just can't stay here. He pedaled off, struggling back to the road through a raked layer of silt, clay, ash.

It beats prison, Rory murmured after him.

Brandnew ninthgraders at Van Luna High School entered a hostile ecological system at the bottom of the teenage food chain. Seniors fed on juniors, juniors on sophomores, and all three upperclasses on eggshell-walking freshmen.

Fortunately, over the summer the highschool principal, David Lustig, opted for early retirement and moved to Arizona. The board of education hired Joel Medders to replace Lustig, making the Medders family's batting average in the game of school-by-school advancement a perfect one thousand. Maggie Vy had never had to attend a facility run by anyone other than her daddy.

Sonny was glad. Mr. Medders' taking control at Van Luna High somewhat mitigated the traditional lowliness of entering freshmen. Maggie Vy underscored her own untouchability in the halls by carrying in her handbag one of her daddy's perforated wooden paddles, whose presence discouraged hazing. In fact, Maggie Vy's untouchability extended to some of her classmates, Sonny included, at least for the first two or three weeks, by which time the dailiness of classes had begun to homogenize the studentbody, counteracting its tendencies to oneupmanship and conflict.

On the personal level, Sonny did no better than he had done as an eighthgrader—worse, maybe. He had no girlfriend, nor any imaginable prospects. Neil Stroyer and Pike Kennerly had drifted without fuss or any apparent harsh feelings out of his narrowing circle of pals. Captain Chili Smith occupied more of Jenniel's time than he did—a relief in one way, but in another a source of repressed puzzlement. Rory Peacock, his uncle on the outskirts, he now viewed as one more rivet in the clanking machinery of Van Luna's city government: a mere nestfeatherer, maybe even a sellout. And after their Christmas vacation, the basketball coach —not Mr. Medders, who had too much else to do, but Jimmy Trube, an elderly toughguy for whom Mr. Medders had once played—cut Sonny from the junior varsity and told him to try out for track instead. (Sonny had no interest in track.) His grades had improved since last year though, especially in composition and social studies, but good grades commanded less respect among his peers than they once had; in fact, among a few lunkheads, they stimulated catcalls, mockery, ostracism. Craig Baldwell, Sonny's best buddy and a good student, endured similar treatment, but dismissed casual hecklers and even more obnoxious tormentors as idiots.

Idiots, Craig said classily. Spitlicking zombies.

Tornado season rolled in that spring with ripening fury. Severe thunderstorm watches gave way to warnings, which either gave way to or combined with funnelcloud warnings, many of them as long as political campaigns. The warnings led to sightings that triggered sirens, radio updates, shelterscrambles among the populations of dozens of bamboozled towns, the deployment of patrolcars, ambulances, heavy yellow equipment.

One afternoon at the highschool, with the watertower siren ululating fiercely, Mr. Medders had his teachers send every student into the building's interior halls, where they sat in morose lines, heads down, fingers locked behind their necks, just as they did for Civil Defense drills simulating the threat and terror of a Soviet ICBM strike.

As Mr. Medders strolled past on an inspection round, Sonny glanced up from his selfprotective huddle. This is just like a bomb drill, he said.

Mr. Medders halted and looked down. (He had a long way to look down.) Why not? he said. This is a war, Peacock. Only the enemy is meteorological rather than ideological and a lot harder to predict than the Rooskies. He tousled Sonny's hair. Hang in there. We'll come through, believe me.

They did. The school—the whole town—survived this scare, but every week brought fresh thunderhead incursions and tornado sorties.

Twice in April the Peacocks ducked into their cellar. On the second such occasion, Captain Chili rousted Sonny from bed and hustled him out to the berm, where Jenniel stood propping the door, her kneelength terrycloth robe and her translucent nightgown whipping about in torrents of rainless wind. Captain Chili sported a Tshirt and jeans, the white of his boxershorts visible in his halfzipped fly. Sonny had not even known he was in the house.

Down in the cellar, Jenniel and Captain Chili covered their embarrassment, or tried to, singing stupid ditties in loud voices: Witch Doctor, Flying Purple People Eater, Itsy Bitsy Teenie Weenie Yellow Polka Dot Bikini, She'll Be Comin Round the Mountain. Sonny listened skeptically to their offkey version of Witch Doctor, tentatively joined in on the next two songs, and enthusiastically conducted the captain and Jenniel on the third.

Then Sonny said, Let's do Row Row Row Your Boat. Jenniel and Chili assented. With the storm buffeting and yowling just above them, Sonny led them through a succession of boisterous rounds, finishing in a gruff baritone: Merrily merrily merrily merrily, Life is but a dream.

The following Saturday, flabbergastingly enough, another tornado watch went into effect shortly before sunset. Jenniel had driven into Wichita to see *Inherit the Wind* with Captain Chili, after earlier instructing Sonny to go to Mrs. Whited's if any sort of emergency arose. He had no plans to report to a babysitter he had long ago outgrown and only a thin curiosity—rather than a crippling fear—about the telegraphically phrased weather bulletins doing intermittent crawls across the foot of their TV screen.

Leaving the set on, he went outside, where he immediately smelled a flood of galvanized air molecules, and climbed onto the roof by way of a ladder that Chili had propped against the house for some raingutter repair. Sonny advanced from the kitchen's sloping roof to the ridgepole of the main roof, then straddled it like a rodeo cowboy gingerly lowering himself onto a Brahma bull.

From there he could see the sun squeezing down at the top of a narrow leaf-fringed street. Tree branches stood out like construction-paper cutouts on a rippled tin mirror reflecting the watery yellow of a lowwattage lightbulb. Lovely. Spooky too. Sonny shifted his butt.

To the east, north, and southeast: prairie. The curve of a high grey lid capped these plains. To the south the jumbled rooftops, linden and maple canopies, and towers of Van Luna (watertower, grain elevator, broadcast antennas) blocked any chance of spotting a funnelcloud spinning toward them over the shiny wet spine of the river.

Cowabunga, Buffalo Bob, said Sonny.

He stood, his hands on his knees, balancing himself with one sneaker on either slope of the roof. Then, fully upright, he heard the watertower siren cycle through its thin repertoire of alarms: loud, louder, loudest. He covered his ears.

The unsteady tip of a waltzing funnelcloud dipped out of the curved grey lid that had advanced on Van Luna from the open plains. This tip tracked from side to side as the svelte ashen oriole's-nest of its body writhed seemingly at crosspurposes to its tip. The cloud and the ambient pewter-rose sky grew hazier and weirder in the long sunset, and in Sonny's own exhilarating wooziness atop the house.

Pivoting, he spied another twister, this one as broad and white as the concrete spillway of a dam, clocking about itself to the northwest. A monster. Van Luna's irregular grid spread out before it vulnerably. The siren keened at its shrillest, and in certain streets silhouetted figures scurried in panic or strolled in postures of fake calm for shelter. The convergence of these funnels, Sonny figured, would signal the town's final battle in this spring's war.

Cmon! he cried, beckoning them with both arms. Cmon, you lousy stinkin twisters!

They came, each from its own direction, but the narrower cloud, the one like an ebony nylon on the leg of a lingerie model, ran faster. It touched its toe to a field beyond town, kicked up a cycloning spray of dirt and cropstubble, and rose again to dizzying height, as if yanked on a garterlike lead. The wider cloud, like an ivory Slinky revolving about itself even as by turns it elongated and flattened, plodded forward. Sonny decided to ignore it. Turning back to the tornado from the southeast, he was astonished to see that it had already crossed into town, obscuring the houses and the lindens on Van Luna's perimeter in a haze of added debris. His amazement also stemmed from looking up into the funnel's evershifting hollow at the secret engine powering it. He could hear nothing but a monumental growl and a ssssssss like the outgassing of a heated precious metal.

What happened next Sonny may have actually done, or he may have only dreamt and later transmuted into delusional reality: he could never decide. Against all reason and despite all obstacles, he reached one hand into the upwardtending well of the tornado and grasped within it a rung of air or iron or wood that enabled him to fly, as the tornado rose again and turbidly redirected itself from Franklin Street to the street on which the Medderses lived. There, as Sonny struggled to stay aboard, the funnel cracked like a bullwhip, flinging him clear of his handhold and bowling him up against the chainlink fence around the family swimmingpool.

An oak behind the house crashed down on the Peace-O-Mind bombshelter, and Sonny labored to his feet. He clambered over the fallen oak's trunk—a trunk as big around as a Volkswagen—and searched amid its snapped branches and torn foliage for the shelter's airpipe. The siren no longer blared. A silence like snow had mantled the town.

Sonny put his lips near the airpipe and spoke in a voice so unlike his own that it unsettled him: A tree's on your exit. It's too big for me to move. Someone down in the bunker spoke, and Sonny replied, Okay okay.

This time no one answered, almost as if Sonny's new voice, distorted by the airpipe, had frightened the Medderses too. But now that these funnelclouds had spun into and through Van Luna, the family was out of imminent peril, for Mr. Medders had stocked the shelter with enough supplies for even a protracted fallout siege.

Sonny still wanted to get them out. Speculating dazedly about his conveyance to Maggie Vy's, he loped off through their yard to his own neighborhood and rushed into his house to make a call. The receiver returned no dialtone. He got his bike out of the garage and set off for the dump, noticing as he rode that Van Luna was strewn with trash, lopped foliage, a thousand other windblown scraplets. The town was torn up in patches, as if the twisters had aimed random hammerblows at it, picking and choosing their targets with the stupidity and nihilism of armed psychotics.

The chain on Sonny's old Schwinn kept slipping. At several intersections he had to pedal over downed powerlines. Vehicles moved in the streets again, folks stood outside surveying their damage. Then, suddenly, pitchdarkness. The only visible light came from automobile headlamps and the candles flickering in the picturewindows and secondstorey bays of the houses that had weathered the pummeling, and even some of those stood in shorn sections, semidemolished. Sonny heard children crying, grown men calling out names, requests for help, angry commands.

The business district—namely, Main Street—had pretty much escaped destruction, but the old clapboard residential neighborhoods between the traindepot and the Methodist church had suffered a hideous melancholy scramble.

Craig Baldwell's family lived in one of the ruined houses, but Sonny, squinting into the darkness—an alien topography superimposed on a townscape he thought he knew—kept pumping, despite his cranky chain. Before reaching the railroad tracks though, he made out several yellow machines, their headlamps crisscrossing eerily, parked next to or grumbling purposefully through the tread-gullied yard of Mayor Goodroe's remodeled Victorian.

Rory Peacock hulked in the midst of the machines, talking to the drivers and holding in his arms a two- or three-year-old child with a bloody gash on its temple. Sonny bumped his bike up onto the faulted sidewalk—an uprooted tree had levered a cracked slab out of the ground—and his chain broke for good, falling completely off. With some care he laid the bike down, then tiptoed fastidiously through the slimy grass.

Uncle Rory! he called. *Uncle Rory!*

The curlyheaded man turned toward him without fully seeing him. What the hell you want? he barked, inadvertently daunting Sonny even as he stroked the cheek of the dazedlooking kid in his arms.

Help, Sonny said. For Maggie Vy's family.

As shadowy men and groaning machines worked at Rory's curt behests, Sonny told about the Medderses and how he had found them trapped in their bombshelter. He left out the part about traveling from his house to theirs while clocking around at the tip of a funnelcloud.

To Sonny's surprise, Rory slapped an ignition key into his palm and nodded toward a parked bulldozer. Take it, Sonnyman. Go git em out.

But—

Think your broken bike's gonna git you there?

Nosir. The chain fell off. But I've never—

Rory interrupted, telling Sonny how to start the machine, how to drive it, how to operate its scoop. He wagered that all Sonny really needed to do was nudge the fallen oak a couple of feet off the bombshelter's hermetically sealed door. Any fool could do it, and Sonny had at least as much greymatter as did a lump of modeling clay.

Just clear the tree and git back here, Rory said. We'll need that ugly yellow trapshun ourselves fore thisere night's over.

Sonny could not credit Rory's handing him the keys to a bulldozer. He could not really picture himself sitting at its controls, much less driving it across town and operating it from its safety cage like an honest-to-God earthmoving man. He did it though, after some embarrassing struggle with the gears and the footpedals; and no one in Van Luna—the confusion being general, the darkness providing cover—called him down for his presumption or griped about a truly horrible misuse of costly city equipment.

At the Medderses', Sonny easily cleared the oak. As the clan ascended from the shelter—Maggie Vy and her mother first, Joel Medders unfolding into the dozer's headlamps after them—Sonny ground out of their backyard in reverse, acknowledging their shouts of thanks with a clanking salute from the dozer's scoop, after which he was content to return to Mayor Goodroe's house without ever having betrayed his identity to the people he had rescued. No one needed to know that Rory had given him the bulldozer's keys. Although he would have relished Maggie Vy's wonderment and praise, he would have also experienced an embarrassment that he still had no arsenal of words or actions to mitigate.

Maggie Vy enjoyed the excitement of going underground for tornado watches. She thought the family bombshelter a silly structure (at least in its ostensible purpose of preserving the Medders clan alive through, and beyond, the forecast nuclear Armageddon), but she liked the privacy that it often afforded her. When blue or thoughtful, she visited the bombshelter for a handy getaway. She had decorated those few spaces in it not given over to foodstorage with bird drawings or posters of her favorite lyric poems—She Was a Phantom of Delight, She Walks in Beauty, La belle dame sans merci, I Died for Beauty—in her own calligraphy: bloodred Olde English script. Her parents, she thought, looked ridiculous in the shelter, Joel her father as cramped as a daddylonglegs thrust into a watchfob, Vivian her mother as gloomy as a deposed queen. So Maggie Vy had not enjoyed their underground confinement on Saturday evening—not because the tornadoes had cowed her but because the oak landing on the shelter's door was an eventuality that she had long ago predicted and that both her parents had ignored as unlikely and alarmist.

Being trapped—whether in a physical space or an unhappy relationship or any degrading situation—she regarded as intolerable.

After the bulldozer freed them, Maggie Vy took her father's arm and thanked him for his part in the rescue. After all, he had told the anonymous wanderer, who had spoken to them through the airpipe, to apply to Rory Peacock for help; obviously, the wanderer had done so.

Don't give me credit, Mr. Medders said. Give the credit to the messenger and whoever ran the bulldozer.

At school on Monday, Maggie Vy gravitated to a table in the cafetorium not far from where six of her male counterparts had set their lunchtrays. Neil Stroyer, Jim Krew, Craig Baldwell, Sonny Peacock, and two sophomores were discussing the storm and its widespread local devastation.

At least we didn't get absolutely wiped the way Fedora did last year, one of the sophomores said. To Sonny he said: What happened to you Saturday evenin, Peacock?

A twister picked me up and set me down in somebody else's yard several blocks away. Sonny grinned. It sucked me right off my rooftop.

I bet it did, Neil said. Sounds more like it sucked your brains out.

Jim Krew said, No doubt a little green man from Mars had taken your twister's controls.

Maybe, Sonny said. Sort of like I took the controls of a dozer and helped my uncle do some cleanup.

You lie like linoleum, Neil said.

The boys at Sonny's table crawled all over him about his bulldozer brag, which offended them even more than had his tale of riding the tip of a funnelcloud. They lambasted him. They could tolerate the obvious whopper but despised with a fury the more plausible lie.

As unobtrusively as possible, Maggie Vy set her own tray down. Out of the corner of her eye she saw that Sonny had bit his lip and flushed a beefsteak-tomato red. He would not reply to any of the other boys' sarcasms. Eventually he knocked his chair over standing up to leave.

The bulldozer claim stayed with Maggie Vy as she ate, and after too. The surprising harshness of Sonny's pals' attacks on this claim certainly stemmed from jealousy: jealousy, envy, the inability of teenage males to imagine a lifelong buddy even marginally good at any adult work unfamiliar to them. Anyway, Maggie Vy remembered.

* * *

That summer three separate but festively ritualistic events occurred to bolster Sonny's spirits and to convince him that in the often demoralizing campaigns of his freshman year—not to mention his more or less secret armored-cavalry sorties during tornado season—he had won a significant steppingstone triumph, something better than a mere armistice. Maggie Vy, although by no means his girlfriend or even an occasional date, went out of her way to talk to him, as she had done in elementary school. Mr. Medders frequently called upon him to carry messages, to do lunchhour filing work, and to act as a student escort whenever visitors arrived for briefings or tours. Neil Stroyer called him a brownnose, and Pike Kennerly made a show of saluting him at their every meeting, but because Sonny never appeared to benefit unfairly from, or to gloat over, these modest instances of preferment, almost no one else asserted any feeling about them but a lowgrade admiration.

The first event of the summer was a private costume party one Saturday night in the highschool cafetorium, a party for members of the rising sophomore and junior classes. Maggie Vy insisted on and singlehandedly organized this party, for which Mr. Medders footed the bill, providing the board of education a guaranty for any damage and writing a check for the utilities that the revelers would necessarily call upon. He also paid a discjockey to spin records, a softdrink supplier to unload pressurized canisters of carbonated drinks, and an assortment of gangpressed lunchroom personnel to manufacture pizzas in the onsite kitchen.

At Uncle Rory's suggestion Sonny showed up in an overlarge threepiece suit, with his hair dyed black and so many dabs of Brill Cream massaged into it that it shone like record vinyl. He also wore a striped repp tie and a pair of hornrims as black as his hair.

Craig Baldwell, as Albert Einstein, asked Sonny, Who're you sposed to be?

Whoduya think?

You look like the man in the greyflannel gunnysack.

He looks like a complete groad, said Pike Kennerly, who had dressed as Li'l Abner but who more closely resembled Skeezix in Gasoline Alley.

Waitnsee, said Sonny, putting his hands in his pockets and assuming a stance of worldly nonchalance.

So they waited, and when, late in the evening, the costume judging finally occurred, Sonny walked to the center of the cafetorium stage, faced the judges, and then, with a startling flourish, tossed away his hornrims and ripped off the ugly suit to reveal the garish blue leotard, the stylized chest insignia, and the enormous scarlet cape of his homemade Superman outfit. He made a short Superman, to be sure, but with no one else on stage to belittle him by towering contrast his compact muscular body—in combination with his flamboyant change from mr. nobody to comicbook superhero—carried off the masquerade, and all the other partygoers burst into cheers.

Never once smiling, Sonny wrapped himself in his scarlet cloak and strode into the wings looking more like Count Dracula than the Man of Steel. Even this out-of-character exit drew a burst of cheers, and the applause at evening's end, when Maggie Vy presented him a big electroplated gold lovingcup containing fifteen silverdollars for Best Costume, sustained itself for a solid three minutes—with only a few mild boos to protest that his costume's victory owed more to its manner of presentation than to its originality.

The hired discjockey shone a red spotlight on the couple on stage and played the Peggy Lee tune, Fever, to which Sonny and Maggie Vy—who had dressed as Maria Tallchief—improvised a clumsy chacha. Dancing, Sonny held the gold cup over his head, inciting fresh applause and some energetic footstomping.

Back down on the floor, Sonny received the backslapping congratulations of old friends and new: Li'l Abner, Albert Einstein, Popeye, Paladin, Dan'l Boone, Lucille Ball, Joan of Arc, etc. Unfortunately Popeye—Neil Stroyer—objected not only to Sonny's first prize in the masquerade but also to his victory dance with Maggie Vy. He bumped Sonny in the jostling crowd, tried to wrest away his trophy, cursed him with a shower of spittle.

A scuffle—a rollicking terrifying flap—broke out, one that locomoted in a swaying tangle from the cafetorium stage to the breezeway exit. Mr. Medders did what he could to bring it under control, but Superman effectively halted the wrangle when he headbutted Popeye and sent him sprawling into a dissolving scrum of bodies. Because Stroyer had focused the room's only true rage, his departure from the flap ended it.

You okay? Albert Einstein asked Superman.

I'm great, said Sonny, glowing. I mean I'm just downright super.

The ballerina Maria Tallchief sought out Superman to return his electroplated cup.

You dropped this. I'm really sorry, but a couple of people seem to've kept the silverdollars they found.

Superman received the cup with almost as much pleasure as he had accepted it earlier. It seemed to him under the gaze of Maria Tallchief that thirteen silverdollars was a fine number, a lucky number. He did not begrudge the thief or thieves their petty windfalls.

The second event occurred during Pioneer Week when the Van Luna Chamber of Commerce sponsored a womanless wedding in the highschool gymnasium as a fundraiser for additional relief for local victims of that spring's onslaught of tornadoes. The chamber deliberately timed these farcical nuptials to coincide with the traditional influx of visitors for Pioneer Week, many down from Wichita, not a few up from Ponca City, Winfield, and Wellington. The money raised would not all come, given these circumstances, from broke Van Lunans who had long ago succumbed to Good Samaritan fatigue.

Anyway, Uncle Rory put up posters advertising the womanless wedding, and the *Van Luna Vanguard* ran stories explaining the idea and urging attendance at the event and generous donations to the relief fund as an admittance fee.

During what Sonny assumed was an accidental encounter on Main Street, Rory said, It's going to be a pioneer wedding. A pioneer shotgun wedding.

Fine, said Sonny. Why're you tellin me?

We want you to play the bride.

Sonny stared at Rory, grimacing his refusal.

A good cause, kiddo. A very good cause.

I don't wear women's clothes, Uncle Rory. It's a principle of mine. He thought this over. I just realized it.

It takes a man to wear a woman's clothes.

That doesn't make a pennyswortha sense, Sonny said. Repeat it and see.

It takes a man to wear a woman's clothes.

Sonny started to walk off.

Rory grabbed him by the elbow. Didn't I help you win that costume prize a while back?

Sonny said, That was different.

Why? Cuz you got to play a superhero?

Sonny looked at his feet.

This time you git to *be* a superhero. Don't you just ache to help your friends and neighbors who took tornado hits?

I'm not an insurance company.

I guess you're not. I guess you're a walker. Rory let go of his arm.

All right, Sonny said after three or four incredibly long beats. Just one thing though.

Rory smiled. Sure. Put a name on it.

If I'm the bride it's not a shotgun wedding. The guy *wants* to marry me.

But the shotgun part makes it funnier.

No. Not to me it doesn't.

You have to have a shotgun at a womanless wedding. People expect it.

That's my only term. Take it or leave it.

To Sonny's surprise Rory shook his hand. Okay, you've got it, Sonnyman. Welcome aboard.

So smack in the middle of Pioneer Days, on a humid Thursday night, Sonny found himself dressed from throat to instep in a beaded gown of antique ivory satin. He wore a wreathlike tiara of gardenias from which hung a lacy snowwhite veil the size and approximate shape of a beekeeper's helmet. This veil had been his second term (he had had his fingers crossed when he claimed to have only one) because he did not wish to appear before either strangers or friends in the guise of a bride, whether a blameless virgin or a knockedup tramp, especially if anybody on hand might recognize him.

As added precautions, under the veil Sonny wore smeared red lipstick, a plastering of rouge, and raccoonlike circles of kohl around his eyes. Entering the gym on the arm of Mayor Goodroe as the bride's railway-tycoon daddy, Sonny sensed that the audience had hoped for a grosser male specimen in his role. Too womanly a bride infected the burlesque with a hint of ambiguity which triggered disquiet rather than bellylaughs. The audience could not whoop unselfconsciously at a classic womanless wedding if one of its members (the bride, no less) looked during the dum-dum-DA-dum processional like a Rose Bowl starlet or a Parisian runway model.

None of the other participants occasioned any doubts about their sex. Mayor Goodroe played and indisputably looked like a man. So did Mr. McKinley, ostensibly the groom, and so did Ingram Zook, ostensibly the groom's father, both of whom wore fringed buckskin, coonskin hats, deerhide moccasins. Other men playing men dressed as an eighteenth-century circuitrider (the preacher), prospectors (the bride's brothers), cavalry officers (the ushers), and railway engineers, trappers, storekeepers, or drovers (the groomsmen).

The men playing women—not including Sonny, that is—also presented figures whose gender the audience could deduce from such visible characteristics as bulk, bodyhair, beards. The bridesmaids, for example, misled no one to suppose that they had just finished a semester at Radcliffe or Vassar. Even in bonnets and anklelength calico dresses they resembled seasoned veterans of the Chicago Bears.

Sonny, however, clearly suggested a chesty wrenlike female, and his progress down the aisle had a subtle rhythmic fluidity inspiring both notice and doubt. Jenniel, who sat in one of the bleacher sections with Captain Chillicothe Smith, assumed the so-called bride an honest-to-God female and hence a thumbed nose at the binding central protocol of the event. She never suspected that Sonny had taken the role, believing that Craig Baldwell and he had pitched a puptent in Craig's backyard for a midsummer campout.

At the phoney altar Sonny joined Mr. McKinley, who leaned into him to whisper: When the preacher pronounces us man and wife you've got to let me throw back your veil for our kiss.

No way, Sonny said.

It's part of what the people here have paid to see. It's part of—

No way.

I like it no better than you. But it's to keep our bargain with the audience. It's—

A load of horsecrap. Sonny had heard it all before. From Rory H. Peacock himself, who at this very moment stood before the couple as the simpering Parson Brown.

It's for charity, Mr. McKinley said. You have to.

Okay. Try me. See what happens.

Rory led them through their vows, speaking loudly enough for the audience to hear him. He asked the couple for their rings. Mr. McKinley's diamond for Sonny resembled an icecube mounted atop a fat gold doughnut. It fit around Sonny's thumb so that even the folks squeezed in under the gym's electronic scoreboard could see it. Sonny flexed it in a broad parody of bridal pride.

I want one just like that, Jenniel told Captain Chili.

Captain Chili said, Maybe right after the ceremony I can mug the bride for hers.

At Parson Brown's okay for the nuptial kiss Mr. McKinley chose discretion over valor and bussed Sonny on the forehead through his veil. However he bent Sonny back about as far as Sonny could bend, and the crowd came to its feet.

Not until a week later did Sonny learn that Neil Stroyer had wanted to do a campy turn as the bride, arguing with some justice that at sixfoottwo he would have made a much funnier impression in that role. Rory had made him play a groomsman though, in the cheap muslin garb and floppy hat of an oxdrover, and after the event, before the crowd's complete dispersal, Neil protested that he had never attended a stupider unfunnier womanless wedding in all his fifteen years.

Later, in the lockerroom, Rory told Sonny that the show had grossed nearly a thousand dollars, including two big anonymous donations, and that Neil's gripes were nothing but sourgrapes.

Then Rory took the ivory gown, the wreath of gardenias, and the snowy veil back from Sonny and packed the gown away in a plastic drycleaning bag and a long cardboard box. He laid the wreath and the veil atop the bag, fitted in some tissuepaper, and set the box's lid.

This gown was your grandmama's, Rory said. Cullison's and my mama's. I've got to take it back to her.

Sure, said Sonny, scrubbing his face and grinning.

You looked delicious in it, Sonnyman.

The lockerroom echoed with the whoops of the other members of the wedding. None felt any better than Sonny did.

In August, not long before Sonny and his rising classmates began their sophomore year, the third ritualistic event of that long summer occurred, namely, the marriage of his mother to the bomberpilot from Chillicothe, Illinois.

Because Jenniel Peacock only rarely attended the greystone Methodist church in which, at age ten, Sonny had arranged his own baptism, she appealed to Mr. Medders for the use of the highschool cafetorium as her wedding site. With the telephone approval of a majority of schoolboard members, Mr. Medders said okay, and, pretty much on their own initiative, Maggie Vy and Mrs. Medders decorated the cafetorium with balloons, flowers, and crepepaper streamers.

Sonny had mixed feelings about Jenniel's plans. Despite Chili's oddly eastern devotion to meditation and vegetarianism and his fondness for wearing his zipperseamed orange flightsuit for knockingabout, the captain was an okay guy. In fact, he had asked Sonny to stand up for him as his bestman, an honor that Sonny recognized and in which he took an ambiguous pride. Chili, who intended to speak his vows in his formal airforce messdress, wanted Sonny to wear a tuxedo. He had even asked Sonny how he would feel about undergoing adoption and changing his surname from Peacock to Smith.

I like Peacock better, Sonny said.

They were watching television, and NBC's trademark for its color broadcasts, an animated peacock fanning its tail, came on the screen at that very moment.

Chili laughed. You've got a spiffier logo than us poor Smiths, that's for sure.

Yessir.

What exactly's wrong with Smith though?

Sonny sat silent.

Cmon. Give. I won't gnaw your foot off.

Everybody's named Smith. Everybody and his automechanic. Sir, he added.

Chili pursed his lips and nodded. Allrighty then. No name change for you. Your daddy'd be proud.

Yessir.

To keep from hurting my feelings though you need to do just one thing for me.

What?

Stand beside me in a sooty black monkeysuit tailored to the Chicago utmost. Deal?

Deal.

From superhero to bride to bestman all in the same summer, thought Sonny. What could possibly come next? Stepson. I'm going to wind up a B-47 pilot's stepson.

This prospect scared him a little. That very month, for example, an American U-2 pilot that Krushchev's missiles had shot down over an unpronounceable Russian city was in Moscow standing trial for espionage and aggression against the Soviet peoples. The *Wichita Eagle* reported that if the military court over there found the pilot guilty, it might sentence him to life in prison or even death. The U-2 in which this man had attempted his mission, Sonny knew, was a highflying piece of frail-looking machinery painted black to make it harder for the Reds to detect and shoot down. Somehow they had detected and shot it down anyway. It occurred to Sonny that in times such as these—an era of missiletests, bombshelters, and espionage trials—he might lose his stepfather to international violence just as he had lost Cullison to a riot in a Colorado prison. He did not want Jenniel to suffer such a repetitive loss. He did not want to suffer such loss again himself.

The blackness of the times seemed mirrored in the tux for

which Chili had had him fitted, and the wedding day itself crackled into activity under a sky of piled blackness. Rain. Waterfalling oceans of rain.

More people attended than Jenniel had expected. Guests included the Medders family; several friends of Chili's from McConnell; and the families of Sonny's gradeschool pals, the Baldwells, the Kennerlys, and the Stroyers. (Sonny knew that Rory had received no invitation and had driven across state to visit his mother in Coronado.) Maggie Vy played an ebony upright moved into place from the musicroom, and Mrs. Whited, Sonny's babysitter as a kid, stood up as maid of honor in a yellow chiffon dress. This dress brightened the room, as did the modest decorations — but no one could fail to hear the rain clattering on the pavement or to notice the hectic flickerings of the cafetorium's fluorescents.

A justice of the peace with the halfironic name of Dulles — not John Foster or Allen, but Timothy — performed the ceremony before about six rows of foldingchairs. Sonny, right on cue, produced the small gold band with the small elegant diamond — nowhere so large as an icecube — with which Chili wed Jenniel, and Jenniel's ring for Chili came to her through Mrs. Whited. By this point in the proceedings however, his role pretty much fulfilled, Sonny had let his mind drift away to the bleakness of the weather and a brief daydream in which a jowly man in an ugly uniform condemned him to life imprisonment in a very cold place. He came back from this disheartening exile when Captain Smith eagerly responded to Mr. Dulles's invitation, You may now kiss the bride. He came back gladly.

If that little twerp's a bestman, I'm John Dillinger! said Neil Stroyer from a seat up front. He withdrew a pelletpistol from his plaid sportscoat and pulled its trigger with a muffled click. Take that, twerp!

Sonny felt a fiery sting in his thigh and clutched it. The sting grew hotter, the heat from it spread like a stain. *Holy cripes!* Sonny cried without meaning to, and he began a vigorous onefooted jig while rubbing the back of his leg as if trying to start rather than put out a fire.

Neil Stroyer, meanwhile, turned his weapon on the balloons suspended overhead. He shot at and burst four of them before one of Chili's officer pals grabbed him and disarmed him. A lull of appalled incredulity gripped nearly everyone, and to keep panic at bay Mr. Medders and the officer said repeatedly, Easy, easy, everything's under control, while Neil's father, maybe the angriest person on the premises, marched Neil outside to one of the noisy breezeways.

Jenniel had her arms around Sonny, whose pain had subsided into a dull throbbing. Mr. Medders strode forward to ask how Sonny was and if he wished to press assault charges against Neil. The wedding—not just the exchange of vows—had ended, and guests milled about whispering or moved toward the exits to await a break in the rain.

Neil's mother sat alone and motionless in her chair, her head in her hands. Jenniel kissed Sonny on the forehead and went to comfort her friend.

Well? said Mr. Medders to Sonny.

Sonny shrugged, but Mr. Medders waited him out.

This is the first time I've ever been shot in a tux, Sonny said. I look sharp and I feel sharp too. He rubbed the back of his thigh.

What about the Stroyer kid?

Sonny could not believe that this man wanted him to reckon Neil's ultimate dispensation before the law. He said, I look sharper than he does. That coat is strictly Bulgarian.

Get serious, Mr. Medders said. Why would Neil come in here and shoot you with a pelletgun?

Probably because he didn't have .357 Magnum.

Mr. Medders' face betrayed his impatience.

Is it up to me? Sonny said. If it is, I don't guess I want him arrested. Mostly I just wish he'd shot me and the balloons in reverse order. Then he wouldn't've shot me at all, if you know what I mean.

Sonny smiled a goodbye and limped over to sit down beside Neil's mother. He and Jenniel bookended the woman. While they were sitting there, a thundercrack rattled the building and the lights flickered out.

Three years later the senior class of Van Luna High received their diplomas on a beautifully blue, beautifully mild evening in early June. Sonny finished fifth in his class academically, and Maggie Vy, the valedictorian, sang You'll Never Walk Alone at the outdoor ceremony on the football field as the graduates filed across the buntingdraped platform to shake hands with her daddy and to accept their diplomas from Mr. Ventura, the county superintendent of schools. To Sonny, Maggie Vy resembled a beauty-pageant princess, with the happy exceptions that she wore a good deal less makeup and stood almost as tall in her pale robe as the chalky statue of the pioneer woman in Buffalo Bill Park.

Rory sat several rows behind Captain and Mrs. Chillicothe Smith in the overlooking bleachers, for no reconciliation had occurred between Jenniel and her former brother-in-law despite the fact that at the beginning of the schoolyear Rory had told her of the existence of a handsome starter fund for Sonny. Since his receipt of his first city paycheck, Rory had put at least fifty dollars a month into this fund, earmarking it all for either Sonny's higher education or his initial expenses as a young man trying to settle on a career.

Jenniel had gotten angry. You can't buy your way back into this family or my affections, Rory. Money is only money. We couldn't accept it from you even if we need it.

It's not goin anywhere, Rory said. I never meant it for anybody but Sonny. It's his. He can have it for the askin any time he wants. I want you to tell him that.

Tell him yourself, Jenniel said.

In the end Sonny decided not to go to college but to spend a year selling ads, reporting news, and writing editorials for the hometown *Van Luna Vanguard*. Ernest Hemingway had not gone to college. He had worked for the *Kansas City Star* and then driven ambulances in Italy for the American Red Cross in World War I. Sonny hoped to advance from the *Vanguard* to either the *Wichita Eagle* or *Beacon* or the *Tulsa World*, earning the kind of journalistic credentials that would take him to Southeast Asia as a warcorrespondent. The conflict there might represent his only shot at validating himself, as Hemingway had so gracefully done, in the muck and the ambiguous glory of twentieth-century warfare.

But the *Vanguard*'s managers considered Sonny indispensable, promoting him to slot after slot through his first eight months aboard. At length he held the day-to-day editorship and turned the rag from a weekly into a twiceweekly publication. Eighteen years old and already a talented presence in town, he purchased a car with the money that Rory transferred unbidden to his bank account, then made frequent weekend trips to Lawrence to court Margaret Vivian Medders, a freshman majoring in music at the University of Kansas. He proposed to her in March, and their wedding took place that June—in the greystone Methodist church in which, with all the questing conviction of his naiveté, he had once pledged allegiance to Christ, a wounded figure who had long since forfeited most of his power to Sonny's far stronger conceptions of his loved ones (Jenniel, Rory, Maggie Vy), but a figure that he hoped to resurrect through honest daily labor and many spendthrift showings of his heart.

Rory, meanwhile, spent most of this year in Coronado seeing to his mother. She had recently turned eightysix, and Rory had helped her celebrate by taking her to his highschool ballfield to watch the Coronado Canaries, nimble in grass-stained yellow uniforms, play an imposing team from Grainfield. After the Canaries' resurgent victory in the bottom of the ninth, he had packed up India's belongings, closed her house, and with the help of her younger sister, Burma, put her in a nursinghome and headed west to Colorado for a twoweek vacation.

The Medderses had mailed him an invitation to Maggie Vy's wedding, but he had decided not to complicate Jenniel's life, or to quench her pleasure in the event, by attending. He had adopted a like strategy four years ago, removing himself from Van Luna during Jenniel's wedding, to which he had received no invitation at all, and visiting Coronado on that occasion had helped to keep him sane. This time, with India in a weakened condition and most of his hometown kin indifferent to both his nearness and his pain, he felt no remorse about heading west.

The wedding went off as scheduled, on a day more propitious than the one that had attended Jenniel's nuptials. Sonny wore the same tuxedo—its trousercuffs and its jacketsleeves let out—in which he had received a pellet below the left buttock. (Neil had since been diagnosed as a borderline schizophrenic, a disorder that a team of doctors in Wichita had mitigated with the ten-year-old psychotropic medication chlorpromazine, which Neil selfadministered on an outpatient basis.) Sonny's shooter was one of his three groomsmen; consequently, both Mr. Medders and Sonny made big shows of patting him down before admitting him to the sanctuary. One measure of Neil's improvement lay in the goodhumor with which he and his family submitted to this burlesque. In fact, Sonny had extended the joke not only by declining to allow his mother to repair the pellet hole, but by accenting it with an inside patch of white silk. Onlookers may have assumed that someone had flicked a droplet of Elmer's Glue on Sonny's trousers.

After the ceremony the reception took place in a grassy courtyard between the sanctuary and the long grey wall of the educational annex. Ivy festooned both of these facades, and the Medderses had rented three funeral awnings to shade those crowding into the courtyard for canapés, cookies, sausageballs, weddingcake. Jenniel, separated from Chili by a postceremony surge of bodies in the sanctuary, was preparing to rejoin him in the courtyard when Rory Peacock—uninvited, steelyeyed, and inappropriately dressed—interposed his bulk and asked if she would go out to the parkinglot with him.

You're not suggesting a fistfight, are you?

No mam. Rory pled with his eyes. Although Jenniel's every nerve cried out for her to shove Rory aside or to summon Chief Loyal, himself a guest, she resisted these urges and followed Rory. In the parkinglot he introduced her to a gaunt man on crutches, whose tresses reminded her of neatly clipped strands of angelhair pasta. The gaunt man's checked trousers and grey knit shirt displayed as many creases and wrinkles as a set of slept-in pajamas. Even as he gripped his crutches for support, he had propped his butt against the trunk of Rory's Buick and pointed his sneakered toes as if to prevent his crumpling to the steamy asphalt.

Hello Mrs. Peacock, the man said. I'm Willie Swetz.

The name sounded distantly familiar, the voice sounded like the uncoiling of a rusted clockspring. It's Smith now, Jenniel said. It hasn't been Peacock for four years.

Willie Swetz swallowed. The effort tightened cords in his underjaw and throat, it also made his lipcorner twitch and just perceptibly glisten.

Sorry, he said. Just wanted to telya— He looked at Rory, who nodded him an oddly mournful go-ahead. Just wanted to tell you that this man here didn't shoot me.

He means me, Rory said.

Swetz ignored this to say, I never even saw this fella. It was, you know, the *other* guy.

Jenniel looked skeptically at Swetz and then at Rory. Rory said that Swetz had fallen to gunfire during the armored-truck robbery that had sent both Peacock brothers to prison. Until six or seven years ago, Swetz said, he had lain in a coma in a care facility in Pueblo, Colorado. Then he'd roused, regaining the use of his crippled limbs through physical therapy, and of his voice through daily practice and a dogged belief in his own recuperative powers. Rory had looked him up on his recent trip to Colorado, and Swetz had corroborated for him and witnesses at the therapy center the truth of Cullison's testimony at the trial. Rory had brought Swetz all the way to Van Luna to give Jenniel a chance to believe.

I don't mean to blacken Cully's memory, he said. He shot Mr. Swetz and messed up a mess of lives in the process, but—

You expect that to make me feel better? Jenniel said. To make me like you better?

But he never lied about it, Rory said. I want you to know Cully never lied about *any* of it. What you think of me, that's your sayso, Jenniel.

Jenniel had to concentrate real hard to keep her eyelids from gumming together. You hungry, Mr. Swetz? She said. You look a little hungry.

Guess so, Swetz said. It's been a while.

Come to the reception. You too, Rory. Help Mr. Swetz through there. She pointed. To the courtyard.

I can make it on my own, Swetz said. He put his crutches under his arms and gimpily departed.

To Rory's surprise, Jenniel embraced him. She also applied a tender pinch to the bulb of his nose, then left him there as she hurried after Swetz. Rory rummaged in his auto's trunk and pulled out a pasteboard box, which he carried to the courtyard and set down on the end of a servingtable. After opening it, he handed Coronado Canary ballcaps to every member and every guest of the wedding, including the photographer, the janitor, the preacher, the organist, and three excited boys attracted by the hubbub and the free eats.

Sonny and Maggie Vy posed behind their weddingcake in their yellow caps. Maggie Vy yanked Sonny's capbill down and said to him sidelong through a mouthful of angelfood:

Even in sixthgrade, honey, you looked sexy as all getout in your yellow hat.

Epilogue

Despite this auspicious beginning, Sonny and Maggie Vy did not live happily everafter.

Sonny's number came up. The army inducted him. He did his basic training at Fort Benning, Georgia. Four months later he was wounded in Vietnam. The blue sky under which he fell so reminded him of the sky over his hometown that he used the last of his strength to reach for it. Somewhere, he figured, it was a good day, a day of promise and color. He would more than likely miss it, but its blue spread above him without striation or limit.

Years later, under a different sky, Rory stood before a black wall and rubbed snow into the gritblasted letters of his nephew's name:

CULLISON H PEACOCK Jr

AUTHOR'S NOTE

My interest in the situation in South Africa is of several years' duration. It would be difficult to compile a comprehensive list of all the sources to which I am indebted. Deserving of special mention, however, are three works of nonfiction that I recommend to anyone attempting to make sense of the absurd tyranny of apartheid: Move Your Shadow: South Africa, Black and White *by Joseph Lelyveld (Times Books, 1985);* Crossing the Line: A Year in the Land of Apartheid *by William Finnegan (Harper & Row, 1986);* and Biko: The Revised Edition *by Donald Woods (Henry Holt, 1987).* I also owe a debt to the eloquent title story in Njabulo S. Ndebele's harrowing collection Fools and Other Stories *(Readers International, 1986). Additional help has come by way of Ray and Joanne Cavender of Washington, D.C., who provided me with a large map of Pretoria, and through Ron GoldKorn, a South African currently resident in Austin, Texas, who vetted some of my terminology and physical details and attempted to set me straight. Let me also thank Randy Loney of Cataula, Georgia, and Terry Bisson of Brooklyn, New York, for providing additional materials. Nevertheless, please lay any and all remaining errors at this writer's doorstep.*

Apartheid, Superstrings, and Mordecai Thubana

The Transvaal, 1988

AN ELEPHANT BLOSSOMED IN HIS HEADLAMPS. AT TWO-thirty in the morning, on the highveld between Pretoria and the northeastern Transvaal, a doddering bull elephant—which had *not* been there—suddenly *was* there; and Gerrit Myburgh, a 38-year-old banker, knew that his imported cranberry Cadillac was going to hit it.

As hard as he could, Myburgh began braking.

The Cadillac, hydroplaning on his astonishment, slid into the elephant. Its tusks flashed like scimitars. Glass shattered. A bewildered, trumpeting bleat echoed over the landscape, and so much plastic, chrome, and steel crumpled around Myburgh that he knew the world had ended.

Well, fine. He was already in his coffin, the flashiest coffin a success-driven Afrikaner could ever want.

Eventually, Myburgh untangled himself, crawled through a broken window, and got to his feet on the debris-strewn asphalt.

It was July, the torso of winter, as clammy-cold as it ever got in this part of the highveld, and his tailored suit was a drafty ruin. His forehead was bleeding, there were bruises on his upper thighs, his left shoe had disappeared. Traffic on this stretch of roadway was seldom heavy, and at this hour his hopes for a quick rescue were laughable.

Myburgh turned about, searching for the elephant. "I hope you're happy!" he shouted in Afrikaans, his words muting themselves in the drizzle. "You've turned my car into a pile of goddamned slag!" Even worse, he realized, his insurance assessor would never believe that he had hit . . . an elephant.

What the hell was happening? There weren't any elephants in this part of South Africa. You had to go to a national park to see them. Out here, where a few *bittereinder* Boers resisted both state and corporate attempts to buy their land (the government to feed it into black "closer settlements," industry to turn it into another hideous factory site), wildlife consisted of stray chickens, stray dogs, stray cattle.

But he had run into it, an elephant. Surely, it had suffered as much damage as—if not more than—the Eldorado. He had heard it bellow its agony. Still, it had managed to totter away from the accident scene. Even when he made a painful circuit of his Caddy, stooping to search for blood or other spoor, nothing on the paving or in the nearby bush reassured him that what he *knew* had happened had actually happened.

At least it wasn't pink, Myburgh thought. At least the damned thing wasn't flying, like Dumbo.

The elephant may have been a phantom, but the gash on his head was real. So were his battered thighs, his lacerated jacket, his blood-smeared trousers. He stood like a scarecrow in the center of the road, guarding the wrecked vehicle and peering about for some sign of a farmhouse, a police van, or a besotted Ndebele tramp who could be bribed to help him.

He took a monogrammed handkerchief from the breast pocket of his jacket and touched his brow. This simple act made him flinch, but he held the handkerchief to the wound, determined both to halt the bleeding and to restore some clarity to his thoughts.

Should he walk back toward his brother's farm or on toward the Pretoria suburb in which he had a condominium flat? Onward, of course. Nothing but wintry veld lay behind him, whereas a hike southwestward would carry him into populated areas, white or black, where he could buy or beg assistance.

God help me, Myburgh thought, calculating—for a quick glance at the mileage counter on the Eldorado's caved-in dashboard told him that Pretoria was still eighty miles away. It would take him days to walk home. He felt too weak to start hiking.

Holding his handkerchief to his temple, Gerrit Myburgh began to cry. He sat down on the wet pavement and hugged himself as if he were his own lost child.

He heard it before he saw it, a raw chugging from the alley of Boer farmland dividing the eastern boundary of KwaNdebele from the western boundary of Bophuthatswana.

It was coming down the road toward him, a blunt-grilled Putco "commuter" bus, one of the armada of state-subsidized motorized argosies that hauled residents of the homelands to and from work in Johannesburg, Pretoria, Witbank, and Middleburg. They ran morning and evening, Myburgh knew, but he was surprised to hear one coming so early. It wasn't yet three o'clock, and surely no one would be riding at this godforsaken hour. Myburgh himself usually arose at seven-thirty, took a leisurely Continental breakfast, and got to the bank by nine. It was an accident that he was still up tonight, the result of his journey to see Kiewit and of his mulish brother's mulish disdain for reason. Otherwise, Myburgh would be safe in his bed in Pretoria.

Myburgh got up off the road, spread his arms, and began waving his clotted handkerchief. Then, seeing that the bus would *have* to stop or slow down for the wreck of his Caddy, he realized that maybe he didn't want to be rescued—not by a bus full of kaffirs on their way to grinding deadend jobs paying them just enough to get potted in a *shebeen* and to listen in ale-beclouded sullenness to rabble-rousing ANC shortwave broadcasts from Lusaka, Zambia. No, he didn't want that at all.

But just as it had been too late to brake for the elephant, it was too late to sidestep the bus. Its wan headlamps picked him out of the darkness, and it squealed to an eardrum-puncturing halt a few meters away, then rocked back and forth on its shocks like a melancholy elephant. Its driver remained invisible, hidden by the tocking blade of a lone windshield wiper and the fuzzy glare of the headlamps.

All right, then. He'd assert himself. He'd force the pathetic kaffirs to help him.

Myburgh limped over to the bus's door. The bus itself, he saw, was painted a chalky blue. A legend in English on its dented flank read GRIM BOY'S TOE. That, Myburgh supposed, was its name —the way wealthy tycoons named their yachts. Whether *Grim*

Boy's Toe carried a full allotment of passengers, he couldn't tell, for the bus's windows were smeared with dried mud and its rear third tailed off into mist and darkness.

The hinged passenger door creaked open. Myburgh peered up and in. He saw—in the wash of a single bulb in a crimson globe—that the bus's driver was a heavyset African with a face etched of ruby shadows. The driver gazed impudently out, as if Myburgh meant less to him than a crippled plowhorse.

Myburgh began to regret not jumping into the roadside *donga* and cowering there until the bus had chugged on by. Its passengers, he suddenly understood, could kill him with impunity, bludgeoning him to a ruddy paste and sticking his body under the collapsed steering column as if he'd died in the accident.

"Go find me help," he said in English, expanding his chest even as he took a half-step back. (Afrikaans, his own tongue, wouldn't do—he didn't trust it here.)

The insolent driver merely stared at him.

"*Get me help!*" Myburgh shouted. "Understand?"

At this, the driver's eyes widened—in astonishment, it seemed to Myburgh. He leaned toward the door, as if to make sure that his eyes weren't playing tricks.

"Didn't you hear me?" Myburgh said. "Find me help."

"No can do, *nkosi*."

"Of course you can. Can't you see I've had an accident? Can't you see—" blotting his forehead "—I've been hurt?"

"*Nkosi*, number 496 has run late three times this week. I can't afford to run late again. There are men in Tweefontein E and other closer settlements who'd kill for my job."

"Why do you run late? Are you a bad driver?"

The driver glanced at Myburgh's wrecked Caddy. "I do as well as many," he said. His expression grew conspiratorially earnest. "A blowout one night, sir. Two nights later, a dope-fiend trucker ran me off the road. And last night—with all the unexpected rain, you see—well, we got stuck."

"Look," Myburgh said, feeling both exposed and ridiculous, "I'm in trouble."

"Yes, and I will help you. But not by going off my route. No, sir. You must climb aboard and ride into Belle Ombre station with the rest of my passengers."

"How long will that take?" Belle Ombre was in the Marabastad neighborhood of Pretoria, once an Indian enclave.

"Three hours. No. Two hours, forty-five minutes."

"That's absurd. You ought to be able to make it in an hour and a half. Two at the most."

The driver laughed, shrugging his bearish shoulders and holding out his hands to indicate the ramshackle condition of number 496. "Not possible, my *baas*. We have more pickups and a Putco checkoff still to do. Really."

"Don't you have a two-way?"

"No, *nkosi*. And no landing gear, either."

Myburgh heard laughter—not obnoxious or general laughter, but the weary guffaws of a few riders near enough to overhear.

"Take me to the Putco checkoff." He gritted his teeth against their amusement. "Somebody there will help me."

"Maybe. Not to get your car towed, though. You should go all the way into Pretoria with us."

Myburgh considered. "Very well—let me on." He climbed aboard and turned to limp down the aisle.

The driver put out a hand. "My name is Ernest Kabini, *nkosi*. Sorry to say so, but you must pay."

"*Pay?*" Should he also introduce himself, as Kabini had just done? Damned if he'd do it.

"Your fare. Everyone must pay, you know. Sixty cents to town, sixty cents back."

"Sixty cents?"

Kabini hesitated. "Half a rand, okay? Ten cents off. Putco doesn't want to screw a fellow down on his luck."

Myburgh dug into his pocket and handed over the fare—the *full* fare. He was a paying passenger on number 496. He turned again to face the kaffirs with whom he was going to be riding for the next three hours and found himself staring as into a huge shotgun bore that seemed to extend all the way to the Transvaal's border with Zimbabwe. The faces peering back were devoid of distinctiveness or personality—like a grainy group photograph of skin-headed National Defense Force recruits. A bulb in a green globe threw sickly khaki shadows over the bodies slumped in the bus's middle rows, while, at the back, a bulb in a yellow globe jaundiced the half dozen riders napping beneath its pale sheen.

If hell had bus service, Myburgh told himself, this is what the inside of one of its buses would look like. He grabbed a seat back for support and silently cursed the inconsiderate elephant that had brought him here.

At this point on the bus's route, Myburgh could have chosen any of a number of seats behind Kabini, but, more angry than grateful, he limped down the center aisle.

His wet sock slapped the metal floor. The twelve to fifteen riders inhabiting the bus seemed to shift from one seat to another without getting up and physically moving.

Meanwhile, *Grim Boy's Toe* leapt into gear and growled around the abstract sculpture of his Eldorado. Myburgh stumbled, caught himself, shakily tottered on.

You've had a blow to the head, he reminded himself. It's not so unusual that you should be seeing things.

But it was troubling. Why wouldn't these seat-hopping kaffirs settle down? No, that was wrong. Why wouldn't his dizziness go away so that he could see things as they really were?

He stopped again. The black faces watching him were no longer popping up in different seats with the same annoying frequency. Maybe he was beginning to get a grip on himself. Maybe the world—or this encapsulated portion of it—was finally beginning to come into focus.

"Sit here, sir."

He looked. The voice belonged to a slender man in a trench coat ridiculously at odds with the filthy woolen cap he was wearing; the coat might have belonged to a movie star, but the cap you could see on any street cleaner or garbage man at work in the city from June through August. This bloke, his thin face almost cadaverous in the dark, scooted over and patted that part of the cracked seat cushion that his skinny bottom had already warmed.

An invitation. A friendly invitation.

Myburgh spurned it. Unfamiliar people—strangers—didn't sit next to each other when there were plenty of seats to choose from. It wasn't racial; it was personal, a way to keep one's identity intact, a means of securing a helpful modicum of privacy. And yet it wouldn't do to stupidly insult the man, even if his pigmentation suggested purple spray paint under a sheen of preserving lacquer. Myburgh eased into the seat in front of the African's, pointedly hugging the aisle.

"Excuse me, sir," said the slender young man, leaning over the seat back as if Kabini had introduced them. "Did you really have an accident?"

What colossal cheek. Myburgh reined in his temper. "What do you think, I *staged* it?"

"Possibly."

"Why in God's name would I do something so stupid—not to say expensive—as that?"

"Forgive me," the man said, placatingly touching his shoulder. "I thought you might be a member of—or, possibly, an advisor to—a Faking Club."

"Faking Club?"

"Yes, sir. A few years ago, until caught without my stinker—" his pass, he meant "—and endorsed out, I lived near Cape Town. At the universities there, students staged accidents—bloody ones—to test public awareness of first aid. Faking Clubs."

"I'm not a member of—or an advisor to—any Faking Club. Why, out here, would you even assume that?"

"So queer an accident. Your car was smashed, but with no sign of any other banged-up vehicle to have caused such damage."

"I hit an elephant."

The man—to Myburgh's relief—withdrew his hand, then simply gazed at the banker sidelong. "My name is Mordecai Thubana, sir. Glad to meet you."

Myburgh grunted. But Mordecai Thubana's gaze was so implacable that he glanced away and began rubbing his thigh as if a pain there had distracted him.

"The blow to your head," Thubana said, nodding at him, "is it bad? Did it make you delirious?"

"Who are you to question me?" Myburgh snapped. "Who are you to imply I'm lying?"

"Mordecai Thubana, sir. And I'm not meaning to be questioning or implying anything."

"If you don't *mean* to, don't *do* it."

"No, sir, I won't. Except, you know, courtesy would hint that maybe you should—forgive me—tell me your name."

"Because you've told me yours?"

Thubana grinned. He had strong, straight teeth. His grin was almost fetching. "One man, one name." He leaned nearer. "When I was in Cape Town, I attended university. I'm not just an ignorant construction worker, sir."

Myburgh pursed his lips. His own name would reveal more than he wanted. *Grim Boy's Toe* was hardly the nave of a Dutch Reformed Church, and its passengers certainly weren't Voortrekkers. But why not tell? Did fear or shame restrain him?

"My name is Gerrit Myburgh," he said defiantly. "My family had a huge farm out here once, on a healthy remnant of which my brother Kiewit continues to live. Three Ndebele families—more than twenty people—still work for him."

"Ah," said Thubana. "But now the government wants it?"

"Yes."

"To make the Ndebele 'homeland' bigger?"

"I suppose."

"And you and your brother are fighting the government's plans to take your land?"

"Kiewit is. I'm not. I think we should sell."

"For the sake of Grand Apartheid?"

"Because we're not likely to get a better offer and they'll end up taking it anyway. Kiewit's a stubborn ass."

"Ah. You argued."

"Would I be out here in the goddamn *bundu* at such an hour if we hadn't?" He meant, as they both knew, Would I be on this Putco bus with all you kaffirs if there wasn't a damned good reason?

"No, Mr. Myburgh. I guess not."

Conversation lapsed. Myburgh was grateful. He didn't know why he'd indulged Thubana as far as he had. Under most circumstances, he would have ignored the man or fixed upon him a withering, mind-your-own-business stare. But Thubana's interest in his plight had seduced him into talking. Weak. Shamefully weak.

Myburgh faced front, clutching his own upper arms. *Grim Boy's Toe* was a real kidney bouncer, even on asphalt, and now the bus was bumping down a dirt track among *enkeldoring* trees to another pickup point.

His bruises had bruises. During the accident, he'd apparently bitten a chunk of mucus-coated flesh from the inside of his mouth, and now that slimy flap of skin was overlapping his tongue. He bit down on it and swallowed. His facial muscles tightened.

Twelve people came aboard at this pickup. All gave him the eye as they bumped down the aisle; all made a point of not sitting next to or across from him. The bus chugged off again. A hubbub of African dialects led Myburgh to suspect that some of these people were talking about him. He refused to turn around. Why give them the satisfaction?

Grim Boy's Toe made three more stops.

At the last one, rows and rows of scrap-wood and corrugated-tin *pondoks*—shanties—grew like crooked architectural cancers. Smoke from Primus stoves billowed into the sky, mistily visible, while a throat-scalding stench eeled into the bus through window cracks and holes in the floorboard.

Although Kabini kept telling the new passengers to move back, move back, several of them bunched at Myburgh's seat. He would either have to stand, as two dozen other people were already doing, or scoot over and share his seat with one of the intimidating construction workers or mechanics waiting for him to make room.

"Hey, my *baas*," said a man in an overcoat, tapping Myburgh's knee, "you saving that spot for your lady?"

"Maybe he's got a disease," said someone else.

"You may have this seat," Mordecai Thubana told the man. He came forward and levered Myburgh over against the window with his hip. The man in the overcoat grunted approval and sat down. The logjam of bodies broke. Myburgh watched as several people placed folded newspapers on the floor, dropped down crosslegged, and gave in, almost instantly, to sleep.

One man in particular drew Myburgh's attention, for, although still young, he was as bald as a stone. Moreover, he held in his lap what appeared to be half a rubber volleyball.

"Hey, Mpandhlani," Thubana greeted the bald-headed man. "How goes it?"

"No reception," said Mpandhlani cryptically. "No reception. A relief, Mordecai. I'm almost grateful." He held the volleyball half in his lap like a vulcanized begging bowl.

The bus jounced off again, through the midnight bush.

Although there were now at least ninety passengers, a third of them in the aisle, conversation had ceased; most were dozing or staring numbly into the Transvaal wastes. One man had affixed a large sponge, or rectangle of foam rubber, to the seat back in front of him, lowered his forehead to its padding, and fallen asleep. Perhaps he was also snoring lightly; the bus's unceasing rattle made it hard to tell.

Damn Kiewit, anyway. With just half the money they'd realize from selling *Huilbloom* (as their great-grandparents had dubbed the family farm), they could emigrate to Australia or Texas and begin life anew, in a place free of the threat of Armageddon.

Suddenly, Myburgh noticed that Thubana had taken a book from a coat pocket and begun to read it with a penlight balanced over his ear and aimed downward. Clever. Or semiclever. Thubana probably hoped Myburgh would ask what he was reading. Africans sometimes liked to impress whites with a show of educability, a demonstration of their debatable love of learning.

Well, the clap on that. If Thubana was reading something, it was probably ANC or PAC propaganda or a book of trumped-up stories about oppression in the townships or an old copy of *Drum*, and he'd be damned if he'd rise to the kaffir's bait. Let him pretend to read all the way to Marabastad.

Thubana spoiled this plan by lifting the book off his lap and holding it up so that Myburgh could see its cover—including title and whimsical three-color illustration. *SUPERSTRINGS*, said the yellow caps above the illustration. And below the title: *A Theory of Everything?* A smooth-skinned English paperback, visibly creased and battered. Myburgh recoiled as if from a contraband AK-47.

"Have you read this yet, sir?"

"What are superstrings?" Myburgh said. "Ordinary strings with impossible ambitions?" Perhaps this subtle insult would sink into the kaffir's pretentious brain, stymieing further talk.

"No, sir. It's physics, Mr. Myburgh. Very deep, fundamental physics. It answers deep questions about how the universe is, and why, and what we may expect of it."

"So you're a physicist, Mr. Thubana?"

"No, sir. I'm a—"

"Every day, you do physics at the university, writing equations with which to solve colossal mysteries."

"Nowadays, Mr. Myburgh, I'm a roofer. At a housing site west of the city. After number 496, I must catch another bus."

"A roofer?"

"Yes, sir."

"Then where did you get this book?" Myburgh rapped it with his knuckles. "And what makes you think you can understand it?"

"I understand it," Thubana said mildly. "Under a different set of circumstances, maybe I *would* be a physicist."

"And if I weren't an Afrikaner," Myburgh said, "perhaps I'd be traveling on the next Soviet Mars flight."

Thubana explained that his immediate boss, an Englishman named Godfrey, had given him the book—as well as the upscale trench coat—and that he had been reading and thinking hard about superstrings for over a month now.

"All right, then," Myburgh said. "Tell me what you know."

"Superstring theory," Thubana said, taking Myburgh at his word, "holds that the building blocks of the universe are not atoms, but tiny strings—tiny strings that twitch and twitch." To illustrate their twitching, Thubana repeatedly crooked a finger.

"Why? To what end?" Myburgh asked only because it was more amusing than staring out the window.

"I don't know, exactly. But the twitching generates matter and energy at the submicroscopic Planck scale. It does this throughout the entire cosmos."

These terms and explanations were unintelligible to Myburgh, as hard to untangle, as indigestible, as a platter of cold spaghetti. "What complete rot. You'd do better to have Mr. Godfrey give you books on bricklaying, tilework, vehicle repair. It's criminal he's encouraging you in this . . . this *nonsense*."

"Because my mind is too dim?"

"Because it's *useless*, young man. Because it's castle-in-the-air elitism."

"No, Mr. Myburgh. It isn't. It's elegant physics. If it's open to attack, it's only on the grounds that experiments haven't yet been able to back it up. Also, the mathematics of the theory require that one suppose ten rather than four dimensions — nine of space and one of time."

Myburgh snorted. What tommyrot.

"Listen, sir. Six of the spatial dimensions must be curled up — 'compactified,' my book says — into a geometrical object called the 'Calabi-Yau manifold.' Otherwise, you see, the mathematics of superstring theory, and its ability to make predictions about the world we live in, fall apart."

"You're giving yourself to utter claptrap, Mr. Thubana. Does it make you feel superior to—" nodding at the other riders on *Grim Boy's Toe* "—your sleepy comrades?"

Thubana turned so that the penlight over his ear shone directly into Myburgh's eyes. "It makes me sorry, sir. And — forgive me for saying so — angry. Quite angry."

"At yourself, I hope," Myburgh muttered, turning his face to the window. Outside, the landscape was graying, quivering like a cloudy aspic in a huge inverted bowl.

Thubana, to Myburgh's surprise, dropped one hand to his knee, his grip like a lobster's claw.

"Let go, kaffir," Myburgh whispered. He took the penlight from behind Thubana's ear and dropped it to the floor.

Thubana released him and picked up the penlight; then he leaned into Myburgh as if they were old chums at a sporting event. But when he turned the penlight on again, no beam shot forth. "That's all right," Thubana hissed. "Darkness is exactly what you want for us, isn't it?"

"Leave me alone."

"Okay. No need for light. I'm not an unintelligent man, and I remember my reading. All of it."

He's crazy, thought Myburgh. A woolhead twice over.

"A superstring expert at Princeton in America—a theorist named Edward Witten—said something profound, sir. He said, 'To have the energy to face a difficult problem day after day, one needs the attitude that victory is just around the corner. But probably it isn't.' Light isn't necessary to remember that. I can remember it just as well in the dark."

"Leave me alone." Myburgh hated the weakness in his voice. It sounded as if he were whistling in Thubana's shadow.

" 'The attitude,' " Thubana grimly repeated, " 'that victory is just around the corner. But probably it isn't.' "

Suddenly, from the vicinity of the center aisle, a barrage of martial music poured forth. This music—drums, bells, trumpets—was so loud that it easily overpowered the continuous rattling of the Putco vehicle. Everyone noticed. Men and women, a moment past slumped and dozing, straightened and looked around: the man who'd rested his forehead on a sponge, the newspaper yogis, a woman who'd scrolled her turtleneck up over her eyes. Everyone —every dead-to-the-world passenger—was instantly resurrected.

Then the music ceased, and a nasal English-speaking voice, made both tinny and scratchy by atmospheric conditions, said, *"This is Radio Freedom, broadcasting to our comrades in Azania from a site we are not at liberty to divulge."*

"Mpandhlani!" cried someone far to the rear. "Mpandhlani, for God's sake, close your mouth!"

"Tonight, we address the issue of education. The policies of the apartheid regime not only deny our people their inalienable rights but also access to universal education. Therefore, hundreds of thousands have left the country just to seek education abroad. The Pan Africanist Congress of Azania, in order to cater for the students and refugees, established the department of education and manpower training so that—"

"Your hat, Mpandhlani! Put it on!"

"Close your mouth! Have pity! Close it!"

Myburgh was at a loss. First the music, then the pontifical radio voice, and finally the shouts of various passengers that the man called Mpandhlani *do* something—shouts that seemed to have no relation to these other events. Looking past Thubana, Myburgh saw that the bald passenger, crumpled in the lotus position not far from Thubana's aisle-side knee, had his eyes closed and his mouth wide open. Nothing bizarre about that. The poor fellow was trying to sleep. In fact, he was *succeeding* in the effort, the only wretch aboard number 496 managing to do so.

And then Myburgh realized that the voice of the announcer on Radio Freedom was issuing from the toothless cavity of Mpandhlani's mouth: "*. . . conscious rejection of the indoctrinated inferiority complex that sparked the Soweto uprising of 1976 when our students said no to the imposition of the oppressor's language. This fight developed into a rejection of an entire system — 'Bantu education' — deliberately designed to keep our people in perpetual subjugation. Therefore, we must enforce a perpetual rainy Monday on every school using these 'techniques of control' and make ourselves — *"

Thubana leaned out into the aisle, put his fist under the bald man's chin, and gently closed his mouth. The harangue from the PAC spokesman continued, but mutedly, as if leaking out of Mpandhlani's earholes and nostrils. Mpandhlani woke up and looked at Thubana in groggy bewilderment.

"What's happening, Mordecai?" His words bled into the report on Radio Freedom like a spooky sort of overdubbing. "Oh, no," he said, pressing the palms of his hands to his temples. He glanced apologetically at several of the other passengers. "Forgive me, my friends. Please, everybody, forgive."

"It's okay," Thubana told him. "Put on your cap." He took the volleyball half from Mpandhlani and crammed it down on his naked and — Myburgh finally saw — grotesquely stitched-up pate. There was silence again, a vacuum quickly filled by the incessant rattling of *Grim Boy's Toe*. Riders fore and aft relapsed into self-protective comas, as if, having survived a crisis, they needed to recuperate. Myburgh felt even more isolated than before.

"Mr. Thubana, I don't understand."

"Perhaps your mind is too dim. — Forgive me. It's just that Mpandhlani — his real name is Winston Skosana — has a metal plate in his head. Sometimes, he picks up radio broadcasts, usually illegal ones from Zambia or Botswana. This is dangerous, especially when he's on a loading platform at the rusks factory. That volleyball — he found it in a KwaNdebele midden — saves him from embarrassment. A matter of physics."

"Dunderheaded physics, surely."

"No, Mr. Myburgh. It works."

"It's nonsense. It's impossible."

Thubana shrugged. He nodded at Mpandhlani — Winston Skosana — who'd already dozed off again.

"Why does he have a plate in his skull?"

"He was arrested by Security Police ten years ago and detained without charge for thirty-two months. Then, one day, while taking him from his cell to an interrogation room, his keepers shoved him down a flight of metal stairs. Suicide attempt, said the Security Police. But Winston didn't die, and some determined ladies from the Black Sash had him released and operated on."

"He was a terrorist, a guerrilla-in-training."

"I suppose." Thubana appeared bored by the possibility. "He could have been a poet."

"Or a physicist?"

Thubana turned back to Myburgh as if he'd reopened an important area of discussion—but, astonishingly, he said, "Mpandhlani once told me that we have no word in our Nguni dialect for *orgy*."

"I beg your pardon."

"African languages are not made to talk about Western mores or contemporary physics. Bantu education—carried out in our tribal tongues—has made it very hard for us to understand the discoveries of men like Einstein and Planck."

"What has that to do with not having a word for *orgy*?"

"If the Ndebele, the Sotho, the Zulu, and others have no word for this *human* activity, how may we—using only Afrikaans and our tribal tongues—grasp interactions among submicroscopic *particles* called fermions, hadrons, baryons, quarks? Impossible!"

"Forget it," Myburgh said. "It's all a lot of horse feathers."

"And now they're saying that these tiny points aren't points at all, but the ends of very small strings—*closed* strings, probably. Only by viewing them as strings may we construct a workable Theory of Everything."

"Theory of Everything?" Thubana's talk was all over the map, an obstacle course of jargon.

"A series of formulae bringing together the four major forces of the universe."

"Right. Given ten dimensions, six of them 'curled up.' Study architecture, man. Study mechanical drawing."

Thubana thumbed through his book. "Gravity, electromagnetism, the weak force, the strong force. Until this theory, Mr. Myburgh, no one was able to *prove* that these four forces were all separate aspects of one underlying force. That's important. We must prove it. I want to *help* prove it."

Myburgh found that the passion with which Thubana was

speaking had touched him. "Not everyone can aid in such discoveries. *I* can't, for instance. But I won't lose sleep over it. I've other interests, other talents."

It seemed a kind of hubris, Thubana's megalomaniacal desire to put himself in the company of Einstein and Planck. Laughable. But Myburgh couldn't laugh. Perhaps—given Thubana's passion—all this superstring business *wasn't* mere crackpottery.

Thubana said, "Gravity is the most powerful force. It works at a distance even on the macroscopic scale, and it has *always* been the problem. Various quantum theories have unified the other three forces, the ones working at subatomic levels, but gravity—damn it most emphatically!—always knocks each potential new TOE, Theory of Everything, out of symmetry. It ruins everything."

"I'm sorry." This was all that Myburgh could think to say, but he meant it. (God, his eyelids were growing heavy.)

Then the African changed tacks. "You whites, Mr. Myburgh, are gravity. Blacks, Asians, and our so-called Coloreds are like the other three forces: magnetism, weak force, strong force. In these cases, though, it doesn't matter much which group I assign to which fundamental force."

Now he's talking trash, Myburgh thought, fighting drowsiness. Has the weird engine of his brain thrown a rod?

Thubana's voice droned on, almost like a lullaby:

"Africans, Asians, Coloreds—it's easy to unify those groups, just as one may construct theories, equations without anomalies, that bring together every major physical force *except* gravity. Gravity's the hang-up. Meanwhile, societally speaking, whites are the biggest obstacle to harmony among peoples. You are gravity, Gerrit Myburgh. You pull everything down. You monkey-wrench the equations."

Before Myburgh could protest this slander, many of the bus's passengers began to second Thubana's remarks.

Incongruously, they did so by singing, *a cappella*, in syncopated rhythms that reminded Myburgh of ancient tribal chants and modern street-corner sing-offs in Soweto, Nigel, Alexandria, and other black townships:

> *Whites are gravity—*
> *They bring us down.*
> *Down, down, down.*
> *Down, down, down.*

> *Whites are gravity—*
> *They bring us down.*
> *Down, down, down.*
> *Down,*
> > *down,*
> > > **down.**

The purity of the laborers' voices—the spine-tingling richness of their harmonies—gave Myburgh a chill. But their voices didn't entirely mask the bankruptcy of the ideas set forth in their stupid little song; and Myburgh, back from the trance into which Thubana's monologue had lulled him, turned around and shouted above the bus's maddening rattle:

"Whites *aren't* gravity! We *don't* bring you down!"

"You act on us over great distances," said Thubana. "You cause us to travel miles. Light-years, so to speak."

"Are you puppets, then?" Myburgh asked. "Mere marionettes?"

" '*Down, down, down,*' " chanted a host of passengers.

"Shut up!" Myburgh cried. "SHUT UP!"

As gently as possible, Thubana pulled Myburgh back down to his seat. "Everyone on this bus—every soul on our planet—is a puppet of superstrings, Mr. Myburgh, for superstrings is a TOE, a Theory of Everything. It explains—it *will* explain—the physical universe to all its living and breathing puppets."

"There's no such thing as your Theory of Everything!" Myburgh replied, shaking off Thubana's hand. "Theories, perhaps. A dozen *different* theories—but not just one comprehensive Theory that can explain everything!"

"Tell him to shut up," a hefty woman in a checkered *doek* told Thubana. "He's giving me the nerves."

"Do you want to be Kentuckied?" Thubana whispered. "You know, *necklaced?* Is that what you wish?"

Of course he didn't. What life-loving person in his right mind would want a used tire lowered over his head, doused in petrol, and cruelly set aflame? Fear rippled in Myburgh's bowels like a school of rapidly finning minnows.

But, bracing himself, he repeated that no one set of equations —no matter how elegant— could offer insight into every interaction in the cosmos.

"Of course not," said Thubana, patting his knee.

Suspicious, Myburgh stared at him.

"Now please apply that principle to the TOE by which the South African state tries to order relations among people."

It suddenly occurred to Myburgh that *Grim Boy's Toe* was really *Grim Boy's TOE.*

Putco bus number 496 carried a moniker that wickedly mocked both the race-obsessed Afrikaners who had devised apartheid and the grim policy itself, a policy on which his ancestors had ingeniously jury-rigged a system of taboos, customs, mores, and laws unlike those anywhere else on the planet.

Damn these kaffirs. Damn them all to the most painful Ndebele hell they can imagine.

"How much longer, Kabini?" Myburgh shouted at the bearish Putco driver.

"Three hours," called Ernest Kabini, over his shoulder. "No. Two hours, forty-five minutes."

"Don't be impertinent." *Coon,* he wanted to add.

"Sorry, *nkosi.*"

Thubana clasped Myburgh's wrist, twisting it around to reveal his watch. Myburgh was dumbfounded to see that its stark crimson readout—which winked as if adequately powered—hadn't advanced beyond . . . 3:15 A.M.

Christ Almighty. Was he dreaming?

Then he gazed past the laborers in front of him and saw, through the streaked windscreen, another Putco bus swerve into 496's headlamps. Immediately, hands braced on the seat back, knuckles whitening, he was on his feet again, shouting at Kabini to hit the brakes before they were all seriously injured.

"Shadow matter," Thubana said, trying to pull him back down by his coat. "Just like us. It can't hurt you, Mr. Myburgh, please believe me."

Shadow matter?

What nonsense! What high-flown, self-deluding claptrap, just like everything else Thubana had told him.

Number 496, as Kabini futilely braked, collided with the other vehicle, striking it resoundingly. Windscreens shattered. Engines anviled together. Bodies flew past one another like players in an avant-garde production of *Peter Pan.* Indeed, Thubana rocketed past Myburgh in the gemmy chaos, clutching his copy of *Superstrings* and smiling as if to say, None of this matters; believe me, sir, not a jot of this means anything at all.

You're lying, Myburgh's dream-self thought. You're lying.

And he was hurled through the broken windscreen of *Grim Boy's Toe* into an endless, entrapping darkness.

When Putco bus 496 pulled up behind the stalled Cadillac (which was blocking the way to Pretoria), driver Ernest Kabini called back to one of his passengers, Mordecai Thubana.

Thubana, shaking himself awake, accompanied Kabini off the bus, and they offered their aid to the policemen in glistening boots and macintoshes walking around the shiny cranberry-colored car.

"Go on about your business," one of the policemen told them in Afrikaans. "There's nothing you can do."

Thubana peered in the Caddy's window at the man slumped behind its steering wheel: a sandy-haired bloke nearing forty. It looked, tonight, as if he would never get there.

Said Kabini, "What happened, my *baas?*"

"A heart attack, we think," the policeman said. He nodded at the road. "Those skid marks show he knew what was happening and fought the car to keep it from going into the ditch. Pretty cool, for a fellow staring disaster in the eye."

Yes, thought Thubana. He saved his deliciously *lekker* car, but he also gave himself a chance—a thin one—to survive the terrible crack-up threatening everything he valued.

The second policeman, his ruddy face shining from his rain hood like a lacquered gargoyle's, approached the Africans. "Situation's under control," he growled. "Get out of here."

Thubana started to reply, but Kabini shook his head.

The two men reboarded number 496, and Kabini wrestled it around the dead man's car on the weather-gouged road.

Finding his seat taken by another man, Thubana slumped to the floor with a book and a penlight. Beside him, a fellow nicknamed Mpandhlani asked him if he thought the dead driver of the expensive American car had gone to heaven or hell. With his steel plate and his unenviable ability to pick up out-of-country radio broadcasts, Mpandhlani often seemed more like a disembodied spirit than any visiting angel would have. In fact, he sometimes gave Thubana the creeps.

"Why do you ask?"

"Because I feel like *three* people got on when you and Kabini came back."

"Really?"

"Yes. Someone else is riding with us, Mordecai."

"Then it's cut-and-dried. The dead man is shadow matter, like you and me and all these others." He nodded at the fatigued bodies all around them. "Get it?"

"Sure," said Mpandhlani "Shadow matter."

" 'Down, down, down,' " sang many of their fellow riders. " 'Down, down, down.' "

It was true of all of them, Thubana thought, but the longer the dead man stayed aboard, the more likely he was to reach Belle Ombre station in the company of his countrymen. The more likely he was to see that the universe's four major forces needed to be unified, tied up with superstrings, and rendered beautiful forever by a TOE equation with no anomalies. The more likely he was to find his own substance again.

Meanwhile, Thubana, his compatriots, and the heartsore ghost of Gerrit Myburgh jounced together across the highveld. And it seemed to Thubana, glancing out the mud-streaked windows, that the eastern sky was beginning to redden. . . .

"*No!*" Myburgh shouted.

The shout jerked him awake. He was sitting next to Mordecai Thubana on the bus called *Grim Boy's Toe*. Although the bus had not wrecked, it was no longer moving. It was parked on a muddy turnout in the middle of nowhere. Glancing down, Myburgh saw that Thubana had draped his trench coat, lined with synthetic fur, over his chest and knees.

"Welcome back, Mr. Myburgh. You had a nice nap?"

"No. I don't think so."

"But you slept. You nodded off while I was trying to explain to you how whites are like gravity."

"I dreamed we had an accident."

"*You* had an accident—earlier. In your lovely, *lekker* car, you hit an elephant."

Myburgh blinked. That collision had happened. This latest one—running *crash!* into another Putco bus—had not. Odd. Very odd. A conundrum inside an enigma.

"I dreamed other things, too."

"Good dreams?"

Myburgh started. "Why are we stopped?"

"Never mind that. Tell me what you dreamed."

"For one thing, I'd . . . died. Heart attack. In my car. But somehow I was you in my dream, Mr. Thubana, and I looked into the window of my car to see me lying in it dead. Then I got on the bus with you and Kabini again. I was a ghost. I was dead, but at the same time I was you seeing me dead and seeing my ghost here on *Grim Boy's Toe*, just another passenger."

"Ah," Thubana said. "Fascinating. You being me and you being your own ghost at the same time."

Myburgh shot Thubana a pleading look. How to tell him that he had taken a weird sort of comfort from hearing Thubana's comrades mock him with their chant? Even from seeing a dream picture of himself in his car, where death had relieved him of both responsibility and culpability? Such things were unsayable.

Myburgh looked down. "You gave me your coat."

"Of course. Your suit's all torn. And I have a sweater." He did: an ugly, ribbed, reddish-brown sweater with more pills than a discount pharmacy.

Myburgh tried to remove the coat and thrust it back at Thubana, but Thubana held it to him with a hard, heavy-veined hand. "Keep it, Mr. Myburgh. Shortly, I fear, you will need it even more than you do now."

What was going on? Myburgh glanced around. Other riders were peering uneasily into the relentless drizzle. Kabini wasn't in his driver's cage. Further, some sort of armor-clad paddy wagon had parked in front of the bus, blocking its way. Africans called such vans "nylons," because of the mesh in their windows. Several men — Myburgh couldn't tell how many — stalked the asphalt and the boggish shoulder. A confusion of moving silhouettes.

"The police?"

"From BOSS," Thubana said. The Bureau of State Security, he meant. Ordinarily, Myburgh would have felt — what? — a frisson of ambiguous pride thinking on these dedicated state functionaries, but this morning, right now, he experienced their presence as all the others on *Grim Boy's Toe* must have — as an ominous interruption, a clamp slowly tightening on the heart. But why? These were men who could help him. Myburgh rapped on his window.

"*In here!*" he called in Afrikaans. "*I'm in here!*"

"They're not looking for you," Thubana said. "Best not to call attention to yourself."

"That's crazy. I *have* to talk to them." Hindered by the seat back in front of him and Thubana's unyielding presence to his left, he tried to stand.

"It will do no good, Mr. Myburgh."

"Nonsense. I'll tell them about my accident. They'll see that I get home." At last, he had allies again. But Thubana would not budge; the only way to reach the aisle would be to shove past him—a distasteful, maybe even a dangerous, option to pursue.

A plainclothes security police agent in a trench coat similar to Thubana's, and a dove-gray fedora, stepped up into the bus. Facing the passengers, he spoke in Afrikaans in a high-pitched voice that unexpectedly conveyed an intimidating authority: "Everyone off the bus! And be orderly about it!"

"Who are you?" said the woman in the checkered headscarf. She spoke in English.

"Major Henning Jeppe," the man said. And again in Afrikaans, "Off the bus, please. Step quickly."

Myburgh pulled himself up and said, "Gerrit Myburgh here. I've had an accident, Major Jeppe. Please help me."

But Jeppe had already gone back down the steps into the night, and the passengers on 496 rose grumbling from their seats or their newsprint mats and shuffled toward the bus's door. Thubana also rose. He took Myburgh by the arm (not so much patronizingly as custodially, as if Myburgh were a polo horse belonging to a doting employer) and guided him into the sluggish stream of bodies. Well, so be it. The sooner he got outside and reported his accident the sooner he could say farewell to these cattlelike Africans and go back to the uneventful life he'd built for himself at the financial institution called Jacobus & Roux.

On the desolate *bundu's* edge (Myburgh's digital now read 4:38, about two hours till sunup), he heard Kabini begging a uniformed policeman not to detain his bus:

"It will be my neck. I'm late as it is. The weather—you see what it's like. Don't be so cruel, *nkosi.*"

The policeman muttered something unintelligible, shoved Kabini around the bonnet of the bus, and disappeared with him behind the scattershot parade of the passengers. Myburgh began searching for Jeppe or some other member of State Security upon whom to dump his story, but all the white policemen had moved to the edges of the shadowy field into which they were herding everyone, depriving him of any chance to make his case. Thubana, settling his coat on Myburgh's shoulders from behind, helped him step over muddy earth toward a stubble-spiked piece of ground so exposed and barren that it stank of its own infertile clay.

"Hullo! My name is Gerrit Myburgh! I'm here by mistake!" In

dry weather, his cry would have echoed. This morning, it had no more impact on the Transvaal than a muffled cough.

"Shhhhh," Thubana said. "Save your breath."

Soon, all ninety passengers had shaped three sides of a square in the field beyond the bus. The fourth edge was the bus itself. Major Henning Jeppe reappeared from behind *Grim Boy's Toe*, where he and two or three policemen in rainslicks had been pumping Kabini for information. To speak to the detained, Jeppe stood in front of 496's tall, inward-pleated door.

"Most of you are honest workers," he said in his stentorian squeak. "But, this morning, at least one terrorist-traitor has ridden from KwaNdebele with you. If the law-abiding residents of your homeland help us identify this person or persons, we will let you reboard and go on to your jobs." He pinched the bridge of his nose, as if his head ached.

Myburgh began waving an arm. "Major Jeppe! Major Jeppe!"

Jeppe ignored him. "If you refuse to help, if you stay silent in the misguided belief that you are observing a higher patriotism, we will detain you here until you piss yourselves or your bladders burst. One or the other. Understand?"

"*Gaan kak in die mielies!*" ("Go shit in the corn!") shouted a squat male passenger only a meter or two from Jeppe.

The black's impertinence stunned Myburgh. The man was crazy. In fact, two policemen in macintoshes rushed into the field, seized him, and chivvied him back aboard the bus with their *sjamboks* and a series of hammerlike blows between the shoulder blades. Inside 496's tin shell, the man, bellowing, begged to be returned to his people in the field.

"Fool," murmured Thubana, shaking his head.

"Major Jeppe, I don't belong here!" Myburgh shouted. He wanted to walk manfully up to the major, but Thubana, sensing this intent, locked an arm through his elbow. "Damn you. Let go."

One of the bus's windows slid down: *Krrrrrrack!* A policeman leaned out. "This isn't the man, sir. He claims our terrorist is someone called Mpandhlani."

Myburgh looked three people to his right and saw Mpandhlani, a raw-boned figure with a face like an inoffensive baboon's, staring at the ground. Actually, his nose was pointing earthward, but his eyes seemed to be rolled back in his head contemplating a dimension where a person could write poetry unmolested. He was wearing his volleyball cap, which made him look like an escapee from either an insane asylum or a circus train.

"Christ," said Thubana.

"Aren't you folks lucky?" Jeppe said, walking into the field in his new boots, unmindful of the mud. "One of you has already come to our assistance. Good. Excellent." Abruptly, he turned back to the bus. "What was that name, Wessels?"

"Mpandhlani, sir. It's a nickname. It means Baldhead."

"Thank you, Wessels." Jeppe did as neat a military pivot as he could manage on the sloppy ground, then strode toward the detainees in Myburgh's crooked line. "Baldhead," he murmured. "Baldhead."

"Psssst, Winston," Thubana said, softly hissing.

A woman beside Mpandhlani nudged him, and he looked at Thubana through glazed, beyond-the-pale eyes.

"Keep your cap on, Winston," Thubana said. "Keep it on."

Myburgh straightened his arm, breaking free of Thubana's elbow lock. "*Here he is, Major Jeppe! The terrorist you want is right here!*" Myburgh stepped out of the line of detainees, leveled an accusing finger at Mpandhlani, and briefly held this stance as if posing for a new statue at the Voortrekker Monument.

"Bring that man out of the bus, Wessels," Jeppe called over his shoulder. "He'll point us to the filthy bugger."

What the hell? Myburgh glanced at Jeppe, then at the policemen strong-arming the informant off *Grim Boy's Toe*, and then at Thubana throwing him a stare of blast-furnace hate.

But Jeppe . . . was he deaf? Was he blind?

One of the fellows who had informed on Mpandhlani (an African, thought Myburgh, not me) had a rugger's body and a flat-cheeked face with a pair of big, liquid eyes. Jeppe's policemen dragged him along each line of detainees until, head down, he stopped in front of Skosana and stood there incriminatingly shame-faced.

"Ephraim," Thubana said. "You shit."

"They already knew," Ephraim said. "Your friend—" nodding at Myburgh "—just fingered him."

"No, he didn't," Thubana said. "He's nothing to his own people this morning. Nothing, Ephraim. He could strip naked in front of these snakes, man. They'd never notice."

"In any case," Ephraim said, "I wasn't the only one who—"

"Watch that talk," said Wessels, angry and puzzled. He slapped Thubana across his lips: a crisp, open-handed blow.

Myburgh turned around. Jeppe, Wessels, Wessels's partner, and the man named Ephraim were all near enough to touch—as, of course, was Thubana. But Myburgh now knew that he was a ghost to the Afrikaners: a person-shaped void. Those he'd expected to rescue him—fellow whites—could not see or hear him, while the blacks—Kabini, Mpandhlani, Ephraim, and so on—had no more interest in him than he had in them. Except (at least until he'd tried to betray Skosana) Mordecai Thubana, who had given him his coat.

Why should I be ashamed? I'm being a good citizen, aren't I? Standing up for stability and order?

Myburgh went to Jeppe and shouted into his pinched, bloodless face: "I've had an accident! My name's Gerrit Myburgh. If you want proof, ring up my brother Kiewit—Kiewit Myburgh—on the farm called Huilbloom! He'll vouch for me!"

Jeppe blinked. He recoiled imperceptibly. That was all. It was as if he'd suffered a mild pang of heartburn or caught a faint whiff of sewage from a settlement upwind. Then he turned about and piercingly commanded all the hangdog laborers from KwaNdebele to reboard their bus. He dispatched Wessels's partner to assist in overseeing the boarding, then approached Mpandhlani with his hands jammed Humphrey Bogart-style in the pockets of his trench coat. All Myburgh could do was skip aside. Then, as 496's riders straggled bemusedly back to the bus at the urging of Jeppe's henchmen, Jeppe eyed Mpandhlani with a rote and clinical ill will.

Over his shoulder, he said, "Don't let the bus go until we've questioned this gentleman."

Myburgh heard Kabini, the driver, cry, "Please, *nkosi*, you've got your man! Let me finish my route!" This plea was followed by a thump, an outraged yell, and the sounds of argument as the police goosed Kabini up the steps to his driver's cage. Myburgh could see only kaleidoscope pieces of their scuffle through the bobbing heads and shoulders of the people stumping back to *Grim Boy's Toe*.

Thubana was not among their number. He stood out in the field with Mpandhlani, Major Jeppe, and the pumpkin-headed cop whom Jeppe called Wessels. Myburgh stood with them, of course, but he seemed not to count, having less impact on the events now unraveling than a stray memory or an unheard song. Should he go back to 496 with the others, strike out on foot for Pretoria, or stand here like an undressed department-store mannequin, humiliated and useless?

Jeppe took note of Thubana. "Go back to the bus, kaffir," he said, abandoning all pretense at courtesy.

"If Winston's a terrorist, I'm a terrorist, Major."

"Then you *are*," Myburgh said. "You *told* me Mpandhlani was held for almost three years for terrorist activity."

Simultaneously, Jeppe said, "Very well. I believe you. Stay here with your bloody accomplice."

Thubana replied to Myburgh: "I told you I *supposed* he'd been a guerrilla. Nothing more."

"Guerrilla, terrorist—it's all the same to us," Jeppe said, squinting perplexedly at Thubana. He turned to Wessels. "Aren't we lucky this fellow's so talkative, though."

"Yes, sir." Wessels had three or four chins. Even in the mud, he seemed to be bouncing lightly on his toes, minutely jiggling his chins in anticipation of the fun he would soon have at the two Africans' expense.

"But no more out of you until we've talked to Mister Baldhead," Jeppe told Thubana. "Understand?"

Thubana merely stared at the major.

Myburgh lifted his arms, dropped them to his sides again. He was invisible to the very authority to whom he should be as plain as a marshmallow in a mug of cocoa. His words were as inaudible to Jeppe and Wessels as the high-pitched piping of dog whistles. He found himself—as he had been on the road right after that elephant demolished his Caddy—on the verge of tears.

Four men in an open field on a damp morning. From nowhere, it seemed, the fancy came to Myburgh that if only they had a folding table and chairs, they could sit down and play a few hands of bridge or canasta. Cards were plasticized, after all—they didn't go soggy on you. He and the others could take partners and play. So what if it wasn't quite cockcrow and he was missing a shoe?

Jeppe ended this absurd reverie by stepping up to Mpandhlani, his eyes level with Mpandhlani's lips, and saying, "Take off that stupid cap, kaffir. When in the presence of a state official, you show respect."

"We're outdoors," Myburgh blurted. "What the devil difference does it make, Major Jeppe?"

Mpandhlani's spirit seemed to have left his body. It had flown away to a thatched Ndebele house with freehand-painted fences and exterior murals, frescoes of wild geometric designs in mint green, lemon yellow, concrete blue. Or that was what Mpandhlani's fallen lower lip and fish-eyed gaze suggested to Myburgh, who thought the man looked catatonic, as if the arrival of the security police had made him take refuge in memory, in a private idyll of childhood.

"Take off your cap!"

"Leave him alone," Thubana told Jeppe.

"Shut up!" Wessels said, and, wincing, he struck Thubana with his rhinoceros-hide whip.

Up, involuntarily, went Myburgh's arms as he flinched away from the unexpected blow. When he looked again, a raw gash on Thubana's cheek had begun leaking scarlet.

Mpandhlani's spirit flew back from his boyhood home (probably only a few kilometers from Huilbloom, the Myburgh family farm) and reanimated his upright corpse: he took off his cap.

Jeppe seized it from him, examined it with distaste (it stank of rubber and man sweat), then hurled it into the twilight with a contemptuous flip. The volleyball half whistled through the air and landed wetly, a sound like two hippopotamuses kissing. Jeppe, noticing Mpandhlani's saddle-stitched pate, gave a squeaky guffaw. Perhaps his laugh embarrassed him: he cut it off immediately.

"My," he said. "What an ostrich egg. I'll bet old Christiaan Wessels here would be glad to scramble it for you."

Now Mpandhlani's eyes were semi-alert. He looked at Jeppe, at Wessels, at Thubana, at Myburgh. It seemed that he started to speak. But what came from his mouth was a staticky tirade:

"... *our express purpose to kill more and more South African security forces, especially the Boers, because unless whites are made to feel unsafe, and until they too are killed, they will yet feel safe to go on killing the Africans. And, in fact, although some whites are among the security forces killed by the Azanian People's Liberation Army, time has almost come when—*"

"Shut up, you bloody kaffir!" Jeppe cried.

"*—for every African killed by the racist security forces, a white person must be killed. One racist, one bullet! Phambili Nomzabalazo Wabantu!*"

At that moment, Mpandhlani stopped broadcasting propaganda and began transmitting a medley of pompous marches. Jeppe and Wessels appeared nonplussed, uncomprehending. But Jeppe seized Mpandhlani by the arms, pulled him to him, and then brutally shoved him toward the roadway. Mpandhlani bent double, clutching his head as if to dam the symphonic battle hymns spilling out.

Headlamps and flashlights reflected off the windshield of *Grim Boy's Toe* like strobes in a Joburg nightclub. Confusion reigned. Myburgh literally had no idea where, or to whom, to turn.

"Take this walking radio station to the van, Wessels. Get the filthy bugger out of my hearing."

"Me, too," Thubana said.

Jeppe nodded. "Of course. You, too." He swept his hand after Wessels and Mpandhlani, a command and a dismissal.

"What about me?" Myburgh asked Thubana. "What am I supposed to do?"

"Go find Winston's cap."

"His cap?"

"I beg your pardon," said Jeppe, glaring at Thubana.

"Sure. Otherwise, the broadcasts he's picking up will drive us crazy before we reach security police headquarters."

Myburgh hobbled deeper into the field, trying to find the spot where their comrade's volleyball cap had made its obscene-sounding, sucking touchdown.

"Hurry!" Thubana yelled after him. "Or we may go off and leave you, Mr. Myburgh!"

"Shut up!" Jeppe said. He twisted Thubana's arm, chivvying the much taller man after Wessels. He appeared to believe that Thubana was playing mind games with him, maybe communicating by means of code words and gestures with a squad of guerrillas deeper in the *bundu*. In fact, Jeppe was royally spooked. Myburgh would have sympathized with him more if his own predicament had not been so outlandish. No one could feel as isolated as he did.

By what seemed pure luck, he found Mpandhlani's volleyball cap, pried it out of the mud, then stumbled back to the roadway to the *bakkie*—the nylon—into which Wessels and two more security agents were herding Mpandhlani and Thubana.

Kabini, sporting a badly swollen eye, waved at Myburgh from his driver's cage on the Putco bus. Although Myburgh thought seriously about boarding 496 again, he decided that, being invisible to the Afrikaners, he'd do better sticking with Thubana, who, however mad, had at least some small insight into the clunkily ratcheting gears of this nightmare.

So Myburgh leapt into the BOSS van just as Wessels was pushing its doors to. The hem of Thubana's coat got caught in the closing doors. Myburgh yanked the hem free and toppled backward. Wessels, cursing, slammed the doors a second time, harder, so hard that the metal walls and loadbed of the *bakkie's* holding cell vibrated like fettered gongs.

Mpandhlani and Thubana sat on narrow benches on either side of this four-wheeled cell.

"Are you all right, Mr. Myburgh?" Thubana said.

"No," Myburgh said. "Of course I'm not."

For added to the trauma of his selective invisibility was the fact that he had lost a stocking: his muddy left foot ached with the pitiless July cold.

Wessels—whom Thubana ridiculed in Afrikaans as *Pampoenkop*, Pumpkinhead—had taken Mpandhlani's coat, leaving his upper body clothed only in a threadbare T-shirt. Meanwhile, Mpandhlani's steel plate broadcast, even inside the nylon, an ANC report on forced removals to impoverished bantustans. Their little cell buzzed with the transmission, a crazily garbled mix of news, exhortation, and music.

"Give him his cap," Thubana said, his naked hand on the *sjambok* cut on his cheek.

"Gladly." Myburgh flipped Mpandhlani the volleyball half and, lying in the center of the floor, watched him settle it on his head like a housewife twisting half an orange onto the fluted reamer of a citrus juicer. At first, it seemed to hurt Mpandhlani to cover his skull, but then the cap muted the transmission, turning it into sounds like voices heard faintly through a heating vent. The bald man's eyes brightened, his lips relaxed. But he still looked cold, hugging himself and hunching forward like someone straining against electrocution.

"May I give him your coat, too?" Myburgh said. "I'm fine now. Well, not fine, exactly. Numb."

"Sure," Thubana said. "Go ahead."

Myburgh rolled out of Thubana's expensive coat and handed it up to Mpandhlani, who nodded his curt thanks and shrugged himself into it. As he put it on, Myburgh saw that neither he nor Thubana had belts now. Wessels had undoubtedly taken them, too, on the grounds that the kaffirs could use them as makeshift weapons, their buckles serving as nasty flails. Well, that seemed smart. A policeman had to watch himself. Wessels would surely have taken their shoes, too, if they hadn't been wearing ratty *takkies*.

"What's going to happen to us?" Myburgh said.

"To Winston and me?"

"Of course."

"Interrogation. Detention. Torture. One of us may fall out a window. One of us may strangle himself."

"Strangle? Strangle yourself?"

"It's hard to say, Mr. Myburgh. I don't know what Winston's supposed to have done. Or what kind of stuff Jeppe and Pumpkinhead will be looking for."

"Someone exploded a bomb near the Armscor factory," Mpandhlani said. "I'm getting a report on it now." He listened to the voices tunneling his gray matter like so many ethereal brain worms. "The blast—a car bomb—did heavy damage to the plant itself."

Myburgh blinked. Armscor was the weapons-manufacturing arm of the South African Defense Force and a profit-making enterprise of the first water. Its plants were among the most heavily fortified in the country. If it had suffered a crippling bomb blast, no place and nobody—no white place and no white person, rather—could rest secure again. So far as that went, though, Myburgh could not recall any time that he had really rested secure. Living in South Africa had always seemed to him like walking through a plush hotel suite past hundreds of whirring electric fans with frayed cords and no safety baskets.

"You didn't have anything to do with that, did you, Winston?" Thubana said.

Mpandhlani—no, better to call him Skosana: Winston Skosana, a man with both a baptismal name and a Ndebele surname, not merely a patronizing Bantu joke name—*Skosana* tilted his volleyball-capped head against the van's wall and laughed in the basso profundo registers of earthquake.

"Don't I wish. Oh, don't I wish, Mordecai."

Thubana grinned sheepishly. "That's what I thought. But . . . hey, man, you know."

"I know. But I'm just an oke at a Simba Quix chips-and-rusks factory, loading trucks and carrying out trash. Oliver Tambo never tells me nothing."

He laughed again. His laughter overwhelmed the hisses and pops still seeping through his earholes, nostrils, and eyes from Lusaka and other points north—*several* points north, Myburgh figured, for occasionally Skosana picked up ANC broadcasts, and sometimes PAC patter, and, more rarely, the revolutionary threats of the Azanian People's Liberation Army. Indeed, Skosana's skull was a broadcast clearinghouse for a variety of anti-apartheid, anti-imperialist voices. Myburgh couldn't look at the man—lean, weathered, battle-scarred—without twinges of both awe and fear. On *Grim Boy's Toe*, he had seemed comic. Here in the nylon's holding cell, though, he suddenly and unaccountably radiated a good-humored self-confidence and strength. Myburgh did not think it was all owing to Thubana's trench coat.

Painfully, Myburgh got up and limped to one of the mesh-covered windows on the nylon's rear doors. He was surprised to see Putco bus number 496 chugging down the highway behind them, its headlamps jittering in the pale light, losing distinctiveness, like fish eyes vanishing into clear water, as the sky reddened through a gauze of blowing clouds and spread out vividly over the Transvaal.

Pretty. Very pretty.

With no closer settlements or factories blighting this part of the Putco route, the land was lovely, an exhilarating desolation. Soon the nylon would enter Pretoria's outskirts, cruise past the jacarandas on its boulevards, and he, well, he would be home.

Bracing himself against any sudden lurches, Myburgh said, "What in God's name happened to me out there?"

"You became shadow matter to them," Thubana said.

"I was shadow matter in my dreams. When Kabini hit that other Putco bus. When I had a heart attack in my Cadillac and got on 496 as my dead self's ghost. Damn it, this is *real!*"

"You look real to me," Skosana said.

"Thank you." Nearly slipping, Myburgh turned back around.

Thubana's hand was blood-streaked from the ragged *sjambok* wound that Wessels had inflicted. Myburgh found the handkerchief he had used to staunch his own bleeding and passed it to Thubana, who took it with no qualms and held it against his cheek.

"I don't get it," Myburgh resumed. "Why didn't I mean anything to those men? What's going on?"

"Winston," Thubana said, gesturing with his free hand, "is my book in one of those pockets?"

Skosana patted the side pockets of the borrowed coat, raised a telltale thump, and pulled out the copy of *Superstrings*. He hefted it as if it were a hand grenade.

"Turn to page eighty," Thubana said.

His eyebrows lifted, Skosana began riffling. When he found the specified page, he bent the book back in his lap.

"Up at the top," Thubana said. "John Schwarz is talking about 'E sub-eight' symmetries. Do you see it?"

" 'E sub-eight'? Christ, Mordecai, did you memorize this whole crazy book?" He waved it. Again, like a hand grenade.

"I've been studying, hard. Find it and read it, okay? Right where Professor Schwarz first mentions shadow matter."

Amused, Skosana shook his head and read: " '. . . a new kind of matter, sometimes called shadow matter, that doesn't interact, or only interacts extremely weakly, with the ordinary matter that we are familiar with. If you wanted to—' "

"Skip down, Winston. Below where it says we can't see shadow matter because it doesn't interact with everyday light."

Skosana grimaced. He ran a finger along the lines of print and finally read: " '. . . it *does* interact with our kind of gravity—we share our gravity with shadow matter.' "

"Yes," Thubana said. "Yes."

"You called me gravity," Myburgh said. "Now you're calling me shadow matter. Make up your mind!"

"I called *whites* gravity," Thubana said. "Not you. I was using analogy to explain a point. Now I'm making another one."

"There's nothing metaphorical about my situation! Damn it, I'm invisible to my own kind!"

"Shadow matter," Thubana said smugly, as if he had just solved a devilishly abstruse equation.

"I can see you," Skosana said. "Clearly."

"Read," Thubana commanded. "Read what the professor says about shadow matter and gravity."

"There's hardly anything, Mordecai. He only says we'd notice a shadow planet by its gravitational effects—but we wouldn't see it with ordinary light."

"I'm not a planet! I'm a person!"

"Person or planet," Thubana said bitterly, taking Myburgh's handkerchief from his cheek and examining it, "you're shadow matter to those fucking Boers." He nodded at the *bakkie's* cab.

"How? Why?"

"Ask God. That's what I do. I ask him every day: 'Dear God, Great Jehovah, how did my people get to be such thin shadows in our own country?' "

"What am I going to do?"

"What are *we* going to do?" Thubana said.

"I yelled in Jeppe's face," Myburgh said. "He didn't hear me. He just leaned away—as if a soft breeze had touched him." The memory of the major's lack of reaction was painful. Humiliating.

"Gravitational effects," Skosana said, sliding the book back into a coat pocket. "Mr. Myburgh has a gravitational effect on the *stormjaers*. They can't see him, but he can—I don't know, *move* them, maybe. Just a little."

Silent tears traced Myburgh's cheeks like liquid fuses; he sat down beside Skosana. When Wessels opened the nylon's doors, he could dismount in front of Pretoria's security police headquarters and walk the formidable distance to his condo or the much shorter distance to the offices of Jacobus & Roux. Even if no one his own color could see him, he could make it home, resume his life, and forget these past few disorienting hours.

But for how long? No one could hear him. He couldn't make a living if the clients for whom he prepared loans, stock options, capital-outlay schemes, and Krugerrand investments could neither see nor hear him. He would have no real existence, he would be a walking cypher, a ghost of blood and bones.

"How did I get this way? When did it happen? I was all right when I left Huilbloom. Physically."

"Hitting that elephant did it," Thubana said. "There aren't any elephants between Pretoria and KwaNdebele."

"This morning, there *was* an elephant—I saw it, I hit it!"

"Okay, okay. But the elephant you hit was . . . a totem from the old times, shadow matter from yesterday. It changed you. It took Kabini a moment or two to pull you into focus when you came up to the bus. Remember? He saw your wrecked car, yes, but after he stopped and opened the door, what he first saw was only mist, night and mist, and then your ghost—which, of course, he *couldn't* see—filled up with Africa, and he *could* see."

"That's poppycock. You're trying to say I'm dead."

"No. I know you're not dead. I'm trying to explain something very hard to explain."

"How do I change back? Explain that."

"Back to what?" Skosana said, finding a packet of Rothman's 30s and a book of matches in Thubana's coat. "A dead man? Maybe you were dead—killed in your wreck—until number 496 came along. What do you think?" He tapped out, and lit, a cigarette.

Myburgh wiped the wet from his face with the torn sleeve of his jacket. He hated Rothman's 30s. He hated any cigarette. To avoid the smoke slipping out of Skosana's head (along with a faint radio speech about the Azanian victory over Armscor), he crossed over to Thubana's bench.

"What I think is, number 496 couldn't resurrect anyone. It can scarcely even go."

"It's still behind us," Thubana said. "It'll make it to Belle Ombre this morning, and back out to KwaNdebele tonight, and back in to Pretoria tomorrow. And so on."

"But how do I change back, Professor Superstrings?"

Thubana, to Myburgh's surprise, folded the bloody handkerchief he'd been using to clot his wound and stuffed it fastidiously into the breast pocket of Myburgh's suit coat. "Right now, Mr. Myburgh, everything is so *befok*, I hardly care."

Lifting his muddy foot up to the bench and arranging himself so that one haunch could warm it, Myburgh was unable to meet Thubana's eyes. He'd got what he deserved. Thubana and Skosana were riding off to detention, interrogation, torture, possibly even (it was a filthy thing to contemplate, a filthier thing to admit) death; and he had badgered Thubana about restoring him to the lofty estate of an upper-middle-class Afrikaner.

Sweet Christ, what weakness. Or what brass. It was hard for him to know exactly how he had erred, but he had definitely erred. The chilly proof of it was Thubana's silence.

Traffic in Pretoria was beginning to thicken, but Jeppe and his driver had beaten the morning rush. From one of the van's windows, Myburgh saw that they had lost *Grim Boy's Toe* and that a great many familiar landmarks were kaleidoscoping past. Then they reached the headquarters of the security police, pulled off a main thoroughfare into a concealing side street, and slammed to a jolting halt. The laughter from the cab made Myburgh suspect that Wessels (or whoever was driving) had braked like that for the sadistic joy of shaking them up.

"*Out! Out!*"

The doors came open. Fists with billy clubs shook insistently at them. Pampoenkop—Lieutenant Christiaan Wessels—appeared among the men waiting to escort them inside. And when Skosana, squinting like a mole, stumbled out onto the pavement, Wessels grabbed him by the trench coat lapels and bullied him up against the wall of the terraced security building.

"Where did you get this coat, kaffir?"

Skosana nodded at the nylon's doors, through which Thubana was now warily coming. "Mordecai let me borrow it."

"He wasn't wearing a coat when we put him in." Wessels looked at one of the agents. "Dedekind, did you leave a goddamned coat in there yesterday?"

"No, Lieutenant Wessels. Absolutely not."

Myburgh had already dismounted. He stood between the tall gray building and the nylon, studying the situation.

Wessels, meantime, stuck his big round head, with its flat pink nose, into Skosana's gaunt face. "Where in fuck did you get this, Baldhead? *Tell me!*"

"I had it in my trouser pocket," Thubana said instead. "Folded up very small. 'Compactified,' one could say."

"It's a coat in ten dimensions, six of them curled up," Myburgh said, amazed to hear himself using back talk similar to Thubana's. Of course, the difference—the telling difference—was that Wessels couldn't hear him.

Wessels shot a disbelieving look at Thubana. "Shut up. You'll have your chance to sing." Then, back to Skosana: "Take it off, kaffir! At once!"

Skosana got help. Two security agents hurried to yank the coat off him, grabbing down on its sleeves. So zealous were they, they almost unsocketed one of his arms. Myburgh heard a nauseating *pop!* and saw both agony and hate flare in Skosana's eyes, with their immense pupils and muddy-yellow whites.

"Leave him alone!" Thubana cried.

A pretty-boy policeman menaced him with a *sjambok*. "You want a star on that other cheek too?"

"All of his cheeks, Goosen," said Dedekind, a thirtyish fellow with close-set eyes. "He wants a star or two to sit down on."

"Just as he wishes," Wessels said. "The filthy bugger."

As a policeman wrapped Thubana's trench coat around his arm, *Superstrings* dropped out. So did the package of Rothman's 30s and the matchbook from an Indian restaurant in a condemned Asian neighborhood. One officer scooped up the book, another bent down for the cigarettes and matches.

Wessels turned aside to examine *Superstrings*. "Well, well," he said. "This could be a find, Schoeman—a code book, maybe. Carry it in with you."

Thubana barked a laugh. "Who's going to decode it?"

This time the policeman with the *sjambok* hit him, but Thubana deflected the blow by lifting a hand and hunching his shoulder. A second man made him pay by billying him in the groin. Thubana fell to his knees in front of the *bakkie's* yawning doors.

I don't have to watch this, Myburgh thought. I can walk home. Who's going to stop me?

Suddenly, Wessels realized that Skosana was again wearing the volleyball cap that, on the road from KwaNdebele, Major Jeppe had hurled off into the night "What the hell is this?" He snatched the cap from Skosana's head, dangled it distastefully.

"... *King, Tutu and Boesak's reformism has been endorsed by the imperialists worldwide. Both King and Tutu received the Nobel Peace Prize for their efforts to restrict our liberation movements to non-violent methods. However, their—*"

"Shut up!" Wessels shouted.

"*—timid political activity can only patch up a few of the more glaring injustices of their morally bankrupt societies. When the armed struggle is at low ebb, they condemn it outright, but when it intensifies and gathers mass support, they cry, 'Negotiate with us, or face them!' This is how they sell—*"

"Shut up!" Wessels slapped Skosana with open palms on both sides of the face, like a man playing cymbals.

"Don't!" Myburgh stepped forward. But, as he knew it would, this heartfelt caution went unheeded.

Skosana, stung, gave Wessels a two-handed shove in the chest, knocking him into Goosen and Dedekind. Meanwhile, his steel plate continued to receive and transmit:

"... *revolutionary organizations like the Black Panther Party and the Dodge Revolutionary Union Movement (DRUM) in Detroit. It is this common history that unifies mass struggle in—*"

Recovering, Wessels jumped back at Skosana with a *sjambok* taken from the agent named Schoeman. His face as red and bloated as a rising sun, he lifted the flail with all the fury of Christ going after the moneychangers.

From his knees, Thubana cried, "He can't help it, you *tsotsis!* Give him back his cap!"

Goosen and Schoeman caught Wessels from behind.

"Not out here, Lieutenant," Goosen said, trembling excitedly. "Save it. You'll have your chance. All of us will."

Hyperventilating, Wessels resembled an inflatable, horror-show van der Merwe, an editorial cartoon of the Bad Afrikaner. Myburgh was simultaneously repulsed and fascinated. When Wessels finally gained control of himself, though, he saw the cap in his left hand and slapped it punishingly into Skosana's palm.

"Put it on!"

Glaring contempt, Skosana obeyed, rendering the broadcast from Zambia as thin and reedy as water trickling through the pipes in an adjoining hotel room.

Wessels appealed to Goosen: "Where did he get it? The major threw it away. I *know* he threw it away."

"He probably had the other half crimped up in a pocket," Goosen said. "That's all."

Myburgh bent down beside Thubana, gripped his elbow, put an arm around his waist, helped him stand.

"It's muddy just like the one Major Jeppe threw away," Wessels said. "He got it back somehow. The same way he got that coat."

"How was that?" said Dedekind, shifting his eyes.

"That old black magic," Thubana whispered to Myburgh. "That I know so well."

Hearing Thubana quote from an old pop song, in a street next to security police headquarters, tickled Myburgh; against his will, he smiled.

"Go home," Thubana whispered. "It only gets worse now. Go on home, Mr. Myburgh."

"*No!*" Skosana said.

Wessels looked up as if Skosana had spit in his face. " 'No' is just what we *don't* want to hear, kaffir. We're in the business of manufacturing yeses."

"Come inside with us," Skosana said, speaking around Wessels to Myburgh.

"Never fear," Wessels said. "Steenkamp!"

A policeman came to grasp Thubana's arm. Myburgh tried to push him aside, to protect his own grip on Thubana, but his efforts only made Steenkamp stumble slightly and glance down as if a stone had tripped him. Then he seized Thubana, brushing Myburgh's arm away as if it were less than a spider's thread.

"Come inside with us," Skosana said again. "And stay, please, with Mordecai. He's never been in before."

Wessels said, "Neither of you kaffirs will be lonesome—don't worry about that. And if your friend's never been in before, it's past time, isn't it?"

"Please," Skosana said. "Come inside."

Myburgh looked at the man pleading with him with such dignity. He looked at Thubana, and at the security police—Wessels & Company—whose eagerness to escort his two comrades upstairs seemed akin to that of small boys on Christmas. Packages to unwrap. New toys to break in.

"All right," he said.

Getting in was easy. Myburgh squeezed through the street-level door beside Thubana and struggled up through the echoey stairwell behind Skosana.

APARTHEID, SUPERSTRINGS, AND MORDECAI THUBANA 99

Each prisoner was bookended by a pair of security agents, who had handcuffed Thubana and Skosana before bringing them in. Didn't this mausoleum have elevators? If so, they weren't for detainees, even in the off-limits parts reserved for suspected terrorists and other enemies of the state. So let the kaffirs climb the stairs to their inevitable comeuppance.

Myburgh could not clearly account for his lack of sympathy for Goosen, Steenkamp, Dedekind, and Schoeman. (Wessels had left them on the first landing, perhaps to check in with Jeppe.) After all, he'd grown up with such men. Men somewhat like them, anyway—the sons of farmers on the properties bordering Huilbloom. Freckled, sunburnt, sandy-haired toughs with callused hands and laughs.

Several times, in fact, as a teenager, he had ventured out as a balaclava man with these fellows. Everyone wore a hood and rode in Anton Smoot's tiny Renault, headlights off, to shoot out the streetlamps and robots—traffic lights—in the black areas near Nylstroom. They had carried real pistols (he and Kiewit juggled Papa Myburgh's Ruger back and forth) and real bullets. And, to this day, Kiewit held that on one outing they had shot a pair of meths-drinking Ndebele drunks along with the streetlamps. Myburgh's memory of these jaunts wasn't as clear as his brother's, nor could he see himself engaging in anything so reckless today. But, once upon a time, he had definitely ridden balaclava. . . .

Jeppe, Wessels, Goosen, Steenkamp, Dedekind, Schoeman, and the others were just doing their jobs. A hard job. A necessary job, albeit a dirty one. And they weren't much applauded for the hard, dirty job they did. Folks didn't want to think about them. Just as a man—a city man, at least—putting away a juicy steak doesn't want to be told that the cow it came from died under the spattering thwack of a sledgehammer.

But Myburgh *did* know the reason for his animosity toward these men. Mordecai Thubana put roofs on houses and apartment buildings in the new white subdivisions in and around Pretoria; Skosana had paid for his crimes against the state long ago. They were kaffirs, sure, but neither of them belonged in this building. Myburgh knew that. A man who wanted to help the world's finest physicists come up with a Grand Unified Theory of Everything, and another who made his living loading snack foods onto trucks.

Such reprobates. Such traitors.

Stop worrying, Gerrit. Despite Thubana's fears ("It only gets worse now"), Jeppe and his men will see their error once they've asked a few questions.

Of course they will. They *must*.

At the third or fourth landing (during his reverie, Myburgh had lost track), the slightly overweight Schoeman, breathing raggedly, asked Dedekind, the ranking agent, if they could rest a while. His request was granted, and Thubana and Skosana positioned themselves at a rail fronting a narrow window looking down on a graveled roof; there, a peeling billboard glistened.

Skosana nudged Myburgh. Read the billboard, his nudge and his lifted eyebrows commanded.

Myburgh studied the sign. It was one he recognized from other venues—street bills, newspaper ads, magazine inserts. It showed a bottle of laundry bleach, with a slogan next to it that struck him this morning with a new, almost brutal, forcefulness: JIK, it said. (A brand-name.) And under that: WITH CONTROLLED STRENGTH, FOR THE WORLD'S WHITEST WASH.

"Oh, Lord, I'm feeling sick," Skosana said, in a self-mocking lilt: "Here in the land of Jik."

Thubana said nothing. The sight of the billboard, along with his friend's doggerel, seemed to dispirit him. And Thubana's funk clouded Myburgh's efforts to regard the situation in an optimistic light. They were all in the land of Jik.

Must I keep on climbing these stairs? Myburgh wondered. Like Schoeman, he was winded. Trotting back down, after a short rest, seemed a more attractive option. If, at least, he could get out again. Did the street-level door automatically lock? Did you have to have a key to go through it again?

Dedekind grabbed Skosana's arm. "That's it," he said. "Let's get moving."

Myburgh, unsure of whether he was a man or a ghost, hurried along after the others. He feared that if they reached an upper floor before he could squeeze through too, he would be trapped in this claustrophobic stairwell for days.

On the fifth or sixth floor (again, Myburgh was unsure), Goosen and Steenkamp strong-armed Thubana in one direction, while Dedekind and Schoeman pulled Skosana in the other. Skosana set himself against their tugging and told Myburgh, "Go with Mordecai, man."

"I said I would, didn't I?"

"Shut up, kaffir," Goosen said over Myburgh's unheard reply. "We know what we're doing."

Steenkamp rolled his eyes to indicate that Skosana was off in the head and that Goosen should ignore him. Myburgh followed the two security agents with Mordecai Thubana. Dedekind and Schoeman took Skosana the other way, off into the well-lit but nightmarish warren of the upper floor.

What happened from that moment on, Myburgh received as if in a dream—a protracted hallucination that complemented his selective invisibility. Much of this experience did not seem real; much was so hurtfully vivid that he almost ran from it. All of it caromed past at fast-forward speeds impossible to slow, or at crazy angles defying his efforts to find in them a coherent pattern.

In an interrogation room off a pair of nichelike halls giving onto the floor's main corridor, Goosen, Steenkamp, and four more members of the security police—men Myburgh had not seen before—immediately began stripping Thubana.

They tore off his heavy, pilled sweater, revealing a light-gray T-shirt on which a complicated series of mathematical equations in red, blue, and yellow danced like thousands of printed footsteps on an impossible fox-trot diagram. A caption under all these symbols read THIS EXPLAINS EVERYTHING.

As two men held Thubana's arms and two others stood by in case he resisted, Steenkamp grabbed the T-shirt at the neck and started to rip it away.

"*Pas op!*" Goosen shouted. Then: "You nincompoop, take it off carefully. Carefully."

"It stinks," Steenkamp said. "And it's—" he nodded at the math-symbol choreography "—nonsense."

"You don't know that, nor do I. Take it off carefully. Lay it over there."

Steenkamp obeyed, pushing Thubana's head forward, unrolling the T-shirt up his back, and spreading the T-shirt out on a metal desk in the corner. The six agents then hurried to strip Thubana of his rubber-soled *takkies*, pants, and baggy, tan undershorts.

"Stop that!" he cried, swatting at them. "Stop!"

Goosen cuffed him viciously. Soon, embarrassed and shivering, Thubana stood naked before them, his ribs touchingly prominent and his knobby-kneed legs like those of a muddy stork. Myburgh could tell at once that he hated this exposure, hated and resented it, even though he'd known from the start that this was the way things would go, for no African entering state custody as a crime suspect or as a political detainee could hope to come out unscathed, either physically or emotionally.

Even Myburgh knew that, but this morning, unable to intervene, he felt like a voyeur. It pained him that Thubana had to undergo not only the impersonal brutality of the policemen's attentions, but the added humiliation of having a third party (the agents were one obsessive entity) see his helplessness. But each time Myburgh turned aside or drifted to a different corner of the room, he felt that he had given in to a cowardly squeamishness.

At last he turned to Thubana and said, "What can I do?"

Thubana's eyes fastened on him. "Don't look at me. But don't leave. That's all."

"We're not leaving," Goosen said, "but we'll look at you all we damned well please." (Lord, the pretty fellow was young!)

Myburgh started to speak, but stopped. He looked aside. Then he crossed to the desk upon which Steenkamp had spread Thubana's THIS EXPLAINS EVERYTHING T-shirt, collapsed into a metal folding chair, and averted his face from Thubana's interrogators.

Occasionally, of course, Myburgh *had* to look, for the sadistic imagination of the agents was a fertile one. In fact, to think of Goosen, Steenkamp, and their accomplices as state interrogators was to whitewash their activities. Call them, rather, torturers. They didn't just ask questions. They did all they could to shame, hurt, and dehumanize their ward without quite knocking him unconscious—unconsciousness would have interfered with their efforts to crowbar the "truth" out of him.

"*Praat, praat, praat!*" ("Talk, talk, talk!") the six men yelled at Thubana.

"*Op die stene,*" Goosen said. ("On the bricks.")

They made him balance on a pair of bricks placed at contrasting slants on the floor, one brick a meter behind the other, so that Thubana resembled a circus performer walking a tightrope. Also, they slipped a yellowish latex hood over his head so that when he let out a breath, the hood ballooned obscenely; when he inhaled, he sucked the rubber back into his mouth and nostrils.

The way he swung his elbows, his wrists tied behind him, showed his terror, as did his muffled pleas to take off the hood. He made this plea whenever any opportunity to reply to the agents' stylized harassment arose—for, darting in and out, they were like hyenas worrying an injured springbok.

"Who prepared the car bomb at Armscor?"
"Who drove?"
"How did they get that *bakkie* past perimeter security?"
"Mpandhlani—your 'friend'—says you were a contact for the ANC guerrillas who planned the attack."
"Would you like to sire your own little *pikkenien* one day?"
"A statement, Mordecai. A statement!"
"List your contacts."
"Everything you did these past six months."
"The hiding places of your fellow terrorists."
"What do you know about ANC plans to decommission the Pretoria Dam?"
"When did you first hear of them?"
"This hood is nothing. Nothing. Wait until you've got a noose around your neck, kaffir."

Seeing that brick-balancing and dogged verbal harassment were not doing the job, Goosen commanded a change in tactics. Steenkamp approached the desk and yanked the chair that Myburgh was sitting on out from under him. Myburgh only narrowly kept from splintering his tailbone. Steenkamp took the chair to Thubana (still trussed in that urine-hued cowl, a baby in a placental membrane), slammed it down, unbound Thubana's hands, and thrust the folding chair into them even as he was trying to rub the soreness from his wrists.

"Over your head," Goosen said.

"*What?*" To counteract the possibility of smothering, Thubana kept puffing against the latex.

"I said, lift the chair over your head. Lift it and hold it. If you let it down, you'll pay."

Major Henning Jeppe and Lieutenant Christiaan Wessels entered the little room. They grinned when they saw what was going on; two of the four men who had been assisting Goosen and Steenkamp clicked their heels, nodded deferentially, and left. Myburgh, rubbing his hip, backed into the corner behind the desk. He watched from this cubbyhole as if standing aloof from the agents' sins would absolve him of any complicity.

Thubana, when Steenkamp prodded him with a billy club, raised the open folding chair over his head. He held it by two legs, his elbows bent.

"All the way up, kaffir! *All the way!*"

Thubana strained, straightened his arms, and pushed the chair up as high as it would go. Its rounded back bumped the ceiling, and Thubana almost toppled from the bricks to which his feet awkwardly clung. As a warning, Steenkamp thrust his billy into the cleft of Thubana's buttocks and jiggled it.

"Hold the chair sideways! Arms up! Up!"

Thubana stuck his chin out, as if to allow more air under the latex cowl, struggled for a fresh grip on the chair, and lifted it as high as it would go in this new position, missing the ceiling and so maintaining his balance. He looked like a monument to the patron saint of contortionists.

"Good," Steenkamp said. "Good."

Jeppe caught sight of the T-shirt spread atop the desk and came over to look at it. Wessels, his head bobbing first to this side and then to that, sought to keep an eye on Thubana as he swaggered over, too. At Jeppe's bidding, he picked up the shirt, smoothed it out in front of him, then minced about clownishly, modeling it.

"Phew!" he said, sniffing the T-shirt.

"Be still," Jeppe said in Afrikaans. Then he read the English words under the run-amok equations: " 'This explains everything.' " He squinted. "Yes, I'd wager it does."

Then, to Thubana: "What is this, kaffir? What kind of treason did you come in here wearing?"

"What is what, sir?" Thubana was hooded and blind. Naked and off-balance and straining to keep a chair aloft. Myburgh could not believe that Jeppe actually expected him to deduce the specifics of his moronic question.

"Your T-shirt, kaffir. These equations."

"That's a GUT, sir." His words were hard to make out, the hood muting and skewing them.

"A 'gut'?"

"Yes, sir. Or a TOE. A T-shirt TOE."

"Is it a 'gut' or a 'toe,' kaffir? Don't trifle with me today; I'm coming down with something."

"A Grand Unified Theory, sir. A Theory of Everything. Except that it . . . it isn't."

Steenkamp jabbed Thubana with his billy again, and Thubana had to lift one foot from its brick to keep from falling and to prevent his interrogators from assaulting him. Indeed, he would never have found the brick again if the policemen hadn't caught him and guided his wayward foot home.

Then, as if to show that this "kindness" has been provisional, Goosen used the end of his billy to lift and then lower Thubana's testicles. Again and again. Gently but menacingly.

"A 'gut,' a 'toe,' or neither, kaffir?" Jeppe said. "Explain to me these scribbles—" flapping the T-shirt "—you claim explain everything!"

"A T-shirt TOE," Thubana said. "A joke, my *baas*—just a joke."

Myburgh was disappointed. Until just now, Thubana had avoided using any kind of kowtowing epithet.

"A joke? How is it a joke?"

"There's no finished Theory of Everything yet, sir. So that's a . . . well, it's a just-pretend TOE."

"What does it *pretend* to mean?"

"Nothing, sir. Nothing real, at least."

Goosen lowered his billy, then rapped it upward into Thubana's groin so fast that Myburgh was not sure he had actually done it. The chair in Thubana's hands slipped and clattered down, striking both Goosen and another man; and Thubana, flailing one arm, toppled from the bricks, landed on his ribs, and rolled over like a man who hears gunfire on a busy street and tries to escape it. But Thubana could not escape.

"*Jy wil baklei, jy wil baklei?*" ("You want to fight, you want to fight?") Goosen cried, wiping blood from his lip and dropping the billy. He hurried to a filing cabinet, removed a piece of green hosepipe whose tube glistened as if cored with diamonds, and stalked back to Thubana. He began to pummel Thubana vigorously about the head and shoulders.

Thubana rolled from side to side under these blows and also the inescapable boots of Steenkamp and the two men whose names Myburgh still had not learned, for they stepped in and out to kick Thubana, like dancers in an intricate musical-comedy number.

"Stop it!" Myburgh shouted.

He rushed from his corner and grabbed Goosen's hosepipe on its backswing. But, after a brief hitch that made Goosen look back as if someone were playing a trick on him, the hosepipe slipped from Myburgh's grasp and crashed down solidly on Thubana's ear.

All Myburgh's subsequent efforts to deflect the hosepipe were failures, leaving burns in his palm but only imperceptibly delaying the adrenaline-charged policeman.

"Damn it, Goosen," Jeppe said, not even raising his voice. "Do you know what you're about?"

Goosen and the three other men backed off. Jeppe walked over to Thubana's huddled body, nudged him in the small of the back with his boot toe, and, letting the tail of the gray T-shirt dangle down mockingly on his shoulder, asked if he were now ready to explain—seriously explain—the formulas imprinted on it. Then, because he clearly wanted an audible reply, he yanked the hood off Thubana and flung it at Steenkamp.

"It's nothing, my *baas*," Thubana wheezed. "It only *looks like* it means something."

"Where did you get it?"

"I had it made. I designed it."

"Designed these equations?"

"Yes, sir." Thubana lowered his arms, sculled backward on his skinny, bruised rump, and propped himself against a wall.

"Who else has seen them?"

"Only a shopkeeper in Marabastad. I gave him the equations on a paper bag, sir. He silk-screened the shirt."

"What do they say?"

Thubana studied Jeppe with visible wariness, as if dealing with an idiot or a psychopath—an entire roomful of such creatures—and Myburgh suddenly feared that it was so.

"Gravity, electromagnetism, the strong force, the weak force."

"Pardon me?"

"A man in America—at Fermilab in Chicago—says the final TOE will fit on a T-shirt. It will be that simple."

"Fermilab?" Jeppe said.

"They have a particle accelerator there," Thubana said.

"Nuclear stuff," Wessels said. "Particle accelerators have to do with . . . you know, nuclear stuff."

Jeppe stiffened. He flapped the shirt out, grasped it by its sleeves, pulled it taut before him, surveyed its just-pretend TOE. "Decode this, kaffir."

"A big fish," Steenkamp said. "We've caught a big fish."

"A joke but not a joke," Thubana said. "One day I hope we have a Grand Unified Theory, a Theory of Everything, but today it's—" He stopped. "Today, my *baas*, it's only a dream."

"*Explain!*" Jeppe said.

When Thubana could not, they laid their bricks about two hand spans apart, prodded Thubana to remount them, forced him to hoist the chair aloft again, and walked around him asking questions and beating him with billies, hosepipes, their open hands. Although Steenkamp repeatedly slapped him across the buttocks with the hood, Thubana was doing better now: he could see his tormentors, he could breathe without fear of choking on rubber.

* * *

Later, after beating Thubana again, they pushed him into a nearby shower and made him stand under a prickly spray of cold water. The pipes clanked, the showerhead ratcheted like a Gatling gun. Typical. Tomorrow's building, yesterday's plumbing.

Myburgh accompanied Thubana to the shower room's threshold, but two security agents, there to make sure Thubana didn't duck out of the spray, kept him from coming nearer. So, like Thubana, he could do nothing but wait for the ordeal to end.

When Thubana finally did stumble out, his dark flesh appeared transparent: a fragile, oiled membrane of veins and welts, bruises and lacerations. It hurt to look at him.

"I'm cold," Thubana said. "Give me my clothes."

But they didn't. They returned him to the room in which they had beaten him, sat him down at the desk, encircled him. But the cold shower, rather than melting his will, had undergirded it. He looked unflinchingly into the eyes of his tormentors.

"Give me my clothes."

"Give us a statement," Jeppe said.

"How?" Thubana said. He lifted his dripping arms to show them the obvious: no writing materials.

At a nod from Jeppe, Goosen went to the filing cabinet, pulled out several sheets of paper and a ballpoint pen, and returned with these items to the desk.

"A towel," Thubana said. "Or I'll ruin whatever I write."

Wessels disappeared into the room near the shower stall, banged around ill-temperedly, and returned with a towel.

A hand towel, not a bath towel.

But Thubana, grimacing, got up, patted down every part of his severely punished body, and, when no one asked for the towel back, spread it out on the seat of the lopsided chair and sat down on the damp cloth as if it were a cushion. He looked up at Jeppe and the others with a stare that made the angry bulge next to one eyebrow seem less a wound than a badge of defiance.

"A statement," Jeppe said.

"Of what?"

"The full extent of your knowledge of and participation in the Armscor bombing. All you know about ANC plans to knock out the dam at Rietvlei. Plus a full—"

"I don't—"

"Quiet."

"But I'm not—"

"And a full breakdown of the *real* meanings behind those T-shirt 'equations.'"

Thubana hesitated. Then: "It will take some time."

"An hour."

"Two," Thubana said.

"An hour. If your statement is helpful but you haven't quite finished, *then* we'll give you more. Understand?"

"I think so."

Amazingly, they left Thubana alone. They carried out their bricks, locked the filing cabinet, blocked passage to the shower stall with a sliding metal grille, set Steenkamp as a guard on the main corridor, then left Thubana alone to draw up a statement, his first respite from their badgering since entering the building.

Myburgh sat down atop the desk, facing away from Thubana as he believed the other man wished. "Sometimes, it's impossible not to look, Mr. Thubana."

"That depends on who you are."

"What they did to you: terrible, barbaric. Mr. Thubana, it's only because—"

"Please be quiet. I must write."

Myburgh shut up, and Thubana began filling up the top sheet of white foolscap. For the next hour, the only sound in the room was the faint scritching of his ballpoint.

The statement was unsatisfactory. It denied any knowledge of the Armscor car-bomb, it pretended not to have any awareness of the planned assault on the dam at Rietvlei, and it interpreted all the arcane mathematical symbols on Thubana's T-shirt as attempts (phony attempts) to unify the four major forces of the universe in a grand Theory of Everything. Moreover, this TOE presupposed that the most basic units of matter were not atoms but tiny, twitchy strings that had sprung into being only seconds after the Big Bang. There was nothing about the ANC, the APLA, or any other revolutionary group.

And so the statement was unacceptable.

Jeppe took Thubana's statement as a personal affront. Wessels acted as if Thubana had sodomized his grandmother.

Goosen, Steenkamp, Dedekind, Schoeman, and a group of men who seemed to live in closets on this floor (so readily did they pop out to do their commanders' bidding) assumed Thubana's questioning; soon enough, they had reduced Myburgh to impotent rage.

He learned the amusing names, and the sickening particulars, of four or five different "interrogation techniques." Although he tried to help, grabbing one or another of the security policemen by the collar and yanking backward with all his strength, he lacked the somatic specific gravity to do anything but strain his back or herniate himself, so that as Thubana screamed, he screamed, and as Thubana begged his tormentors to stop, please stop, Myburgh begged them too, and the "airplane," "Dr. Frankenstein," the "helicopter," and the "wet cap" rolled past him like scenes from a half-dozen ineptly spliced horror movies.

"Bastards!" Myburgh cursed. "*Bastards!*"

When they were finished, and Thubana had told them nothing they wanted to hear (not even confessing that the symbol "E_8" in the book *Superstrings* was mathematical code for a cadre of terrorists in Mozambique, or that "Lie algebras" were a secret means of rating military-aid shipments from Red China), they dragged Thubana out and hurled him into an isolation cell—with bars, a lidless toilet, and a stiff, reed sleeping mat—on the same nightmarish floor.

"Animals!" Myburgh shouted, hobbling after them.

The cry reverberated in his own ears, but Jeppe & Company were infuriatingly deaf to it. Worse, they locked Thubana into the cell and handcuffed him to the lower part of its grille (so that he was unable to use his sleeping mat) without leaving Myburgh enough room to edge into it, too. Invisible to his countrymen, Myburgh was one of them again. Thubana was locked up, but he was free. Except that he was a prisoner, too, in the same building containing a cell that contained Thubana. Boxes inside boxes. Cages within cages. Bantustans within the Fatherland . . .

And then the security agents were gone, and Myburgh, clinging to the bars, was alone with Thubana.

"Go home," Thubana said. He didn't raise his head; he mumbled into the pit of his handcuffed arm.

"I can't."

Thubana moaned, heedless of the misery escaping him.

"Mr. Thubana, I don't think I can. I live, and move, but I don't—" Myburgh searched for the word "—*impinge* on anything. How can I get out of here?"

Thubana did not reply.

Myburgh knelt. He put a hand through the bars and rubbed a finger over Thubana's woolly hair. Rivulets of blood had dried in the tiny gullies in this wool. The side of Thubana's face resembled an inner-tube strip with an infestation of polyplike heat blisters. Myburgh wiped his eyes with a coat sleeve.

"Mr. Thubana—"

"Go home."

"I—"

Thubana lifted his head. His face called up images from battle photography and traffic-safety films. Was the poor man a member of a Faking Club. . . ?

"Try," Thubana said. "You must . . . *try*."

Myburgh pulled himself up, backed away, and wandered through the maze of the upper floor.

Eventually, he located the door to a stairwell, pulled it open, and went through into a shaft as forbidding as a mine stope. There were fluorescents on each landing, and the window overlooking the billboard proclaiming the "controlled strength" of Jik gleamed under anemic spotlights. It was night.

He went down, all the way down, and paused at the street-level door, expecting failure. His success at barging into the stairwell and coming down the steps was a fluke of physics. By all rights, he should have no more impact on the physical structures of this building than a shade—for he *was* a shade, a man-shaped confluence of shadow matter.

Myburgh gripped the push bar on the door. He pushed down on it. It resisted. It resisted as if it understood that his was a conjectural, a ghostly, pressure.

Myburgh examined his hands. The palms were still raw from his attempts to wrest the hosepipe from Goosen. If the hosepipe could do that to him, it seemed logical—in an inevitably symmetrical way—that he could exert some influence on the sort of matter that had scalded him. Tit for tat.

He pushed down again.

Surprise. This time the bar depressed, clicking open the door to which it was attached.

Myburgh stumbled outside, one hand still on the bar.

Traffic noises assailed him.

The air was brisk and damp-feeling, but a glance at the sky, between the tops of the security building and the office building opposite it, showed him an indigo road of stars. If you squinted, if you put your imagination into gear, you could believe that out there beyond those twinkling points of fire vibrated—majestically—a cosmic string light-years in length tying this moment to the instant of creation. That string would be a stretched remnant of a tiny superstring that had blown clear of the Big Bang and escaped into the cosmos. It would be proof that everything on hand in the universe today had exploded from the same blazing Ur-furnace.

Or so Thubana believed. And so he had told Myburgh and Skosana on their not-so-smooth nylon ride into Pretoria.

Christ. Such thoughts.

It would take an hour to walk home from here, Myburgh decided. Or he could walk to Church's Square for public transport to his condominium. If no one could see him, he wouldn't even have to pay the bus driver. . . .

The clap on that. Thubana was upstairs, naked and suffering. And if Myburgh stepped outside, letting go of this door, it would lock behind him. He could tug on it all he liked; it would never budge, no matter how strong his will, how mighty his arms. This door locked on people who were *not* shadow matter, and it would hold Myburgh out even if he rematerialized as a visible Afrikaner, with a thousand questions for Major Henning Jeppe.

So he went back in, let go of the push bar, and trudged back up the six flights of steps to Thubana.

Myburgh took off his coat, pushed it between the bars, spread it over Thubana's shoulders and back. He straightened it as well as he could so that only Thubana's legs and part of his handcuffed arm remained uncovered. Then Myburgh curled up on the floor beside the comatose man and fumbled toward sleep.

In his dream, he was driving a bus—not a municipal bus, but a Putco bus like the one Kabini drove from KwaNdebele every morning and back again every night. His riders were plainclothes security policemen from this very building; the bus was packed with them—Jeppe, Wessels, Goosen, Steenkamp, and maybe ninety more, every one standing or sitting ramrod straight as Myburgh drove them through a teeming closer settlement.

The streets were unpaved and dusty. Angry blacks—many armed with rocks, many shaking their fists, some determined enough to leap in front of the bus and spit at the bus's windshield—crowded in so grimly that it was hard to keep going. Either Myburgh could slow to a walk, letting more and more blacks approach the bus, lay hands on it, and rock it back and forth until it turned over; or he could jam the accelerator, wrestle the steering wheel, and harvest these agitated people like corn.

There seemed to be no other options, only death for his riders or blatant, cold-blooded vehicular homicide. He might have been able to resign himself to the first option if it had not required his own death. He might have been able to adjust to the second one if his passengers had not been Jeppe & Company.

Soon, Myburgh was crying as he drove. He could not tell if his watery vision stemmed from his own tears or the dripping spittle on his windshield. He beeped his horn. He beeped it and beeped it. A rock struck the windscreen, giving it the look of a puzzle-piece spiderweb. His riders—outwardly calm—began sticking handguns through their windows and firing into the streets as if the closer settlement were a huge shooting gallery. Each time a black fell dead or wounded, a bell rang (Myburgh didn't know from where), and Jeppe, sitting behind him, got up to reward the sharpshooter with a stuffed animal: hyena, giraffe, ant-bear, elephant. Jeppe took these animals from a duffel under his seat, and their supply, like that of the shouting Africans, seemed endless.

Then a bomb exploded in the road, a bomb made out of a knot of blacks banished from South Africa's cities. When it went off, body parts and clothing scraps flew up into the sky. (Suddenly, it was night. The Coal Sack nebula, near the Jewel Box cluster, opened up like a hungry pit.) Myburgh tumbled into the whirlpools created by the explosion. Not knowing what else to do, he grabbed the strands of the puzzle-piece web in his windscreen and pulled himself along them to its center.

From this vantage, Myburgh looked down and saw his bus on fire, five or six kilometers below. The strands of the web in which he swung—a hammock now, a hammock attached to the four stars of the Southern Cross—started reeling at high speed, as if a vacuum cleaner light-years away were cracking him apart atom by atom and sucking him into its bag. It wanted him and his galaxy-sized fears to fly into the bag without tearing it. Myburgh turned over in the hammock, clutching at its lengthening, ever-thinning strings.

The hole of the Coal Sack (Kiewit had always called it the Soot Bag) got bigger and bigger. It was like a black widow; no, a black *window*. And what Myburgh saw through it was the body of a stuffed elephant, slowly tumbling. A minute ago, it had been in the lap of one of Jeppe's boys, a prize for marksmanship. Now the beast was growing at the same high speed as the Coal Sack, and he could see that no matter what he did, he was going to hit it, and hitting the elephant (a doddering bull with fractured tusks, not a stuffed toy) would probably destroy him. . . .

"Wake up, man. Wake up."

APARTHEID, SUPERSTRINGS, AND MORDECAI THUBANA 113

* * *

Myburgh roused; his nightmare had disoriented him. Then he saw Wessels—a.k.a. Pampoenkop—glowering down on him, and he began to suspect that his real nightmare was about to start. It seemed that Wessels could see him.

"Who are you? What are you doing here?"

Myburgh blinked. Wessels's head—its size, its slanted brows, its crooked teeth, its fat chins—*did* resemble a jack-o'-lantern.

"Answer me, please."

"What time is it?" Myburgh said in Afrikaans. (Wait. He had a watch. He checked it: 3:45 A.M.)

"Time you answered me," Wessels said. "You're up to your chin, brother-man."

Myburgh did not stand. He rolled over and scooted up against Thubana's cell. Thubana was asleep or comatose. In sleep, he had dislodged Myburgh's coat, exposing most of his back.

"You can see me," Myburgh said.

"I'm not blind. How did you get in?"

Myburgh shook his head to clear it of some confusing images and swallowed to make his ears pop. His left foot stuck out toward the policeman like a big, mottled sausage. Wessels aimed a kick at it, and the back of Myburgh's head banged metal.

A warning. Only a warning.

"I am Gerrit Myburgh, a special-accounts executive at Jacobus and Roux. On the road back from Huilbloom, our family farm, I had an accident. I've come here to report it."

"You need the city police, Meneer Myburgh."

"My accident occurred in the country."

"You are still in the wrong place. This is the special branch, Meneer Myburgh. You have no business here."

Myburgh nodded at Thubana. "That man has clearly been through hell. Why is he naked?"

"Did you give him that coat?"

"He looked cold. He still looks cold."

Wessels was trying hard not to erupt. Maybe he suspected that Myburgh was a member of some kind of governmental Faking Club, sent out to test the humanity of security agents.

Finally, Wessels allowed the dam to burst: "You are a foolish goddamned *kaffirboetie*, Meneer Myburgh."

"This man needs medical attention."

"You have many questions to answer. Get up and come with me."

Myburgh stared insolently at Wessels. He massaged the sole of his naked foot. Perhaps it would have been better to remain shadow matter to his compatriots until he had thought of a way to rescue—if that were possible—both himself and the two innocent Africans now in custody.

"You gave him a coat," Wessels said. "Maybe you gave him other things as well? Instructions, for example?"

"Telephone my brother. Telephone my superiors at Jacobus and Roux. Dozens of people can vouch for me."

"At this hour?" Wessels turned and called down the corridor to an office seemingly kilometers away: "Major van Rhyn. Major van Rhyn, we have a problem."

Major W. K. van Rhyn worked on him all that morning. Wessels assisted, and it was a relief—a surprise and a relief—that they only questioned him. The wallet from inside his jacket (which an unseen policeman brought to van Rhyn's office from Thubana's cell) contained materials identifying Myburgh.

Then a plainclothes agent named Lieutenant Cuyler came in to report that the South African Police had found a Cadillac stalled on the KwaNdebele Road. The car was badly banged up. Plates and serial numbers proved, though, that it belonged to one Gerrit Jozua Myburgh of Pretoria.

"I hit an elephant," Myburgh said.

"Meneer Myburgh," van Rhyn said, shaking his head.

Cuyler came to Myburgh's aid: "That may be true, sir."

"How?" van Rhyn said.

"A Colored from Durban has a fleabite circus: Motilal Prassad's Travelling Big Top. He carts it around to the bantustans and makes a few rand entertaining the stay-behinds while their wage-earners are at work. Three days ago, he was in Bophuthatswana. Seems he lost an elephant there."

"I found it," Myburgh said. "I hit it."

"Not unlikely," Cuyler told van Rhyn.

"What happened to it?"

Both van Rhyn and Cuyler looked at Myburgh as if he had asked a very troublesome question.

"What happened to it?" Myburgh said again.

"We don't know," Cuyler said. "It disappeared."

"An elephant?" van Rhyn said. "To where?"

"If we knew, we wouldn't be saying it's disappeared. Maybe to the proverbial elephants' graveyard."

Myburgh wondered if his Cadillac's collision with the elephant had rendered it shadow matter, a kind of premonitory ghost from an era and a system long since doomed to perish.

He had no time to mull the issue, for Cuyler had to leave, and van Rhyn and Wessels asked him what he knew about the Armscor bombing? About ANC plans to sabotage the Rietvlei dam? Questions that Jeppe and his men had already repeatedly asked Thubana.

Myburgh replied to all these questions in the negative (for he knew nothing), but he was also careful to tell his interrogators what an outrage his detention was and how deeply he resented the slanders implicit in their questions. He was a decent Afrikaner, a patriotic Vaalpens. They should ring up his brother, Kiewit. Or the manager of his condominium. Or his secretary, Pia Delfos.

On the other hand, he railed at van Rhyn, what could he expect of a group of officers who had beaten one of their charges within a fingernail of his life and left him naked in a cold cell? The sort of men who would deny an injured countryman medical help? The sort who would bully that countryman with stupid innuendoes about treason and terrorist collaboration?

"What we do," said van Rhyn coldly, "we do to protect."

Van Rhyn went off duty. Myburgh sat in his office, all alone, for a long time. Exactly how long he couldn't say, for Wessels had taken his watch—plus his keys and pocket change—and retreated to another part of the building.

Longer than an hour, though. Possibly two.

When Major Jeppe came on duty (whey-faced, thin, and struggling with the sniffles and watery eyes), he spoke with Cuyler, Wessels, and one or two others.

Then he left, too, and Myburgh was escorted to a holding room where he stewed for another two or three hours, growing more and more frustrated and impatient.

Why the delay? Did they really think him an ANC collaborator? Apparently, they did. For that reason, they had not released him. For that reason, they had done nothing to see about his cuts or to replace his tattered clothes. Section Six of the Terrorism Act—that was the inappropriate statute they were using to detain him.

At last, Jeppe came back. Goosen, Steenkamp, and Schoeman came with him. All four surrounded Myburgh's table.

"How did you get to Pretoria from your wreck?" Jeppe said.

"I walked," Myburgh said. (A lie, but better than admitting the hard-to-swallow truth.)

"How did you get into the building?"

"Through a street-level door."

"Except for our entrance on the park, our street-level doors are all locked, Meneer Myburgh."

"Not the one I used."

The four men stared at him as if they had reached an impasse; obviously, they had.

"If I can't go home," Myburgh said, "I want some clean clothes and something to eat."

They brought him a plate of food: sausages, rice, and a poached egg. They also brought him a pair of corduroy trousers, a flannel shirt, some heavy brown socks, and a pair of *takkies* that looked as if they had been bleached. Myburgh suspected that this outfit—except for the store-bought socks—had once belonged to a black man detained for political reasons. Where was that man now? In a jail cell? In a township cemetery? In the *bundu*, hiding?

"The man I gave my coat to," Myburgh said: "He needs clothes and food, too. And medical attention."

"*Kaffirboetie*," Goosen said, turning away.

"How do you happen to know him?" Jeppe said.

"I came up the stairs, onto this floor, and I saw him naked and unconscious in that cell down there." He nodded vaguely.

"The man's a terrorist," Jeppe said. "You want nothing to do with him. Nothing. Leave him to us."

When Myburgh finished eating, only Jeppe and Goosen remained with him. Goosen cleared his plate away, returned, and laid the book *Superstrings* on the table exactly where the plate had been.

"What do you know about this?" Jeppe said. "The man you saw up here was carrying it when we captured him."

"Why should I know anything about it?"

"We had a tip, Meneer Myburgh. Our informant told us to take a man or two off a commuter bus from KwaNdebele."

"So?"

"Major van Rhyn's report says you had your accident—hitting that elephant—on the same stretch of road."

Physically, Myburgh felt better, his hunger satisfied and his bruised body clad in snug, warm clothes. But now that Jeppe had made the connection between his wreck on the KwaNdebele Road and the stopping of *Grim Boy's Toe* several miles beyond that roadblock, Myburgh feared that maybe these single-minded men were determined to link him to the same absurd scenario to which they had already linked Thubana and Skosana. If that happened — if they succeeded — his comfortable station in life would evaporate like mist and only his brother Kiewit, a lukewarm friend or two, and some of his more appreciative clients would care at all. He would vanish forever, a statistic of the state of emergency.

"Coincidence," Myburgh said uneasily.

"You've never read this book?"

"No. Why?"

"Certain passages are underlined. We thought you could help us explain their encoded meanings."

"I'm a financial advisor, not a cryptologist."

"But if you were also a traitor and spy?" Jeppe said, smiling. Abruptly, he shouted: "Steenkamp!"

Steenkamp came into the room with Thubana's T-shirt. He spread it out on the table next to the book.

"And this?" Jeppe said. "What about this?"

At that moment, Myburgh heard the familiar staticky tinniness of a resistance radio broadcast: "*. . . and the Ten Point Program of the Unity Movement put forward in 1943. This advance reflected the awakening of the people and departed from a liberal democratic program by posing the issue of the 'Land to the Tiller' as being of paramount . . .*"

Jeppe stood up. "Not again." He went from the room, followed closely by Goosen and Schoeman. Steenkamp remained behind to guard both Myburgh and the seditious T-shirt TOE.

"*. . . only one meaning amongst scientific socialists: seizure without compensation. Lenin in his Agrarian Program repeated this point again and again to distinguish it from . . .*"

"Skosana," Myburgh whispered.

Over the staticky lecture, a scream: "MORDECAI-I-I-I-I-I!"

Myburgh stood up. Steenkamp laid a hand on his shoulder and pushed him back down.

"MORDECAI-I-I-I-I-I!"

Christ, what was going on? He could hear (over both the radio broadcast and Skosana's screaming) the sounds of scuffling, grunts, billy clubs clattering, metal bars gonging.

"Steenkamp!" someone yelled. "Steenkamp, get out here!"

"Stay put," Steenkamp said. He slipped around Myburgh's chair, darted into the hall like a soccer wingman.

The uproar went on: shortwave screeches, screams, the muddled warring of iron and wood and boot leather. Myburgh's heart pounded like a machine press stamping out badges. He told himself to obey Steenkamp's warning and stay put, but when the hubbub persisted and no one returned to check on him, he crept to the door.

"*Mordecai-i-i-i-i-i*. . . !"

Six or seven men at the far end of the corridor were wrestling Winston Skosana around its dogleg, hurrying to get him out of sight and hearing. Myburgh could still hear him calling Thubana's first name, but with less and less energy.

Then the long hall was empty: a bright tunnel of plaster board, tilework, and staggered, ceiling-mounted smoke detectors. Myburgh could not believe the feeling he had. As if he had become shadow matter again, an invisible man in the near-invisible empery of the security police.

In his bleached *takkies*, Myburgh hobbled down the hall. Past van Rhyn's office. Past a pair of closed—what?—storage rooms? Past a lavatory, another shakedown room, and two vertical strips of chrome suggesting that this end of the hall had a purpose different from that of the end he had just left, namely, imprisoning people who knew things that the state needed to know. And then, suddenly, Myburgh was at Thubana's cell again.

Thubana's naked feet hung half a meter off the floor. His body twisted from a light fixture in a noose made from a cracked leather belt.

Thubana's belt was his only article of clothing. Why? Myburgh wondered. A man with no pants didn't need a belt.

Jeppe, blowing his nose into a handkerchief, marched around the corner with Goosen, Steenkamp, and Schoeman. When he saw Myburgh standing outside Thubana's cell, he cursed, waved his handkerchief, and piped congestedly, "Get him!"

Before Myburgh could react, Goosen ran at him and flattened him with a high elbow. Steenkamp kicked him in the ribs. Goosen gave him an exasperated conk as he sought to roll away, for Myburgh was writhing—both from the pain and to avoid further blows.

"Enough!" Jeppe cried.

Myburgh lay under the security men's feet. There was blood on his clean flannel shirt. This angered him all out of proportion to the shirt's value. Maybe because Thubana was dangling in his cell from his own belt.

"You murdered him," Myburgh said.

"A lot of them commit suicide," Jeppe said. "He's just another goddamned kaffir who took the easy way out."

"Where did he get the belt?"

"Perhaps his friend slipped it to him."

"When? You confiscated their belts, didn't you?"

Jeppe paused in his niggling attentions to his nose. "How did you know that?"

Myburgh hesitated. "A deduction. Procedure, isn't it? Aren't you supposed to take their belts?"

"Procedures vary." Jeppe's voice was as unforthcoming as that of a veteran government spokesman.

"You murdered him," Myburgh said again.

Goosen cocked his billy threateningly.

"Don't," Jeppe told Goosen. "Get him back down the hall. He never should have been out here."

"That wasn't my—"

"Shut up."

"I'm bleeding," Myburgh said. "These men assaulted me."

"A cut from your automobile accident," Jeppe said.

"It's a cut I received when that swine there tried to—"

"From your accident. From hitting Motilal Prassad's run-away elephant. Please remember that."

Myburgh was afraid to contradict Jeppe, who should have been at home, taking antihistamines and drinking healthful juices. More or less passively, Myburgh returned to the interrogation room in which Steenkamp had so precipitously abandoned him.

This time, Jeppe had Goosen stand watch. Myburgh studied his guard. Goosen was late twenties or early thirties, a dark-haired fellow who would have been handsome if his eyes hadn't carried in them a perpetual look of unfocused shock, as if almost everything about life offended him. He was hair-trigger, a grenade with the pin pulled.

Or he gave that impression. Maybe it was the job. Maybe he had a wife and babies at home. Or maybe he had the job because something cankered and peeling in him had pointed him to it, and maybe he *still* had a wife and babies at home. So far as Myburgh knew, there was no law on the books against borderline psychopaths marrying and raising families.

Oddly, Myburgh felt fairly safe with the boy. Jeppe was going to let him go. Or else why caution him to remember that the cut on his head had come from an automobile accident, not the attentions of this duty-conscious pretty boy? Something—something beyond the barbarous lynching of Thubana—had happened, and so Jeppe & Company were on the brink of releasing him.

"What's your name?"

Goosen looked at him with stupidly snobbish disdain. "Maybe I don't care to tell you."

"I know your family name. What's your Christian name?"

"All you need to know is Warrant Officer Goosen."

"You look like—" Myburgh pretended to consider possibilities "—a Hans, I think."

Goosen was insulted. "Not a Hans. A Hugo. And you're to keep your mouth shut."

"A while ago you wanted me to talk."

A glint of smug cunning sparked from Goosen's eyes. "You have a statement to make?"

"Where did the hanged man's belt come from?"

"You heard Major Jeppe. That other kaffir, probably."

"From you, far more probably. Or from Wessels, or Steenkamp, or Schoeman."

Goosen merely smiled. "Oh, Meneer Myburgh."

"I think the 'other kaffir' told you his friend had nothing to do with the matters you were investigating."

"Why don't you shut up?" Goosen said, leaning across the table; his breath reeked of cream cheese and beer.

Myburgh ignored the smell: "But you gentlemen had done such lovely hosepipe work on the man it would have been awkward to let him go."

"Such a mind. What a detective. You should join the special branch yourself."

"So you found his belt. And gave it to him. To help him hold up his appendectomy scar, I suppose."

Goosen's brow furrowed. "He had no appendectomy scar."

"No, but you people hanged him naked, anyway. And with his own belt, too."

Goosen went to the room's filing cabinet. Did he plan to take a hosepipe from it?

Wham! Wham!

He kicked the file cabinet, then turned back to Myburgh with comets in his eyes, the red and yellow fallout of Voortrekker Day sparklers. The pupils shining inside these fireworks were those of a man high on his own ill-suppressed rage.

"You'd better stop, brother-man. You'd better just stop!"

"All right, Warrant Officer Goosen. All right." Myburgh held up his hands placatingly.

Given everything that had happened, maybe the best course *was* to keep his mouth shut. To refrain from antagonizing Major

Jeppe, Warrant Officer Goosen, and all the other high-strung men of the special branch. To maintain his composure. And, maybe hardest of all, simply to bide his time.

He had not guessed wrong; they were releasing him. Lieutenant Cuyler, according to Major Jeppe, had done some telephoning and had learned that Myburgh was a clean case. Each reference, though, had needed cross-checking and confirmation. That was why, regrettably, they had held him so long.

"Not because you thought me a terrorist?" Myburgh said.

Jeppe swallowed a cold tablet with a gulp of water. "It isn't often that a man who hits an elephant on the KwaNdebele Road comes into our building to report it."

A tactful way of confessing that they had grilled him because they had been suspicious of him. Thank God they hadn't subjected him to the "refrigerator," the "airplane," "Dr. Frankenstein," the "marionette," and so on. Thank God.

Without warning, Jeppe started. "Meneer Myburgh! Where the hell did you go?" He dropped his glass and looked around the room as if Myburgh had left it. His glass, meanwhile, broke on the floor into a nebula of scattershot shards and chips.

"I'm right here."

Jeppe recovered. "Ah, yes, *there*. You faded out on me. It's this cold, I guess. My vision's bollixed. My head aches. My nose feels like a cherry pepper."

"You should go home," Myburgh said.

But he was frightened. It wasn't Jeppe's cold that had caused him to fade; it was a brief reversion to shadow matter, the result of his again beginning to view things—a little, at least—from the pedestrian focus of Henning Jeppe. He had to cling to Thubana. If he did not, this entire nightmare would cease to signify.

"I *should* go home," Jeppe said. "And so I will. Allow me to drive you to your own place, Meneer Myburgh."

"I can't. It wouldn't—"

"The least I can do. For all the nasty inconvenience."

In the end, Myburgh permitted Jeppe to chauffeur him along the tree-lined boulevards of Pretoria, past the monuments and parks and museums, to his condominium. A good ride. Last week's clouds were only memories. The blue Transvaal sky—a dome of fragile porcelain—made him forget that it was winter, that the jacarandas would not blossom for another three months. Even Jeppe's reminders not to speak of anything that had happened during his confinement seemed benign and sensible, for Myburgh had the odd feeling that his life was beginning anew.

Back in his apartment, hanging his dry-cleaned but ruined suit in a closet, he realized that he had bought his mellow spirits with counterfeit coin. Thubana was dead, the victim of men hostile to the quixotic Grand Unified Theory toward which he had so touchingly—but ineffectively—pointed his dreams.

And Thubana, dead, was a living rebuke.

The dressing mirror on Myburgh's closet door gave back an image that modulated in and out of visibility like the picture on a snow-afflicted TV set. He was there, then he wasn't. He wasn't there, then he was. The degree of reality he had was contingent on forces over which he had no direct control.

Or, at least, so it seemed at the moment.

Myburgh crossed his arms in front of his chest and clutched his own shoulders. Stay put, he told himself; stay put. Arms crossed, he walked into his apartment's living room—a studio decorated with opera posters, ferns, an aquarium with Chinese carp, and a wall of books, few of which he had opened since taking his degree from the University of Pretoria nearly twenty years ago. Today, his reading was almost all business related, with a smattering of international news to keep him abreast of fluctuating trends, and he did the bulk of it in his office at Jacobus & Roux.

Thubana was at the fish tank tapping nutritional dandruff out of a colorful box onto the water for Myburgh's starving carp. The fish rose in pairs or trios, hit at the scaly food, then splashed away through the bottle-green water to allow another greedy pair or threesome to surface and feed.

—They're hungry, Thubana said. —You were gone a long time, Mr. Myburgh.

—I left a key with the manager, Myburgh said. —He promised to take care of them for me.

—It appears he forgot.

Thubana looked exactly as he had hanging in his cell on the top floor of security police headquarters: naked, bruised, grotesquely cinched at the throat with his confiscated belt. Here, though, his body was relaxed, his manner courteous. The end of his belt hung straight down his chest like a tie instead of twisting stiffly away in a makeshift noose. Under the glances of Jeppe & Company, he had been humiliated. Here, he was at ease with his nakedness, relieved that an insufferable ordeal was over.

—Let me get you a robe. You must be cold.
—It's all right, Mr. Myburgh. I can't stay.
—No trouble, no trouble.

Myburgh returned to his closet (dismayed to see nothing in the full-length mirror on its door but the framed poster for *Die Götterdämmerung* opposite it), rummaged distractedly among his hang-ups for a dressing gown, found one, and returned to Thubana. Thubana protested, but took the gown and put it on—more to ease Myburgh's embarrassment, Myburgh felt, than to satisfy propriety or to defeat the cold. Now he looked a great deal like a lanky prize fighter, the undaunted loser of a bout with the world title holder.

—What are you doing here? Myburgh said.
—I must tell you something.
—Out with it, then.
—The challenge is to write one set of equations that will prove the four known basic forces to be separate showings of one even more basic force.
—You told me that on *Grim Boy's Toe*.
—Reminders are necessary, I think. People keep forgetting how important this challenge is.

Myburgh raised and dropped his arms. —You're not really here, Mr. Thubana. Maybe I'm not either.

Thubana ignored this. —Another thing.
—What?
—Someone narked on Winston.
—"Narked"? Do you mean that Skosana was actually involved in the Armscor bombing?
—Could be. Could be.
—I thought he was innocent, a victim.
—Few of us are innocent, Mr. Myburgh. Many are victims.
—A man who plants bombs, or who protects people who do, isn't a victim. He's a perpetrator.

Thubana, hands in pockets, shook his head disappointedly.
—Violence sickens me, Myburgh insisted.
—Sometimes it does. Sometimes. But Winston had a steel plate in his head. It broadcast to him almost continuously. The buzzing of one's own bones is hard to set aside.
—I imagine it is.
—Another thing I wanted to tell you, Mr. Myburgh: Informers are everywhere.
—Who? Do you know who it was?

— Of course. It came to me while helicoptering under the blows of Pampoenkop and his goons.
— Tell me.
Thubana told.

It was still daylight. Lightning Bird (called by the Ndebele of Sebetiela *māsianoke a selwana* and by Afrikaners the *hammerkop*) had done his work; he had brought the highveld rain. The coming summer drought would be easier to bear for his help in July. Now, though, the winter sun shone to the north again, and the people of Pretoria were enjoying both the freshness of the air and the brisk high rage of that rapidly westering sun.

In the same clothes he had worn home from police headquarters, Myburgh went downstairs and hailed a cab. The driver was a young Afrikaner who had probably never heard of the *hammerkop*. Myburgh felt an irrational resentment toward him even as the young man let him in and turned to receive his destination. (Or not irrational, Myburgh thought. Misplaced.)

"Marabastad," he said.
"Are you sure? I don't carry many of our kind there."
"Do you carry any?"
"Yes, sir. Now and again."
"Good. I'm another. Please take me there."
"This is the rush hour. It'll be slow going."
Myburgh showed the cabbie a handful of rand notes.
"Yes, sir," the cabbie said. "Where in Marabastad?"
"Belle Ombre station."

The cabbie started to speak again (Myburgh could see him in the rear-view mirror), but changed his mind and slid the cab into gear.

Because of traffic, the trip needed twenty minutes. During it, Myburgh recalled his final moment with Thubana: nodding goodbye, Thubana had ascended through his apartment's ceiling and beyond, carrying with him both Myburgh's dressing gown and the self-pitying edges of his funk. Now, Belle Ombre station — a kind of soaring, concrete circus tent with attractive parterres and geometries of structural piping painted red, yellow, blue, and green — loomed out of the old Asian enclave like a Transvaaler's Disneyworld.

This was the depot from which the architects of the homeland solution accepted the black "foreigners" from Bophuthatswana and KwaNdebele as day laborers, and from which they expelled them again every night. Bullet trains were the key both to white autonomy and economic self-sufficiency, and this afternoon, almost in spite of himself, Myburgh found himself admiring the sleek, high-tech trains that state planners had commissioned, and bought, to put their dear and preposterous scheme into action.

Unfortunately, not all the high-speed rail lines necessary to make this solution work were operating yet, and to make sure that no "foreigner" spent the night in the city, Putco had to continue to send commuter buses to KwaNdebele and some of the more distant corners of Bophuthatswana.

It was these grime-encrusted buses, not the sexy trains, that Myburgh had come to Belle Ombre to find; and when he saw the ramps leading to the passenger docks, he made his driver stop, gave him both his fare and an extravagant tip, and stepped out among milling armies of weary blacks, who looked at him (if they looked at him at all) with glazed, preoccupied eyes.

A ghostly twilight had begun to draw down.

What business did the white *baas* have here? His clothes didn't identify him as a policeman, nor did they say that he was well off enough to be a bullet-train official or a Putco executive. He was, in fact, an intruder, and Myburgh became more and more aware of his status as an intruder the deeper into the crowd he walked, hurrying to reach Thubana's bus before it filled and left for various closer settlements on its route to the Wolverkraal depot, three hours out of Marabastad.

"Bus four-nine-six," he said, stopping a woman wearing a heavy, unbuttoned coat over a maid's uniform. She merely stared. He said the same thing in English, and she gave him an I-couldn't-tell-you shrug. Not hostile; indifferent.

He let her go, blundered on, asked others, got blank stares or confessions of ignorance, and finally approached a uniformed white policeman who wanted to know where he was going and why. Didn't he know that, at this hour, Belle Ombre was no place for casual sight-seeing? Above the shuffling crowd, speakers piped a Mantovani-ized arrangement of the old Petula Clark hit, "Downtown."

Myburgh, putting his face in the policeman's, explained that he had come to scold a Ndebele roofer for the shoddy work he had done on a Sunnyside housing project. The man had to return tomorrow and repair his labor, or he would forfeit his pay and any future chance to roof in the city's white subdivisions.

"What bus is he riding, then?"

"Number four-nine-six," Myburgh said.

The policeman sighed, as if being asked to find a diamond on a floor strewn with broken glass.

"It has a name, too," Myburgh said: "*Grim Boy's Toe.*"

The policeman nodded. "Ah, yes, I know it."

"You know it?"

"Of course. They're not allowed names. Commercial buses with one-time passengers, yes. But not state-subsidized commuter buses run by good old Putco."

"No? Why not?"

"Names on state-subsidized buses are disrespectful. *Grim Boy's Toe*, for instance. Who'd want to ride that?"

Myburgh thought that even if it were called *Bali Ha'i Express*, he wouldn't be pleased to ride it again (not so far as the Wolverkraal depot, anyway), but he bit his tongue.

"Over that way," the policeman said, pointing across one of the esplanades to a down-sloping ramp. "Driver's busy trying to bring his bus in line with Putco policy."

"This way?" Myburgh said, already walking.

"Yes, sir. Right on over."

Myburgh jogged across the esplanade. He found another nexus of ramps, looked around, selected the one he thought the policeman had meant, and, breathing raspily, jogged down it to the loading dock. People had not yet begun to queue here. Myburgh relaxed a little. He was no longer in a crowd, and Ernest Kabini was standing next to his bus.

A closer look: Kabini was holding a small can of blue enamel and painting out the legend that had personalized number 496 for Myburgh on the drizzly highveld.

"Stop!" he cried.

Kabini glanced up at the white man coming irresistibly down the ramp, his heavy-heeled strut more the consequence of gravity than self-esteem. Myburgh, meanwhile, read confusion on Kabini's face. Not guilt, not panic: confusion.

And then Kabini recognized him, knew him for the unlucky fellow who had wrecked his *lekker* Cadillac on the KwaNdebele Road. His confusion turned into something like both guilt and panic, and his eyes cut from side to side, looking for a way out.

"What are you doing, Kabini?" Myburgh put a hand on the mud-caked bus, almost as if he owned it.

Kabini lifted his brush and paint can. "Covering this unhappy name, *nkosi.*" He smiled. "Very good to see you again."

"Don't cover it."

"Company regulation, my *baas*. Got to finish. Got to finish up before Mr. Krige comes back to check."

"Leave it as it is."

Kabini glowered. He had already glopped out most of the first two words, GRIM BOY. All that was visible now was 'S TOE (whatever that implied). Obviously, he could see no point in leaving only an orphaned possessive and the name of a lowly body part on the bus's side. Mr. Krige would not be pleased. His passengers would laugh.

"Forgive me, *nkosi*, but I must paint it out."

"And I must tell your riders—" Myburgh climbed up into 496 and saw that maybe twenty people were already aboard, waiting for the rest of their fellow commuters to connect and climb on, too. He came back down. "I must tell them you're a paid police informant."

Kabini's puzzlement appeared to grow. "Why would you say that, my *baas*?"

"Because it's true."

Smiling, Kabini shook his head. "No. No, *nkosi*."

"You turned in Winston Skosana. Skosana was a friend of young Mordecai Thubana's. So Major Jeppe took him, too."

"Most unlucky."

"Even unluckier, Kabini, is what happened to your ex-passengers while being detained."

Kabini's usual deference gave way to guarded hostility. Lines clawed from his eyes. His mouth tightened, a piece of string pulled taut. He put his brush into the can of enamel and started to feather blue paint onto the 'S TOE. Myburgh shook his head in warning.

"You're a government informer. Should I tell them?"

"Look at my eye. The police beat me."

"For show. To protect you. But I have details. Details your passengers will believe. God's truth."

Kabini lowered his brush. He looked around. Possibly, he was imagining what it would be like for twenty to ninety outraged Putco customers to stomp him to death on a terminus ramp or maybe to wait until he had driven back to Tweefontein E, or Kameelrivier, to hang a petrol-drenched Firestone around his neck.

"What, my *baas*, do you want from me?"

Myburgh pointed. "Thubana gave your bus that name?"

"Only the word *Toe*. It was called *Grim Boy* even before I began to drive. Thubana made me add—" Kabini nodded at the apostrophe S and the three-letter word after it.

"Then leave it alone, please."

Kabini stuck his brush into the can and threw the can down. It splattered blue on the passenger dock's retaining wall and on part of the bus's undercarriage. Perplexity and distaste had fused to make Kabini surly.

"What else?" he said.

Myburgh wasn't sure. He had to do something else. Wasn't that why he had come out here?

"I want to drive your bus," he said.

"What?" Kabini looked around for help. If he found a security agent who knew what services he had rendered the state, Myburgh was lost. Myburgh knew he had to act quickly.

"Give me the keys to your bus."

Kabini was hugely offended. "Surely not, *nkosi*."

"I'll blow the whistle on you. Loud."

Kabini was at sea, a man in an unexpected gale. "The keys are in the goddamned ignition."

"Thank you."

"Why are you doing this? Are you crazy?"

"I want to take some people on a tour, Kabini. I want them to learn something of what I've learned."

Myburgh climbed in and stood at the top of 496's center aisle. He pulled the handle shutting the double-hinged door. He told his passengers—Kabini's passengers—that although he intended to drive them back to KwaNdebele eventually, their trip this evening would take a little longer because he had an important errand to run in the heart of Pretoria.

All who wished to get off now and wait for Putco to rectify the terrible additional inconvenience he was going to inflict on them were welcome to do so. On the other hand, all who wished to ride with him into the city were welcome to stay on. If the authorities did not arrest him before he could carry out his pledge to finish the KwaNdebele run, he would (he swore) get them home an hour or so before midnight. At least.

"Who are you, my *baas*?" said a woman in a knit hat, like a pink and purple crown. "Some demon-taken drunk?"

"I'm the man who hit the elephant. I'm the friend of Mordecai Thubana. I'm your driver this evening."

Out the window, he could see Ernest Kabini stalking up the ramp in the grainy dusk, bleakly intent.

"Drive us, then," the woman said. "Drive us."

Three or four others asked Myburgh to let them get off, but the rest acknowledged him as the man who had hit the elephant, numbly accepted him as Kabini's stand-in, and allowed him to grind *'s Toe* into gear, leap-frog it out of the loading dock, and carry them out of Belle Ombre in a fit of backfires and roars muffled by a torrent of deadly Muzak and by the pipe-trimmed buttresses of the station's colorful pavilion.

Myburgh drove badly, but he escaped Marabastad heading south on Eleventh Street, chugging through its intersections with Boomstraat and Strubenstraat, and eventually turning east on Vermeulenstraat, within hailing range of the Kruger House Museum, in order to make a rattletrap assault on Pretoria's center. Double-decker municipal buses, as well as European, American, and Japanese passenger cars, jockeyed for position around him, their drivers eyeing him and his out-of-place riders as if the Putco bus had dropped into their town from another cosmos.

Myburgh cracked the window in the driver's cage. "We're going to KwaNdebele!" he shouted. "If you want to see that South African Shangri-la for yourself, meet us at Church's Square!"

A moment later, he added, "By the Palace of Justice!"

(—Gravity, he heard Mordecai Thubana whispering, —is the only universal force. It acts between all particles without exception. Nowadays, though, it is the odd force out.)

"I know!" Myburgh said, shouting at his passengers.

(—Most matter in our universe, said Thubana, an unseen spirit in the driver's cage, —is invisible.)

"Shadow matter. Dark matter."

(—They're not the same thing, Mr. Myburgh, but, yes, there is a truth of sorts in what you suppose.)

"Dark matter, then. Invisible matter."

(—Yes. For years, astronomers have been studying, and calling real, only those parts of the universe defiled by light.)

"Defiled?"

(—Yes, Mr. Myburgh. Contaminated.)

Contaminated, Myburgh thought. Contaminated. Was his Pretoria less real than KwaNdebele? It unquestionably gave off more light, it was giving off light right now, the entire city was blazing, it was blazing with the lovely contamination of streetlamps, electric lights, shiny clock faces, the headlamps of dozens of chrome-plated vehicles. And this blazing—this contamination—was a blow to the head, the kind that ignites fireworks, sparklers, glowing cascades of light, an outward/inward overload that blinds whoever decides to look no farther than the edges of this self-righteous blazing. And that person—every such person—is defiled by the loveliness of the contamination to which he has given his heart, and the night on the highveld contains for him no Southern Cross, no Lightning Bird, no Jewel Box cluster, but only the shadow-matter armies bivouacked in their shameful invisibility out there beyond the electric bonfires, and the cherished stench, of his own high blindness. Contaminated by light . . .

"We're going to KwaNdebele!" Myburgh shouted out the window of his cage. "Meet us at Church's Square!"

(—Mr. Myburgh. Mr. Myburgh, come back.)

"Not yet! I've got to recruit some passengers!"

The claxon of a police cruiser sounded; lights flashed from the turret on its roof. It pulled speedily abreast of 496 and paced it around the immense, palm-dotted memorial park and traffic circle at the center of Church's Square.

An officer was waving angrily, and futilely, at Myburgh, urging him to pull over. Myburgh wasn't ready to do that. He waved back at the policeman. If the officer wanted to stop him before he was ready to stop, then let him call up a roadblock and clog the circle with barricades and police vehicles.

In fact, because that was the only option (other than shooting Myburgh dead and perhaps inflicting injury on bystanders and riders alike) that Myburgh had given the officer, he apparently did just that, for, soon enough, the traffic circle resembled a raceway, and Myburgh's bus was slowing, slowing, as city cruisers surrounded it and nudged it toward the waist-high brick wall on the circumference of the park.

Around him were such familiar landmarks and competitors as the South African Reserve Bank, Standard Bank, and Barclays National Bank. Nearby, too, were the Raadsaal and the Transvaal Provincial Administration Building, every structure looming.

"This man is demon possessed," Myburgh heard the woman in the knit crown tell her fellow riders. "Truly."

He opened the door for the policemen pounding on it. One man stood in the traffic circle with a pistol pointed at him through the window of the driver's cage. The officers on the sidewalk also leveled guns at him.

"Be a hands-upper for me, man," one of them said.

Myburgh kept his hands on the steering wheel. The bus's motor continued to sputter and bang.

"*Hands up!*"

"This bus is called *Everybody's Toe*," Myburgh said. "I'd like to give you a free ride to Tweefontein E in KwaNdebele, gentlemen. Please ask forty or fifty people to go with us. It shouldn't be too crowded."

Two policemen rushed up the bus's steps, dragged him from his seat, and pulled him onto the sidewalk to cuff his hands and hold his face to the paving as they patted him down.

Myburgh was conscious of the riders on *Everybody's Toe* creeping to its windows to observe his takedown. Their faces were shadowy, but not invisible; they seemed far more sympathetic toward him than did the washed-out faces of the policemen. It was night, but the city hurled off too much light for any stars to shine through, and Myburgh understood that the Theory of Everything for which Thubana had been looking was still twisting out there in the vacuum—beyond the contamination, cloaked in darkness, waiting.

"Mordecai," Myburgh said, his cheek on the sidewalk, and he had the distinct sense that someone had heard him.

CRI DE COEUR

cri de coeur \ ˌkredə́ kər \ n. [Fr. lit., cry from the heart]
: passionate protest, appeal, or complaint

WHY, ONCE, DID MOTHS SINGE THE TAPESTRIES OF their wings in candle flames? Why, once, did the cinder-laden parachutes of fireworks so excite us? And, again, why did certain crazies—fools or saints—sometimes steep themselves in petrol and torch themselves to carbon?

Why, in short, do we long to blaze?

Ever since I turned twelve, I've known. Only a minuscule fraction of the stuff of our universe glows. The rest, the bulk, drifts in darkness, unmoored or rudely tugged. The cold vast black of interstellar night cloaks it from our eyes, our telescopes, our roachlike searchings. We belong to the part that does not glow, to the swallowing dark.

Why wonder, then, that a yearning to leap into the furnace, to god-fashion ourselves in fire, drives us starward on the engines of a mute cri de coeur?

"Whurh we guhn?" Dean asked me.

"It's a surprise. Have a little patience."

"Huvh uhliddle—" he grinned up at Lily "—payshuhns."

Excitedly, I gripped one of roly-poly Dean's hands. Lily Aliosi-Stark, my son's mother, a systems specialist, held the other. Dean swung between us like a baby orangutan, a creature habituated *in utero* to a starship's sterile bays, bioengineered for life aboard a space ark.

Except that he hadn't been. After more than an E-standard century of travel, U.N.S. *Annie Jump Cannon* and the other two great wheelships of our colonizing armada pulsed a mere three years from a rendezvous with the Epsilon Eridani system. The brakes were on.

Along with U.N.S. *Fritz Zwicky* and U.N.S. *Subrahmanyan Chandrasekhar, Annie* was slowing to keep from overshooting our target, a world where Dean might find himself ill-suited to cope. Of course, I had to admit, that might prove true of all of us.

I led Lily and Dean up a rampway and thumb-keyed the panel of the topmost room in G-Tower of *Annie*'s rotating wheel, a structure so large that the sight of any portion of it always summons my awe.

We entered the observatory. A scaffold supporting the enameled barrel of the ArkBoard Visual Telescope (ABVT) reared over our heads.

We rode an electric lift up through this scaffolding to a carpeted platform with chairs, handrails, and a large shielded viewport. At the platform's other end, two men stood talking at the base of a ladder to the ABVT's sighting mechanisms. One man I knew only as a fuel-systems specialist whose up-phases rarely coincided with mine. The other man, however, was my friend Thich Ngoc Bao, our mission's chief astrophysicist.

Bao sprinted up the ladder. The fuel-systems man turned toward us brushing invisible lint from his tunic. Dean, who had fixed all his attention on Bao and the ABVT's shiny ivory tube, paid him no mind.

"Whurh are we?" Dean said.

"The observatory," Lily said.

"I go up . . . *thurh!*" Dean pointed at the ABVT.

"No. Sit." I made him sit down in front of the shielded viewport. Dean burrowed into the chair and rolled his head against its cushion, his eyes hungry for new wonders. Clearly, this place excited him.

"Watch," I said.

The shields on the forward viewport retracted, exposing a window into space two meters tall and at least twice that wide. Dean quivered. Gaping, he pulled himself forward, his pudgy legs banging the chair's undercarriage, his pudgy hands bouncing on his knees.

"Holy crow," he said. "Holy crow."

Lily put a hand on his shoulder. "Happy birthday, DeBoy. Many happy returns."

"Whurh iz," straining hard to see, "New Hohm?"

"There." I nodded at the window. "Straight ahead. Among those fuzzy match flames and haloes."

Actually, between *Annie Jump* and the edge of the Epsilon Eridani orrery there now lies an arc of interstellar debris — tumbling chunks of dirt-ice, frozen gas, a chaos of nomadic mongrel rocks — not unlike the Oort Cloud beyond the orbit of Sol's Pluto. Our armada's astronomers, using radio telescopes as well as ABVTs, detected this belt less than five E-years ago. Today, we call it the Barricado Stream. Given the dimensions of this shadowy region, however, Commander Odenwald and his counterparts on *Zwicky* and *Chandrasekhar* foresee no trouble taking even our prodigious arks through its far-flung hazards into the system's heart.

The tech who'd been talking to Bao strolled over and halted in front of Dean. From this new vantage, he stared at Dean. The relentless blankness of his gaze annoyed me so much that I stared pointedly back at him.

"Hello, Mr. —?" I prompted.

"Mikol. Kazimierz Mikol. Children have no place up here."

"Sez who?" Lily said.

"Regs, I'm afraid. Ask Heraclitus." He hitched his thumb at the nearest toadstool unit. "Check for yourself."

Seeing a quick tautening of the cords under Lily's jaw, I said, "Dean's just come off a short ursidormizine nap. He's six. This is his first observatory visit. Why try to squelch his pleasure?"

Mikol shrugged.

"This is his birthday present," Lily said. "Abel wanted to give him—" She stuck.

Mikol superciliously lifted an eyebrow.

"—the stars," Lily finished in some consternation.

"Oh? Is that right? Who's Abel?"

"I am," I said. "Abel Gwiazda. When I was twelve, my adoptive father gave the stars to me for Christmas on my first Mars trip."

Mikol clasped his hands at his waist and smiled. "Ah. The reenactment of a family tableau. How sweet."

Lily and I exchanged a look.

"Of course, the reg in question has its roots in a wholly legitimate concern for mission efficiency," Mikol said. "In addition — as if it mattered in this case — it means to protect our youngest from the deleterious effects of either cosmic rays or overexcitement, I forget which."

Dean kept gaping at the stars, but I gaped at Mikol. I had never known such rudeness, even under the guise of enforcing shipboard discipline, since coming aboard *Annie Jump Cannon* off Luna in 2062. Reputedly, the U.N.'s planners had selected against egregious social blunderers like Mikol. If so, how had he contrived to get aboard?

Pointing, Dean suddenly cried, "I see . . . New Hohm!"

"No," I said. "New Home's sun, maybe. We're still too far away to make out planets."

"Or even the biggest rocks in the Barricado Stream," Mikol told Dean in a grating adult-to-child voice.

Dean twigged next to nothing of the insult. He grinned at Kazimierz Mikol.

Mikol turned to Lily. "Does the boy like rocks? Take him down to the beach garden in hydroponics."

"Abel's done that already," Lily said. "Dean likes it."

"Likes rocks, does he? Good. Maybe we'll grab one with a Colombo tether while crossing the Barricado."

"Whatever for?" Lily said.

"To abandon him on," Mikol said as a parting shot. He strode to the scaffold lift before Lily or I could blink, much less frame a rejoinder.

Dean, heedless, sat there gnomishly. Starlight, modestly color-shifted from our deceleration, washed over his face like melting diamonds.

I was outraged. I stared after Mikol, thankful only that Lily and I could give our son the stars.

Me? Just as I told Mikol, I am Abel Gwiazda. My adoptive parents came to the United States from Poland in the fourth decade of the twenty-first century. My father, a physicist trained in Krakow, and my mother, the science journalist who broke Poland's so-called "Coca-Cola/Cyclotron" scandal in the late twenties, took positions with the ISCA (International Space & Colonization Authority) in Hutchinson, Kansas. After discovering that they could have no children of their own, they adopted me, a nameless Tanzanian child orphaned in the last of the Drought Riots and smuggled to

Puerto Rico by profit-taking babyleggers.

I grew up well-loved, but aimless and deracinated. I spent three years as a teenager in a dome community beneath the great escarpment of Mons Olympica on Mars, learning, more by accident than deliberate application, the agrogeology skills that, upon our joint return to Earth in 2056, I took up formally in Oran, Algeria. With doctorate in hand and recommendations from my well-placed parents, I qualified for, and easily landed a spot in, the Epsilon Eridani Expedition—whose planning, funding, and assembly in lunar obit occupied the entire world throughout the turbulent fifties. You can't go home again, but you can try to make one Elsewhere, and for me the E's in E^3 stand for that very hope.

A part of any home is family. I can't help it: I feel the call of family intensely. So strongly did I feel it before the making of my son Dean that I (respectfully) sought reproductive contracts with a half dozen women in G-Tower—including Etsuko Endo, Nita Sistrunk, and even the menopausal physicist Indira Sescharchari —before Lily Aliosi-Stark, a kindly woman in her late twenties, agreed. Her only stipulation was that I expect and solicit only minimal help from her in raising the child. To raise a child in the habitat tower of an ark, at least one parent must forgo the balm of ursidormizine slumber, submitting to the pitiless depredations of aging to care for, teach, and discipline that child.

"This is what *you* want," Lily said. "I wish to save myself for New Home. I don't want to set foot there feeling achy and antiquated. Understand?"

I did. So Dean is *my* child. I begot the Down's-syndrome boy on Lily during several bouts of fiery lovemaking. Later, in a burst of self- and partner-mocking irony that startled and then tickled me, Lily called our wild sessions a "screwbilee." Aboard *Annie*, I have a reputation for straight-laced stoicism stemming from my Reform Catholicism and the twin concerns of my arkbound work, agrogeology and poetry. The former I do for business (ultimately, the business of survival), the latter for love—just as, looking ahead, I persuaded Lily to conceive a child and then finagled authorization from med services for her to carry it to term.

During our lovemaking, Lily said, "Boy or girl, give it your name. I decline to hang another hyphen around the poor kid's neck."

"Gwiazda-Aliosi-Stark?"

"Absolutely not. Throw in a double first name, Claude-Mark

or Julia-Cerise, and it'd go down like a swimmer in a titanium wetsuit."

So, months before giving birth, Lily renounced any claim on handing the child her surname. This fact comforted me. What if she had waited until the photoamnioscan at the end of the first trimester revealed the embryo's trisomy 21? (Which, of course, it did.) At that point, the imperfect fetus would have thrown her motives forever in doubt. I would have wondered if she had deferred to me not solely out of her wish to set aside the demands of parenting, but also out of scorn for our botched offspring.

Masoud Nadeq, the chief physician in G-Tower, showed us the results of the photoamnioscan and listed our options, namely, to abort the pregnancy, to bring it to term with no effort at gene rectification, or to intervene at the chromosomal level with the highly limited procedures available on board. During the past seven E-years, nearly two hundred other children have been born on the *Annie Jump Cannon* alone, and Nadeq's records show that only one other couple — cosmic rays, variable gravity, and the other gene-crippling aspects of near-light-speed travel aside — has conceived a Down's-syndrome infant.

Lily: "What did they do?"

Dr. Nadeq: "They chose to terminate."

"Is that what you advised?" I asked.

Dr. Nadeq: "For quite good reasons, expedition guidelines strongly advance that option. In cases like yours, however, there's no unappealable directive to terminate."

I said, "To get a directive, our fetus would have to have two heads or no brain. Is that it?"

Dr. Nadeq: "In a manner of speaking."

Lily: "Then our baby is reprieved. Forget your hook."

Dr. Nadeq: "Do you agree, Dr. Gwiazda?"

I said, "Of course. Didn't I lobby this woman to help me call Dean's pent-up spirit from the dark?"

Dr. Nadeq: "That's . . . very poetic."

"My avocation. Didn't I run our application through every nook and switchback in Heraclitus's cybernetic innards?"

Dr. Nadeq: "Then you accept the role of guardian as well as that of sire?"

Lily: "He does."

"I do," I said.

Dr. Nadeq: "Excellent. Sign off on this waiver."

"What waiver?"

Dr. Nadeq: "Of unadulterated community support—once, that is, your child is born and later when we begin to colonize New Home."

I despised the waiver's threat of premeditated abandonment, but I signed off on it. How could I condemn a society under extreme environmental and psychological duress for declining to accept with open arms a handicapped child? Especially when Lily and I chose to bring him to term knowing his handicap and his potentially disruptive needs?

Even so, the waiver galled. I signed it with a trembling hand.

Most voyagers treat Dean with kindness. To date, Kazimierz Mikol comprises a boorish minority of one. Despite recycling and other ingenious reclamation schemes (his reasoning must go), we have finite supplies, and once we achieve planetfall, anyone with a mental and/or physical handicap will represent an outright drag on the colonization process.

Better that Dean had come stillborn from the womb, Mikol must figure. Better, now, that we recommit him to the darkness through an ejector tube.

I think too much on Mikol's hostility. Most people, as I have said, are kind.

Item: Etsuko Endo, a biologist who passes her up-phase time doing adjustment counseling, recently spent four hours casting sticks of different lengths for Dean and helping him lay them out in educational patterns.

"Rhommm-buhz!" he said when Etsuko brought him back to me. "Daddy, I cuhn make a . . . *rhom-buhz!*" So proud. Even as he made, not a rhombus, but a triangle whose unequal sides did not quite touch one another.

Item: Commander Odenwald visited Lily only two hours after Dean was born. Repeatedly since that visit, he has used small portions of his long up-phases (despite enzyme cocktails and downtime cell repairs, his hair has turned cayenne-and-silver) to watch Dean trip-sleep or to guide him around the various facilities in G-Tower. In fact, had I not begged him to leave the observatory to Lily and me, Odenwald would have long ago showed that to Dean, too. I believe, then, that with a simple request I can have Mikol dressed down, if not sent packing to his biorack.

Why bother? If Dean had understood any part of Mikol's insult in the observatory, or read the least shade of disdain in his face, I would do it. But Dean thinks everyone loves him. In a universe of swallowing dark, and despite the eclipse of his reason at conception, he scatters a property so similar to light that it dims my vision.

Until, less than a decade ago, a few of us began to have children, you could seldom find more than twenty people awake at any one time in any single living tower on the ever-clocking wheels of our ships. Ten percent of the expedition's personnel oversaw the armada's running, tracked the stars, maintained ship-to-ship communications, studied their specialties like workaholic monks, and ministered to the quasi-corpses stacked in each ark's bioracks.

Only a few days into these up-phases, loneliness settled. An ineffable strangeness pervaded *Annie*'s labs and corridors, as if a winged fairy tripping along at light-speed had cast a spell over my sleeping arkmates, a dark enchantment over every workroom, crawlspace, and maintenance deck. I could hear this implacable sorcery in the hydrogen hiss of the stars; in the white noise of generators, computer-cooling fans, and hidden air recirculators.

I came aboard U.N.S. *Annie Jump Cannon* as a hotshot Ph.D. of twenty-two. So far, this voyage to Epsilon E has taken a little over 109 standard years—relative, that is, to the arks in our fleet. Had I left an infant child with my parents in Algeria, it would have long since doddered into codgerhood—if it remained alive at all.

As for me, given the periodic metabolic respite of U-sleep, I have aged (Dr. Nadeq tells me) the physiological equivalent of only thirteen years. In short, I am a thirty-five-year-old centenarian. But no one stays up-phase much longer than a month each shipboard year (other than Commanders Odenwald, Roosenno, and Joplin, and a few engineering troubleshooters and continuity personnel), so that, among us would-be colonists, youthful centenarians—of many different ages—register as commonplaces, not freaks.

Of course, in this final decade of our approach to Epsilon Eridani, an expedition policy authorizing the conception, *in utero* gestation, and natural birth of children took effect for screened personnel young enough to carry out their parental obligations on New Home. Six years after Lily and I made Dean, this policy lapsed because "children under four will impact negatively on the efficient settlement of the target world that we call New Home."

Then why permit the arrival of any children at all? Or, at least, the arrival of any offspring under the able-bodied age of, say, sixteen?

Well, the original U.N. planners believed that "in the long term, a generation of colonists reared on the target world's surface from midchildhood, adapting daily to that world, will prove of incalculable benefit to the planting of a permanent human base in an alien solar system." Nobody, of course, had factored Dean into this reckoning.

In any case, with the advent of children, the living towers on our three wheelships seem less like mausoleums and more like chatter-filled atria or aviaries. I have stayed continuously up-phase ever since Dean's birth (Lily, by contrast, opted for ursidormizine slumber soon afterward and comes up-phase only on his birthday). Although Dean takes closely monitored "naps"—to foster cell growth, to husband our various dry-good stores, and to ease the burden on our recirculating systems—I have no desire to down-phase just to match my sleep periods to his. I sleep when I need to, without drugs, and plot ways to sample, test, and seed the unearthly (conjectural) loams, marls, and humuses of New Home.

At other times, of course, I work in G-Tower's polyped, where Dean has become a favorite of his playmates; a mascot, almost. His blockish head, flat nose, spongy tongue, and stubby hands endear him to, rather than estrange him from, the group. The curiosity and altruism of well-loved children has a weird dynamic. It astonishes and uplifts. It soothes. So how can I regret the nearly six extra years that I've aged as a result of going up-phase for Dean?

Simple: I can't.

Meanwhile, the metaphoric seedpods of *Annie*'s towers have begun to rattle and split. Our corridors ring. The children dance, wonder, explore, scuffle, and sing. Kazimierz Mikol, I feel sure, has taken both a powder and a double dose of refined and amplified bear's blood: ursidormizine.

Our G-Tower mess is draped festively about with acetate banners. Through it drifted both a smell like fried ozone and the piped-in strains of an old song called, if repetition of a single phrase means anything, "I'm So Dizzy."

Thich Ngoc Bao, the astrophotographer Nita Sistrunk, and I sat at a table over our trays. Dean huddled in an obsolescent VidPed near the door, spinning the control ball with his palm. (He won't use virch goggles; their simulated environments cut him off too thoroughly from me, and that scares him.) Hiller Nevels, a pilot and maintenance tech, swaggered over from the autodispenser to join us.

"... detected Eppie's heliopause," Bao was saying. "So we *will* in fact rendezvous with the system."

"You doubted we would?" Nita said.

"Eppie's heliopause?" Hiller said. "What's that?"

"Did *you* never doubt, Nita?" Bao took a bite out of his steaming oyster-shell pasta and its garlic-spinach filling. He swallowed. "One down-phase, I had a six-month-long nightmare, complete with sound and motion effects. *Annie* dropped like a stale doughnut into a Kerr singularity and whirled around its glowing mouth for about twelve eternities. Frame-dragging, you know. I mummified in my biorack. So did everybody else."

"Cheerful talk," Hiller said.

"Eppie's heliopause is the very edge of the Epsilon Eridani system," Nita told Hiller. "Where the star's solar wind hits the charged particles in interstellar vacuum."

"Isn't the Barricado Stream the edge?" Hiller said.

A star's energy influence, Bao explained, extends well beyond its farthest planet or cometary cloud. Low-frequency radio emissions can undulate a dozen billion miles into the obsidian emptiness surrounding a star.

As Bao spoke, I watched Dean swaying in the VidPed, slapping the control ball. I could see his virtual self—a chunky two-dimensional figure with a feathered spear—stalking a herd of electronic ostriches on a veldt whose real-world equivalent long ago turned into tourist hotels, tennis courts, and golf courses.

Dean didn't care about that. The control ball was easy to spin; the figures on the screen made him laugh. His chuckle, along with the way his head lurched gleefully, warmed my heart, almost as if Lily had rubbed my chest with a thermotherapeutic cream.

Without alerting the others, I picked a comppad off my tunic's carrypatch and began to punch out some verses. I struggled, recasting each stanza three or four times before moving on. During this effort, *Annie* and my friends ceased to exist for me.

In the end, I had my entire effort almost, if not quite, the way I wanted it:

> *A starchild in a VidPed cage*
> *Unwraps himself, with deadpan glee.*
> *Such fragile tissues disengage,*
> *Such guileless beauty in debris.*
>
> *Bafflingly, he molts and fledges,*
> *Unwrapping in order to dress.*

> *By this divestment, he pledges*
> *To put on a scarecrow success.*
>
> *Never has he touched a bird:*
> *A maypop, an eggling, a flame.*
> *In the beginning cracked a word,*
> *The broken promise of his name.*
>
> *I hear lark song where my fellows*
> *Discern but babble, vocal cheats.*
> *Take away your amped-up cellos,*
> *Leave me only DeBoy's bleats.*
>
> *With no ulterior intent,*
> *He cocks and grins at every sign:*
> *Litmus test or test-tube infant,*
> *Telescope or Colombo twine.*
>
> *So watch his palm atop the ball,*
> *A misfit's flesh on spinning chrome:*
> *Just now a shade on spectral veldt,*
> *But next my son on our New Home.*

I looked up to find my friends eyeing me with amusement. How long had I occupied myself writing my poem? Even Hiller, the last of us to sit down, had polished off his meal and was staring at my comppad.

"Another poem?" Bao said. "Well, you have to let us see it. If it's bad manners to tell secrets in front of one's dinner companions, concealing a poem composed at table is also rude. Surely."

"The rudeness is writing it in front of us," Nita said. "He might as well've sat here picking his nose."

Hiller guffawed. "That depends on the poem. Or the nose."

Bao reached across the table. "Give."

I handed him the comppad. I had no qualms about showing around the product of my fugue. Keats need not fear even a partial eclipse of his immortality, but no other soul this far from home—with the self-proclaimed exception of the Pakistani sferics specialist Ghulam Sharif on U.N.S. *Fritz Zwicky*—can rival my versifying prowess. Other expedition members may scribble confessional, hortatory, or occasional poems (you can find the results of their activity on toadstool units everywhere about), but I (humorously) regard my challengers as amateurs or hacks.

"Prepare to fall at my feet in veneration."

"Cripes," said Nita. "Self-praise is no praise at all."
"I unequivocally agree, Ms. Sistrunk," I said.
"You do?"
"Sure. But *no praise* is also no praise at all. I blow my own horn to add a little dressing to the silence."

Bao began to scroll the comppad. He read each stanza aloud for the others. He did so with a pitch of feeling that humbled me: I could *hear* the hiccups in my poem's flow, the off-speed diction, the bungled metrics—hiccups for which Bao's sensitive reading almost compensated.

"What's an eggling?" Hiller asked.
"A little egg," Nita ventured. "What else?"
I said, "I don't know. Something hard like a stone, dense like a black hole, and life-packed, potentially, like an ovum. See? Eggling."

"What does it mean?" Hiller asked. "Not just eggling, the whole poem?"

"That he loves his son," Bao said. "And looks forward to raising him to manhood on a brave new world."

I could add nothing to that, and when Bao gave me back my comppad, Nita began talking about heliopause again, the savory imminence of planetfall.

Our fleet pulses onward, skimming at a modest moiety of lightspeed the interpenetrating membranes of space-time. The Barricado Stream—inside the hard-to-mark heliopause, outside the orbit of a planetary iceball—rushes nearer.

Toward the end of the twentieth century, perturbations in Epsilon Eridani's motion revealed that it most likely dragged planets, if not a gravity sink, around it. Observations made from the Infrared Lunar Astronomical Telescope (IRLAT) on Darkside in the 2030s, along with the fact that Eppie emits an infrared signal hinting at protoplanetary debris, led scientists to posit that the system had five planets, including one in Eppie's zone of habitability, and possibly an outer dust band. We sent out an unmanned probe to confirm these hypotheses, but our armada—dispatched nearly thirty years later, when Ju Tong technology, multinational money, and worsening environmental/social conditions converged to make the launch seem practical if not imperative—has long since outrun the U.N. probe.

Fortunately, shipboard telescopes and Thich Ngoc Bao's relativistic calculus have validated the presence of these worlds. Even more convincingly, so has a probe that we dropped over the side of *Zwicky* before commencing deceleration; as our arks slowed, this probe kept going, making a full-speed transit of the system and thereby detecting the cometary matter in the Barricado Stream by radar echoes.

In any case, New Home does exist, along with a fiery inner planet that a wag among us tagged Red Hot. Three outer planets received equally silly names: Jelly Belly, Jawbreaker, and Cold Cock. Moreover, spectroanalysis carried out on *Chandrasekhar* indicates that New Home has water.

A couple of days ago, because Dean requires extra work and attention if I wish him to reach his full potential, I took him into the geology bay under *Annie*'s observatory deck. I planned not only to do some elementary professional review but also to show him a grab bag of tray specimens: a quartz crystal, a piece of obsidian, a leaf of limestone, a fossil imprint, a geode. Etsuko Endo, after all, has too much to do to spend her every waking moment amusing Dean or devising therapeutic games to educate him.

I don't. My real work begins when our advance scientific teams set down on Epsilon Eridani II (even the hackneyed New Home seems a better name than that) to map, explore, sample, test, and catalogue. Besides, I'm Dean's father: I insisted that this expedition permit him to be.

Dean handled each specimen with clumsy delight. Except for the collection's lone geode, the specimens are small to the point of parody. In fact, many soil and mineral types exist on *Annie* only as wafer-thin cross-sections on glass slides for microscope viewing.

I half feared that Dean would slice himself on the crystal. (His fingers have the nimbleness of porcelain.) Or would drop the trilobite fragilely preserved in Ordovician clay. Or would lose the stalagmite tip that rested on his single-creased palm like a Lilliputian dagger.

But, chortling, goggle-eyed, Dean managed to hold on to, examine, and return to me every item. He was as respectful of them as, on his sixth birthday, he'd been of the glittery stars in the observatory's viewport.

"Whuh's thiz?"

"Schist."

"Durdy word?"

"No. *Schist*. A flaky, stress-formed rock. Be careful, you'll peel away a mica layer."

"Sch-schid?"

I started to say, "No, *schist*," when I heard a man behind us laughing, just inside the bay's entrance. I looked over my shoulder to see (for the first time since Dean's visit to the observatory) Kazimierz Mikol.

My gut clenched, a spasm of *déjà vu*. What was Mikol doing in a work-and-study laboratory authorized for, if not expressly limited to, *Annie*'s geology contingent? Would he argue that my six-year-old retardate had no business here? No business, for that matter, anywhere?

"He *does* like rocks, doesn't he?" Mikol said.

That remark instantly soured the look I turned on him. "My sweet Jesus," I murmured.

"You mistake me for someone else," Mikol said. "Look. I came up here at Ms. Endo's request. She wanted me to tell a man in here — identity then unknown to me — that his son — ditto — would have a therapy session with her tomorrow at ten-hundred hours."

"Why didn't she intercom?"

"A whole tribe of ankle biters had her occupied. Besides, your sanctorum was on my way. I need to eyeball the harp strings sweeping down from the arc opposite G-Tower. That all right with you?"

Harp strings meant fuel spokes. I stared hard at Mikol.

"Consider yourself duly messaged, Dr. — ?"

"Gwiazda."

"As you like." He pivoted on his heel.

"Wade," Dean said. He meant *wait*, and Mikol turned back to face him.

Dean held up the geode in our collection. He tilted this queer, split rock so that Mikol had to look directly into its crystal-laced cavity. Its hollow glittered like an in-fallen spiderweb in a splash of sunlight, and Mikol stared into it as if hypnotized.

"Spokes," Dean said. "Fyool spokes."

Those words seemed to stun Mikol. He looked from the reflective cavity of the geode to the dull, flat face of the boy that Lily and I, in his view, had selfishly inflicted on the limited resources of our ark.

"He means the crystals," I said. "They remind him of the spokes to our matter-antimatter rocket."

"I *know* what he meant."

"He saw those spokes only once," I insisted. "The same day Lily and I gave him the stars."

"There's a mobile of the *Annie* in the polyped. He's seen that dozens of times, surely."

"Its spokes don't glow like the real ones. In the glare of the exhaust stream, the real ones are . . . magical."

"That doesn't make his *equating* the two a wonderwork."

Mikol refused to look away from me. And, out of atavistic machismo or scientific curiosity, I refused to look away from him. "But he's just linked you, a fuel-systems specialist, to the 'spokes' in the geode."

"He heard me say fuel spokes. So he has a bare-assed modicum of mother wit. Hallelujah."

"What about the associative leap he just made? Not from your words to you, but from the geode's crystals to *Annie*'s weblike fuel lines?"

Dean kept pointing the geode. The way he was gripping it, it reminded me of an exotic weapon. I imagined a burst of energy flashing from it and splitting Mikol's chest open, to reveal . . . what? The gemlike perdurability of his heart? The flowing rubies of his blood? The hard-edged latticework of his myocardia?

"Do you think that on that basis I should declare the kid a genius?" he asked me.

"Human would do. Just human."

"Tiglathpileser was human, it's rumored. And Caligula. So were a whole host of twentieth-century tyrants. So presumably were the brain-dead idiots who turned the Earth into a treeless detention camp. Being human, I'm afraid, doesn't automatically confer demigod status on anyone."

"Human beings made these arks."

"Praise Noah for your insight! Which onboard system did your genius offspring invent?"

This retort shut my mouth; it also had a spirit-dampening effect on Dean. He lowered the geode and made a queer, gargling moan in his throat.

No longer in the geode's sights, Mikol backed out of the workroom. I followed him.

In the corridor, Mikol pointed a finger to hold me at bay. "Two run-ins with Gwiazda and his hairless baboon," he said. "Well, this second run-in was a lot less amusing than the first. A third meeting may result in the total overthrow of my antihostility training, the blanket neutralization of my daily serenotil boosters."

"What's the matter with you, anyway?"

"Nothing. I dislike mongoloids. In my view, an entirely rational prejudice."

"You've overstepped yourself there," I said.

"Well, so what? I'll go down-phase again after solving my

hydrogen-flow problem. And stay zonked until *Annie* enters the Barricado Stream. With any luck, I won't collide with Gwiazda and Son ever again, either aboard this ark or down on New Home, where I plan to homestead a small farm off limits to fat little mongoloids and their selfish Sambo daddies."

"You bastard," I said.

"Check out the little bastard in your lab," Mikol replied. "More than likely, he's accidentally swallowed a rock."

Once again, he strode away before I could seize his arm or mount a reply. Under my breath, though, I murmured, "Honky," not knowing where the word had come from; even so, it seemed a crass betrayal of the Gwiazdas, who, in innocence and love, had bought my life and raised me.

"Whurh's Lily?" Dean asked.

"You know as well as I. Asleep. She's always asleep. It's her calling."

"I wand to see her."

"Uh-uh. You only think you do. We've done this before, Dean. The damned bioracks spook you."

"I *want* to see her," Dean said, struggling to enunciate.

"No you don't."

"Yez. Yez I do. Take me to see her."

Dean and I had long since retired to our mezzanine-level quarters. The hour was nearly midnight (as if you could not legitimately say the same of any hour of our arkboard journey), and I wanted Dean to go as soundly asleep as his mother. But an afternoon birthday party in the polyped, and then an evening of restored and colorized *Our Gang* comedies over our link to Heraclitus's vidfiles, had left him wrought up and obstinate. I could tell that an all-out battle now would snap my brittle self-control faster than would appeasement, even with a visit to the bioracks thrown in as Dean's unwarranted spoils.

(Spoils. Evocative word.)

Actually, Dean seldom tries to stand his ground against me or anyone else. Agreeableness and conciliation define him the way stealth and curiosity define a cat. Better for harmony's sake, I rationalized, to indulge him tonight in this unusual display of resoluteness than to shatter my peace of mind—what peace of mind?—by playing the tyrant.

Ten minutes after midnight, then, we dropped to the lowest level in G-Tower, a fluorescent dungeon of computer monitors and foam-lined ursidormizine pods, and asked the security tech Greta Agostos to pass us through the barred entrance of *Annie's* hibernaculum.

"On what business?" Greta asked.

"Guess. Dean wants to see his mother."

Greta rubbed her knuckles furiously—but not hard—over Dean's head. "She won't be very talkative, DeBoy. And you and your dad will have to submit to a search. You know, a ticklish patting down."

"The only reason I came," I said.

But that "patting down" remark was a standard security-tech joke. In fact, without even touching us, Greta ran an aural fod—*f*oreign-*o*bject *d*etector—around our entire bodies with the impersonal deftness the very opposite of sensual. Her fod, by the way, absolved us of trying to smuggle into the hibernaculum any sort of weapon, drug, or soft-drink IV-drip.

The security bars retracted upward, and Dean and I passed into the eerie twilight mausoleum of the bioracks. The air in this circular hibernaculum has a wintry blue tinge and a biting regulated chill. You can identify our quasi-corpses, by the way, either by reading their nameplates or by looking through the pods' frost-traced visors.

We walked the hibernaculum's perimeter—tap-tap-tapping on its naked metal floor—until we had reached the biorack of Lily Aliosi-Stark. Her pod rests on the chamber's third strata, not quite two meters up, and I always have to lift Dean so that he can gaze through the rime-crazed faceplate at his mother's pale but lovely profile.

"Sleepin beaudy," Dean whispered, full of awe. "My mama's jes like sleepin beaudy."

"I'd wake her with a kiss, DeBoy, but my lips always freeze to the visor."

"Funny."

"Not if it happens to you. All right if we go home now?"

Dean put his fingertips to Lily's faceplate. He chuckled when they didn't stick to it. Instead, they left milky prints, which faded slowly once he'd drawn his hand away.

"Pood me down."

I put Dean down. He ambled along the bottom two strata of bioracks, back toward the hibernaculum's entrance, until he came to an empty pod featuring this legend on its nameplate: *Abel Walter Gwiazda*. Dean rubbed the letters of our surname with a stubby forefinger. Then, as I had feared—as I'd *known* would happen—Dean gulped at the chilly air and went as pop-eyed as a strangler's victim. Why had I supposed that this visit would turn out better than all the others?

"Gone," Dean said. "Holy crow, daddy's gone."

"I'm right here, son. Unlike your ever-drowsing mama, you can't expect me to be two places at once."

On the verge of blubbering, Dean repeated, "Gone," at least a dozen times and then began to wail: a fractured banshee keen that filled this weird crypt for the living like a squadron of angry wasps.

I clutched my shoulders, then covered my ears, then grabbed my shoulders again. Dean's wail stung and restung the snarled thread-ends of my untangling nerves.

"*Damn you, you little defective! Shut up!*"

Dean's eyes dilated hugely. He stopped wailing and retreated. Repeatedly, I shoved him in the chest with my knuckles, herding him toward the exit. On my fifth or sixth such shove, Dean stumbled and collapsed sliding on his bottom. I yanked him up.

"The one place you can't endure for three minutes straight is the one place you insist on coming! Why? You don't have a clue, do you?"

Greta appeared out of the cold indigo fog. She knelt and hugged Dean from behind. He spun about and clung to her as if to the winged savior in a fairy tale unwinding on a private channel in his head. The sight of his fear—the realization of it—staggered me.

"You asked Lily for this, Abel," Greta said. "You asked for just what's got you browned off tonight."

"I, I didn't know," I managed. "Not really."

"I'm taking Dean out front with me. He'll be okay. Go to Lily. Talk to her. Stay for as long as it takes."

Greta picked up Dean and carried him, totally compliant in her arms, around the hibernaculum's circular walk. As I stood there in the shame of Greta's rebuke, they receded into the thickening blue fog.

I returned to Lily's biorack. Our conversation touched on many things, including the essential loneliness of starfaring. Later, back at the U-dorm's entrance, Dean greeted me as if I had never derided his mother or cravenly abused him—as if, in short, I *deserved* his regard.

* * *

Each of our ships carries around sixteen hundred people, two hundred to a habitation tower. Most travel down-phase in banks of computer-monitored bioracks. Over the last few years of our approach, however, with a deliberate effort to bring children into our spacefaring community, we've increased our numbers by almost twenty young persons a tower. I assume that *Zwicky* and *Chandrasekhar* boast comparable population surges, but I've made no real effort to stay abreast of their figures. Dean claims most of my time.

After my flare-up in the hibernaculum, I tried to teach Dean everything I could about our ship, our fleet, our aims, our mystical hopes. He now understands that hydrogen flows from the fuel tanks on *Annie*'s thirty-mile-long wheel to the stores of antihydrogen ice in the rocket dragging us along behind it like a colossal, fixed, empty-bottomed parachute. He knows that once we reach New Home, we will have exhausted every scintilla of fuel available to us, and he also understands, I believe, that to return to Earth or to go on to another solar system (Tau Ceti, say, or Sirius) will require the processing and loading of a volume of hydrogen and antihydrogen ice equal to that with which we left the Moon. He knows. . . .

But I delude myself: Dean has profound physical and mental handicaps; and love, the ultimate paternal blessing and folly, has limited power to add to his brain cells or to pack those he has with liberating knowledge.

In the polyped portion of the G-Tower nursery, Dean and I sat behind a partition draped with a banner depicting the galactic cluster including our own Milky Way. I thumb-moused a gyroscopically interphased replica of *Annie Jump Cannon,* hung above us as a mobile, through a dozen different maneuvers. In its miniature filament harness, the tiny ark canted, wheeled, and strained.

Dean was weary of the drills and demonstrations, enduring them out of puppy-dog loyalty. In fact, I felt that somewhere along the trajectory of this lesson, our roles — of father and son, of mentor and student — had reversed.

"Howfurh?" Dean said.

"What?"

"How furh to New Hohm?"

"I don't know. We're still braking. Commander Odenwald probably has it computed to the nanosecond." (And God has a cockpit in every jumpy quark in every offshoot universe since space-time exploded. . . .)

Etsuko came in and sat down opposite Dean in a chair almost too small even for her. "No matter when we start orbiting New Home," she told Dean, "you'll be at least eight or nine before you visit the planet."

Dean visibly perked—not at Etsuko's words, but at her presence. "Why?" he asked.

"We'll have a lot to do before we let any of you children risk the surface. Surveillance, photography, mapping, testing, a great many things. Understand?"

"Will thurh be monstuhrs?"

"Monsters?"

The wedge of Dean's tongue hung between his lips. Then he said, *"Dyne-o-sours,"* as if the word embodied a vinegary type of lizardly force.

"I doubt that," Etsuko said.

"Then what? Peepul?"

"I doubt that too."

"And if there were people, intelligent beings, they'd look upon *us* as the monsters," I said. "Invaders from outer space, their worst fork-legged nightmares."

Dean's face clouded. His tongue filled his mouth like a gag.

"Abel, you've scared him."

"No great task." I usually avoid sarcasm—my son has no feel for it—but I hadn't slept for over fifty hours (not even a catnap), and Dean's intractable innocence had worn some holes in my cheerfulness. "But suppose, Etsuko, that we do drop down to New Home and find ourselves confronted by a species of gentle sapients."

"Suppose we do?"

I told her how the aboriginal sapients of New Home would inevitably view us as a scourge. Later, I wrote,

down
  we
    fall
deformed invaders
dropping into their midst

so that
at our coming
they reel back
feeling
 blitzed

> *appalled*
> *prey to misshapen raiders*
>
> *noting*
> > *our beaklike snouts*
> > *our eyes of shiny goo*
> > *the rows of gleaming bones*
> > *behind our pouts*
> > *the way our fingers*
> > *sprout like vermicelli*
> > *with half-moon lyre picks*
> > *twanging*
> > *in their knuckled heads*
>
> *and they know*
> > *their hot-pink sods*
> > *glass-sheathed trees*
> > *spiraling geyser creeks*
> > *and dog-masked gods*
> > *crunching fire opals*
> > *on the waves of cliffs*
> > *a destiny made manifest*
> > *by a pale of stars*
>
> *will fall forever*
> *to the uprights—*
> *who but us—*
> *swarming down from*
> > *who knows where*
> > *who knows why*
> > *and couldn't they*
> > *just die*
>
> > > *we hope so*
> > > *oh we hope so*
> > > *don't we*
> > > *ms. etsuko*

Still later, Dean occupied elsewhere, I showed this effort to Etsuko. She read my last little quatrain as an insult.

Without benefit of ursidormizine, I dream of New Home and its dominant species: humanoid creatures unaware that invaders from outer space are eyeing their world. A landing in the capital of their foremost nation-state allows the first U.N. party (oddly, it includes both me and Kazimierz Mikol) down to see that every individual of this species roughly resembles my handicapped son.

"I know what we ought to call this place," Mikol tells me: "Special Olympica."

In a collective journey of a century or more, you cannot expect to reach your destination without losing someone, even if the majority of your expeditionary force spends most of its time in monitored trip-sleep. Seven of *Annie Jump*'s original contingent of sixteen hundred have died in transit, the latest (but one) a woman in A-Tower who failed to survive child birth, although, blessedly, her infant daughter did not die and still lives in the A-Tower nursery.

Arkboard funerals last only minutes; few among us attend them. Each tower has a chaplain well-versed in the rituals of different faiths, those of mainline world religions as well as those of small local cults. If the deceased ascribed to a particular belief system and left unambiguous instructions, the chaplain observes them during the memorial service and the subsequent ejection of the corpse from the ship. (For reasons that should be self-evident, our regs permit neither cremation nor entombment.)

Granted, most of those who have died, both here and on our sibling arks, have professed a generic sort of agnosticism or a science-centered, mystical atheism (no matter how oxymoronish this last term may sound), but one man aboard *Chandrasekhar* asked for and received a voodoo funeral, complete with chants and sprinklings of (symbolic) rooster's blood. According to associates, he believed that one day, far in this expansion/contraction cycle of our cosmos, another starfaring ship would retrieve his mummified corpse. Technospiritually revived, he would walk its decks as the undead prophet of the universe's next systolic blossoming.

In my view, the shame of this bravura credo resides not in its superstition, but in the fact that only four of this man's arkmates attended his obsequies. Of course, those who sleep cannot send off the sleeper.

The point of this digression? Several weeks after taking Dean to visit his sleeping mother, a woman by the name of Helena Brodkorb, a floral geneticist in D-Tower, died in her biorack. Despite a complex fail-safe system, her monitors had not alerted her tower's med-unit personnel of her measurable physical deterioration under ursidormizine. By the time anyone noticed, she had slipped away.

A small scandal ensued. Odenwald suspended two up-phase med techs and ordered an investigation. He did not intend to have one more sleeper under his command die in a malfunctioning biorack.

This death would have meant little to me, and nothing to Dean, if, a few hours later, I had not learned that Helena Brodkorb was—or had been—Kazimierz Mikol's aunt, an aunt two years younger than he. Further, Ms. Brodkorb had no other kin on *Annie* or our sibling arks. (Effecting a passenger exchange between two huge wheelships moving at point-ten C is a doable but risky venture.) Excepting spouses and the children born during our decade-long approach to Epsilon Eridani, few people in our expedition have relatives aboard our arks. Therefore, Odenwald felt that Mikol, down-phase again in G-Tower, should know that Ms. Brodkorb had died, even if—maybe *especially* if—it reflected badly on arkboard fail-safe systems. Mikol might elect to attend her last rites.

Quickly, then, Mikol was up-phased, and Odenwald personally broke the news of his aunt's demise.

Mikol, groggy from both the ursidormizine and its sudden neutralization, began to weep. (I have this fact from the med techs who revived him.) He had loved Helena Brodkorb. The disorientation common to the newly awakened may have influenced him, but, still, Mikol's tears had a strong emotional, not just a narrow physiological, wellspring.

I had difficulty crediting this report, of course, but it cheered rather than surprised me. I wanted to believe it—not that a smart and productive woman had died, but that Mikol had reacted to her passing less like an automaton programmed for cynical efficiency than like . . . well, someone's warm-blooded nephew.

I have reconstructed Kazimierz Mikol's activities on the day before Helena Brodkorb's memorial service from an account he gave me later. The most surprising things about this turn of events, of course, are that he deliberately sought Dean and me out in a spirit of reconciliation and that he and I did in fact reach a wary accord.

On that morning, then, Mikol dressed in paper coveralls and a pair of plastic slippers. He added a disposable dove-grey tunic. Every item in his make-do wardrobe emitted a soft grey incandescence. Dove grey. Mourning-dove grey. The colors of civilized dolor, gentlemanly grief.

The chaplain in D-Tower had scheduled Helena's funeral for 0900 hours the next day—after a noninvasive autopsy and med-tech analysis. Mikol had received assurances that he would be unable to tell that anyone, or anything, had so much as pinched Helena's eyelid back or calipered her elbow. He would find her lying serenely in state on the retractable lingula, or tongue, of a waste-disposal ejector.

Tomorrow.

In the meantime, Mikol had a small mission to carry out. He tried to recall what amusements—games, toys, icons—young boys found amusing, and which still pleased *him*, as an adult. No rocks, though. No fake beaches in hydroponics. No shiny precious or semiprecious stones. No geode. Nothing, in fact, pertaining to geology, the professional realm of Dean Gwiazda's father.

Mikol thought a long time. Then he took a lift from the transphase lounge to the mezzanine-level cubbyhole of a pilot and maintenance tech. This, not altogether coincidentally, was a pack rat named Hiller Nevels. Hiller gave him the items he wanted as a kind of consolation gift.

Gift in hand, Mikol rode back down and crossed the G-Tower atrium, a lofty cylinder housing vitrofoam benches, a vegetable garden, exotic ferns, parrot-colored orchids and bromeliads, and a regulated population of purple finches. Heedless of its plants and birds, Mikol hiked through this pocket wilderness to the catwalk outside the polyped.

He found Dean and me playing a game of cards (Go Fish, if I remember correctly) at a toadstool unit well removed from the other children. I greeted him with a look betraying my outrage and suspicion:

"Yes?"

"I came—" Mikol told me later that he could feel his words scratching his throat like a rusty sword blade "—I came to make peace."

"Why?" I said.

"You need a reason?"

"If I'm not to regard this as a shabby trick, yes."

"Such generosity of spirit."

The cards on Dean's screen fanned out before him like so many canceled tickets, and he gave Mikol a toothy, distracted smile.

"Dr. Gwiazda, the truth is, I've undergone a—"

"A change of heart?"

"Perhaps."

"Because your aunt has just died?"

"Word certainly travels."

"Yes, it does. At a healthy fraction of light-speed."

Dean pushed away from his toadstool console. "*Hullo!*" he cried. "*Mistuh Mickle!*"

Mikol knelt beside Dean and pulled a small, foam-lined carrypress from his pocket. After thumbnailing its lid open, he held it on his palm so Dean could see the faceted seeds inside it. They looked like four pieces of sparkly gravel. This was a coincidence of appearances, though, not a surrender to the insult theme—*rocks in the head, out on a rock*—that had so far typified his run-ins with Dean and me.

"What . . . what are they?"

"Eye-eyes," Mikol said. "Impact inflatables."

"They're so . . . liddle."

"The better to bring aboard a vessel where closet space is tight. Touch one."

"No!" I said. "Mr. Mikol, those things are illegal aboard *Annie*."

"Not so," Mikol said from his crouch. "Would I endanger our ship? Or hooliganize your son? You see, *these* eye-eyes will fall back to portable grit as quickly as they burst to their full dimensions—the latest in amusement engineering just before our launch."

Dean held a finger over the carrypress: expectant, unsure, ready for direction. His psychic investment in electronic Go Fish had long since bottomed out.

"No," I told him.

"Ease off, Dr. Gwiazda," Mikol said. "I'm trying to make amends, not get the boy bioracked for reckless mischief."

Although still skeptical, I thought this over and nodded at Dean. "Go on, then. Take one. Just one."

Dean's hand trembled over the carrypress. Mikol seized it and guided his forefinger to one of the eye-eyes. Sweat and surface tension lifted the eye-eye clear. Dean stared at the grit on his fingertip in what looked to me like goggle-eyed dumbfoundment.

"Roll it between your thumb and forefinger," Mikol said. "Then throw it against the floor or the wall." He stepped aside to give Dean room.

Dean flicked the eye-eye feebly past my head. It struck the

polyped's deck, skittered to a standstill, and began to emit a faint, melodious hiss.

When Mikol picked it up, it quieted. "More *oomph!*" he advised. "Try again." He gave the eye-eye back to Dean, who looked to me for guidance.

"Go ahead. Hurl it. Hard."

Dean obeyed me, tossing the eye-eye with such an awkward shoulder snap that I could imagine him whining for weeks about the lingering soreness. A hard expulsion of breath through his nostrils sounded a lot like a squeal.

But the eye-eye hit the wall behind me and impact-inflated on the rebound.

Wham! Revolving in the polyped was a balloonlike replica of an Allosaurus as large as Mikol himself. It hissed as it tumbled, that crimson and turquoise effigy of a giant lizard, and hissed more loudly than the eye-eye from which it had burst. At length, it righted and settled on its hind legs to the deck.

Dean had begun to scream.

Mikol might have guessed that a dinosaur exploding into view would traumatize a child of Dean's makeup, but, of course, he hadn't. He grabbed the effigy and thrust it to one side—as if removing it a few centimeters would calm Dean. It didn't. Dean went on wailing, his hands at chest height in heedless parody of the Allosaurus's forepaws.

"It's all right, Dean," Mikol was saying. "Look. It's okay. A make-believe lizard. See. A plaything."

Despite the threat of ear damage, I picked Dean up.

Meanwhile, Etsuko Endo, Thom Koon, and Sidonia Montoya came rushing in to us from the main polyped. A covey of children in bright paper tunics, muumuus, dhotis, or jumpsuits crowded in behind the adults to satisfy their own curiosity. One little girl patted Dean's rump and said, "Shhh, shhh," as I also tried to shush him, but the others either flocked to the dinosaur or clamped their palms over their ears.

"Holy crow!" Dean screamed. "*Mon-stuhrrr!*"

"He could mean you," I told Kazimierz Mikol.

Mikol moved one hand in a rapid back-and-forth arc to keep the kids from the dinosaur. "I'm sorry, Gwiazda. You can't think I wanted *this*. I figured the instant manifestation of a dinosaur would, well, tickle him." He slapped the knuckles of Danny Chung-Barnett, who had weaseled far enough into the corner to grab the effigy's turquoise scrotum.

"Can't you de-pop it?" Etsuko asked over Dean's spookily modulating wail.

"Of course. See this." Mikol pointed to a navy-blue spot behind the balloon's left eye. "Watch."

He jabbed the spot. With a flatulent keen, the Allosaurus collapsed, rekernelized itself, and began to hiss—so that we could find it again. Mikol grabbed up the tiny eye-eye before the Chung-Barnett kid could pounce on and flee with it.

Dean stopped wailing. Chagrined, Mikol told Etsuko, Thom, and Sidonia what had happened. Herding children before them, they went back to the polyped's main activity area, leaving Mikol to struggle with the necessity of apologizing to Dean. To his credit, Mikol apologized.

Insofar as I had perceived him as an enemy, in the next few moments Kazimierz Mikol ceased to exist. The cynic who had viewed my son as a deadly obstacle to our colonizing mission to Epsilon Eridani vanished as suddenly as had the eye-eye dinosaur, leaving behind no speck of grit to flash-reconstitute his hostile persona.

"If carnivorous lizards are out," he said, "what would make a good present for Dean?"

"Stars," I said. "Try stars."

After the debacle in the polyped, Mikol actually resolved to do as I had suggested. He would bestow upon Dean a gift of stars—not by escorting him to an observatory viewport, but instead by allowing Dean to accompany him to Helena Brodkorb's last rites in D-Tower. This trip, over a fifteen-mile arc of the top side of *Annie*'s wheel, would take a good half hour and expose Dean to all the stars salted into the engulfing bowl of space. Seen from the bubbletop on our perimeter car, these stars would prickle, blaze, shimmer, dim, and flare out again: an unceasing festival of light. Dean would watch it all as if bewitched.

"I don't know," I said. "A ride in a perimeter car may terrify him as much as—"

"A dinosaur from the late Cretaceous?"

"Exactly."

"He's had a good look at stars before. You and his mother made sure of that on his birthday."

"But he's never set foot outside G-Tower."

Mikol appealed to Dean. "You don't want to spend the rest of your life in G-Tower. When we go into parking orbit around New

Home, you don't plan to nest in the polyped while everybody else is down exploring the planet. Do you?"

"No surh." Puzzlement and hurt clouded Dean's face. "Not if . . . I doan have to."

"Good for you. So. Would you like to go for a little ride in Peeter?"

Peeter was the name I'd given the perimeter car officially allotted to Towers G–H. Take *rim* from *perimeter*, and you have our magnetic conveyance's pet monicker. It's a silly sort of joke. We call *Annie*'s other three perimeter cars Pauli, MARE (Magnetic Arc-Ranging Elevated), and Albertina. In any case, Mikol spoke the name Peeter on purpose — to flatter me? — even though, as he later confessed, he could not decide if it were genuinely clever or only unbearably cute.

"Yez," Dean said. "I want to ride."

"But he doesn't want to attend the funeral," I said. "Just the sight of sleepers in bioracks—"

"Then he doesn't have to," Mikol cut in. "He can go to the polyped and virch with the other ankle biters."

"Then I'll ride along too."

"Master Gwiazda, do you want your silver-tongued old man to go over to D-Tower with us?"

Solemnly, Dean nodded.

"Then it's settled," Mikol said. "To give ourselves plenty of time, we'll leave at 0750 hours."

Peeter, our magnetic bubbletop, tracked along the front top edge of *Annie Jump*'s breathtaking wheel of underslung hydrogen tanks. From our perches in the car, we could see *Fritz Zwicky* running parallel to us, a ring of diamonds twinkling beyond the silver Möbius strip of our own ark. *Subrahmanyan Chandrasekhar* was an opalescent sheen somewhere off to port. The other two arks were dimly visible to us, of course, only because of their running lights and the mirrored glow from the exhausts of their braking rockets.

Three distinct motions had their common vectors in our rim car: the bubbletop's tortoiselike crawl toward D-Tower, the gravity-producing circumvolution of *Annie*'s fuel ring, and the starward progress of our ark at point-ten C. It seemed to me that these countervailing forces should have ripped us from limb to limb, that our brains and entrails should have flown outward like loose meat in a centrifuge. Instead, we journeyed without incident, three casual travelers poking along the edge of a hurricane slingshot at high speed at infinity.

Dean couldn't keep his eyes off the sky. Starlight sluiced over us like quinine water and guava punch. An alien vista of the Milky Way, familiar but wildly intense. Whorls of gas and dust, a trail of spun sugar crystal. Individual stars guttered and prickled, twinkled and blazed. Nearer to hand, across from us, the underside of *Annie*'s fuel wheel gleamed like the tracks of an archangelic railroad.

"All right, cowboy," Mikol said. "Whaddaya think?"

Dean, his eyes aflicker, continued to gape into the sprawl of God's candelabra.

"Mr. Mikol asked you a question, Dean."

"My friends call me Kaz," Mikol said.

(I'd wondered if he *had* any friends. Bao referred to him only as a professional colleague, and a nettlesomely frosty one at that.)

"Suhr?" Dean said, fuddled.

"Mr. Mikol—Kaz—wants to know what you think of all this."

A second or two lapsed before Dean could find the words he wanted: "Priddy. Holy crow, very priddy."

Kaz patted Dean's knee and laughed.

Peeter inched ahead—in a steep, gleaming silence that held the three of us like prehistoric waterwalkers in a blister of see-through resin. The wheel turned as Peeter inched as *Annie* leapt gully after gully of the interstellar chasm. . . .

Then Kaz—our old nemesis, Kazimierz Mikol—began to talk, his hands in his lap, the methodical wheel of his mind dipping memories from the millstream of his boyhood:

"My grandfather was an immigrant from the liberated Warsaw Pact nations of eastern Europe. He settled in newly democratic Cuba and set up a small factory in the foothills of the Sierra Maestra, manufacturing a vehicle of his own design that ran on a nonpolluting, replenishable fuel distilled from pig shit and sugar-cane fibers. Cuba had lots of pig shit and sugar cane. Grandfather Alexej's oldest son, Milan, who attended university in Poland in the double-twenties, developed the Mikol Process, a type of nanomechanization that brought down the price of the Sabio, our most popular model, so that even streetcleaners in Havana could afford to buy and drive one. In fact, Milan Mikol, my father, stands in relation to my birth century, at least in Cuba, as Henry Ford stood to the twentieth century in North America."

Kaz had apparently aimed this speech at me, for Dean had

tuned him out right after the second mention of pig shit. In our bubbletop, Dean hung beneath the stars like an Earth kid on a midsummer swing.

"I grew up with a sister, Marisa, afflicted with a host of weaknesses that forced my mother to devote herself to her like a nurse. You or I would say that Marisa had cerebral palsy, with severe hemiplegia and ataxia. Mama denied this and said her disabilities stemmed not from brain trauma at birth, but from the influence of an invidious toxin made in the States and sprayed relentlessly on the cane crops of our province. No matter. Marisa had many handicaps; at first, not even constant attention and coaxing enabled her to learn to speak."

Kaz's story had begun to make me uncomfortable. I looked past Dean, who sat between Kaz and me, and asked, "Why tell me all this?"

"Just listen, okay?" Annoyed, he resumed: "The year I was thirteen, Marisa turned eight, and my mother's youngest sister, Helena, just then ten or eleven, jetted over with the Brodkorbs from Poznan—for a visit and a reunion. Helena spelled Mother with Marisa. She spelled me, too, because, hating the task, I now often found myself acting as a care provider. I may have welcomed little Helena to Ciudad Sabio even more vigorously than my mother had, because Helena's presence freed me to swim, hike, and play *beisbol.*

"That same autumn, a movie company from Florida built an amusement park on Pico Torquino, the tallest mountain in Cuba, only a few kilometers from our Sabio factory. The jewel of this set was a Ferris wheel that the filmmakers erected as close to Torquino's summit as they could safely get it. Then, once production had halted, the company's publicity department let it be known, in and around the Sierra Maestra, that locals could ride the Ferris wheel for the equivalent of fifteen American dollars a person on the last three days of October. After the last ride, the company would dismantle the device and return Torquino to its more or less natural state, prior to production.

"Marisa heard of the Ferris wheel. By this time, she had a computer that gave her a voice—a lilting little girl's voice—and she told Mama that she wanted to ride Vireo Films' greatly ballyhooed amusement. She wanted this boon as a birthday gift, before Vireo's roustabouts broke the wheel down and shipped it back to Florida. But, of course, if my parents granted Marisa this wish, they couldn't allow her to ride the Ferris wheel's gondola alone.

"I would have to go with her. I despised North American films and the nauseating hoopla that went with them, and so I absolutely hated this idea. In fact, I had a perverse nostalgia for the days of Fidel Castro, the sort of socialistic idealism that only the well-off son of a millionaire capitalist could afford to indulge. I didn't want to go. I didn't want to take Marisa.

"Helena intervened. She said *she* would ride with Marisa, if Diego, our household's major-domo, drove the two of them up Pico Torquino to Vireo's make-believe amusement park. (Even at thirteen, I heard this last phrase as an egregious bourgeois tautology.) She said it was fine if I chose to stay home, for the combined altitudes of the peak and the Ferris wheel would probably simply cause my snotty nose to bleed. This insult—reverse psychology?—worked, and I angrily offered myself up as Marisa's guardian on this expedition after all. Two evenings later, Diego drove Marisa, Helena, and me up the mountain so we could ride in one of the bright gondolas of the film company's Ferris wheel."

I began to see—dimly, at least—where Kaz was going with this story.

"We rode the wheel—Marisa, Helena, and I. We rode it an hour after sunset. Marisa sat between me and her pretty young aunt from Poznan. What can I say? My nose didn't bleed, but the combined heights of Torquino and that stately illuminated wheel made me tremble like a palmetto leaf in the salty October wind. Believe me, I shivered uncontrollably. Marisa, however, loved the entire experience.

"When our gondola stopped at the top of the wheel and swung back and forth in its gyros, with the south Cuba coast and the smoky mirror of the sea arrayed below us like glossy infrared photographs, Marisa barked her approval—a clipped, excited gasp; a call from the heart. The wheel itself blazed, and the stars of autumn . . . *Dios mió*, some of them seemed to swim in and out of view, shyly, like bronze or pewter carp."

Kaz fell silent.

I laughed nervously. "Remind me never to challenge you to a duel of similes."

"What I understand now," Kaz finally went on, "is that in that Ferris wheel gondola, poised above the darkened island, I loved Marisa, I loved Helena, and I loved the simple day-to-day astonishments of living. Down from Pico Torquino, however, the world—my world, anyway—seemed to change. The Brodkorbs went back to Poland. My mother returned to fussing over Marisa and ignoring the rest of us.

"By the following February, my parents had divorced. Mama, taking Marisa with her, rejoined her sister's family in Poznan, and my father immersed himself in design revisions, production goals, marketing strategies. He died four years later, on a business trip to New York, when Sashimi, a guild of militant Japanese whalers, exploded a pocket nuclear device in a subway tunnel under Grand Central Station. I was in my first year at Havana Tech, gearing up to study particle physics and vacuum propulsion systems."

Even though it seemed that he had just begun another story, Kaz stopped.

"Is that all?" I asked.

"All my life, I blamed Marisa for the loss of my parents. Two days ago, upon learning of Helena's death, I remembered something I couldn't quite remember. Please don't laugh. You see, this incomplete memory softened me. Only when we boarded Peeter and started crawling toward D-Tower did the memory come totally back to me. I have just told it to you, Dr. Gwiazda."

"Abel."

"Abel, then."

Peeter docked with the observatory complex at the summit of D-Tower. Dean had a crick from staring heavenward during our crossing—so, while ambling through the docking connector, he bemusedly rubbed his neck.

In D-Tower, despite *my* misgivings, I believe it gratified Kaz— oddly gratified him—when Dean insisted on going with us to Helena's memorial service: the voiding. (This last term offends me even more than does *ejection*, but, over our trip's past quarter century, it has gained currency and a certain cachet; the puns it embodies are, if nothing else, vivid and expressive.) Kaz realized that Dean wanted more to keep him, his new-found friend, in sight than to attend the funeral of a stranger, but I set aside my objections, and all three of us turned up on part of the observatory deck given over to, well, voidings.

To Kaz's obvious surprise, thirteen people, including our party from G-Tower, had come to honor Helena, who lay, just as promised, on the lingula of the ejector tube.

Commander Stefan Odenwald himself, looking distinguished but gaunt, headed this group of mourners, which also comprised Chaplain Mother Sevier and eight of Helena's friends and colleagues. The service, which I thought dignified and moving, featured brief prayer readings by Odenwald and Chaplain Mother Sevier, a few words by a fellow geneticist, and a holovid of fifteen-year-old Helena singing *"Dona Nobis Pacem"* in a soprano as clear and chilling as ice water.

The holovid scared Dean, but didn't send him careening away from the ceremony. He grabbed my arm and held to it like Quasimodo clinging to a bell rope, his gaze shifting back and forth between the shimmering image of young Helena crooning like an angel and her decidedly aged corpse, recognizable even to Dean as a transfigured but silent version of the beautiful hologhost. Adding to the eeriness of this experience was the fact that young Helena sang her part in rounds with an unseen orpianoogla and an invisible mixed choir. Indeed, their anthem echoed hauntingly throughout the deck.

At its conclusion, Odenwald said, "Mr. Mikol, as Helena Brodkorb's only living relative aboard *Annie Jump Cannon*, you have—if you wish it—the privilege of eulogizing her."

Kaz walked to the lingula, to stand in almost exactly the spot where the hologhost had sung. Bending, he kissed Helena's cold temple.

"From Pico Torquino to Epsilon Eridani," he said, standing erect again, "Helena Brodkorb was not afraid of heights. She dwelt on them. Like Harry Martinson, she knew that 'space can never be more cruel than man, / more than its match is human callousness.' And so, unlike me, she was never cruel."

Which was all Kaz could steady himself to say. He put a hand over his mouth and stared at Helena's sunken eyes and lovely complexion. Meanwhile, Dean threaded a path through the other mourners to stand next to Kaz in mute condolence.

Odenwald said, "Shall we commend her now to the stars?"

Kaz nodded.

The lingula on which Helena Brodkorb lay retracted into its tube. A maintenance tech among the mourners used a remote to seal the tube and activate its plunger. Although no one on the deck could see her go, Kaz's dead aunt hurtled outward like a torpedo—far beyond the gravitational attraction of any of the armada's wheelships.

"Because we're decelerating," Commander Odenwald observed, "Helena Brodkorb will reach Epsilon Eridani before us."

"And eventually pass on out of the system into interstellar space again," said a colleague.

The company fell silent again. No one appeared to want to move.

After a time, I said: "May I speak?"

When Chaplain Mother Sevier nodded, I recited:

*"So very human,
To grieve and to entomb.*

*This ardent woman
We cremate in the cold.*

*No longer may we hold
Her from her spacious home."*

"Amen," said Chaplain Mother Sevier, crossing herself.
Finally, we funeral goers broke up and departed.

Back in G-Tower, Kaz opted to remain up-phase for the remainder of our armada's voyage. He has been spelling me with Dean as once, years ago, Helena Brodkorb spelled his mother and him with his handicapped sister, Marisa.

We have entered the Barricado Stream, a region a good deal less clogged with debris than a few of our astronomers had earlier supposed. The probe dropped by *Zwicky* has determined recently that the Stream hosts only one substantial cometary mass per each sphere the approximate size of the Earth's orbit around Sol. Good news. Very good news.

"There's hardly any chance at all we'll hit a comet," Nita Sistrunk said yesterday in the G-Tower mess.

But Bao added, "It isn't the comet-sized bodies we must fear. Remember, though, if *big* masses whirl around out here, there may also be smaller but more perfidious bodies impossible to detect at a distance."

"What do you mean?" I asked.

"You don't really want to know." And Bao deftly changed the direction of our talk.

In any event, more and more personnel aboard our three wheelships have come up-phase. We still have some journeying to do to reach New Home, at least another standard year's worth, but excitement mounts. Also, the staggered awakening of adults from the enchantment of ursidormizine slumber has delighted the children, and each pulse of our matter-antimatter engines seems a quickening heartbeat. The peculiar atmosphere of a seminar-cum-carnival has gripped *Annie*; also *Chandrasekhar* and *Zwicky*. I wonder if Pharoah's royal architect had a like sense of culminating accomplishment upon realizing that only a few more blocks would complete his master's pyramid.

Lily has come up-phase. She still can't believe that nasty Kazimierz Mikol has ingratiated himself with Dean—altogether sincerely, however—as a kind of uncle. Nor does she believe that Kaz and I have become friends. And, in fact, I prefer Thich Ngoc Bao's company to his, or Nita Sistrunk's, or Matthew Rashad's, a compatriot among the geologists. Our personalities (mine and Kaz's, that is) scrape against rather than complement each other's.

Nevertheless, we've hammered out a crumpled sort of mutual respect. Lily can't imagine how. I've told her about Helena Brodkorb's death and our rim-car trip to and from D-Tower, but, not having experienced these herself, she remains skeptical of everything about Kaz except his clear, if startling, affection for Dean.

"It's like the tiger and the lamb on the same bed of straw," she says. "A fearful symmetry whose opposing balances I can't quite grasp."

"Don't try," I tell her. "Just enjoy."

Lily simply shakes her head and laughs, a gruff chuckle so like Dean's that I gape. My look prompts more laughter and a sudden peck on my cheek.

"I like you more today than when we first met," she says. "More than on DeBoy's last birthday, even."

"Why is that?"

"You've started going gray," Lily tells me. "I've always liked older men."

Commander Stefan Odenwald stood in *Annie*'s pilothouse, supervising its computer-aimed passage through the Barricado. Our other two arks ran parallel to *Annie*'s course at port and starboard distances of about seventy kilometers. Nonetheless, each of the other ships remained dimly visible to everyone in the pilothouse, either on TV monitors or through the shielded viewports of the domelike bridge. A simultaneous look at the two vessels depended, of course, on the pilothouse's rotating to either the top or the bottom of the fuel wheel's orbit vis-à-vis the headlong motion of the other two ships, but this happened often enough to thrill Dean and me, and seldom enough to increase our anticipation.

For a long time, I guess, Odenwald had realized that Dean enjoyed looking at the stars as much as anyone else aboard; therefore, he had invited us into the pilothouse, a structure midway between Towers A–B and G–H on the ever-clocking fuel ring, and had there installed Dean in the thronelike chair that inevitably, and a bit sardonically, we call the Helm, as if it willy-nilly grants its occupant both authority and navigational savvy.

The Helm swallowed Dean. His feet dangled half a meter from the deck, and his chunky little body resembled that of a ventriloquist's dummy. Thankfully, he took no notice of the chair's scale, but turned his neckless head from side to side, ceaselessly ogling the universe.

"You look like—" Odenwald began. He turned to the other officers in the pilothouse. "Who? You know, that holovid space explorer, what's-his-name?"

"I'm almost completely ignorant of such entertainments," I admitted—with an undercurrent of pride that Odenwald did not seem to find off-putting. It suggested, as it should, that I had better things to do.

On the other hand, I had often petitioned Odenwald for this audience, here in *Annie*'s control center, for my handicapped son, and surely that petition told him more about me than did any cheap slam at the junk on holovid.

"Can I?" Dean said. "Can I steer?"

"Have you mastered astronavigation, wheelship helming, and the rights and obligations of cybernetic command?"

"No suhr," Dean told Odenwald meekly.

"Well, then, you can't steer. But you're the only person besides myself to occupy that chair since we left lunar orbit in our own solar system."

"So far as you know," I put in.

Odenwald laughed. "Yes. So far as I know."

The TV monitor taking transmission from the *Subrahmanyan Chandrasekhar* showed all of us on the bridge the face of a haggard Caucasian male. I recognized him as one of Commander Joplin's lieutenants, Wolfgang Krieg.

"*Attention!* Commanders Odenwald and Roosenno, *attention!*" the haggard face said. "We appear to be on a collision course with a stream of frozen debris—gravel, call it—that initially composed a single mass about two meters in circumference. This stream of material—"

Odenwald took the mike. "*Initially?*" he said. "What do you mean, initially? What happened to it?"

"When we radar-sighted the object, we could see it would hit us," Krieg said. "Having no time to change course, we used our laser to try to deflect it."

"By vaporizing one side of the body to push it in another direction?" Odenwald theorized.

"Yessir," Krieg said.

"But, instead of moving aside, the object fragmented?"

"Yessir. The resulting stream of debris will strike us in two minutes fifty-three seconds."

Odenwald said, "How may we assist?"

"Get yourselves out of here," Krieg replied. "You might also want to pray."

Odenwald gave an order to activate the siphons to draw fuel from the C–D to E–F hydrogen tanks down the spokes to their matter-antimatter propulsion system. Kaz appeared from nowhere to do exactly that, while Odenwald ran the ignition programs. Bridge officers on *Zwicky* followed suit. Despite their size, both wheelships shoved agilely ahead, out of the energy-saving coast marking the latest stage of our years-long deceleration process.

"Don't look at the exhaust trail!" I told Dean.

But Dean *was* looking at it, a blazing bore of magnesium-white light that had already turned our wheel's opposite inner arc into an eye-stinging mirror. If he kept looking at it, he'd burn out his retinas. Blessedly, just as I started to push his face into his lap, Dean averted his gaze.

At that instant, the monitor receiving from *Chandrasekhar* filled with popping kinetic snow. *Chandrasekhar* itself, one instant past a platinum ring on a bolster of sequined black felt, flashed out like a miniature nova, a wound of radiance even brighter than *Annie*'s exhaust trail. Then, after the flash, in the place where the space ark had been: nothing but blackness. Every light on its rim, every light in its habitat towers, snapped out.

Immediately, though, a series of explosions on the wheel went off in astonishing sequence, like a silent Fourth of July gala with Roman candles, phosphorus bombs, and self-shredding parachutes of light. The sight of these distant fireworks froze me in place, for, as the disaster unraveled, there was nothing that anyone on either of our sibling arks could do—except imagine both the terror and the agony of our companions aboard the splintering ship.

Later, Bao and others postulated, the biggest chunk of the fragmented rock tracking *Chandrasekhar* had hit and severed its rim. Simultaneously, the gravel from Krieg's misguided attempt to deflect this object ripped into the fuel spokes *cum* support cables. Then centrifugal force took over, tearing the vessel apart. Broken tentacles of diamond writhed in the blackness. The electromagnetic levitation tanks holding the antihydrogen ice clear of the ordinary matter making up the ark's set-apart propulsion unit took ricocheting hits of their own, emitting, as a result, such hot bursts of radiation that the sky flared again and many of the ark's buckled compartments actually began to melt.

This catastrophe stunned me. I could think of nothing like it in the history of spacefaring. The *Challenger* disaster might qualify, or the fate of the Chinese ship *Wuer Kaixi* off Titan late in 2057, but these events seemed so remote, and so happily limited in their life-taking scale, that the emptiness off to starboard, the afterglow of so many doomed lives, left me groping for some competent or humane response.

"Whuh?" Dean murmured. "What happen?"

Odenwald looked at him. Dean, in turn, looked to him for some hopeful reordering of the chaos that had inflicted itself on the sky outside our blister.

The incandescence, then the cold.

The kaleidoscopic brightness, then the dark.

"Please tell him, sir," I said. "And don't sugarcoat it."

Voices from *Fritz Zwicky* rattled in the pilothouse. Radio operators in the communications well bent to their tasks. Two of Odenwald's lieutenants rushed in from the attached day room and lounge. Their concern—their activity—could not reverse the fate of *Chandrasekhar* or rescue a single person in any of its radiation-drenched habitation towers. All, like data in an irretrievably crashed program, were gone or going, already almost less than ciphers.

But it was Kaz, not Odenwald, who finally knelt in front of Dean's chair. "They hit something, or something hit them. A chunk of ice about like so." Kaz made a circle of his arms. "Maybe even a little smaller. Which split into pieces when the people on *Chandry* tried to move it."

"But how. . . ?"

"As fast as we're going, hitting an object that size makes a bang like the burst of a fission device." Kaz looked at me. "Sorry. He's never heard of Hiroshima, right? Or the Sashimi attacks on New York and L.A.?"

"Can it happen to uz?"

Kaz looked to me for permission. I nodded.

"Yes, it could," Kaz said. "At the moment, though, we're outrunning the blast. If this helps at all, Dean, we should go fairly quickly if we hit something."

Dean began to cry. "I'm sorry that happen," he said. "I'm sorree-sorree."

"Me too," Kaz said.

Odenwald came over and said he wanted Dean and me off the bridge. I picked Dean up, and Odenwald advised us to retreat to the day room while he spoke with Roosenno and some of his lieutenants about the morale and logistical implications of the disaster.

Dean and I left.

Two hours later, when it seemed to Odenwald and his closest advisors, including Bao, that we'd outrun any pursuing debris, our ships cut their engines and drifted back into the coasting mode of our long advance on Epsilon Eridani II.

If we survive the Stream, none of us will ever forget what has happened out here. Ever.

Mere chance enabled Dean to witness the destruction of a wheelship. Nonetheless, I blame myself for putting him in a place to see the spectacular melting or vaporization of sixteen hundred human beings.

And Dean? He understands that *Chandrasekhar* and all its passengers have passed into physical oblivion. Kaz and I both tell him it's possible that God has received their souls, but, despite my religion, I remain a militant skeptic on this point, and Dean no longer asks if the victims of the disaster have gone to heaven. It both frets and wearies him to hear me say, "Dean, I don't know."

He also grasps, by the way, the peril of traveling at even a mere fraction of light-speed. He knows that *Annie Jump* or *Fritz Zwicky* could blaze out, novalike, as Commander Joplin's wheelship did. This knowledge has penetrated his awareness as deeply as, if not more deeply than, anything else he has ever learned. Sometimes (for me, red-letter occasions for guilt and moroseness), he remembers the catastrophe, bolts upright, and begins to rock and sway.

"Why?" he says. "Why?"

The basic existential inquiry.

And I wonder if Lily and I sinned against Dean, ourselves, or the incessant nag of the life force by bringing him to be in this precarious flying tin can.

Kaz says to ice the gloom-and-doom, the self-debates, the ontological kvetching.

A word to the wise? Not with *this* target audience: I don't qualify.

An arkboard month has passed. We have broken clear of the Barricado Stream—computationally, if not in our hearts. Our learned astronomers inform us that we have wide riding ahead, unobstructed glissading to New Home. Scant solace to the dead, of course, and scant comfort to either Dean or me.

More than once I've tried to eulogize the victims of this prodigious calamity. My words back up on me; my rhymes, even the off ones, don't quite slot; my rhythms, sprung or unsprung, drill like drugged acephalics in jackboots. At last I wrote a stanza:

> *With a charged, chance suddenness,*
> *The all of spinning* Chandrasekhar,
> *The all of its ark, flashed to dark and spun to less*
> *Than a heat-dead, hooded star:*
> *A nova, an aura, an aroma of light-speed-sizzled thought,*
> *Brains broiled, skin fried, the atomizing mystery and mess,*
> *Actinic sabotage of each blind arrogance we bought*
> *With the hardware-software-psychware of our ever-shoving-onward high-tech-tied success.*

Yesterday Bao asked if I've made any headway on the elegy everyone assumes I'll write. Reluctantly, I showed him this stanza. "Read it aloud," he said. There in the G-Tower mess, I lowered both head and voice and recited it.

Only Bao, thank God, could hear me. Kaz would have flung my comppad aside and stalked off, to seek better company in the finch-filled atrium.

"That's pretty," Bao said. A dig.

"So was the little mishap that triggered it."

"True. But I would have never taken you, my friend, for a Hopkins enthusiast."

This remark startled me. Bao had realized from the get-go that the paradigm for my stanza was an elegy by Gerard Manley Hopkins. I sat back and stared at him.

"Nor I you," I said.

Bao laughed. Then, with no physical prompts whatsoever, he recited:

> *"With a mercy that outrides*
> *The all of water, an ark*
> *For the listener; for the lingerer with a love glides*
> *Lower than death and the dark;*
> *A vein for the visiting of the past-prayer, pent in prison,*
> *The-last-breath penitent spirits—the uttermost mark*
> *Our passion-plunged giant risen,*
> *The Christ of the Father compassionate, fetched in the storm of his strides."*

"How can you do that?" I said. "Remember it all?"

Bao laughed again. "Stanza thirty-three. Because I've had Heraclitus call it up repeatedly since the accident. Balm from a long-dead Jesuit."

"I would have never taken you for an incarnationist, Bao, and certainly not one of a papist stamp."

Nothing marred Bao's hollow-cheeked amiability. "The wise take their comfort where they can."

"The wise seldom choke down such bilge."

Bao, grunting, grabbed his chest as if I'd just slipped a blade into his heart. He recovered at once, a fey smile on his lips. "Your stanza clatters where the Jesuit's sings, my dear unable Abel."

"Then I guess I'd better delete it."

"Ah, a wiser man than I'd supposed." He put a hand on my wrist. "Don't, though. Save it, as a ward against hubris." He released me, finished eating his vegetable shell, and, with a smile and a bad parting joke, excused himself. None of Bao's observations on either wisdom or comfort-taking had recast my own opinions; however, sitting and talking with him had cheered me. I kept the lone stanza of my come-a-cropper elegy, but attempted no others.

Later, in a geology carrel, I had Heraclitus call up "The Wreck of the Deutschland" and read it twice from beginning to end. If mere language can redeem a disaster, I believe Hopkins redeemed his.

Fuel rings turning like mountain-high Ferris wheels, *Annie Jump* and *Fritz Zwicky* have completely traversed the Barricado Stream. We have penetrated the orbit of Epsilon Eridani V, the system's outermost planet, an ice ball known to every member of our expedition as Cold Cock. New Home lies nearly 5.7 billion kilometers farther in, in the direction of Eppie herself; and our fleet, calamitously dispossessed of one of its arks, flies at a scant percentage of light-speed, a million kilometers per hour. At this rate, given the need to slow still more, it will take almost a year to reach our destination.

The hydrogen harvesters we deployed shortly after entering the Barricado, great funnels of molecularly strengthened mylar, will not only add calibrated drag to our deceleration, but resupply the exhausted tanks on the rim arcs between habitat towers. From the G-Tower observatory, it sometimes appears that we haul behind us the iridescent bladders of immense Portuguese men-of-war. Floats or wings? No one seems to know how to regard them. Sometimes, we can't see them at all. In any case, gathering hydrogen makes little sense, given that, by the time we reach New Home, our ships will have almost wholly depleted the antihydrogen ice required by our matter-antimatter rockets for further travel.

Ours not to reason why. . . .

Days (or arkboard hours comprising their equivalent) ghost past as our last two vessels simultaneously plummet and wheel through this alien system. Up-phase scientists, technicians, engineers, and support personnel work methodically to prepare for planetfall and the colonization of New Home. Much of this preparation—plan comparisons, logistical projections, computer simulations—has to do with adjusting for the loss of the vital skills and labor units destroyed along with Commander Joplin's *Subrahmanyan Chandrasekhar*. On the other hand, our expedition's organizers factored in an atoning redundancy: personnel on any one ark can meet and overcome, by themselves, the environmental challenges of our target world. If a disaster befalls *Zwicky*, then *Annie* has the wherewithal to succeed.

And, of course, vice versa.

Less than halfway to the gas giant Jawbreaker (named for its bands of umber, licorice, and cherry, as well as for the fact that it has more than twice the mass of Jupiter), an astronomy group met with Odenwald in the observatory. This group (as Thich Ngoc Bao told me later that same evening) consisted of Nita Sistrunk, Indira Sescharchari, Pete Ohanessian, and Bao himself.

Actually, after putting Dean to bed in our cubicle on the mezzanine level, I hitched a lift to the observatory for some private time to unwind and found Bao slumped in a swivel chair in a consultation bay not far from the ABVT. The door to this bay stood open, and, upon sighting Bao, who had made himself uncharacteristically scarce for the past seventy-two hours, I slipped in and greeted him.

"Hey."

Bao jumped as if I'd popped an eye-eye in front of him. Recognizing me, he composed himself and gave me a wan grin. His skin looked sallow, drum-tight.

"Doctor," I said, "what's up?"

"The jig," said Bao. "Old American expression. The game is over. Our hopes are dashed. Or, at least, a hefty plenty of them."

I sat down in a swiveler across from Bao, in front of an HD screen as big as a door. "We're surfing different wavelengths, friend o' mine."

"Tonight," Bao said, "our group presented to Odenwald the radio, spectrographic, and visual evidence that New Home may not be habitable to human beings."

My gut corkscrewed around itself. "Come again?"

"We did so—Indira, Nita, Pete, and I—as if discussing mutation rates in fruit flies. Very professionally. As if our findings had only hypothetical significance to our arkmates and the people on *Zwicky*. In truth, we all felt blown away, Abel—nuked, one could say."

I leaned forward. "Bao, are you violating confidentiality telling me this?"

"I hardly think so. Tomorrow morning, the news will have spread all over both ships."

"Then go ahead. Tell me."

Bao rocked back, resting his ankle on his knee. "All right. Nita showed Odenwald a series of photographs—computer amplified and enhanced—revealing New Home as an ugly-looking marble, a hard little sphere rotating under drifting rinds of reddish-brown dust and ejecta. The water we discovered by spectrographic analysis while outside the Barricado lay hidden under enmantling dust. Odenwald stared at us—his magi, so to speak—as if we'd led Herod right to him."

"*Ejecta?*" I said. "What's going on? Volcanic activity? A worldwide dust storm?"

"Odenwald asked the same question, and Nita said, 'The dust storm's real enough, but Bao worries more about its causes.'

" 'What do you think's happened?' Odenwald asked me.

"I told him that not long ago—possibly just before we drew within the orbit of the fifth planet—an asteroidal object the size of Mexico City burned through New Home's atmosphere and impacted with the surface. The stratospheric blizzard wrapping the planet derives from material crater-blasted upward by this nomadic body's impact.

"Odenwald turned over one of Nita's lovely gloomy photos, as if its other side would nullify my words. When it didn't, he thoughtfully replaced it in its sequence.

" 'What does this mean for us?' he asked. 'As refugees in search of a livable world?'

" 'Nothing good,' Pete Ohanessian said.

" 'Itemize, please,' Odenwald insisted.

"Nita reached over and touched his wrist—trying, you see, to console him. Meanwhile, though, she told him that infrared absorption spectroscopy would give us the best look at current conditions on the planet.

" 'Dr. Sescharchari has the results,' she said. 'Indira?' "

Here, Indira had showed him a slide. So Bao punched a button, and the very slide in question flashed up on the HD screen behind me. When I swung about in my chair to look at it, an arrow jumped onto the screen over New Home's latest IR absorption spectrum.

Bao resumed his story:

"Indira said, 'This slide compares data taken on the trip out with more recently obtained info. This peak at around ten microns—' " the arrow landed on it " '—is carbon dioxide, and you can see from the corresponding peak here—' " the arrow bounced again " '—that the atmosphere's carbon dioxide content has risen dramatically as a result of the collision. We hypothesize that the vaporization of a lot of carbonate rock—namely, limestone—from the asteroid strike triggered the jump in CO_2. You can also add to that the CO_2 produced by the combustion of biomass—grasses, trees, who knows what else?—in the resulting firestorm. But even more alarming is that the levels of carbon dioxide continue to rise.'

" 'Why?' Odenwald demanded."

Indira told him she'd get back to that and noted that the second peak on the spectrum represented the absorption from the NO_2 molecule, nitric oxide. Bao, quoting Dr. Sescharchari, said that fumes from nitric oxide present two real problems for would-be colonists. First, the acid has a bite. Only idiots would try to land with it contaminating the ecosphere. Second, and even worse, the nitric acid has apparently begun to release even more carbon dioxide from New Home's limestone. To get an idea of the process, think of sodium carbonate—ordinary baking soda—in a bath of vinegar, fizzing away.

"Cripes, Bao, you've got to be kidding."

"I wish." He got up and began to pace. "Pete Ohanessian took over from Indira and told Odenwald that the most efficient natural mechanism for removing CO_2 from a world's atmosphere is probably photosynthesis. Unfortunately, Abel, we think the asteroid strike and the firestorm have wiped out all but about five percent of New Home's vegetation. God, or Fate, has smashed the thermostat on that planet. When New Home comes out of its Ice

Age—below-freezing temperatures everywhere, all a result of the dust cloud shrouding it—Pete thinks the planet could fall victim to the runaway greenhouse effect."

In this scenario, Bao told me, atmospheric CO_2 provokes warming via standard greenhouse action. Carbon dioxide levels in cold water drops with added temperature, even more CO_2 outgasses as CO_2 once dissolved in polar oceans comes out of solution. Hence, even faster warming. As temperatures keep going up, the seas begin to evaporate, and H_2O is a more powerful greenhouse gas than CO_2. Water and carbon dioxide working together slow the escape of infrared energy into space. The hotter New Home grows, the more water vapor in its atmosphere: a steady amping up of the greenhouse effect. Many thick blanketlike layers swaddle the planet, letting solar heat in but trapping the heat generated below. Eventually, New Home's equatorial seas start to boil.

"New Home seems to be something of a misnomer," I said.

Bao chuckled mirthlessly. "Well, perhaps not. We've done some very careful modeling to establish how close the planet is to the edge of Epsilon Eridani's habitable zone. It does lie on the inward edge of the zone, but at sufficient distance from Eppie to avoid a complete greenhouse runaway."

"Won't things ever get back to normal?"

"What's normal?" Bao said. "But, of course, that's what Odenwald wanted to know. Pete told him that a counterbalancing geological process could reverse the situation." Bao grinned a dare at me. "Any idea what it is, *Dr. Gwiazda*?"

The question caught me off guard. "Weathering?"

"You're the geology man. I'm asking you."

"Weathering," I said more forcefully.

"Care to explain it?"

"Spectroscopy implies New Home's mantle consists of calcium and magnesium silicates, right?"

"I guess so. Pete, at least, concurs."

"Then the planet's atmospheric CO_2 will react slowly with these silicates to make calcium and magnesium carbonate. The process speeds up in hot, damp air, binding carbon dioxide into the planet's limestone. Temperatures drop. With this cooling, water vapor precipitates out. The greenhouse effect decreases, along with the temperature. In the end, New Home returns to 'normal.' How long will it take? I don't know. My specialty is soils. And we still don't know the percentage of anorthitic rock in New Home's exposed crust."

Bao smiled. "Maybe you should have briefed Odenwald too."
"What time-scale estimate did Pete offer?"
"He hemmed and hawed. I don't blame him. We lack solid values for anorthitic rock and the rate of vulcanism."
"Come on, Bao."
"A century or so. For sure, less than two hundred years. Maybe as few as fifty."

Hearing this, I thought first of Dean, now asleep in Lily's care. Such news would crush him. Lily, too. It was crushing *me*, like sixteen tons of granite on my chest. Had we traveled more than a century to reach a world that would accept us as colonists only after we had stewed in our bioracks another one hundred years?

"Yes," Bao said. "New Home's something of a misnomer." He punched a button on the arm of his chair and the speakers next to the HD screen activated. A recorded discussion garbled past on fast-forward. Bao stopped it. "After Pete talked, some of my colleagues got silly. Listen."

Nita: "Dead End might be a better name."
Indira: "Or Crater Quake."
Pete: "Or Pot Hole. Or Acid Bath."
Nita: "Gloomandoom!"
Indira: "Bitter Pill! Or maybe—"
Bao: "That's enough!"
Odenwald: "Easy, Bao—I was about to propose an irreverent name of my own."
Bao: "Sir, the purpose of this session is to brief you, not to divert ourselves."
Odenwald: "Maybe we should divert *Annie* to another planet in this system."
Nita: "Which? Jelly Belly? Red Hot?"
Pete: "The gravity on Jawbreaker would crush us. We'd do as well to set down on Eppie herself."
Nita: "Or as ill."
Bao: "We should continue to New Home. First-hand studies of the environmental aftermath of an asteroid strike this large are virtually nonexistent. We should follow up."
Indira: "But for whose sake?"
Odenwald: "You all have your work. I have mine. And my first duty is to break the news."
Nita: "You'll break hearts as well."
Pete: "A better time might be—"

Odenwald: "Traveling at nearly a million klicks per hour, there's no time like the present."

Bao halted the recording.

"Nita was right," I said. "The news has broken my heart. And it's sure to break others."

Bao toasted me with an imaginary shot glass, then slugged back its imaginary contents.

Lily broke the bad tidings to Dean. She insisted on her prerogative in this. In his self-appointed role as goduncle, Kaz tagged along.

We took Dean to a glade in the atrium, a stand of sycamores bonsai'd artfully near a waterfall encased in a sort of panpipe of clear plastic. In this secluded place, the falling water, pump-driven and -recirculated, made its tremulous woodwind and brook music.

Kaz lifted Dean to a notch in one of the sycamores and then tactfully wandered away. Lily took up a post beside Dean, to catch him if he slipped, while I sat on a bench masquerading as a ledge on the face of our miniature cascade.

Finches warbled, and, not far away, another party murmured among themselves, their talk a faint counterpoint to the water noise and the nonstop background hum.

"DeBoy, I have to tell you a very unpleasant thing," Lily began. "New Home won't be our new home, after all." She told him about our discovery of the recent asteroid strike and its meaning for everyone aboard our remaining ships—namely, either a frustrating wait until environmental conditions improved on Eppie's second planet or another long interstellar journey to another solar system with potential for settlement, most likely the Tau Ceti system.

None of this seemed to impress Dean. He sat in the dwarf sycamore gazing upward, and all around, for a glimpse of one of the finches.

"Do you understand me?" Lily asked. "We've come all this way, DeBoy, and New Home may be denied us."

"Yessum." Dean gave her a grudging, shifty-eyed nod.

"It's all right to feel sad. It's even all right to cry."

Our ingrate son kept rubbernecking for birds.

"*Dean!*"

So quickly did Dean's gaze snap back to Lily that he had to grab a limb. "I *like* it here," he said. "Now that evvybody's ub . . . *up* . . . I like it jes fine."

Almost against my will, I guffawed.

Lily shot me an I'm-going-to-kill-you glare that modulated, almost against *her* will, into a defeated grin.

Whereupon Hiller Nevels, a botanist named Gulnara Golovin, and Milo Pask, a habitat engineer, came strolling toward us, arguing or at least expostulating among themselves. Golovin had her hand consolingly on Pask's arm, and none of the three seemed at all aware of our own family group, not even when Kaz trudged back into the clearing and halted in some puzzlement at the sight of them.

". . . *won't* get over it!" Pask was saying. "To travel over a century and learn on your final approach that a stupid rock from the sky has turned the planet of your dreams into a gas chamber! Why did I come? I'm supposed to build habitat geodesics, water and sewer systems. Now, I can't. I've come all this way for no reason!"

Golovin said, "You can't do your job *now*, that's all this setback means. Wait for the dust and the acid rain to settle out. A kind of normality will return to New Home. What's another year—even two—given all our years in transit? Milo, from the very beginning we knew we were living with a deferred ambition."

"Besides," said Hiller, "we had no guarantee any planet out here would prove a cozy place to camp."

Pask brushed Golovin's hand from his arm and rounded on Hiller. "Maybe not when we set out. But the closer we got to Eppie and the more that thick-headed gook and his star-gazing cronies learned, the more flowery they got about how New Home was Shangri-la and how grandly the place would welcome us. We hadn't come all this way just to rot in our biovracks. So they told us. The incompetent buggers!"

"Except for the asteroid strike, I think they appraised New Home accurately," Golovin said. "I don't see how you can hold them responsible for an act of God."

"We can't even hold *God* responsible for an act of God!" Pask raged. "So I'm scapegoating Thich and his sickening ilk. Do you mind?"

"Irrationality doesn't become you, Milo," Golovin said. "Stop it."

"No. But I become it, don't I?" Finally catching sight of Dean, Pask strode over with a weird glimmer in his eyes. "Who could have predicted this turn of events? This kid? Yeah, the kid. *Annie*'s resident . . . gnomic gnome."

Lily said, "Lay off, Milo."

Pask reddened as if she'd disparaged either his engineering skills or his virility, not simply rebuked him for bullying a child.

"What're the odds?" he asked. "What're the odds that New Home would take a lousy asteroid hit during our expedition's final approach?"

"I have no idea," Lily said.

"Well, I'll tell you. Statistically, Dr. Aliosi-Stark, the chances are something like a trillion to one. *A trillion to buggering one!*"

"I don't think so," Lily said.

"You don't, do you?"

"Given the event itself, I'd say that, statistically, the chances are one hundred percent."

Now Pask looked at Lily as if she'd slapped him. His face crumpled. Without attempting to mitigate or hide the fact, he began to cry. Dean followed suit. I took Dean out of the tree and held him. Lily hugged Pask.

"I want to leap into the same swallowing blackness everyone on *Chandrasekhar* leapt into," Pask said.

"You should talk to someone," Lily told him.

"I've talked to Hiller and Gulnara," Pask said. "Now I'm talking to you. Talk doesn't heal, it just turns into more of itself." Regaining a degree of control, he wiped his eyes and reset his twisted features.

Seeing Pask calm himself, Dean quieted.

"That may be," I said. "But you should still sit down for a while with Etsuko Endo. Soon."

Pask wouldn't commit to this, but Golovin agreed to contact Etsuko on his behalf. Then she and Hiller led him out of the glade, and out of the atrium, in search of someone to dismantle his dread.

Kaz took Dean from me, and Dean leaned his head on Kaz's shoulder. "I like it here," Dean said.

Whether he meant his nook of the atrium or life in general aboard the ark, I had no idea.

New Home—or Acid Bath, or Dead End, or Bitter Pill, as the more mordant of our expedition's surviving members insist on calling the world—has no moon. Not long ago, *Annie Jump* and *Fritz Zwicky* took up orbits about ten thousand kilometers out, orbits that bestow on them—in the minds of our astronomy specialists and a few of our anonymous dreamers—exactly that status.

The two great ships, their own wheels rotating, turn about New Home like diamond-lit satellites, *Annie Jump* half a klick farther out—higher—than *Fritz Zwicky* but otherwise in rough parallel with its sibling. If any sentient species lives on the world below, and if roiling dust didn't veil the night sky from the ground, the sight of our two staggered wheels turning overhead would surely prompt stillness and then awe among their unknowable kind.

Aboard *Annie*, I imagine myself swinging in the gondola of a Ferris wheel on a lofty New Home peak, gazing into the night at this manmade binary cluster. In fact, I go on to imagine myself imagining myself as a passenger on one of our glittering rings. Lost in this double fantasy, I prefer the image of myself in New Home's transfigured sky: Orion orating in the heavens, not some mute Sherpa in the Himalayas.

I want to blaze, not to slog and grapple. Given my choice, I want to god-fashion myself in fire—even if the attempt slays me, even if no one but the greedy homunculus in my own breast hears my Promethean cri de coeur.

At 0800 hours tomorrow—measuring time by Greenwich mean time, as we still do aboard *Annie*—we will boost away from New Home and park ourselves nearer her sun, to begin the refueling process that will eventually take us to Tau Ceti.

The majority of us will travel down-phase, in ursidormizine slumber. Commander Stefan Odenwald will yield the bridge and his primary continuity-preserving duties to Hiller Nevels and a fresh team of self-sacrificing troubleshooters, all volunteers, for Odenwald hopes to wake with legs fresh enough to climb a lovely new peak on the world that we discover and colonize in the Tau Ceti system.

Who can blame him? He has aged beyond any of the rest of us, excepting only Commander Roosenno, who will stay here in the Epsilon Eridani system, and Commander Joanna Diane Joplin, who ceased aging forever in the fatal millrace of the Barricado Stream.

As noted, the personnel aboard *Zwicky* will remain in orbit around New Home for as long as it takes to outlast the surface inferno brought about by the impact of the asteroid that Bao has named Epimenides, after a figure in Greek mythology who, while seeking a lost sheep, fell asleep for fifty-seven years and on awakening resumed his search unaware that so much time had passed. The oracle of Delphi then recruited Epimenides to cleanse Athens of a plague. Bao sees parallels between our slumbers and Epimenides', and between *Zwicky*'s task upon coming awake and that of the ancient Greek shepherd.

Briefly, Roosenno, like Odenwald, plans to send most of his would-be colonists down-phase until planetary conditions permit their revival. Then they will undertake the daunting task of turning New Home into a permanent human colony. Blessedly, the ark-to-ark redundancy of our skills makes the separate agendas of our ships both feasible and attractive. The survival of our kind, we feel, depends not only on diversity, but also on our projection across as much of the inhabitable or terraformable galaxy as we can reach.

How did we make these decisions? Mostly democratically, in the extraordinary session I will now describe.

Twelve days ago, when Odenwald first broached this plan in the auditorium of *Annie*'s A-Tower, few of us could credit that he wanted us to vote on an "option" as hare-brained as *resuming* our expedition. We had gathered, after dozens and dozens of rim-car trips, to discuss the issue in face-to-face assembly (rather than from separate electronic carrels), and the first question from the floor surprised no one, least of all Stefan Odenwald himself.

"How can we go to another solar system when by most cogent reckonings, we've nearly exhausted our supplies of antihydrogen ice?" Thom Koon asked this for everyone but about thirty techs and/or scientists already in the know.

At the head of our banner-hung auditorium, Odenwald asked Thich Ngoc Bao to reply. Bao stepped to the podium to address us: "Good evening."

I had Dean in my lap, for Odenwald had told us that no one should miss this gathering; that, in fact, children should also attend.

So when Bao said, "Good evening," we replied in kind, like children answering a teacher.

Dean, waving crazily, called out, *"Bao! Bao! Bao!"* until I brought his arm down and whispered as quietly as the noise level allowed, "Hush, DeBoy. Hush."

Dean hushed.

"Hydrogen is no problem," Bao said confidently, his reedy voice echoing. "We harvested this fuel during the deceleration process, from the Barricado on in."

"What about antihydrogen?" Thom cried. "Do you guys plan to turn regular hydrogen molecules inside out?"

Bao shifted his weight. "You should know that every ship in our armada, including *Chandrasekhar—*" he briefly shut his eyes "—was built with the capacity to generate antihydrogen for travel *beyond* the Epsilon Eridani system."

This news stunned most of us in the A-Tower auditorium. I had certainly never supposed us to have the ability to journey to another system, perhaps even back to Earth. And none of my friends—with the conspicuous exception of Thich Ngoc Bao—had suspected it either.

"How can we do that?" somebody shouted.

"Each ark is also a cyclotron, a particle accelerator," Bao said. "Each accelerator runs right down the underside of the fuel wheel itself, around its circumference. Given enough time and energy, the cyclotron belting *Annie Jump* will produce the hydrogen antiprotons necessary to fuel our journey from here to Tau Ceti."

Across the hall from where Lily, Dean, and I sat, Milo Pask stood up and shouted, "You geniuses kept this a *secret*? Why? Are the rest of us simply freeloaders? Idiot peons unworthy of consultation?"

Odenwald rejoined Bao at the podium. "Please recall that when the U.N. originally began planning a mission to Epsilon Eridani, we didn't know for sure if any planet out here would prove suitable for colonization. We thought it highly likely, of course, but didn't really know."

"Sir, what's your *point*?" said Milo Pask.

"Our mission's first mandate was hopeful exploration. Originally, then, U.N. planners allotted us only *two* ships, both of which were to have antimatter factories so that they could return to Earth after exploring the target star system. In that scenario, I'll remind you, *Annie Jump Cannon* didn't even exist."

Pask, peevishly flushed, was still on his feet, and an undercurrent of impatience—lapping the commander, not Pask—ran through the hall.

"During this initial planning," Odenwald went on, "off-Earth telescopes on Luna and the moons of Mars strengthened the case for a habitable planet here in EE. As a result, our mission changed, from one of exploring and establishing a permanent base if conditions allowed, to one of pure colonization. That change led us to add a third ship and extra people, not only because many more nations were clamoring to take part but also because planting a colony requires a diverse gene pool and a third ship would give us insurance against an act of fate. In this, by the way, you can see how prescient the U.N. planners proved themselves."

"What about the antimatter factories?" Pask yelled.

"When we added *Annie*, mission costs skyrocketed. The most effective way to cut costs was to dump the notion of putting an accelerator on each vessel. Bao here, along with Trachtenberg and Arbib, considered that suicidal; the manufacturers of our wheelships thought it a kind of sacrilege—namely, bad design—and worked fiendishly to come up with a dirt-cheap redesign that would save the antimatter factories. They did. Then they shunted their costs into other systems, at least on disk, and actually built the accelerators. Unfortunately, they couldn't test them without betraying their presence, and they had no money for testing anyway. So the planners kept them a secret—to prevent protests, work stoppages, maybe even the collapse of the entire project."

Pask was having none of this. "Why keep the accelerators a secret once we'd fled our Earthbound debts? It all smacks of a sleazy elitism!"

"Damned straight!" people cried.

"*¡Eso es verdad!*"

"Go get 'em, Milo!"

"*¡Claro que sí!*"

Like a bidder at a noisy auction, Odenwald raised his arm. "True, once we were on our way, no one on our dirty, anarchic planet was going to stop us. We had what we needed, and we ran so far beyond Earth's jurisdiction as to become a species apart from those left behind. So we stayed mum, both over the radio and aboard our ships, out of respect."

"*Respect?*" several people cried incredulously.

Odenwald increased the gain on his mike. "We didn't want to rub our patrons' noses in either our early defiance or our present freedom. More important, we were afraid the cyclotrons might not work. We had no reason to try them while in transit and no desire to raise false hopes about their capabilities if the trip to Eppie went forward smoothly, as it did until we hit the Barricado. And even the painful loss of *Chandrasekhar* did nothing to persuade Commander Roosenno or me we should tell you the accelerators existed. What for? Epsilon Eridani Two—New Home—still looked to be a viable colony site. So our silence about them was meant to keep everyone up-phase focused on our prime destination, *not* to relegate any of you to the status of steerage riders."

"But that's what it did!" Pask shouted. "Knowing we could go from this system to another, and maybe even from Tau Ceti to yet another one, would've eased our minds! It would've saved *me* a lot of anxiety!"

Pask looked around. Odenwald's explanation had quieted the bulk of the hall. Reluctantly, Pask sat down, and Bao moved up to the podium again to speak:

"Recent tests of the accelerators on *Annie Jump* and *Fritz Zwicky* confirm their reliability. Tau Ceti is closer to Eppie than Eppie is to Sol. We can accomplish the trip without undue emotional stress or physical hardship—in about half the time it took to come here. I have nothing else to add unless some of you have technical inquiries that would fall within my areas of expertise."

"Wonderful!" someone not far from me shouted—Thom Koon, I think. "A mere half century!"

"Ursidormizine slumber will turn that half century into a sleep and a forgetting," Bao said smoothly.

Too smoothly, I'm afraid.

The med techs responsible for maintaining the bioracks and their monitoring systems had seats on a catwalk to Bao's left; a dozen of them stood up and booed. Several other maintenance specialists—down on the floor with Lily, Dean, and me—joined the med techs in jeering Bao's proposal.

"*Booooo! Booooo!*" The auditorium echoed with this ugly rumbling. A few people began to stamp their feet.

"It's Bao, not Boo," Bao told us. "You're using the wrong diphthong."

Not many of Bao's auditors—if you could call them that—caught this witticism. In fact, the booing and foot-stamping got louder. Here and there throughout the hall, people stood to voice their dissent, if not their outrage.

When the woman in front of me rose, Dean struggled out of my lap and held himself upright with his feet on my thighs. I could no longer see the podium.

"*Quiet!*" I heard Odenwald's amplified voice say. "*Resume your seats!*"

In the face of this esteemed authority, the mutiny more or less ended. Silence settled. People sat back down. Tension, however, left an inaudible buzz in the air; and if Pask or some other aggrieved renegade chose to challenge Odenwald, I feared that chaos—out-and-out insurrection—would erupt in full and undefeatable cry.

Meanwhile, Dean continued to balance himself erect on my

thighs. When I tried to tug him back down, he seized the chair back in front with one hand and, with the other, fended off my frustrated tugging.

"*Bao!*" Dean shouted into the silence. "*Bao! Bao! Bao!*" He pistoned his right arm, an emphatic machine, up and down. "*Bao! Bao! Bao!*"

At the mike again, Bao said, "Of all the learned people in this gathering today, only young Gwiazda seems to know how to pronounce my name. Thank you, Dean."

"*Bao!*" Dean shouted again. "Bao, holy crow, you are really welcome!" Then eased back into my lap.

A ripple of applause and a drizzle of cheers boomed into a tidal swell of acclamation. Single-handedly, so to speak, Dean had scotched any threat of mayhem.

Lily rolled her eyes at me. She patted Dean on the leg. Under her breath, she murmured, "Way to go, Tiny Tim. And God bless us, every one."

Bao had control of the meeting again. He pointed out that even if we moved *Annie* ten times closer to Eppie than New Home orbited—to make use of the energy generated by the solar cells affixed to the hydrogen tanks covering our fuel wheel—we would still require about eighty-five days to create a single ton of antihydrogen. Given *Annie*'s overall weight and the speeds that we had to achieve to complete our journey to Tau Ceti in fifty years, it would take another half century, up front, to concoct the 370 tons of antimatter necessary for our trip.

If Bao had given us this news a moment ago, an all-out riot would have broken out. As it was, we began to hear hostile—if not downright bloody—murmurings again.

Greta Agostos stood up. "That puts us back to where we were when we left Earth—a century away from our destination! Possibly more!"

"If I could lessen the time and energy requirements," Bao said, "believe me, I would. But some things are givens. You either deal with them or pitch an infantile tantrum. I urge the former."

"Amen," said Milo Pask. "Amen." And his consent, after the outrage he'd so angrily voiced, seemed to bring a rational truce upon the convocation.

Odenwald took over good-naturedly from Bao, secret-keeper par excellence, and let it be known that Commander Roosenno and he favored a plan whereby *Fritz Zwicky* stayed in orbit around New Home until it became habitable again and *Annie Jump* went on to the Tau Ceti system. However, within certain well-defined parameters, they would permit personnel exchanges between our ships: the trade-offs mustn't drastically unbalance the skills available to either the would-be colonists or the interstellar voyagers. Whatever we did, long stretches of ursidormizine slumber lay ahead of us, as did a host of catch-as-catch-can repairs. Our wheelships, after all, were *old*. On Earth, we'd regard them as antiques.

"But the plan favored by Commander Roosenno and me isn't a *fait accompli*," Odenwald said. "I called you here to vote on, not merely to endorse, it, and I trust you to discuss and pass on the question like intelligent adults."

I squeezed Dean's leg and whispered to Lily, "Do our less than genius kids get a vote too?"

"Ask him," Lily said *sotto voce*.

But before I could, Kaz had risen to his feet. "Sir, why don't we return to Earth—not just *Annie Jump*, but *Fritz Zwicky* too? Tau Ceti may well lack a colonizable planet, and New Home may never recover from its asteroid strike."

"Are you making a motion that we return to Earth?"

"No, sir. I'm putting it forward as an option worthy of debate. The Sol system bred and gave us birth. Neither Tau Ceti nor Epsilon Eridani can say as much, and some of us now have children. Who wishes to doom them to death in an alien star system with no provision for basic human needs—food, air, water, a sense of belonging?"

Kaz sat down, and we debated the matter. Few wanted to return to Earth. In a quick poll, even our children rejected that option. We had fled Earth to explore, to claim new and rejuvenating territories for our species, not to bail out when that very enterprise—as we had known it would do and so had tried to anticipate—threw obstacles in our way. Besides, we all owed the universe a death, and better to pay up seeking a fruitful tomorrow than retreating to a polluted cradle.

When Odenwald actually called the vote, less than a hundred people selected the return-to-Earth option. Not even Kaz voted for it. He had raised the question with an eye on the future of the innocents born in transit to New Home, and I respected his love and scrupulosity in this. He had completely overcome his early bias against Dean.

After that, the final vote was easy. *Annie Jump Cannon's* personnel overwhelmingly approved Commander Odenwald's plan to resupply ourselves with antihydrogen ice and then to set out for

Tau Ceti. A gathering like ours on *Fritz Zwicky* approved Roosenno's plan to remain in orbit, waiting out the dust storm and the greenhouse effect on New Home. If we were all equally lucky, *Annie* would leave for Tau Ceti about the time those on *Zwicky* ventured to the surface for the initial steps of their colony planting.

"*Hooray!*" cried Dean, clapping, when Odenwald announced the results of our vote. "*Bao! Bao! Bao!*"

At the end of this same meeting, Odenwald congratulated us not only on our decisions, but also on having participated in humanity's first successful venture to another solar system. Whatever happens to us in the coming weeks, months, and years, we have made history, and no one can take that achievement away from us.

"So Commander Roosenno and I agree that we should *celebrate* our arrival here," Odenwald told us. "We therefore decree a three-day festival, to begin officially at 0800 hours the day after tomorrow."

And so it has happened—namely, an alternately solemn and gala commemoration of what we've done, featuring personnel exchanges between our wheelships and continuous ship-to-ship TV broadcasts. Our revelries have included songfests, skits, mess parties, musical competitions, art shows, vidouts, seminars, and, most important to me, poetry head-to-heads.

Thich Ngoc Bao on *Annie Jump* and Bashemath Arbib on *Fritz Zwicky* organized competitions in the writing of ballads, odes, sonnets, sestinas, and haiku, among other forms, and required contestants to use different astrophysical phenomena as their poems' subjects or controlling metaphors.

Inevitably, Ghulam Sharif and I found ourselves squared off in three categories, the most amusing a haiku-writing contest. We wrote in our cubicles aboard our own ships, but the finished poems flashed onto toadstool units everywhere as well as onto the huge softscreens in our A-Tower auditoriums.

In her broadcast introduction, Arbib explained, "In its classical form, the Japanese haiku evokes a season. So each contestant must write four poems, using astrophysical phenomena for their primary metaphors. . . ."

Ghulam and I had ten minutes for each haiku, after which we screened them simultaneously (despite their staggered display here), on penalty of disqualification. Their progression ran winter, spring, summer, fall:

Sharif	Gwiazda
Interstellar planet *ice glistens in star-lit dark:* *does it dream of spring?*	
	Each vast aggregate *glitters, a many-armed flake:* *beautiful, unique*
Hydrogen ions *chirp and twitter microwaves* *making nests: the stars*	
	Plasma stirs and jets: *a furnace catalyzer* *in cold birth-throe depths*
Swelling blue-white star *outshines the bright galaxy* *spraying iron, salt: us*	
	Warm fireflies float *amid the midnight showers:* *blaze and drop, then gone*
Hoard scant hydrogen *against the final darkness:* *stars, like leaves, turn red*	
	A jack-o'-lantern *hisses in its black sky loam:* *baleful, squat, too red*

I leave to you the discovery of the astrophysical concepts used metaphorically in each haiku, but note that both sequences conclude with the word *red* as a combination of coincidence and contest design.

Three hundred persons—150 from *Zwicky*, a like number from *Annie*—selected the winning sequence in a blind electronic vote, Sharif triumphing 167 to 132. (Attribute the lost vote to an abstainer who adjudged both sequences "insufficiently imaginative" to bother choosing.) But I take some consolation from the fact that, in a separate vote, my haiku for summer was the overall favorite.

And then Epsilon Eridani Days, an entertaining success in nearly every way, concluded.

Once again, every member of our great expedition must face the realities of our present circumstances and the obligations of our choices.

Among my friends and acquaintances, Milo Pask, Etsuko Endo, Indira Sescharchari, Masoud Nadeq, and my arkboard lover, Lily Aliosi-Stark, have chosen to transfer to Roosenno's ark to wait for the dust cloud from Epimenides to settle. The defection that stings most painfully, of course, is the last.

"Abel, I've been down-phase in umpity-ump extended comas here on *Annie*," Lily told me a few hours ago. "I could handle another U-nap or two, but after I come up-phase again, I want to *stay* up-phase. I want to get on with my life. Is that so selfish a wish?"

"No more than my own," I said. "What about Dean?"

"We made him together, Abel, but he's yours. You have his life in your hands—insofar as *any* of us has control out here—and I expect you to do right by him."

"He's going with me."

"Of course he is. Nothing else makes sense. But I still expect you to do right by him."

"I won't let him forget you."

"That's one right thing you can try, but sooner or later he'll forget. Don't *force* him to remember. I won't mind if I'm just a nagging piece of grit in his memory. Eventually, if he has you to count on, that's all I should be."

"What crap," I said. "You sound like Joan of Arc praying amidst the flames."

For an instant, Lily's gaze darkened. Then she began to laugh. "I do, don't I? Well, good for me."

Using Colombo tethers and transfer dinghies, those leaving *Annie* carried their bodies across to *Zwicky*, sundering their souls from ours. But before these leave-takings, we took our melancholy last farewells. Dean, Kaz, and I met with Lily at the G-Tower docking station.

"It's like you guys're dying," Lily told us. "I'll never see you—any of you—again."

I kissed Lily. Hard. I kissed her again, caressing her hair. When I let go, Dean—DeBoy, as Lily had always called him—clung to her like a sorrowful young orang. If Kaz had not distracted him, she would have probably had to have emergency surgery to pry him loose.

Later, I watched from the G-Tower observatory as Lily and the others made their slow-motion glides across to or over from *Zwicky*. It seemed to me, though, that the dinghy containing my lover drew across the dark with it, in a harness of fireflies, a vein from my own clamoring heart.

A delusion, of course; a trick of the vacuum.

Nonetheless, it made me remember a haiku that Ghulam Sharif had written in the wake of our contest and sent over to me with a friend as a parting gift:

> *Iron cinders of stars*
> *cool in expanding darkness:*
> *too late for regrets*

"Guh-bye!" cried Dean, one hand on the viewport. "Guh-bye, Mama!"

Odenwald had okayed Dean's presence upstairs, and as his doting goduncle, Kaz had carried him up — for, under the present circumstances, kids had plenty of business in the observatory. Plenty.

"Guh-bye, guh-bye! Holy crow!"

Without Lily bodily before him, DeBoy truly understood only that *Annie Jump Cannon* was going on another long trip and that he was going with.

Death and Designation Among the Asadi

Death
and Designation
Among
the Asadi

Sundry Notes for an Abortive Ethnography
of the Asadi of BoskVeld,
Fourth Planet of the Denebolan System,
as Compiled from the Journals (Both Private and Professional),
Official Reports, Private Correspondence, and Tapes
of
Egan Chaney,
Cultural Xenologist,
by his Friend and Associate,
Thomas Benedict

The Press of the National University of Kenya, Nairobi

PART ONE

PRELIMINARIES: REVERIE AND DEPARTURE

From the private journals of Egan Chaney: There are no more pygmies. Intellectual pygmies perhaps, but no more of those small, alert, swaybacked black people, of necessarily amenable disposition, who lived in the dead-and-gone Ituri rain forests; a people, by the way, whom I do not wish to sentimentalize (though perhaps I may). Pygmies no longer exist; they have been dead or dying for decades.

But on the evening before the evening when Benedict dropped me into the singing fronds of the Synesthesia Wild* under three bitter moons, they lived again for me. I spent that last evening in base camp rereading Turnbull's *The Forest People*. Dreaming, I lived again with the people of the Ituri. I underwent *nkumbi*, the ordeal of circumcision. I dashed beneath the belly of an elephant and jabbed that monstrous creature's flesh with my spear. Finally, I took part in the festival of the *molimo* with the ancient and clever BaMbuti.

All in all, I suppose, my reading was a sentimental exercise. Turnbull's book had been the first and most vivid ethnography I had encountered in my undergraduate career; and even on that last night in base camp, on the hostile world of BoskVeld, a planet circling the star Denebola, his book sang in my head like the forbidden lyrics of the pygmies' *molimo*, like the poignant melodies of BoskVeld's moons.

A sentimental exercise.

What good my reading would do me among the inhabitants of the Synesthesia Wild I had no idea. Probably none. But I was going out there; and on the evening before my departure, the day before my submersion, I lost myself in the forests of another time, knowing that for the next several months I would be the waking and wakeful prisoner of the hominoids who were my subjects. We have killed off most of the "primitive" peoples of Earth, but on paradoxical BoskVeld I still had a job.

And when Benedict turned the copter under those three antique-gold moons and flew it back to base camp like a crepi-

---

* This was Chaney's private and idiosyncratic term for the rain forest the rest of us called either the Calyptran Wilderness or the Wild. T. B.

tating dragonfly, I knew I had to pursue that job. But the jungle was bleak, and strange, and nightmarishly real; and all I could think was *There are no more pygmies, there are no more pygmies, there are no*

Methods: A Dialogue

From the professional notebooks of Egan Chaney: I was not the first Earthling to go among the Asadi, but I was the first to live with them for an extended period. The first of us to encounter the Asadi was Oliver Oliphant Frasier, the man who gave these hominoids their name — perhaps on analogy with the word *Ashanti*, the name of an African people who still exist, but more likely from the old Arabic word meaning lion, *asad*.

Oliver Oliphant Frasier had reported that the Asadi of BoskVeld had no speech as we understood the concept, but that at one time they had possessed a "written language." He used both these words loosely, I'm sure, and the anomaly of writing without speech was one that I hoped to throw some light on. In addition, Frasier had said that an intrepid ethnographer might hope to gain acceptance among the Asadi by a singularly unorthodox stratagem. I will describe this stratagem by setting down here a conversation I had with my pilot and research assistant, Thomas Benedict. In actual fact, this conversation never took place — but my resorting to dialogue may be helpful at this point. Benedict, no doubt, will forgive me.

BENEDICT: Listen, Chaney, what do you plan on doing after I drop you all by your lonesome into the Wild? You aren't thinking of using the standard anthropological ploy, are you? You know, marching right into the Asadi hamlet and exclaiming, "I am the Great White God of whom your legends foretell"?

CHANEY: Not exactly. As a matter of fact, I'm not going into the Asadi clearing until morning.

BENEDICT: Then why the hell do I have to copter you into the Wild in the middle of the goddamn night?

CHANEY: To humor a lovable eccentric. No, no, Ben. Don't revile me. The matter is fairly simple. Frasier said that the Asadi community clearing is absolutely vacant during the night; not a soul remains there between dusk and sunrise. The community members return to the clearing only when Denebola has grown fat and coppery on the eastern horizon.

BENEDICT: And you want to be dropped at night?

CHANEY: Yes, to give the noise of the Dragonfly a chance to fade and be forgotten, and to afford the opportunity of walking into the Asadi clearing with the first morning arrivals. Just as if I belonged there.

BENEDICT: Oh, indeed yes. You'll be very inconspicuous, Chaney. You'll be accepted immediately—even though the Asadi are naked, have eyes that look like the murky glass in the bottoms of old bottles, and boast great natural collars of silver or tawny fur. Oh, indeed yes.

CHANEY: No, Ben, not immediately accepted.

BENEDICT: But almost?

CHANEY: Yes, I think so.

BENEDICT: How do you plan on accomplishing this miracle?

CHANEY: Well, Frasier called the stratagem I hope to employ "acceptance through social invisibility." The principle is again a simple one. I must feign the role of an Asadi pariah. This tactic gains me a kind of acceptance because Asadi mores demand that the pariah's presence be totally ignored; he's outcast not in a physical sense, but in a psychological one. Consequently, my presence in the clearing will be a negative one, an admission I'll readily make—but in some ways this negative existence will permit me more latitude of movement and observation than if I were an Asadi in good standing.

BENEDICT: Complicated, Chaney, very complicated. It leaves me with two burning questions. How does one go about achieving pariahhood, and what happens to the anthropologist's crucial role as a gatherer of folk material: songs, cosmologies, ritual incantations? I mean, won't your "invisibility" deprive you of your cherished one-to-one relationships with those Asadi members who might be most informative?

CHANEY: I'll take your last question first. Frasier told us that the Asadi don't communicate through speech. That in itself pretty much limits me to observation. No need to worry about songs or incantations. Their cosmologies I'll have to infer from what I see. As for their methods of interpersonal communication, even should I discover what these are, I may not be physically equipped to use them. The Asadi aren't human, Ben.

BENEDICT: I'm aware. Frequently, listening to you, I begin to think speechlessness might be a genetically desirable condition. All right. Enough. What about attaining to pariahhood?

CHANEY: We still don't know very much about which offenses warrant this extreme punishment. However, we do know how the

Asadi distinguish the outcast from the other members of the community.

BENEDICT: How?

CHANEY: They shave the offender's collar of fur. Since all adult Asadi have these manes, regardless of sex, this method of distinguishing the pariah is universal and certain.

BENEDICT: Then you're already a pariah?

CHANEY: I hope so. I just have to remember to shave every day. Frasier believed that his hairlessness—he was nearly bald—was what allowed him to make those few discoveries about the Asadi we now possess. But he arrived among them during a period of strange inactivity and had to content himself with studying the artifacts of an older Asadi culture, the remains of a temple or a pagoda between the jungle and the sea. I've also heard that Frasier didn't really have the kind of patience that's essential for field work.

BENEDICT: Just a minute. Back up a little. Couldn't one of the Asadi be shorn of his mane accidentally? He'd be an outcast through no fault of his own, wouldn't he? An artificial pariah?

CHANEY: It's not very likely. Frasier reported that the Asadi have no natural enemies; that, in fact, the Synesthesia Wild seems to be almost completely devoid of any life beyond the Asadi themselves, discounting plants and insects and various microscopic forms. In any case, the loss of one's collar through whatever means is considered grounds for punishment. That's the only offense that Frasier pretty well confirmed. What the others are, as I said, we don't really know.

BENEDICT: If the jungles are devoid of living prey, what do the poor Asadi live on?

CHANEY: We don't really know that, either.

BENEDICT: Well, listen, Chaney, what do *you* plan to live on? I mean, even Malinowski condescended to eat now and again.

CHANEY: That's where you come in, Ben. I'm going to carry in sufficient rations to see me through a week. But each week for several months you'll have to make a food-and-supply drop in the place you first set me down. I've already picked the spot. I know its distance and direction from the Asadi clearing. It'll be expensive, but the people in base camp—Eisen, in particular—have agreed that my work is necessary. You won't be forced to defend the drops.

BENEDICT: But why so often? Why once a week?

CHANEY: That's Eisen's idea, not mine. Since I told him I was going to refuse any sort of contact at all during my stay with the Asadi—any contact with you people, that is—he decided the weekly drop would be the best way to make certain, occasionally, I'm still alive.

BENEDICT: A weapon, Chaney?

CHANEY: No, no weapons. Besides food, I'll take in nothing but my notebooks, a recorder, some reading material, a medical kit, and maybe a little something to get me over the inevitable periods of depression.

BENEDICT: A radio? In case you need immediate help?

CHANEY: No. I may get ill once or twice, but I'll always have the flares if things get really bad. Placenol, lorqual, and bourbon, too. But I insist on complete separation from any of the affairs of base camp until my stay among the Asadi is over.

BENEDICT: Why are you doing this? I don't mean why did Eisen decide we ought to study the Asadi so minutely. I mean, why are you, Egan Chaney, committing yourself to this ritual sojourn among an alien people? There are one or two others at base camp who might have gone if they'd had the chance.

CHANEY: Because, Ben, *there are no more pygmies.* . . .

—End of simulated dialogue on initial methods.

I suppose that I've made Benedict out to be a much more inquisitive fellow than he really is. All those well-informed questions! In truth, Ben is amazingly voluble about his background and his past without being especially informative. In that, he is a great deal like me, I'm afraid. . . . But when you read the notes for this ethnography, Ben, remember that I let you get in one or two unanswered hits at me. Can the mentor-pupil relationship go deeper than that? Can friendship? As a man whose life's work involves accepting a multitude of perspectives, I believe I've played you fair, Ben.

Forgive me my trespass.

CONTACT AND ASSIMILATION

From the private journals of Egan Chaney: Thinking *There are no more pygmies, there are no more pygmies, there are no* . . . I lay down beneath a tree resembling an outsized rubber plant and I slept. I slept without dreaming, or else I had a grotesque nightmare that, upon waking, I suppressed. A wrist alarm woke me.

The light from Denebola had begun to copper-coat the edges of the leaves in the Synesthesia Wild. Still, dawn had not quite come. The world was silent. I refused to let the Wild distort my senses. I did not wish to cut myself on the crimsons, the yellows, the orchid blues. Nor did I have any desire to taste the first slight treacherous breeze, nor to hear the dawn detonate behind my retinas.

Therefore, I shook myself awake and began walking. Beyond the brutal fact of direction, I paid no attention to my surroundings. The clearing where the Asadi would soon congregate compelled me toward it. That fateful place drew me on. Everything else slipped out of my consciousness: blazing sky, moist earth, singing fronds. Would the Asadi accept me among them as they negatively accepted their outcasts? Upon this hope I had founded nearly five months of future activity. Everything, I realized, floundering through the tropical undergrowth, derived from my hope in an *external* sign of pariahhood; not a whit of my master strategy had I based on the genuine *substance* of this condition.

It was too late to reserve either my aims or the direction of my footsteps. You must let the doubt die. You must pattern the sound of your footfalls after the pattern of falling feet—those falling feet converging with you upon the clearing where the foliage parts and the naked Asadi assemble together like a convention of unabashed mutes. And so I patterned the sounds of my footfalls after theirs.

Glimpsed through rents in the fretworkings of leaves, an Asadi's flashing arm.

Seen as a shadow among other shadows on the dappled ground, the forward-moving image of an Asadi's maned head.

The Wild trembled with morning movement. I was surrounded by unseen and half-seen communicants, all of us converging.

And then the foliage parted and we were together on the open jungle floor, the Asadi clearing, the holy ground perhaps, the unadorned territory of their gregariousness and communion, the focal point of Asadi life. The awesome odor of this life—so much milling life—assailed me.

No matter. I adjusted.

Great grey-fleshed creatures, their heads heavy with violent drapings of fur, milled about me, turned about one another, came back to me, sought some confirmation of my essential *whatness*. I could do nothing but wait. I waited. My temples pulsed. Denebola shot poniards of light through the trees. Hovering, then moving away, averting their murky eyes, the Asadi—individual by individual, I noticed—made their decision and that first indispensable victory was in my grasp: *I was ignored!*

XENOLOGY: IN-THE-FIELD REPORT

From the professional tapes of the library of the Third Denebolan Expedition: I have been here two weeks. Last night I picked up the second of Benedict's food drops. It's fortunate they come on time, arriving on the precise coordinates where Ben first set me down. The Asadi do not eat as we do, and the Synesthesia Wild provides me with foodstuffs neither in the way of edible vegetation nor in that of small game animals. I cannot tolerate the plants. As our biochemists in base camp predicted, most of them induce almost immediate vomiting. Or their furry bitterness dissuades me from swallowing them. A few may be edible, or a few may have juices pleasing to the palate—Frasier, after all, discovered the tree from which we have distilled the intoxicant called lorqual—but I'm no expert at plant identification. Far from it. As for animals, there simply are none. The jungle is stagnant with writhing fronds. With the heat, the steam, the infrasonic vibrancy of continual photosynthesis. Rainwater I can drink. Thank God for that, even though I boil it before considering it truly potable.

I have reached a few purely speculative conclusions about the Asadi.

With them nothing is certain. Their behavior, though it must necessarily have a deep-seated social/biological function, does not make sense to me. At this stage—I keep telling myself—that's to be expected. But I persist. I ask myself, "If you can't subsist on what BoskVeld gives you, how do the Asadi?" My observations in this area have given me the intellectual nourishment to combat despair. Nothing else on BoskVeld has offered a morsel of consolation. In answer to the question, "What do the Asadi eat?" I can respond quite truthfully, "Everything I do not."

They appear to be herbivorous. In fact, they eat wood. Yes, wood. I have seen them strip bark from the rubber trees, the rainthorn, the alien mangroves, the lattice-sail trees, and ingest it without difficulty or qualm. I have watched them eat pieces of the very hearts of young saplings, wood of what we would consider prohibitive hardness even for creatures equipped to process it internally.

Three days ago I boiled down several pieces of bark, the sort I've seen so many of the young Asadi consume. I boiled it until the pieces were limply pliable. I managed to chew the bark for several minutes and finally to swallow it. Checking my stool for nearly a day later, I found that this "meal" had gone right through me. Bark consists of cellulose, after all. Indigestible cellulose. And yet the Asadi eat wood and digest it. How?

Again, I have to speculate. I believe the Asadi digest wood in the same manner as earthly termites; that is, through the aid of bacteria in their intestines, protozoa that break down the cellulose. A symbiosis, Benedict might say, being versed, as he is, in biological and ecological theory. . . .

This is later. Tonight I have to talk, even if it's only to a microphone. With the coming of darkness the Asadi have disappeared again into the jungle, and I'm alone.

For the first three nights I was here, I too returned to the Wild when Denebola set. I returned to the place where Benedict had dropped me, curled up beneath the overhanging palm and lattice-sail leaves, slept through the night, and then joined the dawn's inevitable pilgrimage back to this clearing. Now I remain here through the night. I sleep on the clearing's edge, just deep enough into the foliage to find shelter. I go back into the jungle only to retrieve my food drops.

Although the Asadi disapprove of my behavior, because I'm an outcast they can do nothing to discipline me without violating their own injunction against acknowledging a pariah's existence. As they depart each evening, a few of the older Asadi—those with streaks of white in their mangy collars—halt momentarily beside me and breathe with exaggerated heaviness. They don't look at me because that's apparently taboo. But I don't look at them, either. Ignoring them as if *they* were pariahs, I've been able to dispense with those senseless and wearying treks in and out of the clearing that so exhausted me in my first three days here.

To absolve myself of what may seem a lack of thoroughness, I suppose I ought to mention that on my fourth and fifth nights here I attempted to follow two different Asadi specimens into the jungle—in order to determine where they slept, how they slept, and what occupies their waking time when they are away from the clearing. I wasn't successful, however.

When evening comes, the Asadi disperse. This dispersal is complete: No two individuals remain together, not even the young with their parents. Each Asadi—I believe—finds a place of his or her own, one completely removed from that of any other member of the species. This practice runs counter to my experience with almost every other social group I've ever studied—although it's somewhat analogous to the solitary nest building of chimpanzees as observed frequently in the Gombe Stream Reserve in East Africa. Female chimps, however, *do* sleep with their young. Perhaps, now that I think of it, Asadi females do, too. . . . In any case, I was humiliatingly outdistanced by the objects of my pursuit. Nor can I suppose I'd have any greater success with different specimens, since I purposely chose to follow an aged and decrepit-seeming Asadi on the first evening and a small, scarcely pubescent creature on the second. Both ran with convincing strength, flashed into the trees as if still arboreal by nature, and then flickered from my vision and my grasp. . . .

Two moons are up, burnt-gold and unreal. I'm netted in by shadows and my growing loneliness. Field conditions, to be frank, have seldom been so austere for me, and I've begun to wonder if the Asadi were *ever* intelligent creatures. Maybe I'm studying a variety of Denebolan baboon. Ole Oliver Oliphant Frasier, though, reported that the Asadi once had both a written language and a distinctive system of architecture. He wasn't very forthcoming about how he reached those conclusions—but the Synesthesia Wild, I'm certain, contains many secrets. Later I'll be more venturesome. But for the present I've got to try to understand those Asadi who are alive today. They're the key to their own and the distant Ur'sadi past.

One or two final things before I attempt to sleep.

First, the eyes of the Asadi: These are somewhat as Benedict described them in the imaginary dialogue I composed two weeks ago. That is, like the bottoms of thick-glassed bottles. Except that I've noticed the eye really consists of two parts: a thin transparent covering, which is apparently hard, like plastic, and the complex, membranous organ of sight that this covering protects. It's as if each Asadi is born wearing a built-in pair of safety glasses.

Frasier's impression of their eyes as "murky" is one not wholly supported by continued observation. What he saw as murkiness probably resulted from the fact that the eyes of the Asadi—behind the outer lens or cap—are almost constantly changing colors. Sometimes the speed with which a yellow replaces an indigo, and then a green the yellow, and so on, makes it difficult for a mere human being to see any particular color at all. Maybe this is the explanation for Frasier's perception of their eyes as "murky." I don't know. I'm certain, though, that this chameleonic quality of the Asadi's eyes has social significance.

A second thing: Despite the complete absence of a discernible social order among the Asadi, today I may have witnessed an event of the first importance to my unsuccessful, so far, efforts to chart their group relationships. Maybe. Maybe not. Previously, no real order at all existed. Dispersal at night, congregation in the morning—if you choose to call that order. But nothing else. Random milling about during the day, with no set times for eating, sex, or their habitual bloodless feuds. Random plunges into the jungle at night. What's a humble Earthling to make of all this? A society held together by institutionalized antisocialness? What happened today leads me irrevocably away from that conclusion. Maybe.

This afternoon an aged Asadi whom I'd never seen before stumbled into the clearing. His mane was grizzled, his face wizened, his hands shriveled, his grey body bleached to a filthy cream. But so agile was he in the Wild that no one detected his presence until his strangely clumsy entry into the clearing. Then, everyone fled from him. Unconcerned, he sat down in the center of the Asadi gathering place and folded his long, sparsely haired legs. By this time, all his conspecifics were in the jungle staring back at him from the edge of the clearing. Only at sunset had I ever before seen the Asadi desert the clearing *en masse*.

But I haven't yet exhausted the strangeness of this old man's visit. You see, he came *accompanied*.

He came with a small, purplish-black creature perched on his shoulder. It resembled a winged lizard, a bat, and a deformed homunculus all at once. But whereas the old man had great round eyes that changed color extremely slowly, if at all, the creature on his shoulder had not even a pair of empty sockets. It was blind, blind by virtue of its lack of any organs of sight. It sat on the aged Asadi's shoulder and manipulated its tiny hands compulsively, tugging at the old man's mane, then opening and closing them on empty air, then tugging once again at its protector's grizzled collar.

Both the old man and his beastlike/manlike familiar had a furious unreality. They existed at a spiritual as well as a physical distance. I noted that the rest of the Asadi—those who surrounded and ignored me on the edge of the communion ground —behaved not as if they feared these sudden visitors, but rather as if they felt a loathsome kinship with them. This is difficult to express. Bear with me. Maybe another analogy will help. Let me say that the Asadi behaved toward their visitors as a fastidious child might behave toward a parent who has contracted a venereal disease. Love and loathing, shame and respect together.

The episode concluded abruptly when the old man rose from the ground, oblivious to the slow swelling and sedate flapping of his *huri*, and stalked back into the Wild, scattering a number of Asadi in his wake. (*Huri*, by the way, is a portmanteau word for *fury* and *harpy* that I've just coined.)

Then everything went back to normal. The clearing filled again, and the ceaseless and senseless milling about resumed.

God, it's amazing how lonely loneliness can be when the sky contains a pair of jagged, nuggetlike moons and the human being inside you has surrendered to the essence of that which should command only your outward life. That's a mouthful, isn't it? What I mean is that there's a small struggle going on between Egan Chaney, cultural xenologist, and Egan Chaney, the quintessential man. No doubt it's the result more of environmental pressure than of my genetic heritage.

That's a little anthropological allusion, Moses. Don't worry about it. You aren't supposed to understand it.

But enough. Today's atypical occurrence has sharpened my appetite for observation, temporarily calmed my internal struggle. I'm ready to stay here a year, if need be, even though the original plan was only for six months. Dear, dear God, *look* at those moons!

The Asadi Clearing: A Clarification

From the professional notebooks of Egan Chaney: My greatest collegiate failing was an inability to organize. I'm pursued by the specter of that failing even today. Consequently, a digression of sorts.

In looking over these quirkish notes for my formal ethnography, I see I may have given the reader the completely false idea that the Asadi clearing is a small area of ground, say fifteen by fifteen meters. Not so. As best I'm able to determine, there are approximately five hundred Asadi individuals. This figure includes mature adults, the young, and those intermediate between age and youth, although there are no "children" or "infants," surprisingly enough. By most demographic and anthropological estimates, five hundred is optimum tribal size.

Of course, during all my time in the Wild, I've never been completely sure that the same individuals return to the clearing each morning. It may be that some sort of monumental shift takes place in the jungle, one group of Asadi replacing another each day. But I doubt it. The Wild encompasses a finite (though large) area, after all, and I have learned to recognize a few of the more distinctive Asadi by sight. Therefore, five hundred seems about right to me: five hundred grey-fleshed creatures strolling, halting, bending at the waist and glaring at one another, eating, participating in loveless sex, grappling like wrestlers, obeying no time clock but the sun, their activities devoid of any apprehensible sequence or rationale. Such activity requires a little space, though, and their clearing provides it.

The reader may not cheerfully assume that the Asadi communion ground is a five-by-eight mud flat between a BoskVeld cypress and a malodorous sump hole. Not at all. Their communion ground has both size and symmetry, and the Asadi maintain it discrete from the encroaching jungle by their unremitting daily activity. I won't quote you dimensions, however, I'll merely say that the clearing has the rectangular shape, the characteristic slope, and the practical roominess of a twentieth-century football or soccer field. This is pure coincidence, I'm sure. Astroturf and lime-rendered hash marks are conspicuously absent.

A Dialogue of Self and Soul

From the private correspondence of Egan Chaney: The title of this exercise is from Yeats, dear Ben. The substance of the dialogue, however, has almost nothing to do with the Old Master's poem of the same name.

I wrote this imaginary exchange in one of my notebooks while waiting out a particularly long night on the edge of the Asadi clearing (just off the imaginary thirty-yard line on the south end of the field, western sideline), and I intend for no one to read it, Ben, but you. Its lack of objectivity and the conclusions drawn by the participants make it unsuitable for any sort of appearance in the formal ethnography I've yet to write.*

But you, Ben, will understand that a scientist is also a human being and may perhaps forgive me. Because I've withheld my self from you in our many one-sided conversations (you dominate them, I realize, because my silence is a spur to others' volubility; they speak to fill the void), here I mean to show you the mind

---

* Even though we shared a dormitory room for a time, Chaney "mailed" me the letter containing this dialogue. We never discussed his "letter." T. B.

these silences conceal. But since you can't tell the players without a program, I herewith provide a program. The numbers on the backs of the players' metaphysical jerseys are Self and Soul.

PROGRAM

Self = The Cultural Xenologist
Soul = The Quintessential Man
Manager(s): Egan Chaney

SELF: This is my eighteenth night in the Synesthesia Wild.

SOUL: I've been here forever. But let that go. What have you learned?

SELF: Most of my observations lead me to state emphatically that the Asadi are not fit subjects for "anthropological" study. They manifest no purposeful social activity. They do not use tools. They have less social organization than did most of the extinct earthly primates and hominids, and not much more than chimpanzees and baboons. Only the visit, three days ago, of the "old man" and his frightening companion indicates even a remote possibility I'm dealing with intelligence. How can I continue?

SOUL: You'll continue out of contempt for the revulsion daily growing in you. Because the Asadi are, in fact, intelligent—just as Oliver Oliphant Frasier said they were.

SELF: But how do I know that, damn it? How do I know what you insist is true is *really* true? Blind acceptance of Frasier's word?

SOUL: There are signs, Chaney. The eyes, for instance. But even if there weren't any signs, you'd admit that the Asadi are as intelligent, in their own way, as you or I. Wouldn't you, Egan?

SELF: I admit it. Their elusive intelligence haunts me.

SOUL: No, now you've misstated the facts—you've twisted things around horribly.

SELF: How? What do you mean?

SOUL: You are not the one who is haunted, Egan Chaney, for you're too rational a creature to be the prey of poltergeist. *I* am the haunted one, the bedeviled one, the one ridden by every insidious spirit of doubt and revulsion.

SELF: Revulsion? You've used that word twice. Why do you insist upon it? What does it mean?

SOUL: That I hate the Asadi. I despise their every culturally significant—or insignificant— act. They curdle my essence with their very alienness. And because they do, you, too, Egan Chaney, hate them—for you're simply the civilized veneer on my primordial responses to the world. You're haunted not by the Asadi, friend, but by me.

SELF: While you, in turn, are haunted by them. Is that it?

SOUL: That's how it is. But although you're aware of my hatred for the Asadi, you pretend that that portion of my hatred which seeps into you is only a kind of professional resentment. You believe you resent the Asadi for destroying your objectivity, your scientific detachment. In truth, this detachment doesn't exist. You feel the same powerful revulsion for their alienness that works in me like a disease, the same abiding and deep-seated hatred. I haunt you.

SELF: With hatred for the Asadi?

SOUL: Yes. I admit it, Egan. Admit that even as a scientist you hate them.

SELF: No. No, damn you, I won't. Because we killed the pygmies, every one of them. How can I say, "I hate the Asadi, I hate the Asadi," when we killed every pygmy? — Even though, my God, I do. . . .

PART TWO

DAILY LIFE: IN-THE-FIELD REPORT

From the professional tapes of the library of the Third Denebolan Expedition: Once again, it's evening. I've a lean-to now, and it protects me from the rain much better than did the porous roof of the forest. I've been here twenty-two days now. Beneath this mildewed flesh my muscles crawl like the evil snakes BoskVeld doesn't possess. I'm saturated with Denebola's garish light. I'm Gulliver among the Yahoos.

This, however, isn't what you want to hear.

You want facts, my conclusions about the behavior of the Asadi, evidence that we're studying a life form capable of at least elementary reasoning and ratiocination. The Asadi have this ability, I swear it—but only slowly has the evidence for intelligence begun to accumulate.

Okay, base-camp huggers. Let me deliver myself of an in-the-field report as an objective scientist, forgetting the hunches of my mortal self. The rest of this tape will deal with the daily life of the Asadi.

A day in the life of. A typical day in the life of.

Except that I'm going to cap my reporting of mundane occurrences with the account of an extraordinary event that took place just this afternoon. Also, I'm going to compress time to suit my own artistic/scientific purposes.

At dawn the Asadi return to their football fields. For approximately twelve hours they mill about in the clearing doing whatever they care to do. Sexual activity and quirkish staring matches are the only sort of behavior that can in any way be called "social" —unless you believe milling about in a crowd qualifies. Their daylight way of life I call Indifferent Togetherness.

But when the Asadi engage in coitus, their indifference dissolves and gives way to a brutal hostility. Both partners behave as if they desire to kill each other, and frequently this is nearly the result. (Births, in case you're wondering, must take place in the Wild, the female self-exiled and unattended.) As for the staring matches, they're of brief duration and involve fierce gesticulation and mane shaking. The eyes change color with astonishing rapidity, flashing through the entire visible spectrum, and maybe beyond, in a matter of seconds.

I'm now prepared to say these instantaneous changes of eye color are the Asadi equivalent to human speech. Three weeks of observation have finally convinced me that the adversaries in these staring matches control the internal chemical changes that trigger the changes in the succeeding hues of their eyes. In other words, patterns exist. The minds that control these chemical changes cannot be primitive ones. The alterations are willed, and they're infinitely complex.

Ole Oliver Oliphant was right. The Asadi have a "language."

Still, for all the good it does me, they might as well have none. One day's agonizingly like another. And I can't blame my pariahhood, for the only things even a well-adjusted Asadi may participate in are sex and staring. It doesn't pain me overmuch to be outcast from participation in these. To some extent, I'm not much more of a pariah than any of these creatures. We're all, so to speak, outcast from life's feast. . . .

Unlike every other society I've ever read about or seen, the Asadi don't even have any meaningful communal gatherings, any festivals of solidarity, any unique rituals of group consciousness. They don't even have families. The individual is the basic unit of their "society." What they have done, in fact, is to institutionalize the processes of alienation. Their dispersal at dusk simply translates into physical distance the incohesiveness by which they live during the day. How do the Asadi continue to live as a people? For that matter, *why* do they do so?

Enough questions. As I mentioned earlier, something extraordinary took place today. It happened this afternoon, and, I suppose, it's *still* happening. As before, this strange event involves the old man who appeared in the clearing over a week ago. It also involves the huri, his blind reptilian companion.

Until today I'd never seen two Asadi eat together. As an Earthman from a Western background, I find the practice of eating alone a disturbing one. After all, I've been eating alone for over three weeks now, and I long to sit down in the communal mess with Benedict and Eisen, Morrell and Yoshiba, and everyone else at base camp. My training in strange folkways and alien cultural patterns hasn't weaned me away from this longing. As a result, I've watched with interest, and complete lack of comprehension, the Asadi sitting apart from their fellows and privately feeding—as if, again, they were merely an alien variety of chimpanzee or baboon.

Today this changed. An hour before the fall of dusk, the old man staggered into the clearing under the burden of something damnably heavy. I was aware of the commotion at once. Like last time, every one of the Asadi fled to the edge of the jungle. I observed from my lean-to. My heart, dear Ben, thumped like a toad in a jar. The huri on the old man's shoulder scarcely moved; it appeared bloated and insentient, a rubber doll. During the whole of the man's visit it remained in this virtually comatose state, upright but unmoving. Meanwhile, the aged Asadi—whom I've begun to regard as some sort of aloof and mysterious chieftain—paused in the center of the clearing, looked about, and then struggled to remove the burden from his back. It was slung over his shoulders by means of two narrow straps.

Straps, Eisen: S-T-R-A-P-S. Made of vines.

Can you understand how I felt? Nor did the nature of the old man's burden cause my wonder to fade. He was lowering to the ground the rich, brownish-red carcass of an animal. The meat glistened with the failing light of Denebola and its own internal vibrancy. The meat had been dressed, Eisen, and the old man was bringing it to the Asadi clearing as an offering to his people.

He set the carcass on the dusty assembly floor and withdrew the straps from the incisions he'd made in the meat. Then, his hands and shoulders bloodstained, he stepped back five or six steps.

Slowly, a few of the adult males began to stalk into the clearing. They approached the old man's offering with diffident steps, like thieves in darkened rooms. Their eyes were furiously changing colors. All but those of the old man himself. I could see him standing away from the meat, and his eyes—like unpainted china saucers—were the color of dull clay. They didn't alter even when several of the Asadi males fell upon the meat and began ripping away beautifully veined hunks. Then more and more of the Asadi males descended upon the carcass, and all about the fringes of the clearing the females and the young made tentative movements to claim their shares. I had to leave my lean-to to see what was going on. Ultimately, I couldn't see anything but bodies and manes and animated discord.

Before most of the Asadi were aware, Denebola set.

Awareness grew, beginning with the females and the young on the edges of the clearing and then burning inward like a grass fire. A few individuals flashed into the Wild. Others followed. Eventually, in a matter of only seconds, even the males contesting for the meat raised their bloody snouts and scented their predicament. In response, they bounded toward the trees, disappearing in innumerable directions, glimmering away like the dying light itself.

And here is the strange part, the truly *stranger* part. The old man didn't follow his people back into the Synesthesia Wild. *He's sitting out there in the clearing right now!*

When all of the Asadi had fled, he found the precise spot where he'd placed his offering, hunkered down, lowered his buttocks, crossed his legs, and assumed sole ownership of that sacred piece of stained ground. The moons of BoskVeld throw his shadow in three different directions, and the huri on his shoulder has begun to move a little. This is the first night since I came out here that I haven't been alone, base-camp huggers, and I don't like it. I don't like it at all. . . .

Personal Involvement: The Bachelor

From the private journals of Egan Chaney: My meeting of The Bachelor, as I called him almost from the beginning, represented an unprecedented breakthrough. It came on my 29th day in the field—although, actually, I had noticed him for the first time three days prior to his resolute approach and shy touching of my face. As far removed from a threat as a woman's kiss, that touch frightened me more than the first appearance of the old chieftain, more than the nightmare shape of the huri, more even than the chaos of rending and eating that followed the old man's gift of the flame-bright carcass. I'd been alone for weeks. Now, without much preamble, one of the Asadi had chosen to acknowledge my presence by . . . by *touching me!*

I must back up a bit—to the night the Asadi chieftain, against all custom, stayed in the clearing. My first realization that he intended to stay was a moment of minor terror, I'll confess, but the implications of his remaining overrode my fear. Wakeful and attentive, I sat up to study his every movement and to record whatever seemed significant.

The old man didn't move. The huri grew restive as the night progressed, but it didn't leave the old man's shoulder. To be painfully brief, they stayed in the clearing all that night and all the following day, sitting on the stained ground, guarding the spot. Then, when twilight fell on that second day, they departed with all the rest.

I despaired. How many days would I have to suffer through before something else unusual occurred?

Not long, apparently. On my 26th day on the clearing's edge I saw The Bachelor. If I'd ever seen him before, I'd certainly never paid him any real attention, for The Bachelor was a completely unprepossessing specimen whom I judged to be three or four years beyond Asadi adolescence.

Grey-fleshed and gaunt, he had a patchy silver-blue mane of so little length the others must surely consider him a virtual outcast. In fact, in all the time I knew him he never once took part in either coitus or the ritualized staring matches of the full-maned Asadi. When I first felt his eyes upon me, The Bachelor was on my imaginary twenty-yard line looking toward my lean-to from a pocket of his ceaselessly moving brethren. He had chosen me to stare at. That he didn't receive a cuffing for violating the one heretofore inviolable Asadi taboo confirmed for me the negligibility of his tribal status. It was he and I who were brethren, not he and the other Asadi.

In one extremely salient particular The Bachelor didn't resemble the vast majority of Asadi at all: his eyes. These were exactly like the old man's—translucent but empty, enameled but colorless, fired in the oven of his mother's womb but as brittle-seeming as sun-baked clay. Never did The Bachelor's eyes flash through the rainbow spectrum as did the prismatic eyes of his conspecifics. They were always clayey and cold, a shade or two lighter than his flesh.

And it was with these eyes, on my 26th day in the field, that The Bachelor took my measure. The noonday heat held us in a shimmering mirage, our gazes enigmatically locked.

"Don't just stand there making google faces," I shouted, beckoning at him. "Come over here where we can talk."

My voice had little effect on either The Bachelor or the teeming Asadi. Although a movement of the head indicated that he had heard my invitation, The Bachelor regarded me with no more, and no less, interest than before. Of course, he couldn't "talk" with me. My eyes don't have even the limited virtuosity of traffic lights, and since The Bachelor's never changed colors, he couldn't even "talk" with his own kind. He was, for all intents and purposes, a mute.

When I called out to him, though, I believed his dead, grey eyes indicated a complete lack of intelligence. It didn't then occur to me that they might signal a physical handicap, just as dumbness in human beings may be the result of diseased or paralyzed vocal cords.

"Come on over here," I urged him again.

The Bachelor, still staring, didn't approach. He stared at me for the remainder of the afternoon. I tried to occupy myself with note-taking, then with a lunch of some of the rations Benedict had dropped, and finally with cursory observations of other Asadi. Anything to avoid that implacable gaze. It was almost a relief when dusk fell.

But that evening my excitement grew as I realized that something truly monumental had happened: *I had been acknowledged.*

The next day The Bachelor paid me little heed. He wandered forlornly in and out of the slow, aimless files of his aimless kindred, and I was sorely disappointed he didn't demonstrate the same interest in me that he had the day before.

On the 28th day he resumed his shameless staring. I was gratified, too, even though he now pursued a strategy different from that of the previous day: He moved tirelessly about the clearing, weaving in and out of the clusters of Asadi, but always staying close enough to the western sideline to be able to see me. His eyes remained as dead as the insides of two oyster shells. I was fighting stomach cramps and bouts of diarrhea, and by late afternoon his stare had grown annoying again.

I felt better the following morning, my 29th day. The light from glowering Denebola seemed softer, the tropical heat less debilitating. I left my lean-to and went out on the assembly ground.

Bathed in the pastel emptiness of dawn, the Asadi came flying through the lianas and fronds of the Synesthesia Wild to begin another day of Indifferent Togetherness. Soon I was surrounded. Surrounded but ignored. Great ugly heads with silver, or blue, or clay-white, or tawny manes bobbed around me, graceless and unsynchronized.

At last I found The Bachelor.

Undoubtedly, he had had me in his sight all that morning—but, moving with circumspection among his fellows, he had not permitted me to see him. And I had fretted over his apparent absence.

Then Denebola was directly overhead. Our shadows were small dark pools around our feet, like fallen trousers. The Bachelor threaded his way through a dissolving clump of bodies and stopped not five meters from me, atremble with his own daring. I, too, trembled. Would The Bachelor fall upon and devour me as the Asadi males had fallen upon and devoured the old chieftain's gift of meat?

Instead, The Bachelor steeled himself to the task he had set and began his approach. My shadow wrinkled a little under my feet. The grey head, the patchy silver-blue mane, the twin carapaces of his eyes—all moved toward me. Then the long grey arm rose toward my face and the perfectly humanoid hand touched the depression under my bottom lip, touched the most recent of my shaving cuts, touched me without clumsiness or malice.

And I winced.

A RUNNING CHRONOLOGY: WEEKS PASS

From the professional notebooks of Egan Chaney:
Day 29: After this unusual one-to-one contact with the Asadi (hereinafter referred to as The Bachelor), I did my best to find some method of meaningful communication. Words failed. So did signs in the dirt. Hand signals attracted and held his attention, but I have no training in the systematic use of American Sign Language or any of its several variants and so eventually gave this method up, too. I don't really believe it's a likely solution to our communication problems.

Nevertheless, The Bachelor couldn't be dissuaded from following me about. On one occasion, when I left the clearing for lunch, he very nearly followed me into my lean-to. I was almost surprised when at dusk he left with the others, he had been so doggedly faithful all day. Despite this desertion, I'm excited about my work again. Tomorrow seems a hundred years off. . . .

Day 35: The Bachelor continues to follow me around, never any more than eight or nine paces away. His devotion is such that I can't take a pee without his standing guard at my back. He must think he's found an ally against the indifference of the others, who blithely ignore us. I've begun to weary of his attentions.

Day 40: I'm ill again. The medicine Benedict dropped during an earlier bout of diarrhea is almost gone. It's raining. As I write this, lying on my pallet in my lean-to, the odor of the Asadi's morose, grey dampness assaults me like a poison, intensifying my nausea. In and out they go, back and forth. . . .

I have formulated an interesting notion that their entire way of life, in which I've had to struggle to see even one or two significant patterns, is itself the one significant and ongoing ritual of their species. Formerly, I had been looking for several minor rituals to help me explain this people. It may be that *they are the ritual.* As the poet said, "How tell the dancer from the dance?" But having formulated this new and brilliant hypothesis about the Asadi, I'm still left with the question, *What is the significance of the ritual the Asadi themselves are?* An existential query, of course.

The Bachelor sits cross-legged in the dripping, steam-silvered foliage about five meters from my lean-to. His mane clings to his skull and shoulders like so many tufts of matted, cottony mold. Even though he's been dogging my footsteps for eleven days now, I can't get him to enter my shelter. He always sits outside and stares at me from beneath an umbrella of leaves. Even when it's raining. His reluctance to come under a manufactured roof may be significant. If only I could make the same sort of breakthrough with two or three others I've made with The Bachelor.

Day 50: After the Asadi fled into the jungle last night, I trudged toward the supply pickup point where Benedict leaves my rations and medicine each week. The doses of Placenol I've been giving myself lately, shooting up the stuff like a junkie, have gotten bigger and bigger—but Eisen, at the outset of this farcical expedition, assured me that P-nol, in any quantity, is absolutely nonaddictive. What amazes me beyond this sufficiently amazing attribute of the drug, though, is the fact that Benedict's been dropping more and more of it each week, providing me with a supply almost exactly in tune with my increasing consumption.

Or do I use more because he drops more?

No, of course not. Everything goes into a computer at base camp. A program they ran weeks ago probably predicted this completely predictable upsurge in my "emotional" dependency on P-nol. At any rate, I'm feeling better; I've begun to function again.

Trudging toward the pickup point, I felt a haunting uneasiness seeping into me from the fluid shadows of the rainthorn trees. I heard noises. The noises persisted all the way to the drop point: faint, unidentifiable, and frightening. I believe, however, that The Bachelor lurked somewhere beyond the wide leaves and trailing vines where those noises originated. Once, in fact, I think I saw his dull eyes reflect a little of the sheen of the evening's first moon. I don't know.

A typed note on the supply bundle: "Look, Dr. Chaney, you don't have to insist on 100% nonassociation with us base campers. You've been gone almost two months. Let us drop you a radio. A little conversation with genuine human beings won't destroy your precious ethnography, sir. You can use it in the evenings. If you want it, send up a flare tomorrow night before Balthazar has risen and I'll copter it out the next day."

The note was signed by Benedict. But of course I don't want a radio. Part of this business is the suffering. I knew that before I came out here. I won't quit until things have begun to make a little sense.

Day 57 (Predawn): I haven't been asleep all night. Yesterday, just six or seven hours ago, I went into the jungle to retrieve Benedict's eighth supply drop. Another typed note on the bundle: "Dr. Chaney, Eisen says you're a pigheaded ninny. That you don't even know how to conjugate your own first name. It should have been *Ego*, he says, and not *Egan*. Have you started preaching neo-Pentecostal sermons to the trees? What a picture. Send up a flare if you want anything. Ben."

On the way back to the clearing I heard noises again. The Synesthesia Wild echoed with the plunging greyness of an indistinct form—The Bachelor, spying on me, retreating clumsily before my pursuit. Even with a backpack of new supplies weighing me down, I determined to follow these suspicious tickings of leaf and twig. Although I never overtook my prey, I was able to keep up! It had to be The Bachelor. None of his fellows would have given me so much as a glimpse of the disturbed foliage in the wake of their disappearance. I went deeper and deeper into the Wild, farther away from the supply drop and the assembly ground. Two hours. Three.

At last, panting with the sheer momentum of my pursuit, I broke into an opening among the trees. All at once I realized that the noises drawing me on had ceased. I was alone, and lost, and confused.

Filling the clearing, rising against the sky like an Oriental pagoda, there loomed over me the broad and impervious mass of something *built*. The resonances of Time dwarfed me. Thunderstruck, I felt panic climbing hand over hand up the membranous ladder in my throat. Oliver Oliphant Frasier had studied the *ruins* of one of these structures, learning only that the Asadi may once have had a civilization of some consequence. I was staring at a huge, intact relic of that civilization. Amethyst windows. Stone carvings above the entablature. A dome. A series of successively smaller roofs as the eye went up the face of the structure. At last I turned, plunged back into the jungle, and raced wildly away, my backpack thumping.

DEATH AND DESIGNATION AMONG THE ASADI 217

Where was I going? Back to the assembly ground, I hoped. Which way to run? I didn't know, but I didn't have to answer this question. Blindly, I moved in the direction of the suspicious tickings of leaf and twig that had resumed shortly after I fled the pagoda. The Bachelor again? I don't know. I saw nothing. But in three hours' time I had regained the safety of my lean-to. . . . Now I'm waiting for the dawn, for the tidal influx of Asadi. I'm exhilarated, and I haven't even touched my new supply of P-nol.

Day 57 (Evening): They're gone again. But I've witnessed something important and unsettling. The Bachelor didn't arrive this morning with the others. Could he have injured himself in our midnight chase through the Wild? By noon I was both exhausted and puzzled — exhausted by my search for him and my lack of sleep, puzzled by his apparent defection. I came to my lean-to and lay down. In a little while I was sleeping, though not soundly. Tickings of twig and leaf made my eyelids flicker. I dreamed that a grey shape came and squatted on the edge of the clearing about five meters from where I lay. Like a mute familiar, the shape watched over me. . . .

Kyur-AAACCCCK!

Groans and thrashings about. Thrashings and hackings. The underbrush beside my lean-to cracked beneath the invasion of several heavy feet. Bludgeoned out of my dream by these sounds, I sat up and attempted to reorient myself to the world. I saw The Bachelor. I saw three of the larger and more agile males bearing him to the ground and pinioning him there. They appeared to be *cooperating* in the task of subduing him!

Ignoring me with all the contemptuous élan of aristocrats, the three males picked up The Bachelor and bore him to the center of the clearing. I followed this party onto the assembly ground. As they had during the old chieftain's two unexpected visits, the Asadi crowded to the sidelines — but without disappearing into the jungle. They remained on the field, buffeting one another like rabid spectators at a World Cup event. I was the only individual other than the four struggling males in the center of the assembly floor, however, and I looked down at The Bachelor. His eyes came very close to changing colors, from their usual clay-white to a thin, thin yellow. But I couldn't help him, couldn't interfere.

They shaved his mane. A female carrying two flat, beveled stones came out of the crowd on the eastern perimeter of the field. She gave these to the males. With these stones the males scraped away the last sad mangy tufts of The Bachelor's silver-blue collar. Just as they were about to finish, he gave a perfunctory kick that momentarily dislodged one of his tormentors, then acquiesced in his shame and lay on his back staring at the sky. The entire operation took only about ten minutes. The three males sauntered off from their victim, and the satisfied spectators, aware that the barbering was over, filtered back into the clearing with all their former randomness. But now, of course, they ignored The Bachelor with a frigidity they had once reserved for me. I stood in the center of the clearing waiting for him to get to his feet, but for a long time he didn't move. His narrow head, completely shorn, scarred by their barbering stones, looked unnaturally fragile. I leaned down and offered him my hand. A passing Asadi jostled me. Accidentally, I think. The Bachelor rolled to his stomach, rolled again to avoid being stepped on, curled into the fetal position—then unexpectedly sprang out of the dust and dodged through a broken file of his uncaring kin.

Did he wish to attain the edge of the Wild? Intervening bodies blocked my view, but I suppose that The Bachelor disappeared into the trees and kept on running.

What does all this signify? My hypothesis is that the Asadi have punished The Bachelor for leading me last night, whether purposely or inadvertently, to the ancient pagoda in the Synesthesia Wild. His late arrival in the clearing may have been an ingenuous attempt to forestall this punishment. Why else, I ask myself, would the Asadi have moved to make The Bachelor even more of an outcast than he already was?

Patience, dear God, is nine-tenths of cultural xenology. Mystified, I pray for patience.

Day 61: The Bachelor has not returned. Knowing that he's now officially a pariah, he chooses to be one on his own terms.

During The Bachelor's absence, I've been thinking about two things: 1) If the Asadi did in fact punish him because he led me to the pagoda, then they fully realize I'm not simply a maneless outcast. They know I'm genetically different, a creature from elsewhere, and they consciously wish me to remain ignorant of their past. 2) I would like to make an expedition to the pagoda. With a little perseverance it shouldn't be exceedingly difficult to find, especially since I plan to go during the day. Unusual things happen so rarely in the Asadi clearing that I can afford to be gone from it a little while. One day's absence should not leave any irreparable gaps in my ethnography. If all goes well, that absence may provide some heady insights into the ritual of Asadi life.

I wish only that The Bachelor would return.

Day 63: Since today was the day of Benedict's ninth scheduled drop, I decided to make my expedition into the Wild early this morning. Two birds with one stone, as Ben himself might put it. First, I would search for the lost pagoda. Second, even failing to find it, I would salvage some part of the day by picking up my new supplies. I left before dawn.

The directional instincts of human beings must have died millennia ago: I got lost. The Wild stirred with an inhuman and gothic calm that tattered the thin fabric of my resourcefulness.

Late in the afternoon Benedict's Dragonfly saved me. It made a series of stuttering circles over the roof of the jungle. Once I looked up and saw its undercarriage hanging so close to the treetops that a sprightly monkey might have been able to leap aboard. I followed the noise of the helicopter to our drop point. From there I had no trouble getting back to the clearing. Today, then, marks the first day since I've been in the Wild that I've not seen a single member of the Asadi, and I continue to miss The Bachelor. . . .

Day 68: I went looking for the pagoda again. Very foolish, I confess. But the last four days have been informational zeroes, and I had to take some kind of positive action. I got lost again, terrifyingly so. Green creepers coiled about me. The sky disappeared. How, then, did I get home, especially since Benedict's helicopter isn't due for two more days? Once again, the suspicious tickings of leaf and twig: I followed them, simply followed them, confident again that The Bachelor is still out there and steadfast in my decision to make no more expeditions until I have help.

Day 71: The Bachelor is back!

Day 72: The Bachelor still has very little mane to speak of, and the Asadi treat him as a total outcast. Another thing: The Bachelor, these last two days, has demonstrated a considerable degree of independence in his relations with me. He follows me less often. He no longer hunkers beside my lean-to at all. Does a *made* structure remind him of the pagoda to which he led me and for whose discovery to an outsider he was publicly humiliated? I find this new arrangement a felicitous one, however. A little privacy is good for the soul.

Day 85: The note on yesterday's supply bundle: "Send up a flare tomorrow night if you wish to remain in the Wild. Eisen is seriously considering hauling you out of there. Only a flare will save you. My personal suggestion, sir, is that you just sit tight and wait for us. Your good friend and subordinate, Ben." I've just sent up *two* goddamn flares. Day 85 will go down in cultural-xenological history as Egan Chaney's personal Fourth of July.

Day 98: I'm holding my own again. I've survived an entire month without venturing away from the assembly ground. Most of my time has been devoted to noting the individual differences among the Asadi. Since their behavior, for the most part, manifests a bewildering uniformity, I've turned to the observation of their physical characteristics. Even in this area, though, most differences are more apparent than real; beyond the principles of sex and the quality of the mane (length, color, thickness, and so on), I've found few useful discriminators. Size has some importance, certainly—but no matter how tall the Asadi, his or her body usually conforms to an ectomorphic configuration.

The ability of the eyes to flash through the spectrum is another discriminator. Of sorts. The only Asadi who don't possess this ability in a complete degree are the old chieftain and The Bachelor.

Still, I can recognize on sight several Asadi other than these prominent two. I've tried to give descriptive names to these recognizable individuals. The smallest adult male in the clearing I call Turnbull because his stature puts me in mind of Colin Turnbull's account of the pygmies of the Ituri and of my own work among that admirable people, now gone and unrecoverable. A nervous fellow with active hands I call Benjy, after Benedict. The old chieftain continues to exert a powerful influence on my thinking. His name I derived by simple analogy: Him I call Eisen Zwei.

The Bachelor now seems intent on retaining his anonymity. His mane has grown very little since the shaving. I would almost swear he plucks it at night, keeping it short on purpose. These last few days, after ascertaining my whereabouts in the morning and then again before sunset, he's completely avoided me. Good. We're both more comfortable.

Today was another drop day. I didn't go out to retrieve my

parcels — too weary. But I've sworn off Placenol, and the psychological lift attendant on this minor victory has made my physical weakness bearable. As I've tapered off the "nonaddictive" drug, the amount of P-nol in each drop has correspondingly decreased. To hell with the base-camp computer. I refuse to let the predictability of my victory detract from its beneficial effects on my mental health.

Tonight I'm going to read Odegaard's official report on the Shamblers of Misery. And then I'm going to sleep. Sleep, sleep, sleep.

Day 106: Eisen Zwei, the old chieftain, came back today! I first saw him enter this clearing ninety days ago. Has a pattern begun to emerge? I can't interpret its periodicity. I don't even know what sort of life span the Asadi have.... But to come back to the issue at hand, Eisen Zwei entered the clearing with the huri on his shoulder, sat down, remained perhaps an hour, then stalked back into the Wild. The Asadi, of course, fled from him — motivated, it seemed, more by loathing than fear. How long will I have to wait until ole E.Z. returns?

Day 110: The behavior of the Asadi has undergone a very subtle change, one I can't account for.

For the last two days every member of this insane species has taken great pains to avoid stepping into a rather large area in the center of the clearing. As a result, the Asadi have crowded themselves into two arbitrary groups at opposite ends of the field. These "teams" — if I may only half facetiously call them that — do not comport themselves in exactly the same way as did the formerly continuous group. Individuals on both sides of the silently agreed-upon no-man's land exude an air of heightened nervousness. They sway. They clutch their arms across their chests. They suffer near epileptic paroxysms as they weave in and out, in and out, among their fellows. I sometimes believe they writhe to the music of an eerie flute played deep in the recesses of the jungle.

Sometimes staring matches take place between individuals on opposite sides of the imaginary chasm. But neither participant puts a foot inside the crucial ring of separation, which is about thirty meters long and almost the entire width of the clearing. Not quite, mind you — because there's a very narrow strip of ground on each sideline through which the two "teams" may exchange members, one member at a time. These exchanges occur infrequently, with a lone Asadi darting nervously out of his own group, down one of these unmarked causeways, and into the "enemy" camp. Do they avoid the center of the clearing because that is where Eisen Zwei once made his bloody offering of flesh? I don't know.

The Bachelor has reacted to all this by climbing into the branches of a thick-boled tree not ten meters from my lean-to. From dawn to sunset he sits high above his inscrutable people, watching, sleeping, maybe even attempting to assess the general mood. Occasionally he looks in my direction to see what I make of these new developments. But I'm only good for a shrug. . . .

Day 112: It continues, this strange bipartite waltz. The dancers have grown even more frantic in their movements. Anxiety pulses in the air like electricity. The Bachelor climbs higher into his tree, wedging himself in place. The nonexistent flute that plays in my head has grown shrill, stingingly shrill, and I cannot guess what the end of this madness must be.

Day 114: Events culminated today in a series of bizarre developments that pose me a conundrum of the first order. It began early. Eisen Zwei came into the clearing an hour after the arrival of the Asadi. He bore on his back the carcass of a dressed-out animal. His huri, though upright on his shoulder, looked like the work of an inept taxidermist, awkwardly posed and inanimate. The people in the clearing deserted their two identically restive groups, fleeing to the jungle around the assembly ground.

The Bachelor, half hidden by great lacquered leaves, unsteady in the fragile upper branches, leaned out over the clearing's edge and gazed down with his clay-white eyes. Surrounded now by the curious, loathing-filled Asadi who had crowded into the jungle, I clutched the bole of the tree in which The Bachelor resided, and all of us watched.

Eisen Zwei lowered the burden from his back. But now, instead of stepping away and permitting a few of the braver males to advance, he took the huri from his shoulder and set it upon the bleeding lump of meat. The huri's blind head did not move, but even from where I stood I could see its tiny fingers rippling with slow but well-orchestrated malice. Then this hypnotic rippling ceased, and the huri sat there looking bloated and dead, a scabrous plaything.

Without a farewell of any sort, Eisen Zwei turned and stalked back into the Synesthesia Wild. Foliage clattered from the efforts of several Asadi to get out of his way. No one else moved.

Denebola, fat and mocking, crossed a small arc of sky and made haloes dance in a hundred inaccessible grottos of the Wild. An hour had passed, and Eisen Zwei returned! He had simply left the huri to guard his first offering. Yes, first. For the old chieftain had come back with still another carcass slung across his bony shoulders. He set it down beside the first. The huri animated itself just long enough to shift its weight and straddle the two contiguous pieces of meat. Then the old Asadi departed again.

An hour later he returned with a third piece of meat—but this time he entered the clearing from the west, about twenty meters up from my lean-to. I realized that he had first entered from the east, then from the south. *A pattern is developing,* I told myself. *Now he'll depart once more and reenter from the north.* Many peoples on Earth ascribe mystical characteristics to the four points of the compass, and I was excited by the possibility of drawing a meaningful analogy.

But Eisen Zwei remained on the assembly floor, shattering my hopes. (In fact, as on my 22nd night in the Wild, he still has not left. Under the copper-green glow of Melchior the old chieftain and his huri squat on the blood-dampened ground waiting for the dawn's first spiderwebbings of light.) Instead, he made one complete circuit around the clearing, walking counterclockwise from his point of entrance. The huri did not move.

This done, Eisen Zwei rejoined his familiar at midfield.

Here, the second stage of this new and puzzling ritual commenced. Without unloosening the third carcass from his back, E.Z. bent and picked up the huri and put it on his shoulder. Kneeling, he tied straps through the two pieces of meat over which the huri had kept watch. Next, he began to drag these marbled chunks of brown and red through the dirt. He dragged the first into the southern half of the clearing, unslipped the strap by which he had pulled it, and set the huri down once more as his guardian. This procedure he duplicated in the northern half of the clearing, except that here he necessarily stood guard over the second offering himself. The final carcass he still bore on his back.

Eisen Zwei stepped away from the second offering. Deep in his throat he made a noise that sounded like a human being trying to fight down a sob. This noise, I suppose I should add, is the first and so far the only example of *voiced* communication, discounting vague growls and involuntary moans, I've heard among the Asadi. The huri responded to Eisen Zwei's plaintive "sobs"—undoubtedly a signal—by hopping off the object of its guardianship and then scrabbling miserably through the dust toward the old man, its rubbery wings dipping and twisting. (I've almost decided the huri is incapable of flight. Perhaps its wings represent an anatomical holdover from an earlier stage of its evolution.) When both E.Z. and his wretched huri had reached their sacred patch of ground at midfield, the old man picked up the beast and let it close its tiny hands over his discolored mane.

Then the wizened old chieftain extended his arms, tilted his head back, and, staring directly at the sun, made a shuddering inhalation of such piteous depth it seemed either his lungs would burst or his heart break. The clearing echoed with his sob.

At once, the Asadi poured out of their hiding places onto the assembly ground—not simply the adult males, but individuals of every sex and age. Even now, however, in the midst of this lunging riot, the population of the clearing divided into two groups, each one scrimmaging furiously, intramurally, in its own cramped plot of earth. Manes tossed, and eyes pinwheeled with inarticulate color. The hunger of the Asadi made low sad music over the Wild, like summer thunder.

Slashing and sometimes half maiming one another, the Asadi quickly devoured the two carcasses. *Like piranhas*, I thought.

Then E.Z., inhaling mightily, moaned again, and the confusion ceased. Every lean grey snout turned toward him. The dying went off to die alone, if any were in fact at the point of death. I saw no one depart, but neither did I see anyone lying helplessly injured in the dirt. The Asadi waited. The Bachelor and I waited.

The third and final act of today's baroque ritual: Eisen Zwei lowered the last carcass from his back, sat down beside it, and, in full view of his bemused tribespeople, ate the monstrous thing piece by piece. He gave the huri nothing, and the huri, inert but clinging, did not protest this selfish oversight. Meanwhile, terribly slowly, Eisen Zwei ate.

Eventually I retired to the shade of my lean-to, emerging at fairly frequent intervals to check the goings-on in the clearing. By the second hour the Asadi had begun to move about within their separate territories. By the third hour these territories had merged, making it impossible to distinguish the two distinct "teams" of previous days. The old pattern of Indifferent Togetherness had reasserted itself, except that now the Asadi moved with incredible sluggishness, suspiciously eyeing their chieftain and refusing to encroach on the unmarked circle containing him.

I noticed that The Bachelor had come down out of his tree, but I was unable to find him in the clearing. All I saw was E.Z., isolated by a revolving barricade of legs, peeling away the last oily strips of meat from his dinner and chewing them with an expression of stupid pensiveness. The huri flapped once or twice, but the old man still did not feed it.

Finally, sunset.

The Asadi fled, but Eisen Zwei—no doubt as surfeited as a python that has just unhinged its lower jaw to admit a fawn—slumped in his place and did not move.

Now a single alien moon dances in the sky, and I'm left with a question whose answer is so stark and self-evident I'm almost afraid to ask it: *From what sort of creature did the old man obtain and dress out his ritual offerings?* Huddled beneath the most unsubstantial of roofs, I am unable to fend off the frightening ramifications of the Asadi way of death. . . .

SPECULATIONS ON CANNIBALISM: AN EXTEMPORANEOUS ESSAY

From the unedited in-the-field tapes of Egan Chaney: It's a beautiful day, and if I hold my microphone out—I'm holding it out now, extending it toward the Asadi—all you'll be able to hear is five hundred pairs of feet slogging back and forth through a centimeter of hot dust. There. Hear that? Perhaps you don't. Nevertheless, Eisen, it's a beautiful day.

It's four days since your counterpart, Eisen Zwei, stirred things up with his disorderly three-course banquet. Since then, nothing.

I'm walking. I'm walking among the Asadi. They fail to see me even though I'm just as solid, just as *real* as they are. Even the ones I've given names to—Campy, Werner, Gus, Oliver, and the others—refuse to grant me the simple fact of my existence. This is hard, Ben. This is difficult to accept. Nonetheless, I continue to feel a paternal tenderness toward these few Asadi—Jane, Thelma, Dianne, Celeste, and the others—I've been able to recognize and name. . . .

I've just walked by Celeste. The configuration of her features gives her a gentle look, like a Quaker woman wearing a parka. Her seeming gentleness leads me to the topic of this commentary: How could a creature of Celeste's mien and disposition actually eat the flesh of one of her own kind? God help me if these aliens are intelligent and self-aware, base-camp huggers, because I'm walking among cannibals!

They encircle me. They ensorcel me. They fill me with a sudden dread, an awe such as the awe of one's parents that consumes the child who has just learned the secrets of conception and birth. Exactly thus, my dread of the Asadi, my awe of their intimate lives.

Turnbull is missing. Do you remember him? I named him Turnbull because he was small, like the pygmies the first Turnbull wrote about, like the pygmies I worked among. Now I can't find Turnbull. Little Turnbull, squat and sly, is nowhere among these indifferent, uncouth people. I'd have found him by now, I know I would. He was my pygmy, my little pygmy, and now these aloof bastards—these Asadi of greater height than Turnbull—have eaten him! Eaten him as though he were an animal! a creature of inferior status! a zero in a chain of zeroes as long as the diameter of time! May God damn them for their impious rapacity!

[*A lengthy pause during which only the shuffling of the Asadi can be heard.*]

I think my shout unsettled some of them. A few of them flinched! But they don't look at me, these cannibals, and I don't know whether to be outraged or gratified. A cannibal may never go too far toward acknowledging the existence of another of his kind, so uncertain is his opinion of himself. A cannibal's always afraid he'll ascribe more importance to himself than he deserves. In doing so, he discovers—in a moment of hideous revelation—where his next meal is coming from. He always knows where it's coming from, and he's therefore nearly always afraid.

Cannibals—the civilized sort—are the most inwardly warring schizophrenics in all of Nature. On the one hand, Eisen, it requires a colossal arrogance to think oneself enough better than another member of one's own species to eat him. On the other, this same act demonstrates the abject self-abasement of the cannibal in his readiness to convert the flesh of his own kind into— well, let's be blunt about this, into *shit*. Grandiose haughtiness versus the worst sort of voluntary self-degradation. Have the Asadi incorporated these polar attitudes into the structure of their daily life? Does their indifference to one another result from the individual's esteem for himself? Could it be that the individual's lack of regard for his kind precipitates the practices of pariahhood and public humiliation? A schizophrenic society? Does the pattern of indifferent association during the day and compulsive scattering at night mirror the innate dichotomy of their souls? After all, who's more deluded than the cannibal? His every attempt to achieve union with his kind results in a heightened alienation from himself.

[Chaney's microphone picks up the incessant shuffling of Asadi feet and the low sighing of a breeze in the rain forest.]

Yes, yes, I know. This is all very bad anthropology. But I'm not really speaking anthropologically. I'm speaking metaphorically, and maybe I'm not talking about the Asadi at all. I realize full well, gang, that among human populations there are two types of cannibalism: exocannibalism and endocannibalism. I haven't forgotten *all* my training.

Exocannibalism, Ben, usually occurs in a context of continuing warfare between tribes that are dependent to some extent on agriculture for their livelihoods. They war, you see, to protect their sedentary way of life or to expand their holdings into areas where the soil hasn't been depleted by overuse. Enemies eat one another to steal their adversaries' strength and to gain power over them. In such a context, cannibalism is patriotic, and human flesh is invariably kosher.

The Asadi, not being agriculturists, and having no natural enemies here in the Synesthesia Wild, are not adherents of exocannibalism. Instead, Ben, they practice endocannibalism. Is that clear?

What this means, in short, is that the Asadi regularly eat members of their own tribal unit, the only tribal unit on BoskVeld. Usually, this form of cannibalism signifies an attempt on the part of the deceased's relatives and friends to incorporate the dead one's memories and spirit by a ritual ingestion of his flesh. Eating the dead under such circumstances, then, is an act of homage and a visible expression of the community's desire to insure the continuity of its life-style and its membership. Christians, by the way, participate in symbolic endocannibalism every time they celebrate Holy Communion. *Eat this — drink this — in remembrance of Me.*

Why, you may wonder, does the endocannibalism of the Asadi so offend and demoralize me? Because, God help me, I've begun regarding them as alien projections of my own consciousness, and, expecting better of myself, I expected better of them. Does that make sense? I'm afraid you'll think it doesn't. But, damn it, just when I'd begun to see glimmerings of something lofty in their make-ups, old E.Z.—like some nineteenth-century Indian headman putting on a potlatch—comes dragging three carcasses into the clearing and unleashes the ravenous animal in every one of his goggle-eyed subjects! It's more than I can stand. The Asadi ignore me. It's hot out here, and they ignore me. They go by, they go by, revolving about me like so many motorized pasteboard cutouts. And Turnbull's not among them, he doesn't revolve anymore, he's been butchered and consumed. *Butchered and consumed,* do you hear? With the same wanton self-centeredness that we used to poison the Ituri and rout out the people who lived there. Turnbull's dead, base-camp huggers, and *There are no more pygmies, there are no more pygmies, there are no*

PART THREE

THE RITUAL OF DEATH AND DESIGNATION

From the final draft of the one complete section of Egan Chaney's otherwise unfinished ethnography:

DEATH

On Day 120 the old chieftain, whom I called Eisen Zwei, took ill. Because it had been several days since he had gorged himself during the general "feast," I then supposed that his sickness was unrelated to his earlier intemperance. I am still of this mind. For five days he had eaten nothing, although the other Asadi refused to observe his fast and began eating whatever herbs, roots, flowers, bark, and heartwood they came across. They ignored the old man, and the old man's huri, much in the way they ignored The Bachelor and me.

Eisen Zwei's sickness altered this pattern. On the afternoon of the first day of his illness, he abruptly rose and made the horribly glottal, in-sucking noises he had used to summon his people to the meat six days before. I came running from my lean-to. The Asadi moved away from their old chieftain, stopped their shuffling and shambling, and stared with great platterlike eyes whose pinwheeling irises had stalled on a single color. A spastic rumbling replaced the old man's in-sucking noises, and he bent over at the waist, his arms above his head, to heave and heave again—until it seemed he would soon be vomiting into the dust the very lining of his bowels. Out of his mouth came the half-digested crimson oddments of his spectacular, six-day-old meal. Abashed by the sight, stung by the odor, I turned away. The heaving continued, and since the Asadi stared on, I turned back to observe their culture in action. Duty is a harsh mistress.

The chieftain's huri flew up from his shoulder and flapped in the air like a small, wind-collapsed umbrella. I had never seen it fly before, and was surprised that it was capable of flight. Its ungainly flapping excited the already well-aroused population of the clearing, and together we watched the huri rise above tree level, circle back, and dip threateningly toward the branches of the trees on the western perimeter. The old man continued to vomit, but now every pair of color-stalled eyes followed the uncertain aerial progress of the huri, which, at one point, plummeted toward the perch where The Bachelor sometimes sequestered himself.

But The Bachelor wasn't there, and I had no idea where he could be.

Crashing downward through the branches, the huri caught itself up and returned with blind devotion to the airspace over its master. An ugly joke, it sardonically defied gravity.

I thought that at last the huri was going to feed, that its sole diet might well consist of Eisen Zwei's vomitings. I expected the starved creature to fall to earth upon these—but it did not. Somehow it kept itself aloft, flapping, flapping, waiting for the old man to finish.

Finally, it was not the huri that waded into the vile pool of vomit, but the old man's shameless conspecifics. My curiosity overcame my revulsion, and I watched the Asadi carry away their portions of the half-digested mess as if each semisolid piece were an invaluable relic. No fighting, no elbowing, no eye-searing abuse. Each individual simply picked out his relic, took it a short distance into the jungle, and deposited it in some hidden place for temporary safekeeping.

During the solemn recessional, the huri quickened the air with its wingbeats and an anonymous Asadi supported Eisen Zwei by clutching—tenderly clutching—his mane. When everyone had taken away a chunk of regurgitated flesh, the chieftain's attendant laid him down in a dry place, and the huri descended to squat by its master's head.

I should mention that The Bachelor was one of those who appeared in the mourning throng to select and depart with some memento of Eisen Zwei's illness. He came last, took only a palm-sized morsel, and retreated to the clearing's edge. Here he climbed into the tree above which the huri had flown its nearly disastrous mission only minutes before. Until sunset The Bachelor remained here, observing and waiting.

On Days 121, 122, and 123, Eisen Zwei continued in his illness, and the Asadi paid him scant attention. They brought him water twice a day and considerately refrained from stepping on him. The huri sat by the old man's head. It seemed to be waiting for him to die. It never ate.

At night the Asadi deserted their dying leader without a glance, and I was afraid he would die while they were gone. Several times, looking out at his inert silhouette, moonlight dripping through the fronds, I thought he *had* died, and a mild panic assailed me. Did I have a responsibility to the corpse?

But the old man did not die, and on Day 124 another change

occurred. Eisen Zwei sat up and stared at Denebola as it crossed the sky—but he stared at the angry sun through spread fingers, hands crooked into claws, and he tore impotently through the blur of light that Denebola must have seemed to him. The huri sat smug and blindly knowing, as always. But the Asadi noticed the change in the old man and reacted to it. As if his writhing dissatisfaction with the sun were a clue, they divided into two groups again and formed attentive semicircles to the north and south of Eisen Zwei. They watched him wrestling with the sun's livid corona, tearing at its indistinct streamers of gas with gnarled hands.

At noon the old man rose to his feet, stretched out his arms, sobbed, clawed at the sky, and suddenly sank back to his knees. A pair of Asadi from each group went to his aid. They lifted him from the ground. Others on the clearing's edge selected large, lacquered palm leaves and passed these over the heads of their comrades to the place where the old man had collapsed. The Asadi supporting Eisen Zwei took these leaves, arranged them in the shape of a pallet, and then placed the old man's fragile body on the bed they had made.

The second cooperative endeavor I had witnessed among the Asadi, the first having been the shaving of The Bachelor's mane. It was short-lived, though, for aimless shambling replaced chieftain-watching as the primary activity within the two groups on either side of his pallet. Denebola, finally free of the old man's gaze, fell toward the horizon.

I walked unimpeded through the clearing and bent down over the dying chieftain, careful to avoid the huri that eyed me with its uncanny, eyeless face. I looked down into the genuine eyes of its master.

And experienced a shock, a physical jolt.

The old man's eyes were burnt-out, blackened holes in a hominoid mask. Utterly dead they were, two char-smoked lenses waiting for the old man's body to catch up with their lifelessness.

And then the diffused red light that signaled sunset in the Wild came pouring through the foliage, and the clearing emptied.

Alone with Eisen Zwei and his huri, I knew that it would be during the night that the old man died. I tried to find some intimation of life in his eyes, saw none, and withdrew to the cover of the Wild and the security of my lean-to. I did not sleep. But my worst premonitions betrayed me, and in the morning I looked out to see Eisen Zwei sitting cross-legged on his pallet, the huri once again perched on his shoulder.

And then, filtering through the jungle, the tenuous, copper-colored light signaling sunrise and rejuvenation on BoskVeld. The Asadi returned, once again taking up their positions to the north and the south of their dying chieftain. Day 125 had begun.

I call the events of Day 125, taken as a cumulative whole, the Ritual of Death and Designation. I believe that we will never fully understand the narrowly "political" life of the Asadi until we can interpret, with precision, every aspect of this Ritual.

The color of the eyes of every Asadi in the clearing—only The Bachelor's excepted—declined into a deep and melancholy indigo. And stalled there. Profound indigo and absolute silence. So deeply absorbent were the eyes of the Asadi that Denebola, rising, could throw out scarcely a single dancing, shimmering ray. Or so it seemed. The morning was an impressionist painting rendered in flat pastels and dull primaries. A paradox.

And then the Asadi's heads began to rock from side to side, the chin of each individual inscribing a small figure eight in the air. The heads moved in unison. This went on for an hour or more as the old chieftain sat nodding in the monumental morning stillness.

At last, as if they had inscribed figure eights for the requisite period, the Asadi broke out of their groups and formed several concentric rings around the old man. The members of each ring began to sway. The inaudible flute I had once believed to be in the Wild had now certainly been exchanged for an inaudible bassoon. Ponderously, the Asadi swayed, their great manes undulating with a slow and beautifully orchestrated grief. And The Bachelor—all by himself, beyond the outermost ring—swayed also, swayed in lugubrious cadence with the others. The rhythmic swaying lasted through the remaining hours of the forenoon and on toward the approach of evening.

I retired to my lean-to, but thought better of just sitting there and climbed the tree in which The Bachelor had often perched. I forgot about everything but the weird ceremony in the clearing. I gave myself up completely to the hypnotic movements of the grey, shaggy-headed creatures that a bewildering universe had given me to study. . . .

I nodded but I did not sleep.

Suddenly Eisen Zwei gave a final sob, maniacal and heartrending, and grabbed the beast clinging with evil tenacity to his mane. He grabbed it with both palsied hands. He exerted himself to what seemed his last reserve of strength and, strangling the huri, lurched out of the dust to his feet. The huri flapped, twisted, and freed one wing. The old man squeezed his hands together and attempted to

DEATH AND DESIGNATION AMONG THE ASADI

grind the life out of the creature who had imprisoned him even as it did his bidding. He was not successful. The huri used its tiny hands to scour fine crimson wounds into Eisen Zwei's withered cheeks and buckled forehead. Then it flapped out of the old man's grasp and rose to tree level.

I feared it would dive upon me in my borrowed perch, but it skirted the perimeter of the clearing, dipping, banking, silently cawing. Its imaginary screams curdled my blood. Meanwhile, Eisen Zwei fell sideways across his pallet and died.

The Asadi chieftain was dead. He died just at sunset.

I waited for his people to flee into the Wild, to leave his brittle corpse for an Earthman's astonished scrutiny. They did not flee. Even though the lethal twilight was gathering about them, they stayed. The attraction of the old man's death outweighed their fear of exposing themselves in an open place to the mysteries of the darkness.

In my arboreal lookout, I had witnessed two things that I had never seen among the Asadi: death and a universal failure to repair.

DESIGNATION

The Ritual of Death and Designation had passed into its second stage before I truly comprehended that stages existed. I ignored my hunger and put away the thought of sleep.

The Asadi converged upon the old man's corpse. Those of smallest size were permitted to crowd into the center of the clearing and lift the dead chieftain above their heads. The young, the deformed, the weak, and the congenitally slight of stature formed a double column beneath the old man's outstretched body and began moving with him toward the northern end zone.

Arranged in this fashion, they forced a new revelation upon me. These were Asadi whose manes were a similar texture and color: a stringy, detergent-scum brown. They bore the corpse of Eisen Zwei with uncomplaining acquiescence. The larger, sleeker specimens of Asadi—those with luxuriant silver, silver-blue, or golden manes—formed single columns on each side of their lackluster counterparts; and together these two units, like water inside a moving pipe, flowed toward the north—

—The one direction from which Eisen Zwei had not entered on the day he brought those three dressed-out carcasses into the clearing.

Driver ants in Africa use just this sort of tubular alignment when they wish to move great distances as a group: the workers inside the column, the warriors without. And nothing on that immense dark continent is more feared than driver ants on the march. With, of course, the singular and noteworthy exception of Humankind.

Almost too late I realized that the Asadi would move out of the clearing and beyond my reach unless I abandoned The Bachelor's tree. Nearly falling, I scrambled down. As if viewed through a photographer's filter, the foliage through which the mourners marched gave off a soft gauzy glow. I ran. I found that I could keep up with very little effort, so cadenced and funereal was the step of their procession. I slowed to a walk behind it.

Trudging in the wake of the mourners, incorrigibly hangdog in his pariahhood, was The Bachelor. Meanwhile, the twilight reverberated with the footfalls and leaf nudgings of a host of single-minded communicants.

I saw the huri flying above the part of the procession where its master was being borne forward on the shoulders of the smaller Asadi. Avoiding branches, the huri turned an inadvertent cartwheel in the air, righted itself, and landed on Eisen Zwei's bony chest. Here it did a little preening dance, for all the world like an oil-coated rooster wooing a hen. Then the column snaked to the left, the Wild closed off my view of the marchers, and darkness began drifting in like black confetti.

How long we trudged, I have no idea. An eternity of infinitesimal moments. I won't attempt to estimate. Say only, quite a long time. Finally our procession flowed into another clearing.

There in the clearing, rising against the sky like an Oriental pagoda, loomed the broad and impervious mass of something *built*, something *made*. All three moons were up, and the solid black bulk of this structure was spotlighted in the antique-gold claret shed by the three moons together. Even before those of us at the end of the procession had exited the jungle, we could see the lofty, winglike roofs of this sudden artifact and its high, deep-violet windows. Was I the only one whose first inclination was to plunge back into the nightmare forest? I don't believe so.

As we approached, members of both the inner and the outer columns began to sway from side to side, marching and swaying at once. The Bachelor's head, in fact, moved in wide arcs; his whole marching body trembled as if from the paroxysms of ague. If he had been punished for once leading me to this place, perhaps he trembled now from fear. On the other hand, if the Asadi wished this temple kept inviolate, wouldn't they somehow punish me if they discovered my presence?

I almost bolted back the way the Asadi had led me, but the pagoda had captured my imagination and I resisted the impulse to run. However, I did have the good sense to climb a tree on the edge of the clearing fronting the pagoda. From this vantage I watched the proceedings in relative safety.

Grey shadows moved in the deep shadow cast by the Asadi temple. And suddenly two violently green flames burned in the iron flambeaux on either side of the top step of the immense tier of stone steps leading to the temple's ornate doorway! The torch-lighters—formerly the moving grey shadows—came back down the steps. Once again I was stunned with wonder and disbelief. This sophisticated use of both flambeaux and a starting agent I couldn't even guess at destroyed a multitude of my previous conclusions about the Asadi. Fire! They understood fire!

By this time the four columns of Asadi had ranged themselves in parallel files before the stairway of the ancient pagoda, and six slightly built menials bore the corpse of Eisen Zwei—now an uncanny apple green in the torchlight—up the broad stone steps to the stone catafalque before the door. Here they set the corpse down and lined up behind him, staring out over their waiting kinspeople, facing the cruel ambivalence of the Wild, three on each side of the old man. Unaccustomed to such tawdry grandeur, I began to think that Placenol, or something more sinister, was flowing through my veins. Surely this was all hallucination!

The moons cried out with their silent mouths. The flambeaux uttered bright screamings of unsteady light.

But the ritual did not conclude. The night drew on, the moons rolled, and the four files of Asadi tribesmen shuffled in their places. Some stretched out their hands and fought with the tumbling moons just as Eisen Zwei had wrestled with Denebola, the sun. None left the clearing, though I felt that many wanted to. Wrestling with their own fears, they waited. The pagoda commanded their awesome patience. Wedged like a spike into my tree, I watched as Melchior drifted down the sky toward the jungle. The Bachelor fidgeted, and the two iron torches began to gutter like spent candles.

Dawn delayed.

Two vacuums existed: the vacuum in Nature between the end of night and the beginning of day, and the vacuum in the peculiar hierarchy of the Asadi tribal structure. Night and death. Two vacuums in search of compensatory substance. When would dawn break? How would the Asadi designate their dead chieftain's successor?

A commotion in the clearing! Looking down, I saw that the four neat files of Asadi had dissolved into a single disorganized mass of milling bodies. A chaos, an anarchy—as on their original assembly ground. How could a vacuum of "leadership" exist in such an arbitrary melange of unrelated parts? Only the pagoda had solidity, only the pagoda did not move.

Then, looking up, I saw the old man's huri floating high above this disorder, floating rather than flailing: a gyrfalcon rather than a pelican. It rode the prismatic, predawn breezes with uncommon grace, flew off so effortlessly that in a moment it had dwindled to a scrap of light far beyond the temple's central spire.

Then the huri folded its wings behind it and plummeted dizzyingly down the roseate sky. I almost fell. My feet slipped through the fork that had supported me, and I was left dangling, arms above my head, over one edge of the pagoda's forecourt. The anxiety-torn communicants were too caught up in their panic to notice me.

Meanwhile, the huri rocketed earthward. It dived into the helpless crowd of Asadi and skimmed along their heads and shoulders with its cruel, serrated wings. Dipping in and out, it flapped, once again, like a torn window shade, all its ephemeral grace turned to crass exhibitionism (I don't know what else to call it) and unwieldy flutterings. But the creature did what it sought to do—it scarred the faces of several of the Asadi. A few tried desperately to capture the huri. Others, more reasonably, ducked out of its way or threw up their arms to ward it off. The huri did not discriminate. It scarred all those in the way of its bladed wings, whether they attempted to catch it or to flee. The eyes of the harassed Asadi flashed through their individual spectral displays, and the heat from so many changes made the clearing phosphorescent with shed energy.

The fact that The Bachelor's eyes remained cool and colorless subtracted nothing from the heat of those thousand burning eyes. The Bachelor. I had nearly forgotten him. He stood apart from his panicked comrades and observed, neither grappling for nor fleeing from the huri. His eyes were clay white, mute, devoid of all intellect or passion. As for the huri, it flew up, flew down, performed a wobbly banking movement, and slashed with its murderous pinions at everything. Finally, it shot up through the shadow of the pagoda, wildly flapping, then pitched over and dived upon The Bachelor.

It flew into his face. It bore him to the ground and battered him with countless malicious wingbeats.

To the last individual, the Asadi quieted, queued up randomly, and watched this penultimate act in their day-long ritual. It took me a moment to understand. Then I realized:

The Bachelor was the designee, the chosen one, the chieftain elect. Somehow it seemed an inevitable choice.

My arms aching, I dropped from the tree onto the floor of the clearing. In front of me were the narrow backs of twenty or thirty Asadi. I couldn't see The Bachelor at all, though I could still hear the churning of the huri's wings and the altered breathing of the tribespeople.

Suddenly a figure, insanely rampant, disrupted the smooth surface of the crowd and darted through a quickly closing gap of bodies to my right. The Bachelor, having regained his feet, struggled to fight off the huri. The two of them thrashed their way up the tier of steps in front of the temple. Soon they had reached the paving beside the catafalque where Eisen Zwei still lay. On that sacred, high place The Bachelor surrendered to the inevitable.

He collapsed to his knees, lowered his head, and ceased to resist. The huri, sensing its victory, made an air-pummeling circuit over the body of the dead chieftain, sawing devilishly at the faces of the corpsebearers and rippling like dry brown paper. At last it settled on The Bachelor's head. Beating its wings for balance, it faced the onlooking multitude, and me, with blind triumph.

No one breathed. No one acknowledged the dawn as it revealed the caustic verdigris coating the pagoda like an evil frost.

Slowly, painfully slowly, The Bachelor got to his feet. He was draped in his own resignation, in the invisible garb of an isolation even more pronounced than that he had suffered as an outcast. He was the designee, the chosen one, the chieftain elect.

The huri dropped from The Bachelor's head to his shoulder, entwined its tiny fingers in the tufts of his butchered mane. Once again inanimate and scabrous, there it clung.

Now the Ritual of Death and Designation was nearly over. Two of the six corpsebearers on the temple's highest tier moved to complete that ritual. They touched the head and feet of Eisen Zwei with the tips of the two great flambeaux, and instantly the old man's body raged with green fire and the raging flame leaped up the face of the temple as if to abet the verdigris in its more patient efforts to eat the building away.

The Bachelor stood almost in the very blast of this conflagration. I feared that he, too, would be consumed. But he was not. Nor was the huri. The fire died, Eisen Zwei had utterly disappeared, and the corpsebearers came back down the steps and joined the shaggy anonymity of their revitalized people.

The Ritual of Death and Designation had ended.

For the purposes of this ethnography I will minimize the significance of what then occurred and report it as briefly as I am able.

Several of the Asadi turned and saw me in the pagoda's clearing. They actually looked at me. After having been ignored for over four months, I did not know how to react to the signal honor of abrupt visibleness. Out of monumental surprise, I returned their stares. They began advancing upon me, hostility evident in the rapid blurring of colors manifest in their eyes. Behind me, the Synesthesia Wild. I turned to escape into it. Another small group of Asadi had insinuated themselves into the path of my intended escape, blocking my way.

Among this group I recognized the individual whom I had given the name Benjy. Cognizant of nothing but a vague paternal feeling toward him, I sought to offer him my hand. His own nervous hand shot out and cuffed me on the ear. I fell. Dirt in my mouth, grey faces descending toward me, I understood that I ought to be terrified. But I spat out the dirt, the manes and faces retreated as quickly as they had come, and my incipient terror evaporated like alcohol in a shallow dish.

Overhead, a familiar flapping.

I looked up and saw the huri returning to The Bachelor's outstretched arm. He had released the creature upon his fellows in order to save me. An action illustrating the mind-boggling complexity of the relationship between the Asadi chieftain and the huri. Which of them rules? Which submits to command?

At that moment I hardly cared. Denebola had risen, and the Asadi had dispersed into the Wild, leaving me dwarfed and humbled in the presence of their self-sustaining pagoda and the reluctant chieftain who stared down from its uppermost tier. Although he remained aloof, before the day was out The Bachelor had led me back to the original assembly ground. Without his help, I ought to add, I never would have found it. I would be out there still today.

PART FOUR

An Introduction To "Chaney's Monologue"

Thomas Benedict speaking: I have put this paper together out of a complicated sense of duty. As one of the few people who had any substantial contact with Egan Chaney before his defection, I am perhaps also the only man who could have undertaken this task — despite my limited qualifications in the area of cultural xenology. But this is not really the place to discuss the strange *fait accompli* of our collaborative monograph. Suffice it to say that I owed Chaney my dedication to this project.

The section you have just read—"The Ritual of Death and Designation"—Chaney wrote in our base-camp infirmary while recuperating from exposure and a general inability to reorient himself to the society of human beings. In one of our conversations, as well as here in the monograph itself, he compared himself to Gulliver after his return from the land of the Houyhnhnms. At any rate, beyond Part Three of this monograph Chaney never wrote anything about the Asadi for publication, although immediately after his release from the infirmary I believe he intended to write a book about them. This monograph is the ghost of that unwritten book.

After returning to the original assembly ground of the Asadi, Chaney stayed two more weeks in the Calyptran Wild. On Days 126 and 133 I made supply drops, but, just as Chaney had requested, I did not fly over the clearing in the vain hope of spotting him and thereby determining the state of his health. It was enough to verify his robustness, he told me, from the fact that each week when I coptered in his supplies I could note that he had dutifully picked them up and carried them off. The argument that he was not the only creature in the Wild capable of hauling away the goods intended for him impressed Chaney not at all.

"I might as well be," he wrote on one of his infrequent notes left in a canister at the drop point. "The Asadi have all the initiative of malaria victims. More horrible than this, friend Ben, is the face-slapping truth that there is no one else out here. *No one else at all.*"

I am now the sole owner of the personal effects of Egan Chaney. These include his private journals and professional notebooks, a number of unfiled "official" reports, a series of in-the-field tapes, and a small bit of correspondence. Those records concerning the Asadi that I don't own myself I have access to as a result of my affiliation with the Third Denebolan Expedition as Chaney's pilot and aide. I tell you this only because I know for an incontrovertible fact that during his last fourteen days in the Wild, either Chaney did not make a single entry in any of his journals or notebooks, or he so completely effaced these dubious entries that they may as well have never existed.

We have only one complete report of any kind dealing with this final phase of Chaney's field work. It is a tape, a remarkable tape, and I believe Chaney would have destroyed it, too, had we not taken his recorder from him the instant we picked him out of the jungle.

I have listened to this tape many times — in its entirety, I should add, since doing so is a feat requiring almost supernatural patience. On the one occasion I tried to discuss its contents with Chaney (several days after his release from the infirmary, when I believed he could handle the terror of the experience with a degree of objectivity), he protested that I had imagined those contents. He told me he had never recorded the least word in the tape's running account of The Bachelor's . . . "*Metamorphosis?*" he asked. "Is that the word you used?"

I promptly played the tape for him. He listened to ten minutes of it, then got up and shut it off. His face had gone unaccountably lean and bewildered, and his hands trembled.

"Ah," he said, not looking at me. "An elaborate practical joke, Ben. I made it up because there was nothing better to do."

"The sound effects, too?" I asked incredulously.

Still not looking at me, he nodded his head — even though the circumstance of his rescue belied this clumsy explanation, exploded it, in fact, into untenable shrapnel. Chaney remained mute on the subject. In all of his writings and conversations in those last three months among us, he never mentioned or even alluded to the sordid adventure of his final two nights. I present here a transcript, somewhat edited, of the tape in question.

Chaney's Monologue: Two Nights in the Synesthesia Wild

Preliminaries

CHANEY [*enthusiastically*]: Hello all! What day is it? A day like any other day, except that you happen to be along for the ride. I'm going to be leading you on an expedition, you see. How often do I lead you on expeditions?

It's Day 138, I think, and yesterday The Bachelor returned to the clearing—the first time he's been back since the huri anointed him, so to speak, with the fecal salve of chieftainship. I'd almost given him up. But he came back into the clearing yesterday afternoon, the huri on his shoulder, and squatted in the center of the assembly ground just as old Eisen Zwei used to do. The reaction among his Asadi brethren was identical to the one they always reserved for E.Z. . . . Everybody *out* of the clearing! Everybody *out!*
. . . It was old times again, gang, except that now the actor holding down center stage was a personal friend of mine. Hadn't he saved my life several times? Certainly he had.

After the heat, the boredom, and the rainfalls, my lean-to leaking like a colander, I couldn't have been more gratified.

Following the pattern Eisen Zwei established on one of his visits, The Bachelor spent the entire afternoon in the clearing, all of last night, and maybe an hour or so this morning. Then he got up to leave.

I've been following him ever since. Denebola hovering overhead, I'd judge it to be about noon. The Bachelor permits me to follow him. Moreover, it's easy. I'm not even breathing hard. *[Simulated heavy breathing.]* I'm recording as we walk. If this were a terrestrial wood, you could hear birdsong and the chitterings of insects. As it is, you'll have to content yourselves with the sounds of my footfalls in the rustlings of leaf and twig . . . Here's a little rustle for you now.

[The sound of a branch or heavy leaf slapping back. General background noises of wind and, far less audibly, distant running water.]

The Bachelor is several meters ahead of me. You may not be able to hear him—he walks like one of James Fenimore's stealthy Indians. *Pad, pad, pad.* Like that, only softer. I don't care to be any closer than I am because the huri's riding The Bachelor's shoulder, clinging to his mane. It is *not* a winsome creature, base-camp huggers; no, indeed it's not. Since it hasn't any eyes, you can't tell whether it's sleeping—or awake and plotting a thousand villainies.

That's why, jes' strollin' along, I'm happy back here.

Let me impress you with my cleverness. *[A heavy thump.]* That's my backpack. I've brought provisions for three or four days. You see, I don't know how long we're going to be out here. I don't know where we're going. But in The Bachelor I trust. Up to a point, at least. This backpack also houses my recorder—Morrell's miniaturized affair, the one that has a capacity of two hundred forty hours. Or, as Benedict might phrase it if he knew me better, ten solid days of Chaney's uninterrupted blathering.

I've rigged it so my voice will trigger the recording mechanism whenever I speak. The absence of my voice for a ten-minute period automatically shuts it off. That's to conserve recording time—not that I plan on talking for ten straight days—and to keep me from fiddling with buttons when there might be other things to do. I can always go manual if I have to, of course, countermanding the exclusive lock on my own voice, but so far none of the Asadi has been particularly voluble. Only Eisen Zwei. And his voice would not be apt to woo the ladies.

I've been thinking. And what I wouldn't give for a copy of one of those centuries-old works no one reads anymore. *The Brothers Karamazov*, say. Surely The Bachelor is none other than the Asadi equivalent of Pavel Smerdyakov, the illegitimate son who destroys himself out of his innate inability to reconcile the spiritual and the intellectual in his nature. Such passionate despondency! He cannot escape—nor can he accept—the dictum that the individual is responsible for the sins of all.*

The First Night

I. CHANEY [*whispering*]: It's quiet in here, as still as the void. And though you probably can't believe it, I've held my peace for the entire afternoon. Maybe I said, "Damn!" two or three times after scraping my shin or tripping over a root gnarl—but that's all. In here I scarcely feel it's appropriate to talk, to raise my voice above even this hoarse whisper.

[*Chaney clears his throat. There is an echo, a hollow sound that rings and fades.*]

We—the three of us—are inside the pagoda in front of which The Bachelor became the designated "leader" of his people. I feel free to talk only because he and the huri have gone up a narrow iron stairway inside the temple's central vault. They're climbing toward the small convex interior of the onionlike dome from

---

* There follows a totally irrelevant analysis of the ways in which The Bachelor resembles the character of Smerdyakov in Dostoevski's novel. This remarkable analysis, delivered extemporaneously while Chaney follows the Asadi chieftain through the Wild, lasts better than an hour. To spare the reader, I've deleted it. I believe that the passage which follows was recorded almost six hours later. T. B.

which the outside spire rises. I can see them from here. The stairway makes a tremendously wide spiral up toward the dome, and The Bachelor is trudging upward toward it. The huri, meanwhile, is flying in languid circles inside the spiral of the stairway, staying even with The Bachelor's head. The strange thing here is that I can barely hear its wings flapping.

It's preternaturally cold in here, too. Cold and dead. Like the interior of no other building ever erected in a tropical rain forest. My whispers echo, but the huri's flapping is silent.

Outside, it's nearly dark. At least it was nearly dark twenty minutes ago when we came through the heavy doors that the Asadi, twelve days ago, didn't even open. Now at least one of the moons must be up. Maybe a little moonlight falls through the dome overhead. . . . No, no, Chaney. The light in here comes from those three massive globes in the metal ring suspended several meters below the dome like a Spartan chandelier. The Bachelor's climbing toward that huge ring, the spiraling stairway mounts toward it. Light also seeps into this place from the amethyst windows set high in all the walls. Listen. Listen to the light seep through. . . .

[There is no sound for several minutes, perhaps a slight amplification of Chaney's breathing. Then his voice descends conspiratorially.]

Nevertheless, Eisen, I think—I don't know, mind you, but I think—I think that both the chill and the luminosity in here originate in those globes up there. Just a feeling I have. Winter sunlight. The *texture* of the light reminds me of the glow around probeship ALERT and EVACUATE signs, a cold but hellish sheen.

All right. Let's move to where we can see.

[Silence. Rhythmic breathing. Footfalls echoing hollowly off polished stone.]

I'm looking straight up the well of the stairway. *[An echo: "Way way way way . . ."]* Come on, Egan, keep it down, keep it down. . . . Better, much better. . . . I can see the huri flapping up there, noiselessly, and The Bachelor's legs ascending the spiral. The staircase seems to terminate in a glass platform off to one side of and just a little below the suspended ring of the "chandelier." I'm looking up through the axis of the dome, right up through the chandelier ring hanging beneath it.

Outside, above the dome, there's a spire pointing at BoskVeld's sky. Inside the dome, depending from its apex, there's a sort of plumb line—of what looks like braided gold—dropping down the central shaft of the pagoda to a point, well, about half a meter above the suspended ring. I can't tell for certain, my depth perception's not that good. Been in the jungle too long. Just as the pygmies of the Ituri used to have trouble adjusting their vision to open savannah.

I apologize for the complicated description of the upper recesses of this temple, but the *arrangement* is intricate. Also, that's where The Bachelor's going. I can make sense neither of the architecture nor of his intentions. And, my head tilted back like this, my neck's getting sore. I need a rest, base-camp huggers. 'Deed I do.

II. CHANEY [*conversationally, but still in something of a whisper*]: Me again. About an hour ago The Bachelor reached the glass platform beneath the chandelier ring. He's been standing up there like a Pan-Olympic diver ever since. Insofar as I can tell, he appears to be looking at the braided gold plumb line dangling slightly above him, its far end attached to a hook or threaded through some invisible grommet high in the dome. He can't quite reach the plumb line from his platform, though clearly he would like to. He seems to be hypnotized by it.

Let me leave him there for a moment and take a walk about the interior of this pagoda. I'll be your tour guide, base campers. Follow me.

[*The sound of footfalls as, apparently, Chaney walks.*] This pagoda seems to be a museum. Or, perhaps, a mausoleum. At any rate, a monument to a dead culture. I'm reminded of the Palace of Green Porcelain in Wells' *The Time Machine*. . . . The walls around three sides of the bottom of this place are lined with tall spindly cabinets, glass display cases of a wildly improbable design. Each one consists of fan-shaped shelves that fold out from a central axis and lock into place on different levels from one another. [*Chaney blows.*] Dust. Dust on everything. But not particularly thick. And on these shelves—which have the fragile warmth of mother-of-pearl—there are specimens of various kinds of implements and artwork.

[*A click, like stone on stone.*] I'm holding a statue that's about as tall as my forearm is long. It represents the Asadi male, full-maned and virile. . . . But the statue depicts him with a kind of cape around his shoulders. A garment, if you can imagine that. Very strange. . . . Here's an iron knife, with a wooden handle carved so that the top resembles the skull of an early terrestrial hominid. An Asadi skull, no doubt. . . . The statue's definitely an anomaly here; everything else in the cabinet looks like a weapon or a heavy tool.

I'm going across the chamber, past an open corridor leading off down the pagoda's western wing and into darkness. *[Footfalls. Echoes.]* I'm going toward the one wall in here without any of these spindly cabinets against it. The Flying Asadi Brothers are still up there, more rigid than the statue I just picked up. I'm passing directly beneath them now, beneath the iron ring and its energy globes. There's a huge circular pattern on the polished flagstones I'm walking upon. Inside this circle I feel I'm trespassing on sacred territory. . . . Ah, I'm out of the circle and heading toward the horn-colored wall beyond the helical stairway. There are no cabinets on that wall. Instead . . .

Damn this light! this hollowness! Let me get closer. . . . On the wall are what appear to be rows upon rows of tiny plastic wafers. Rows of wafers hung from a couple thousand silver rods protruding for several centimeters at right angles to the wall. . . . The wall's just one big, elegant pegboard glowing like a monstrous fingernail with a bonfire behind it. The rows of these wafers — cassettes, cigarette cases, matchboxes — whatever you want to call 'em — begin at about waist level and go up two or three hands higher than I can reach. Asadi height, I suppose.

[For three or four minutes only Chaney's breathing can be heard. Then, slowly]: Interesting. I think I've figured this out, Eisen. I want you to pay attention. . . . I've just unfastened this intricate, ah, *wing nut,* say, from the end of one of these protruding rods and removed the first of several tiny cassettes hanging from it. . . . *Wafer* was a serendipitous word choice, because these little boxes are as thin as two or three transistor templates welded together. The faces of the things are about seven centimeters square. . . . I've counted fifty of them hanging from this one rod, and, as I said, there are probably three thousand rods on this wall. That's about 150,000 cassettes altogether, and this section of the pagoda, more than likely, is just a display area.

But I want to describe the one I've got in my hand, tell you how it works. Maybe, if I can restrain myself, I'll let you draw your own conclusions. Okay, then. In the center of this wafer — which, by the way, does seem to be made of plastic — there's an inset circle of glass with a diameter of about a centimeter, maybe a little more. A bulb or an eye, call it. Beneath this eye there's a rectangular tab that's flush with the surface of the cassette. Above the bulb, directly under the hole through which the wall rod passes, there's a band containing a series of different-colored dots. Some of the dots touch each other, some don't. The spacing, or lack of it, between dots probably has significance.

And here's how this little crackerbox works. *[Chaney chuckles.]* Oh, Eisen, don't you wish Morrell were here instead of me? I do, too, I really do. It's purposely simple, though. Even a cultural xenologist can figure it out. . . . All you do is hold your thumb over the right half of the tab at the bottom of the cassette. Then the fireworks begin.

[A pleased laugh, and its subsequent echo.] Ah, yes. Right now the eye in the center of the wafer is flashing through an indecipherable program of colors. Reds, violets, greens. Sapphires, yellows, pinks. All premeditatedly interlaced with pauses. Pregnant pauses, no doubt. . . . In this dimness my hands are alternately lit and shadowed by the changing colors. Beautiful, beautiful. That's just about it, in fact. The entire system probably sacrifices a degree of practicality on the altar of beauty.

There. I've shut it off. All you do is cover the *left* half of the control rectangle with your thumb. It may be possible to reverse the program—rewind it to a desired point, so to speak—but I haven't stumbled on the method yet. At least I don't think I have. It's impossible for me to remember the sequences of colors— though it probably wasn't a bit difficult for the Asadi, or Ur'sadi, who composed, manufactured, and used these things, however long ago that may have been.

They're *books*, or the Ur'sadi equivalent, as I'm sure you've already guessed. *[A thumping noise.]* I'm pocketing six of them, putting them in my backpack. For the greater glory of Science. To set the shirttails of ole Oliver Oliphant aflame with envy, may his ghost go angrily blazing across the heavens. Not to mention the fact that they'll be just one more thing for Morrell to put his screwdriver to.

[Musingly]: Look at that wall. Can you imagine the information on hand here? Or the level of technology necessary to devise a storage-and-retrieval system for a "language" that consists of complicated spectral patterns? One fifteen-minute program in one of these cassettes probably represents the equivalent of a three hundred-page book. . . . By the way, what do you suppose I was "reading"? I'd guess that the band of colored dots above the eye is the description of the contents. The title, so to speak. Maybe I was scanning a sex-and-sadism tract by the late Marquis de Asadi—my

hands had begun to sweat while the program was running.

[*Sober again*]: No, no, the eyebook—let's call 'em eyebooks—was the first one on that particular rod. Maybe it's their *Iliad*, their *Divine Comedy*, their *Origin of the Species*, their *Brothers Karamazov*. And what the hell have they done with it? Stuck it in a forgotten, godforsaken temple in the middle of the Synesthesia Wild and left it to commemorate their fall! What colossal waste! What colossal arrogance!

[*Shouting*]: Where the hell do you creatures get off neglecting the accumulated knowledge of millennia? You're animals! ANIMALS!

[*A cacophony of echoes. A prolonged, painful ringing.*]

Forgive me, Eisen, Benedict, all of you. Forgive me. [*Chaney's voice drops to a whisper, scarcely audible.*] And you, you Asadi aerialists, that's right, pretend I don't exist, pretend you can't hear me, ignore the voices of your ancestors whispering to you from their deaths. [*Venomously*]: And may God damn you both to hell!

III. CHANEY [*in a lifeless monotone*]: I think I slept for a while. Under the rows upon rows of eyebooks. Maybe an hour. Then a noise woke me, a ringing of iron.

Now I'm on the helical stairway high above the museum floor. I'm in a curve of the stairway a little below and opposite the glass platform where The Bachelor was standing. He's no longer there. A moment ago he chinned himself up to the cold ring of the chandelier, gained his feet, and balanced on the ring, quite precariously. Then he reached out and grabbed the plumb line that drops down from the dome.

The huri, meanwhile, squats on the foremost globe in the triangle of globes set in the great iron ring. He's been there awhile.

The Bachelor, after grabbing the gold braid, fashioned a noose and slipped his neck into it. Then he swung himself out over the floor so that his feet are hanging a little below the ring of the chandelier. I'm watching him hang there, his feet inscribing a circle inside the larger circle of the globe-set energy fixture.

But he isn't dead, not a bit dead. The noose is canted so that it catches him under the throat in the plush of his mane. In the two weeks since his designation his mane has thickened considerably, especially along his jaw and under his throat, and the new fur cushions the steadily constricting braid. So now he's just hanging there. The dangling man.

[*Listlessly*]: A pretty damn interesting development, I suppose.

At least the huri acts as if it's interesting. The huri's watching all this—should I say *watching,* considering its eyelessness?—with either excitement or agitation, beating its wings sporadically and skittering to stay atop the globe it's perched on. See if you can hear it. I'll hold the microphone out for you. [*A vaguely static-filled silence, followed by a distant scratching sound.*] That's it, the huri's claws scrabbling on the globe. And the sound of The Bachelor's feet turning north, northeast, east, southeast, south, south-southwest. . . .

[*After almost ten minutes of static-filled silence*]: The huri's been joined by two of its fellows. They flew up silently out of the lower darkness of the pagoda, I don't know precisely from where, and settled like miniature brood hens on the other two energy globes. As soon as they had arrived, the original huri—The Bachelor's huri—fluttered to the Asadi's head, grabbed his mane with its claws, and began crabwalking around his shoulders and upper body like a steeplejack. After a couple of minutes had passed, I noticed that a kind of milky cobwebbing had begun to net in The Bachelor's head and that the huri was paying out this glistening fiber from a pair of axillary spinnerets beneath its half-open wings. The huri's tiny hands pulled out the thread, stretched it around the dangling Asadi's shoulders, and looped the stuff so expertly and with such gentle speed that the beastie appeared to be spinning cotton candy out of its armpits. Wingpits, make that. In any case, this is still going on, base-camp huggers, although the other two huri have spelled The Bachelor's huri a couple of times apiece already and The Bachelor has begun to resemble a huge, nylon-pile-lined sleeping bag turned inside out and made strangely translucent. I no longer know which huri is which, they've alternated their spinning chores so many times. . . .

[*Unawed*]: Beautiful. Beautiful and grotesque at once. I'll bet you think I'm drunk or drugged. Making silk out of a souse's fears, so to speak. Not so. I've imbibed no bourbon, played with no Placenol, and I wish it was you, Eisen, or you, Morrell, who was sitting up here on this cramped stairway watching this ritual unraveling of three huri's innards. Is it silk cable or a kind of solid, filamentous milk payed out through these creatures' axillary mammaries? Who knows? The show is beautiful and grotesque, grotesque and beautiful, but at this stage my principal reaction seems to be one of, well, of disgust. [*Unemotionally*]: God, but my patience has been tried. . . .

[*Several more minutes pass. A faint flapping commences, continues for a time, ceases, and commences again.*]

One of the three huri—don't ask me which—let a strand of silk drop down The Bachelor's body and through the axis of the dome until it damn near reached the floor. Another of the huri flew off its globe and caught up a section of the strand in its claws. Then, with both its claws and hands, flapping in higgledy-ziggledly circles, it covered The Bachelor's feet, his ankles, and his shins. After that, it settled on the old boy's wrapped feet. Now, its wings outspread and its spinnerets, I'd imagine, virtually exhausted, the huri's hanging up there like a bat and still bravely mummy-wrapping its master. It's got help, though. The other two huri are also single-mindedly crawling his body, getting The Bachelor ready for Christmas. And all three of them, mind you, as blind as . . . as a besotted cultural xenologist. Good boy, Chaney, no more clichés than the experience itself calls for.

I don't know how long it'll take—not much longer, apparently—but in a while The Bachelor will be completely encased in a murky chrysalis, a sheath which the huri look as if they would like to finish and tie off as soon as they can. Already they're binding in the Asadi's hands, tightening thread around his thighs, thickening and padding the glowing gauze of his enormous sleeping bag. Soon The Bachelor will be nothing but a lopsided pupa hanging from a golden cord inside the eerie loft of his ancestors' rickety barn. I guess. So to speak.

[Chaney grunts. Shuffling sounds. Perhaps the weary shifting of a burden.]

I guess. Don't ask me. I won't watch any more of this foolishness. I'm dizzy. I'm fed up with this nonsense. . . . If I can make it down these steps in the half-light, the hell-glow, I'm going to lie down beside the wall of eyebooks, where I was before, and go to sleep. Directly to sleep. Before the worm turns. . . .

[Footfalls on the iron steps. Unintelligible mumblings.]

Interlude: Early Afternoon of Day 139*

CHANEY *[speaking conversationally]*: Hello. I'm talking to Benedict alone now. Ben? Ben, you're supposed to make a drop tomorrow. Your twentieth. Can you believe that? No, I can't either. It doesn't seem like more than ten or twelve years that I've been out here.

---

* From the end of the previous section to the beginning of this one Chaney engaged in a great deal of irrelevant "blathering." I have deleted it. Altogether, about twelve or fourteen hours of real time passed, time during which Chaney also slept and ate. In this "Interlude" I have taken the liberty of borrowing small sections from the deleted passages in order to provide a continuity which would not otherwise exist. T.B.

Twenty drops. Well I may not pick up this latest one. Not for a while, anyway. God knows when The Bachelor will choose to lead me out of here and back to the clearing. At the moment he's occupied. Let me tell you how.

First, let me tell you what's going on. I'm standing here by one of the dusty display cases. All its shelves are folded up against the central axis, like the petals of a flower at night. But it's early afternoon, Ben, there's dull light seeping through the swirling violet windows between the separate stories of the pagoda's exterior column. Even so, every cabinet in the place is shut up like a new rose. Every one of them. It happened, I guess, while I was sleeping. The fires have gone out of the three globes overhead—they're as dead and as mutely mottled as dinosaur eggs. I don't know exactly when that happened, either. The eyebooks still work, but everything else in here is dead.

The pagoda's dead. That's all there is to it. And I have the feeling it won't come alive again until Denebola has set and BoskVeld's moons climb the sky. Moonlight is reflected light, indirect light, and this place seems to function best when the light comes at you cockeyed and filtered. Don't ask me why. . . .

But The Bachelor. You want to know what happened to him. Again, I don't know exactly. During the night the plumb line from which he fashioned the noose and then hung out over the pagoda's floor while a trio of huri wrapped him in silk—that golden line, I tell you, has lengthened and dropped through the ring of the chandelier so that it's now only a meter or so off the floor. It descended, I suppose, of its own accord. *[A chuckle.]* Now the ungainly pupa hangs in the daylight gloom of this chamber and turns slowly, slowly, first to the right, then to the left, like the gone-awry pendulum in a grandfather clock. . . . That's it, Ben, my somber Big Ben, this whole building's just an outsized timepiece. You can hear BoskVeld ticking in its orbit. Listen. . . .

As for the huri, only one of last night's three remains. The original huri, I have to assume. It crouches on the uppermost node of the pupa, the point at which the braid breaks through, and rides The Bachelor's mummified head as it used to ride his shoulder. Each time the wrapped body turns this way I feel the huri's staring at me, taking my measure. If I had a pistol, I'd shoot the damn thing, I swear I would. Even if it meant that the concussion would split the seams of this temple and send it crashing down on my ears—every fragile cabinet shattering, every eyebook bursting open. So help me, I would. Which is probably why I didn't bring a weapon out here with me in the first place. . . . But now the little beastie's clawing nervously at the silken membrane, unhinging its wings and shaking their outstretched tips. I think, gang, we're going to get some action. Give me a few minutes, just a few. . . .

[Several minutes pass.] Action, indeed. The huri's moving in its own catch-as-catch-can fashion down the swaying cocoon that houses The Bachelor. As it moves, it peels back pieces of the membrane, snips them off with its feet, transfers the pieces to its greedy hands, and eats them. That's right, *eats* them. . . . I'd been wondering what the little bugger subsisted on, and I have to continue to wonder. Viable food chains do *not* result from a creature's feeding on its own excreta. Too much is lost . . . Nevertheless, the huri's feeding on the husk of The Bachelor's metamorphosis, on the rind of its master's involuntary change. Maybe that's phrasing it a little too philosophically, but I can't help thinking the huri's eating The Bachelor's former self. It's crabwalking in a spiral down the cocoon, a spiral mirroring the great corkscrew of the pagoda's staircase, and it furiously shovels in and gobbles up the membrane that it's snipping away.

Now the huri is at the hollow of The Bachelor's chest, and I can see the outline of my old friend's head through the milk-blue film that remains even though the silken outer layer has been eaten away. This film clings to his features like a hood. It's moist and trembly, and through it I can see the death mask of his face.

Ben, Ben, you can't expect me to stay here and watch this. Tell the others not to expect that of me. The bitch-goddess of xenology's fucked me over too many times already, and I'm nauseated with fatigue. With disgust. It's worse than last night. There's an odor in the temple, a smell like excrement and rot and the foul discharges of the glands. I don't know what I'm. . . .

[A retching sound, painful and prolonged. Then, a rapid succession of footfalls, suggestive of running.]

The doors. I've got to get to the doors. . . .

The Second Night

I. CHANEY *[his voice thin but genial]*: We're in the Wild again. Out in the open. Out among the singing leaves, the dancing moons, the glittering winds. The humidity's horrible. It makes my sinuses act up. After spending one sore-necked night in the refrigerated vault of that Asadi warehouse, though, and one stomach-turning day in it when it changed from a warehouse into a charnel house — well, the humidity's a welcome relief. Let my nose run as it may, where it may. Even though I don't know where the hell the face it's running on is running to. Actually, we're not running at all. We're moving quite leisurely through the trees, The Bachelor and the huri and I. In no hurry at all.

[Clinically]: I feel pretty well now. The horror of this afternoon has evaporated. I don't know why it made me ill. It wasn't that bad, really. I should have stayed and watched. That's what I came out here for. But when the smell got so bad, well, I had to get out of there. My system's been under a strain.

I bolted for the pagoda's entrance, pushed aside the heavy doors, and ran down the tier of steps. The sunlight increased my nausea and I threw up again. But I couldn't go back inside, Ben, and as a consequence I'm not entirely certain what the final circumstances of The Bachelor's removal from the cocoon were. Like a little boy waiting for the library to open, I sat on the bottom step of the pagoda and held my head in my hands. I was ill. Really ill. It wasn't just an emotional thing. . . . But now I feel better, and the night — the stars twinkling up there like chipped ice — seems like my friend.

[Wistfully]: I wish I could navigate by those stars. But I can't. Their patterns are still unfamiliar to me. They don't tell me where we are. Maybe we're going back to the clearing, maybe elsewhere.

[Throughout this section of Chaney's monologue the sound of wind and leaves corroborates his testimony that they are out of doors, out of the temple.]

The Bachelor's striding ahead of me, the huri on his shoulder. I know, I know, you're wondering what he looks like, what his disposition is, what his metamorphosis accomplished for him. Well, gang, I'm not sure. You see, he looks . . . about the same. As I said, I didn't go back into the museum, I waited outside until the sun had set, thinking all the while that I'd go back up the steps when the darkness was complete. I knew that my two disarming friends couldn't get out any other way, that I wouldn't be stranded there alone. At least I didn't see any other doors while I was inside. The ancient Asadi — the Ur'sadi, damn 'em — apparently didn't see any need to leave themselves a multitude of outs. The end they've come to supports that hypothesis. But before I could steel myself to reentering the pagoda — just as the twilight began to lose its gloss — The Bachelor, looking not much different, appeared on the highest step.

And came down the steps. And walked right by me.

He didn't look at me, and the huri, clinging to his mane, had the comatose look I remember it possessing when Eisen Zwei came into the Asadi clearing for the second time. Now I know why it looked so bloated and incapable of movement—it had just ingested the old man's huri-spun pupa, if indeed a trio of huri had for reasons of their own so encased Eisen Zwei. God help me. I still haven't figured this out. I may never figure it out.... Anyhow, I noticed only two small changes as he stalked by me in the jungle, two small changes in The Bachelor, that is. First, his mane's now a full-grown collar of fur, not just a bib under his throat. It's still a little damp from the filmy blue substance that lined the chrysalis. And second, a thin cloak of film stretches between The Bachelor's naked shoulder blades and falls in folds to the small of his back. Probably it just hasn't dropped away yet.

And that's it. His eyes are still as mute, as white, as uncommunicative, as they ever were.

We're in a kind of tunnel. We've been walking, slipping beneath the vines and hanging bouquets of flowers, for about thirty or forty minutes. A while ago we came upon what seems to be a footpath, a beaten trail where we can walk upright. The only such trail I've seen in the Synesthesia Wild, ever. The Bachelor's moving down it easily, and once again I'm having trouble keeping up.

[Singing softly]:

> The Wild is lovely, dark, and deep,
>   Its grottos free of war's alarms—
> But would I were in my bed, asleep,
>   And all Earth in my arms.

I'm lost. *[Pensively]*: All the time I've spent in the Asadi clearing, all that time watching them amble around and wear down their heels to no purpose—it seems like centuries ago. No kidding, Ben, Eisen, that time in the clearing just doesn't exist right now. Lost as I am, I feel I could follow The Bachelor down this narrow trail forever.

But his metamorphosis—or lack of it—bothers me. I've been thinking about it. My considered, but not necessarily considerate, opinion is that the old grey mayor—mayor, chieftain, what's the difference?—is exactly what he used to be. Anatomically speaking, that is. Maybe the very brief time he spent hibernating in that homemade sleeping bag altered him psychologically rather than

physically. Perhaps it put him more closely in tune with his huri and his huri with him.
Who's to say, gang? Who's to say?
[Ten minutes of wind, water, and shush-shush-shushing feet.]

II. CHANEY *[whispering]*: There's something in the trees ahead of us. A crouched grey shape. The Bachelor just turned on me, Ben—he wouldn't let me approach with him. If I don't stay fairly close, though, I'll be lost out here. Damn you, you hulking boonie, I won't let you sneak away. . . . We're off the trail, we've been off it a good while, and the trees, the lianas, the swollen epiphytes— hell, everything's the same, one spot's like another. . . . I'm disobeying the bastard. I'm staying close enough to keep him in my sight. He's out there in a ragged hallway of rainthorn leaves moving toward the thing in the tree. A tumor in the branches, a lump that the moonlight gives a suspicious fuzziness. . . . You should see the way The Bachelor's approaching the thing. He's spread his arms out wide, and he's taking one step at a time, one long easy step. Like an adagio S.S. man. The membrane between his shoulder blades has opened out, too, so that it makes a fan-shaped drapery across his back. Shadows shift across it, shadows and moonlight. . . . What a weird goddamn boonie. You should see him. He's a kind of moving, blown-up version of the drunken huri clinging to his mane. . . . We're closer now. That thing up there, whatever it is, it's either dead, or inanimate, or hypnotized. Hypnotized, I think. It seems to be one of the Asadi from the clearing. A grey shape. Ordinarily you don't get this close at night. You just don't. The Bachelor's hypnotized it with his slow-motion goose step, the filmy rippling of the membrane across his back and arms, maybe even with his empty eyes. . . . Now we're just waiting, waiting. I'm as close as I can get without jeopardizing the purity of this confrontation. . . . I can see eyes up there, Asadi eyes, stalled on a sickly but reflective amber. *[Aloud, over a sudden thrashing]*: The damn thing's just jumped out of the branches! It's one of the Asadi all right, a lithe grey female. The Bachelor's wrenching her backward to the ground, the huri's fallen sidelong away from him! It's fluttering, fluttering in the thicket beneath the rainthorn tree! *[A heavy bump. Continued thrashing. Chaney's voice skyrockets to an uncontrolled falsetto]*: I knew it! I knew what you were! Dear lord, I won't permit this! I won't permit your hideous evil to flourish! DAMN YOU! *[Scuffling. Then, indignantly]*: Stay where you are. Don't approach me. Stay where you. . . . *[Violent noises. Then a hum of static and prolonged low breathing.]*

III. CHANEY *[panting]*: My head aches. I've been sick again. I didn't think I could throw up again, my stomach's so tight and empty, but somehow I managed. . . . It's sweet here, though. I'm kneeling in fragrant grass under the lattice-sail trees by the edge of the pagoda's clearing. . . . I've been sick again, yes, but I've done heroic things. *Semi*heroic things, perhaps. In any case, I'm vaguely proud of myself. . . . Even though I'm sick, down on my hands and knees with cramps. . . . You can hear me, can't you? I'm talking out loud—OUT LOUD, DAMN IT!—and he's not about to stop me. He's just going to sit there opposite me with his long legs folded and take my reproaches and evil stares. Aren't you, boonie? Aren't you? That's right, that's a good boonie. . . . He's appalled by what I've just done, Ben. As a matter of fact, so am I. I've freed him from that scabby little battlecock of his. . . . There's blood on the grass. Dark, sweet blood. Too sweet, Ben. I've got to get up.

[Chaney moans. A rustling of clothes, then his strained voice]: Okay. Fine. A little bark to lean against here, a tree with spiny shingles. *[A stumping sound.]* Good, good. . . . I refused to let myself get disoriented, Ben. We came slogging right through that opening there, that portal of ferns and violet blossoms. . . . Oh, hell, you can't see where I'm pointing, can you? Never mind, then. Just know that we slogged to this place from that direction I'm pointing, and I kept my head about me all the way here. My head, by the way, continues to ring from the bashing The Bachelor gave me back in that—that other place. He bloodied me, damn him, when I tried to stop him from slaughtering this poor woman here, the one lying here butchered in the grass. . . . He knocked me down and I couldn't stop him. Then he whirled her up over his shoulder, grabbed the huri out of the undergrowth by its feet, and took off through the jungle. Because of my bruised head, my aching eye, the Wild rang like a thousand wind chimes. To keep from getting lost, I had to follow him. Dear God, Ben, I had to hobble along after that crazy Asadi crew. . . . Then we reached this little patch of grass among the swaying lattice-sail trees—the pagoda's right over there—and The Bachelor threw the dead woman on the ground and disemboweled her. He opened her belly with his teeth. I saw him hovering over her as I stumbled up through the root gnarls and hanging tropical moss after him. I got to this place just as he was making an incision down her abdomen

with his canines. . . . I collapsed and watched. The enormity of what he was doing scarcely fazed me. Holding my bad eye and squinting through the other, Ben, I watched. In ten or twelve minutes I'd forgotten what it all meant, and the woman didn't look like an Asadi any longer—but a deep-red, a blood-black slab of meat. Now the grass is littered with her, and I didn't even attempt to interfere. But, Ben, I couldn't help that, it was all owing to my fatigue and my bruised head, I wasn't thinking straight, I didn't realize he was butchering a human being. As soon as I could, I remedied the situation. And that's why I'm still a little sick. . . . But my head's clear now; it aches, but it's clear. And the boonie isn't about to strike me again. Are you, boonie? All he can do is sit and stare at me. I've intimidated the hell out of him. He thought I was some kind of maneless Asadi vermin, apparently, and now he's unable to reconcile that image of me with his memory of what I've recently accomplished. Poor mute bastard. My semiheroic deed kicked him right in his psychological solar plexus.

[Bemusedly]: As the night is my witness, Ben, I killed the huri. No, the boonie can't believe it either. Nevertheless, it's true.

Look at him. He's making slow figure eights with his chin. He thought me just another low Asadi dog, but I've boggled him past recovery. When he was finished carving up that pitifully helpless woman, that sweet, long-legged lady, he set the huri atop her carcass and busied himself devouring her viscera, the sweet discarded bones of her limbs and skull. . . . I had to do something then, of course. I pulled myself up—but the huri was sitting there on her butchered body staring at me blindly and daring me to move. I wasn't supposed to move, you see; I was supposed to be a good cannibal and wait until dinner was properly served. . . . But I'm not an Asadi, and I paid no heed to the boonie's stupid sentinel, Ben. I killed it. That's the heed I paid it. I ran up and kicked the huri with my boot, it fluttered backward, and I was upon it with my reinforced heel, grinding its filthy little no-face into the grass. Its body split open. Pus spilled out of the lesion like putty from a plastic tube, stinking to the skies. Strands of the stuff coagulated in the gelatinous mass, grew silken and feathery in the air. The smell was intolerable . . . That's what made me sick, I'm afraid, the sight and the stink of the huri's silk-making innards. I stumbled away, fell to my knees, and heaved until I thought my guts would wrench loose inside me. You can't imagine what it felt like. . . .

The Bachelor never moved. Killing the huri had given me a hold over him, a power. He just sat, like he's sitting now, half hunkering, half flat-assed on the ground, and watched me be sick. The smell of the grass revived me, convinced me of my own feeble heroism, and that's when I had to tell you about it, when I started talking through my sickness and the heavy, too-sweet smell of the grass.

[A period of silence, during which only the wind in the tropical vegetation and an ambiguous, intermittent rustling are audible.]

Hello. Are you still there, still with me? The Bachelor just stood up, uncoiled from his crouch, and faced me like an enemy. I thought I was dead, I really did. I know that's a turnabout—you don't have to require consistency of me under these circumstances, do you? . . . But he didn't attack. He merely stared at me for a minute, then turned and walked across the open clearing toward the temple. He's climbing the steps right now, very slowly, a grey shape remarkably like the grey shape he killed.

Every moon is up. The three of them ripple his shadow down the tier of steps behind him. Balthasar, Caspar, and Melchior arrayed in virtual conjunction. The pagoda itself, in this light, scarcely has substance. It looks to have been built of water, water frozen not into cloudy masonry blocks of ice but into a transparent crystalline structure contiguous with the very atmosphere. How to say this? It seems to be merging with the jungle, Ben, Eisen, everyone. The pagoda is slipping out of my vision like a scarf slipping from my hand, just that easily and casually.

[Shouting]: Damn you! You can't leave me here in this gut-strewn glade! I'm coming after you! Do you hear me! I'm coming!

IV. CHANEY: Where is it, Eisen? You said we could see it from this hemisphere, you said it was visible. But I'm standing here, standing out in front of the Asadi's fading temple where there aren't any branches to block my view, and, damn you, Eisen, I don't see it! Just those blinding moons dancing up and down and a sky full of flaming cobwebs. Where's Sol? Where's our own sun? Nowhere. Nowhere that I can see.

[Suddenly resolute]: I'm going back into the temple. Yes, by God, I am. The Bachelor's abandoned me out here. Twenty minutes I've been out here alone. I don't intend to die in this place. I killed his huri, and my suspicion is that he wants me to die for my deed. But is a man who kills a huri the sort to accept a passive death? I hope not, Ben. I've taken too much shit, heaved up too much of myself, to sit cross-legged under the trees and wait for either my own death or the onset of the corrupt hunger that

would keep me alive. . . . I won't eat his offering, and I won't stay out here in that poor butchered lady's company. I can't.

There's a beautiful golden cord in the pagoda, a beautiful golden cord. That should do it. If the boonie's still too shaken up with his loss, his stinking bereavement, to lead me back to the clearing—the Asadi clearing—well, that plumb line ought to serve. I've worked with my hands, I can fashion a noose as well as any dumpling-hearted boonie. And then carry it through where he couldn't. . . .

[The movement of feet in the dirt, Chaney's short-windedness as he climbs the temple's steps, the groaning utterance of a heavy door. From this point on, Chaney's each word has the brief after-echo, the telltale hollowness imparted by the empty volume of a large building's interior.]

It's cold. You wouldn't believe how cold it is in here, Ben. Cold and dark. There's no light filtering through the high, jewellike windows, and the chandelier—the chandelier's out! My eyes aren't accustomed to . . . *[A bump.]* Here's a cabinet. I've scraped my elbow. The shelves are down, and I scraped my elbow on one of the shelves. The cabinets give off their own faint light, a very warm faint light, and I'll be able to see a good deal better if I just stand and let my pupils adjust. *[A scraping sound, somewhat glassy.*]* Wait a minute. The bottom petals of this cabinet have been broken off, torn away. I'm standing in the shards. And I'm not the vandal, Ben. That little bump I gave the cabinet couldn't have done this. Someone had to work energetically at these shelves to break them away. The Bachelor, maybe? The Bachelor's the only one in here besides me. Did he want an axe to stalk me with? Did he need one of his ancestors' ornamental knives before he felt brave enough to take on the pink-fleshed Asadi outcast who killed his huri? *[Shouting]:* Is that it, boonie? You afraid of me now? *[Echoes, crashing echoes. When they cease, Chaney's voice becomes huskily confidential]:* I think that's it, Ben. I think that's why the globe lamps are out, why this place is so dark. The boonie wants to kill me. He's stalking me in the dark. . . . Well, that's fine, too. That's more heroic than the cord, an excellent death. I'll even grapple with him a little, if it comes to that. Beowulf and Grendel. It shouldn't take very long. The lady he killed felt almost nothing, I'm sure of that. *[Shouting]:* Over here,

---

* Just one of the many apparently unsimulated sound effects that convince me of the authenticity of the tapes. How much of what Chaney reports is hallucination rather than reality, however, I'm not prepared to conjecture. T. B.

boonie! You know where I am! Come on, then! I won't move!

[*A forceful crack, followed by a tremendously amplified shattering sound, like a box full of china breaking.*]

My God! The pagoda's flooded with light now, flooded with light from the three globes in the great iron fixture that yesterday hung just beneath the dome. It's different now. The iron ring's floating almost two meters from the floor, it's humming oddly, you can hear the hum if you listen, and The Bachelor's inside the ring stabbing at one of the globes with a long-handled pick. . . . He's already chipped away a big mottled piece of its covering, and that piece has shattered on the floor. . . . All three globes are pulsating with energy, angry energy, they're filling the temple with electricity. A deadly chill. Anger. I'm sure they've generated the field that's keeping the iron ring afloat, the ring hovering like a circular prison around The Bachelor's shoulders. . . . The plumb line whips back and forth as he jabs, it's damn near entangled him, and he's caught inside the ring and keeps jabbing at the foremost globe with his pick. . . .

[*The jabbing sounds punctuate Chaney's headlong narrative. Apparently, another piece of the globe's covering falls to the floor and shatters.*]

What's he doing? Why the hell doesn't he duck out of there? Is he trapped in that field? I can see he's too damn busy to be worried about me, gang. Too damn busy to want to kill me. Instead, he seems to want to kill the pagoda, to destroy its energy source and free himself from the odd hold it has over him.

I think his actions are having precisely the opposite effect, though. All the cabinets are open, all the shelves are down. I can see them. The temple seems to be alive again. Angry. Indignant. All it took was the dark and a little violence. . . . The foremost globe's split wide open; The Bachelor has knocked the crown off it, and spilling from that artificial caldera in the globe, erupting from it and flowing into the pagoda's central chamber with us, is a terrible, violet radiance! It's almost more than I can look at. . . . He persists, though. The ring is canting to one side, and his shaggy body is a flaming silhouette behind that hellish radiance! What does he think he's doing? . . . There's a smell in here, an odor that seems almost to be a concomitant of the light. It's like . . . like the smell when I ground out the guts of The Bachelor's huri. Terrible!

[*A fluttering which is distinctly audible over both Chaney's voice and the persistent tapping of The Bachelor's pick.*]

Lord, they're driving him out of the lofty darkness of the dome —two or three enraged, murder-intent huri. Clumsy beasts a little larger than the one I killed. They're stooping on The Bachelor as a raptor stoops on a field mouse, diving upon him with their claws wide and their wings canted so as to slice him up maliciously each time they pass. He's trying to fight them off, waving the pick overhead, swinging it madly—but they perceive its presence and somehow compute the length and direction of its arc and thereby manage to elude its blows and inflict their anger physically upon The Bachelor. Despite their seeming clumsiness, he's no match for them, no match for them at all. . . .

I'm getting out of here, Ben. I'm going to go tumbling down the steps and out of this place while it's still within my power to do so. What a madhouse, what a sacred, colossal madhouse. Ole Oliver Oliphant should bless the solitary comfort of his grave for sparing him from this. BoskVeld crawls with a strangeness we don't want to be a part of. . . . Or perhaps it's a world beckoning to us across thresholds of insanity and terror for which our sweet lost Earth already has sufficient analogues. . . . Why commit ourselves to a madness the likes of which we've been trying for millennia to flee? . . . Don't listen to me. Who knows what I'm saying? I've got to get out of here. . . . I'm coming home, I'm coming home to you. To you, all of you, my kinsmen. . . .

[Footfalls, a heavy wooden groaning, and then the unechoing silence of the night as Chaney emerges into the Wild.]

V. CHANEY *[exhilarated]*: God, look at them go off! I'm unloading my backpack. I'm lobbing them toward old Sol, wherever the debbil he at. Another Independence Day! My second one. *[Four or five successive whooshing sounds.]* I'm coming home, I'm coming home. To you, Ben. To you, Eisen. To Morrell, Yoshiba, and Jonathan. You won't be able to say I didn't perform my duties with a flair. *[Laughter.]* God, look at them stain the sky, look at 'em smoke, look at 'em burn away the reek of Asadi self-delusion and the stench of huri arrogance!

No, by God, we don't destroy every race we come across. Maybe the pygmies, maybe we did it to the pygmies—but the Asadi, bless 'em, they're doing it to themselves, they've been doing it to themselves for aeons. With help, perhaps. With assistance from their weird, imported familiars from beyond this solar system. It's not ourselves at fault, though. No one can say it's us.

But, God, look at that clean phosphorescent sky! I only wish

I knew which direction Sol was in; I'd like to see it. Eisen, you said we could see it. Where? Tell me where. I'd like to see it like a shard of ice glittering in the center of those brilliant, beautiful, flaming cobwebs. . . .

Last Things

Thomas Benedict speaking: We saw the flares and picked Chaney up. Moses Eisen was with me in the copter. We had come out extremely early on the morning of Day 140 in order to complete Chaney's customary supply drop and then to circle the Asadi clearing with the thought of making a naked-eye sighting of our colleague. Captain Eisen had ordered this course of action when it became apparent that Chaney wasn't going to communicate with us of his own accord. Eisen wished to apprise himself of Chaney's condition, perhaps by landing and talking to the man. He wanted Chaney to return to base camp. If it had not been for these unusual circumstances, then, Chaney's flares might have gone off for no audience but an empty sky. As it was, we saw only the last two or three flares he sent off and had to reverse the direction of our copter to make the rendezvous.

By the time we reached him, Chaney was no longer the exhilarated adventurer that the last section of his monologue paints him. He was a tired and sick man who did not seem to recognize us when we set down and who came aboard the copter bleary-eyed and unshaven, his arms draped across our shoulders.

By removing his backpack we came into possession of the recorder that he had used for the last two days and the eyebooks he had supposedly picked up in the Asadi temple. And that night I went back to the Asadi clearing alone to retrieve the remainder of his personal effects.

Back at base camp, however, we committed Chaney at once to the care of Doctors Williams and Tsyuki and saw to it that he had a private room in the infirmary. During this time, as I've already mentioned, he wrote "The Ritual of Death and Designation." He claimed, in more than one of our conversations, that we had picked him up not more than four or five hundred meters from the pagoda which he describes in this brief paper. He made this claim even though we were unable on several trips over a large area of the Wild to discover a clearing large enough to accommodate such a structure. Not once in all of our talks, however, did he ever claim that he had been *inside* the pagoda.

Only in the confiscated tape does one encounter this bizarre notion; you have just read the edited transcript of the tape and can decide for yourself how much credence to give its various reports. One thing is certain: The eyebooks that Chaney brought out of the Calyptran Wild with him *do* exist. And they had to come from somewhere.

The eyebooks are a complete puzzle. They look exactly as Chaney describes them in the tape, and they all work. The cassettes are seamless plastic, and the only really efficient way we've been able to get inside one is to break the bulb—the glass eyelet—and probe through the opening with an old-fashioned watch tool. We've found nothing inside the cassettes on which their dizzying spectral patterns could have been programmed and no readily apparent energy source to power such a rapid presentation of spectral patterns. Morrell has suggested that the programs exist in the molecular structure of the hard plastic casing themselves, but even this intriguing hypothesis resists confirmation. To date, computer analysis of the eyebooks' color displays has established no basis for "translation" out of the visual realm and into the auditory. We lack a Rosetta stone, and because we do, the eyebooks remain an enigma.

As for Chaney, he apparently recovered. He would not discuss the tape that I once—only once—confronted him with, but he did talk about putting together a book-length account of his findings.

"The Asadi have to be described," Chaney once told me. "They have to be described in detail. It's essential we get down on paper every culture we find out here. On paper, on disk, on holographic storage cubes. The pen's mightier than the sword, and paper's more durable than flesh."

But Chaney didn't do his book. Three months he stayed with us, copying his notes, working in the base-camp library, joining us only every sixth or seventh meal in the general mess. He kept to himself, as isolated among us as he had been in the Asadi clearing. And, I suppose, he must have done a lot of thinking, a lot of somber, melancholy, fatalistic thinking.

He did something else that few of us paid much attention to. He grew a beard and refused to have his hair cut.

Later we understood why.

One morning we couldn't find Egan Chaney anywhere in base camp. By evening he still had not returned. Eisen sent me to the dormitory quarters we shared and told me to go through Chaney's belongings to see if I could determine his whereabouts from an explicit note or a random scrawl—anything he might have left behind in farewell. Already, you see, we were beginning to believe Chaney had defected to the Wild.

"I really don't think he'll be back," Eisen told me. He was right about that, but he was wrong in supposing that Chaney would have left his farewell amid the clutter of our dormitory room.

It wasn't until the next day, when I checked my mailbox in the radio room, that I found what Eisen had told me to look for. Knowing that there had been no probeship deliveries or private light-probe transmissions, I checked my box merely out of habit. And I found the note from Chaney. The only comfort it gave me was the comfort of knowing my friend had not decided to commit suicide—that he had successfully fought off a subtle but steadily encroaching madness.

Eisen disagreed with me in this assessment, believing that Chaney had committed suicide as surely as if he'd taken poison or put a bullet through his brain.

Read the note he left behind, however. It expresses a peculiar sort of optimism, I think, and if you don't see the slender affirmative thread running through it, well, I would suggest that you go back and read the damn thing again. Because even if Chaney *has* committed suicide, he has died for something he believed in.

CHANEY'S FAREWELL

I'm going back to the Asadi clearing, Ben. But don't come after me, I won't let you bring me back. I've reached a perfect accommodation with myself. Probably I'll die. Without your supply drops, that seems certain, doesn't it?

But I belong among the Asadi, not as an outcast and not as a chieftain—but as one of the milling throng. I belong there even though that throng is stupid, even though it persists in its self-developed immunity to instruction. I'm one of them. I feel for them.

Like The Bachelor, Ben, I'm a great slow moth. A tiger moth. And the flame I choose to pursue and die in is the same flame that slowly consumes every one of the Asadi. Don't forget me, Ben, but don't come after me, either.

Good health to you,
Egan

Four thousand copies of this book have been printed by the Maple-Vail Book Manufacturing Group, Binghamton, NY, for Golden Gryphon Press, Urbana, IL. The typeset is Elante, printed on 55# Sebago. The binding cloth is Arrestox A. Typesetting by The Composing Room, Inc., Kimberly, WI.

Additional Titles from Golden Gryphon Press . . .

Terminal Visions

Richard Paul Russo
Foreword by Karen Joy Fowler

Richard Paul Russo is known for his dark and sinister views of the future and the human spirit. In his first collection of short fiction, Russo presents a wide variety of tales—"More Than Night" and "In the Season of the Rains," tales of gritty alien encounters, and the ultimate road story, "Just Drive, She Said." In other stories, the hopelessness of the human condition is examined—on Earth in "Cities in Dust," in space in "The Open Boat," and in an alternate reality in "Prayers of a Rain God." Of the fourteen tales, eleven are set on Earth—and Russo's Earth can be far more alien than other worlds.

"Russo has an excellent eye for the urban landscape [and] the crime writer's well-tuned ear for vernacular."
—Asimov's Science Fiction Magazine

Richard Paul Russo is the award-winning author of several novels that have developed a cult following, most notably *Carlucci's Edge* and *Carlucci's Heart*. He lives in Seattle, Washington.

237 pages, 1st Edition • ISBN 0-9655901-3-5
Cloth: $23.95 postpaid

Golden Gryphon Press
3002 Perkins Road • Urbana, IL 61802

Additional Titles from Golden Gryphon Press . . .

High Cotton
Selected Stories of Joe R. Lansdale

Joe R. Lansdale

This collection of Joe R. Lansdale stories represents the best of the "Lansdale" genre—a strange mixture of dark crime, even darker humor, and adventure tales. The stories are varied in setting and theme, but they are all pure Lansdale—eerie, amusing, and occasionally horrific. In "The Pit," modern gladiators square off against one another using Roman methods. An alternate-history tale called "Trains Not Taken" shows Buffalo Bill as an ambassador and Wild Bill Hickok as a clerk. Landsdale's love of large lizards and humor are evident in the stories "Godzilla's Twelve Step Program" and "Bob the Dinosaur Goes to Disneyland."

"Lansdale is an immense talent. His ability to generate side-splitting laughter and gut-wrenching terror on the same page is unique in modern fiction. There's something special going on here, and it ought not be missed."
—Booklist

Joe R. Lansdale has received the American Mystery Award, five Bram Stoker Awards from the Horror Writers of America, the International Crime Writer's award, and a *New York Times* Notable Book award. He lives in Nacogdoches, Texas.

267 pages, 1st Edition • ISBN 0-9655901-2-7
Cloth: $23.95 postpaid

Golden Gryphon Press
3002 Perkins Road • Urbana, IL 61802

Additional Titles from Golden Gryphon Press . . .

Beluthahatchie and Other Stories

Andy Duncan
Foreword by Michael Bishop
Afterword by John Kessel

This collection of fiction includes two never-before-published pieces in addition to a Hugo- and Nebula-nominated story. The title story spins the tale of a guitarist who refuses to disembark the train at Hell and his adventures at the next stop, Beluthahatchie. Other stories include plot lines about the career concerns of a member of "The Executioner's Guild" and graveyard romances in "The Premature Burials." These science fiction and speculative stories are told with a flair for Southern patois and are followed by comprehensive author's notes.

"I suspect we'll be seeing a lot more from Andy Duncan in years to come."
—Michael M. Levy, *The New York Review of Science Fiction*

288 pages, 1st Edition • ISBN 0-9655901-1-9
Cloth: $23.95 postpaid

Golden Gryphon Press
3002 Perkins Road • Urbana, IL 61802

MAR 2006